THE
TWO
OF
SWORDS

"You've got cards?"

"Of course I've got cards. I'd sooner go out without my trousers on."

There had been a time – one which she tried not to think about, because of other, unrelated issues – when she'd made a comfortable living playing Shields with men in coaches, or on ships, or in way stations and inns. Oida, she knew for a fact, had plenty of money, whereas she was uncomfortably aware of not having a single stuiver to her name until she got back to Rasch.

She clicked her tongue. "Oh, go on, then," she said.

By K. J. Parker

The Fencer trilogy
Colours in the Steel
The Belly of the Bow
The Proof House

The Scavenger trilogy
Shadow
Pattern
Memory

The Engineer trilogy
Devices and Desires
Evil for Evil
The Escapement

The Company

The Folding Knife

The Hammer

Sharps

The Two of Swords:
Volume 1
The Two of Swords:
Volume 2
The Two of Swords:
Volume 3

By Tom Holt

Expecting Someone
Taller
Who's Afraid of
Beowulf?
Flying Dutch
Ye Gods!
Overtime
Here Comes the Sun
Grailblazers
Faust Among Equals
Odds and Gods
Djinn Rummy
My Hero
Paint Your Dragon
Open Sesame
Wish You Were Here
Only Human
Snow White and the
Seven Samurai
Valhalla
Nothing But Blue
Skies
Falling Sideways
Little People
The Portable Door

In Your Dreams
Earth, Air, Fire and
Custard
You Don't Have to be
Evil to Work Here, But
It Helps
Someone Like Me
Barking
The Better Mousetrap
May Contain Traces of
Magic
Blonde Bombshell
Life, Liberty and the
Pursuit of Sausages
Doughnut
When It's A Jar
The Outsorcerer's
Apprentice
The Good, the Bad
and the Smug
The Management
Style of the Supreme
Beings

Dead Funny:
Omnibus 1

Mightier Than the
Sword:
Omnibus 2
The Divine Comedies:
Omnibus 3
For Two Nights Only:
Omnibus 4
Tall Stories:
Omnibus 5
Saints and Sinners:
Omnibus 6
Fishy Wishes:
Omnibus 7

The Walled Orchard
Alexander at the
World's End
Olympiad
A Song for Nero
Meadowland

I, Margaret

Lucia Triumphant
Lucia in Wartime

K. J. PARKER

THE Two OF SWORDS

VOLUME
TWO

orbit

www.orbitbooks.net

ORBIT

First published in Great Britain in 2015 by Orbit
This paperback edition published in 2017 by Orbit

1 3 5 7 9 10 8 6 4 2

Copyright © 2015 by K. J. Parker

The moral right of the author has been asserted.

Excerpt from *The Two of Swords: Volume 3* by K. J. Parker
Copyright © 2017 by K. J. Parker

A CIP catalogue record for this book
is available from the British Library.

ISBN 978-1-84149-928-4

Typeset in Horley by M Rules
Printed and bound in Great Britain by
Clays Ltd, St Ives plc

Papers used by Orbit are from well-managed forests
and other responsible sources.

MIX
Paper from
responsible sources
FSC® C104740

Orbit
An imprint of
Little, Brown Book Group
Carmelite Houe
50 Victoria Embankment
London EC4Y 0DZ

An Hachette UK Company
www.hachette.co.uk

www.orbitbooks.net

For Rosie Buckman, with thanks

Declaration

When it comes to processing the dead, there is no more respected name than Siama Ocnisant. For thirty years, Ocnisant's Emerald Caravan has followed closely in the wake of every major war, performing such vital services as burying the fallen, treating and repatriating the wounded, clearing up and making good the mess, liaising with and reassuring local farmers and landowners – all without costing the combatants' hard-pressed taxpayers a single stuiver. Strictly neutral and impartial, the Emerald Caravan finances its entire operation (without compromising in any way on quality of service) by retrieving and selling abandoned military equipment, which would otherwise go to waste or fall into the hands of undesirables. By reselling war materiel at sensible prices, Ocnisant also helps keep military spending down and make war affordable – a vital consideration in an age of protracted multi-theatre conflicts. "I simply don't know how he does it for the money," the Eastern emperor is reported to have told his close advisers. "Without exaggeration, we simply couldn't have kept the war going this long without him."

Poverty

"The good news," he said, "is that they found you not guilty of witchcraft." He smiled. "All the evidence was circumstantial, no positive identification, therefore no case to answer."

He paused.

"And?" she said.

"The bad news is," he said, "they convicted you on three of the five counts of spying, and they're going to hang you in the morning. I tried to lodge an appeal, but it appears there is no right of appeal in espionage cases, so there's not a lot I can do." He hesitated again. "I've asked the ambassador to petition the court for clemency, but—"

"He's a busy man?"

"Very. And in any case, clemency would mean forty years minimum in the slate quarries, and nobody lasts more than three years down there, so it's as broad as it's long, really. I'm very sorry," he said. "But there you are. Is there anything I can do for you?"

Outside it was raining again. She thought for a moment. "Apparently not."

He frowned slightly. "It goes without saying," he said, "that the Department will look after your children and dependent relatives—"

"I haven't got any."

"No? Well, that's something, isn't it? Now, you can nominate who gets your back pay, death-in-service gratuity, any money you may have paid in to a funeral club, your share of plunder, spoil and prizes, if any—" He waited for a moment. "Or, if you don't nominate, it all goes to the Benevolence. It's a good cause; they do splendid work."

"That's all right, then."

His frown deepened, but he persevered. "Now, if you haven't made a will, you can dictate one to me now and I can get the dispensation from proper procedure. I strongly advise you to: you don't want to leave your family a mess to clear up."

She smiled at him. "I haven't got anything to leave."

"Really? Ah well." From his sleeve he produced three rolls of parchment, a quill pen and a brass ink bottle. "In that case, I just need you to sign these forms, and that's pretty much everything covered."

He handed her the rolls of parchment. She unrolled them, glanced at them and tore them up. He sighed. "Any last message you'd like me to pass on?"

"Actually, yes."

He nodded briskly. "Fire away."

She told him. He looked at her. "I'm sorry you feel that way," he said. "But, after all, you knew the risks when you—"

"Yes."

"Well, then. I know this is a very difficult moment for you, but I would remind you that even in the final extremity, you still represent the Service, and what you say and do reflects on us all. It'd be a great shame to tarnish an otherwise exemplary record at the last moment, so to speak." She looked at him, and he got up and banged on the cell door with his fist. "I'm sorry," he said.

"Why? It's not your fault."

"The duty chaplain—"

"Goodbye."

A key turned in the lock and the door swung open. He looked at her, opened his mouth, closed it again and left. The door closed and the lock turned. She breathed out slowly.

Five hours later, she started banging on the door. "Keep it down, will you?" she heard the jailer say on the other side. "You'll start them all off."

"I want to see the chaplain."

A pause; then, "Yes, all right," in a resigned voice. She sat down on the bed and waited. Some time later, the door opened and the chaplain came in. He was a tall man, thin, bald, somewhere between sixty and seventy; he wore nothing but a tunic, for security reasons.

"I want to confess," she said.

He hadn't shaved recently, and there were crumbs in the folds of his tunic. "Of course," he said, and perched on the end of the bed.

She looked at him for a moment, then said, "I have committed murder, theft and arson. I have lied and carried false witness. I have wounded and practised torture, both physical and mental. I have forged documents, including sacred and liturgical records."

His face didn't change. He nodded.

"I have blasphemed and ridiculed the articles of the faith. I have preached heretical doctrines. I have neglected to assist fellow craftsmen in their time of trial."

He closed his eyes, just for a moment. Then he opened them again. "I understand," he said. "Your sins are forgiven." He stood up and knocked three times. The door opened. The guard stood aside to let him pass; as he did so, he drew the sword from the guard's scabbard and stabbed him in the throat, at the junction of the collarbones. The guard dropped to the floor; the chaplain stuck his head out of the door, then came back into the cell. "All clear," he said.

She nodded. "Thanks," she said.

He gave her a filthy look. "You'd better take me with you," he said. "I don't know what to do."

"That's fine," she assured him. "I do. Stick with me, you'll be all right." She took the sword from his hand. "Where does this corridor lead to?"

"How should I know? I only ever come down the stairs."

She breathed out through her nose. "Fine," she said. "We'll go *up* the stairs."

"You can't. There's a guard."

"Of course there is." She grabbed his ear with her left hand, pulled his head back and rested the edge of the sword against his neck. "Just in case anyone sees us," she said.

The stairs he'd talked about proved to be a narrow spiral staircase, without even a rope to hold on to, so she let go of him while they climbed. As soon as they reached the top, she grabbed him again. There was no guard.

"I thought you said—"

"There should be. There is usually."

They were in a long gallery, with arrow slits every five yards. She stopped and peered out through one of them, but it was pitch dark and she couldn't see anything. After a while, they came to a small door – more of a hatch, really – in the wall. "What's that?"

"It's a garderobe. Where they empty the chamber pots."

"Splendid." She let go of him, dumped the sword on the floor and pulled open the door.

"You can't go that way. It's a hundred-foot drop."

She smiled at him. "Thanks for everything," she said. "I hope you don't get in any trouble."

"Don't be bloody stupid. If you aren't smashed to bits, you'll drown."

"My risk," she said. "Now, go and tell them I got loose and took you hostage."

The door slammed behind her before he could answer. He stood for a while staring at the closed door, then turned and headed back down the gallery. After about ten paces it occurred to him to break into a run and start shouting.

The guards who found him sent for the castellan, who ordered two men to go down the garderobe shaft on ropes. They came back up after a while, white-faced and foul-smelling; no sign of anyone down there, they said, but it's got to be ten feet deep and no handholds; if she fell into that, she drowned, no question about it. Hell of a way to go, one of them added, though if she was lucky she hit her head on the wall on the way down. The castellan asked them: Are you sure? Oh yes, they told him. Positive.

She heard most of their conversation, since the tunnel amplified sound quite wonderfully. She was still climbing. It was desperate work, with her back arched against the opposite wall, her fingers and toes crammed into mortar cracks between the stones – fortunately the builders had lined the garderobe with undressed stone, which gave slightly more purchase. Halfway between floors she came to the conclusion that she'd made a dreadful mistake and she wasn't going to make it, but she kept going nevertheless. She found the door on the upper storey by resting her back against it, thinking it was solid wall; it swung open, she lost her grip, actually slid down the best part of a yard before finding a crack with one wildly scrabbling foot. For a moment her weight was too much for four toes to bear, but she found a handhold just in time, and then another, and then got the tips of three fingers over the sill of the door. It was pure luck that the upper gallery was empty, at a time of day when there should have been a sentry there; but he'd gone down the stairs when the alarm was sounded on the floor below.

Well; she was officially dead and nobody was actively looking for her, but it still wasn't wonderful. Fortunately, she had a resource that most escaping prisoners are denied: she was female and women carrying baskets of washing don't attract attention in the inhabited parts of castles, particularly if they're supposed to be dead. She searched until she found the cupboard where the dirty linen lived, grabbed a big armful that covered most of her face and staggered along the gallery looking for the backstairs. Three guards took no notice of her whatsoever, and then she was trotting down a proper square-section stairway, bare-walled and imperfectly whitewashed, which could only lead to the kitchens, laundry and other tactically negligible facilities where fighting men rarely go.

She came out eventually into a lantern-lit courtyard. A quick glance upwards told her that she was now in the very centre of the castle, surrounded on all four sides by impenetrably thick stone walls, at the junction of all routes of communication and access used by the garrison and the castle servants. Best-quality Mezentine armour wouldn't have saved her, but the armful of washing made her invisible. The difficulty was that a laundry maid had no lawful excuse for leaving the castle, even by daylight; in the middle of the night, forget it. Nor could she spend the rest of her life wandering around with an armful of dirty sheets.

A castle is a fair-sized community, larger than many villages, almost the size of a small town. Even in a small town, of course, everybody knows everybody else, unless their faces are obscured by washing. But she was exhausted, bone-weary and finding it increasingly difficult to think about anything except finding somewhere to sit down and rest. It was only later, in hindsight, that she realised that the exhaustion and the indifference almost certainly saved her life – it made her impersonation of a laundry maid in the last quarter of the night shift far more convincing than mere acting could ever have done. If she'd had to walk past the sentry on the gate between the middle and outer courtyards, almost inevitably she'd have given herself away, if she'd been acting natural. Instead, she caught her foot on the lintel out of sheer weariness, stumbled into the guard, scraped the back of her hand on the stonework, squealed at the pain, mumbled an apology and trudged away, unchallenged, sworn at for clumsiness and completely accepted as genuine.

The outer courtyard was another world entirely, and as soon as she emerged into it she realised she'd made a mistake. A laundry maid could believably carry dirty washing from the outer yard to the middle, but not the other way round. She calculated that she had five, maybe ten seconds to deal with the error before someone noticed. She made her mind up in three.

There were two sentries posted outside the doors to the Great Hall. She headed straight for them, well aware that they'd noticed her. "Excuse me," she said, "but I'm new here and I'm lost. Which way to the laundry, please?" They laughed and told her. That posed another problem. The route she'd been given to the laundry meant going back the way she'd just come, past the guard she'd bumped into. Here the bone-weariness was unquestionably her salvation. She left the guard thinking she was mad or drunk or probably both, but that was fine. Even with her back to him as she walked away, she could tell he wasn't looking at her.

Well, she thought; and what would a worn-out laundry maid do next, if she was as tired as me? The answer was perfectly obvious; she'd caught her own maid doing it once, about a thousand years ago in another life, and given her a tongue-lashing for being lazy. She found a dark corner under some stairs, crawled into it, pulled the shirts and sheets up round her until she looked from a distance like a pile of discarded laundry and closed her eyes. Just for two minutes, that's all.

When she woke up, bright light was streaming in from a window high up on the stairs. She made herself stay perfectly still, and listened, and tried to think. At this time of day, in a well-run castle, where would everybody be? The chambermaids would be in the bedchambers; the kitchen staff would be fixing the midday meal; the laundry maids would be doing yesterday's washing before the chambermaids brought down today's. None of them would be using the backstairs. If anyone came and saw her, they'd know at once that she was an anomaly. But why would anyone come? They all had work to do somewhere else.

If there was an alternative, she couldn't think of it. From the pile of washing she pulled out a plain off-white linen smock, property of some ladies' maid from the third or fourth floor — now there was a group she hadn't taken account of; too late now, she was naked on the stairs, one foot in the smock. She hauled it up round her and knotted the belt, then clawed at her hair in the vain hope of getting it into some sort of order; realised that she'd just made another serious mistake; caught sight of a white mob cap in the pile of discarded washing, thanked God for saving her from her own stupidity, pulled the cap on, settled it firmly and tucked stray hair under the headband. The rest of the laundry she kicked into the shadows under the stairs; didn't matter if it was found and commented on; the laundry maid who'd left it there no longer existed. She noticed her filthy, grimy hands and skinned knuckles, tucked them into her sleeves. The hem of her smock covered her feet. Saved again.

The wonderful thing about ladies' maids is that they can be strangers, in service to guests. They can also go almost anywhere, because their mistresses can order them to do all manner of improbable things at inappropriate times — get me a drink of water, an apple, six yards of fine green silk, scissors (no, you stupid girl, *sharp* scissors, the *other* scissors), sixteen cheese scones, a half-bottle of the '06 Pirigouna, something to help me sleep, I want to see the doctor, my coachman, my dressmaker, the castellan, go and find where my useless lump of a husband's got to, quickly, *now*. More freedom than any other category of servant; more freedom than the fine lady herself, come to that. Being a ladies' maid is next best thing to being a man.

But not enough freedom to get her across the yard, through the gate and out the other side. For that she was going to have to spill blood, or be very clever, or athletic, or all three. She chose a doorway at random, climbed the stairs to the very top and barged open a long-closed door out on to the roof.

Having caught her breath, and making sure she kept her head down below the level of the parapet, she turned her mind to contemplation of the principles of military architecture. The aim of castle building is primarily to keep people out; but the same principles and functions do a very good job of keeping people in, which is why castles make such good prisons. Theoretically, she could spend the rest of the day getting hold of a rope and then, once night had fallen, lower herself down off the tower, swim the moat and run for it, if she still had the energy.

Alternatively— her mind went back to lectures at the Tactical Institute at Beal; fat, one-eyed General Tirza. The weakest part of any defensive structure is the man standing in front of it. There were two guards on the main gate: she could just see the tops of their helmets. The first one would be easy – walk up to him, say "Excuse me" in a little-girl voice, then stab him in the eye as he bent forward to listen to her. But the second one was stationed on the other side of the gateway (fifteen feet? There or thereabouts). Lesson one: space is time. Even if she was wonderfully quick about killing the first guard, she had no guarantee of getting to his colleague before he had time to realise what had just happened, lift his shield and level his spear. True, she didn't actually want to fight him: she wanted to get past him and away, but— She did the mental geometry, and three times out of seven the numbers came out badly. And besides, stab the guard in the eye with what? She'd grown so used to having a knife up her sleeve that she'd forgotten it wasn't there any more. No, too many conditions precedent. Think of something else.

Then, in the distance (no, be precise; in the Great Hall, on the other side of the yard) someone started to play the violin. Her eyes opened wide, and then she laughed.

She woke him up with the gentlest of pricks, from the tip of his own dagger, in the hollow under his left ear. He grunted and his eyes opened; otherwise he stayed perfectly still.

"Hello, Oida," she said.

He moved his hand out from under the sheet, pinched the tip of the knife between forefinger and thumb and moved it away an inch or so. "You're dead," he said.

"Something of a grey area," she replied. "What the hell are you doing here?"

He turned his head and looked at her. His eyes seemed much smaller than usual; and then the thunderbolt hit her. How long had she known him? And never noticed. "You wear eyeshadow."

"What?"

"Admit it," she said. "Go on."

"That's the most ridiculous—"

"Admit it."

He sighed. "Yes, all right. Just a suggestion, to make my eyes look bigger. What's that got to do with anything?"

"You wear *make-up*. Like a girl."

"For crying out loud," he said, and raised himself on one elbow. "Honestly," he said. "They told me you were dead. I was *upset*."

"You were playing the violin."

"Well, I had to put on a show, obviously."

A terrible thought struck her; she tried to shrug it off, but it clung like the mud of a newly ploughed field, and she had to ask. "Are you here to rescue me?"

"Yes."

"Well, you would say that."

He looked convincingly hurt. "It's true."

"You made a pig's ear of it, then. I'm dead. You said so."

"Only because you insisted on trying to escape and fell down a toilet. If you'd stayed put and waited, like a rational human being—"

"Make-up, for God's sake." She realised she was still holding the knife. She put it down on the bedside table; it rolled off and landed on her bare foot, fortunately pommel first. "That's just so—"

"It's an ancient tradition among performing artists," he said irritably. "Goes right back to Perditus. Entirely legitimate." He paused. "You won't tell anyone."

"Oida—" She got a grip and breathed out through her nose. "Tell me the truth. Did you come here to rescue me?"

"Yes. That and other things. But let the record show, I was here in plenty of time, and if you hadn't screwed everything up—" He stopped and frowned. "How did you get in here?"

She nodded quickly over her shoulder. "Window. You needn't have bothered," she added sweetly. "I had the whole situation under control."

He scowled at her. "Fine," he said. "In that case, you carry on. See you in Rasch. You can buy me a drink."

"Keep your voice down," she hissed, though she knew there was no real need; the walls were stone, two feet thick, and the door was four-ply oak. "I'm sorry, I'm being ungracious. Of course you can rescue me, if you want."

He swung his legs out of the bed, pushing her aside. "Easier said than done," he snapped. "My idea was to intercede on your behalf, get you pardoned, and ride out of here in a coach in a civilised manner. Now, thanks to you killing a guard and then dying, that's going to be rather difficult. Why do you always feel this morbid urge to take charge all the time?"

She looked straight at him. "You really did, didn't you? Come here to rescue me."

"Yes."

"You clown."

He flushed with anger, forced a grin. "Well, why not?" he said. "You're a competent operative who happens to be female. And now, one of these days, you'll feel obligated to do the same for me."

Which was true. "In your dreams," she said, but she decided she didn't have the energy for much more sparring. "How are we going to get out of here?" she said.

"We," he repeated. "Well, I'm going to ride out through the front gate in a coach." He frowned; he'd thought of something, but decided against it. Now all she had to do was figure out what it was.

"Did you bring the spinet?"

"What?"

"Your stupid show-off portable spinet. Tell me you brought it. You never go anywhere—"

"No."

"Liar."

"Yes, all right, I brought it. It's in its box, in the coach. But I'm damned if I'm going to—"

She gave him a beautiful smile. "That's all right, then. We'll have to drill air holes in the roof of the box, but you should be able to manage that. Perfect."

"The hell with that," he said angrily, "have you any idea how much that thing cost?"

"Two thousand angels," she replied promptly. "You told me yourself. Several times. But that's all right. You can buy another one. You've got plenty of money."

He was floundering for an objection. "Fine," he said. "So we smuggle you out in my box and leave the spinet behind. And, of course, nobody notices a unique, world-famous musical instrument lying about the place—"

"Oh, that's not a problem. We can break it into small bits and toss it down the garderobe."

Just for a moment she thought he might actually refuse. But then he said, "Oh, right. And how exactly do we get it up here?" and she knew she'd won.

"Oh, that's easy. Tell them you want to practise, or tune it or something. They'll bring it up here for you. In the box. And then they'll carry it back down again, still in the box, and strap it on to the coach roof. And off we'll go, and nobody need ever know anything."

"Two *thousand* angels, Tel. Do you honestly believe you're worth that much to anyone?"

She frowned at him. "That's not a very nice thing to say."

"I was thinking, I could lower you from a window on a rope."

She didn't hit him, though she was tempted. "Get dressed," she said.

"Why? It's the middle of the night."

"Because you're going to send down to the kitchens for some food. I'm starving. I haven't eaten in days."

"There you go again," he sighed, "giving people orders. It's not an attractive attribute, you know."

"Who is there in this room I might possibly want to attract?"

A steward brought wheat bread, cheese, smoked pork sausage and a small slab of partridge terrine. "No apple," she said, with her mouth full.

"Everyone knows I don't eat apples."

"That's you all over. Self-centred as a drill-bit."

He pulled on his boots. She noticed that they were new since she'd seen him last; the finest quality calf, decorated with seed-pearls and little gold stars. "However much do you spend on clothes?"

"People expect it of me."

"I don't think I could ever respect a man who spends more on clothes than I do. And wears more make-up."

"How would it be if you stopped talking for a while? Just to see if you can."

She drank all the water in the bedside jug— "Hey, I was going to shave in that"; she gave him a pretty smile. "I'll shave you if you like," she said. "I'm good with blades."

"Not likely. Dry shaving gives me a rash."

"Well, we can't have that."

He sent for the spinet and she enjoyed herself tremendously breaking up the thin boards and pulling apart the exquisitely glued joints without making any noise at all. "I can't lug all that down to the garderobe," he said, pointing to the pile of wrecked timber. "I'd need a wheelbarrow."

"Fine. Get a fire lit."

"This time of year?"

"You're an eccentric genius. You can have a fire if you want."

He growled and knelt down by the hearth. "Won't it look just a little bit strange," he said, "a grate full of ash, and yet nobody delivered any fuel to this room?"

"You've always got to make difficulties, haven't you?"

"You mean, I think things through before plunging in."

She clicked her tongue. "Get it lit."

"Tinder's damp."

"Oh, for pity's sake. Give it here."

The thin sycamore board burned very well indeed, but the ivory keys just charred and made a horrible smell. She scooped them out of the grate with the tongs and put them in the small velvet bag he kept his razor and toothpicks in. "Sling that down the garderobe on your way out," she said. "Is it my imagination or is it hot in here?"

He was wet with sweat, and there was no water left to wash in.

She could see how distressed being sweaty made him feel, and she tried to remember if she'd ever seen him with dirty hands or mud on his trousers. "If it matters that much to you, I'll give you two thousand angels," she said. "Just so long as you stop looking so miserable."

He looked at her as though she'd just poked him with a stick. "You haven't got that sort of money."

"As a matter of fact I have." She hadn't meant to tell him that. It was something nobody knew. "Some of us save, you know, for our old age. We don't spend it all on poncy boots."

Something told her he wasn't going to forgive her that easily, and she was right. "You seem to think you're going to have an old age," he said. "I wouldn't bet on it, the way you go on."

It was just fencing, but it stopped her short, like the botched parry that sticks your opponent's unpadded leg. "I got caught. No matter. I was dealing with it. I could've managed without you."

"No doubt."

She looked at him curiously, as if a favourite book had just grown an extra chapter. "Did you really come here to rescue me?"

He rolled his eyes, but he was acting. "I told you so, didn't I? Though, actually, I happened to be in the neighbourhood. I didn't come all this way *specially*."

"I didn't think you did," she said quietly. "There wouldn't have been time for you to get here. But you made a detour. You went out of your way, a bit." She paused, then added, "You inconvenienced yourself. Just to save me."

He looked – what? Scared? "Forget about it, all right? It was just, you know. Fellow craftsmen—"

"Of course."

Which, she reflected, was probably true, up to a point. The prison chaplain had risked his life and his career for her, a perfect stranger, for that one all-compelling reason; he'd been miserable and resentful as hell about it, but he did it, because not doing it would've been unthinkable. But there's a fine line, thin as gossamer and just as strong. You save a fellow craftsman if asked to do so; you can't refuse. But she hadn't asked, had she? If she'd smuggled out a message to him to come at once, he'd have been obligated. But she hadn't even known he was in the area.

"Right," he said. "Get in the box."

She looked at it, and it occurred to her that maybe the plan wasn't going to work after all. The spinet had proved to be rather more compact than she'd remembered; also squarer, not as long. I'm not going to be able to get in that, she told herself; and we'll have burned his beautiful spinet, all for nothing.

"Come on," he said. Then he looked at her. "Don't tell me," he said. "You have problems with confined spaces."

"No."

"Yes, you do, I can see it in your eyes. For God's sake, woman, it was your idea."

"I don't have a problem. It's just, the box isn't as big as I thought it'd be."

"It's plenty big enough. You'll just have to cuddle up a bit, that's all."

Getting in the box wasn't the hardest thing she'd ever done, not by a deplorably long way. But when the lid went on she couldn't help it; she kicked and punched at it and knocked it out of his hands. "You idiot," he said, and she saw that the flying lid had hit him in the face; he'd have a fat lip for a day or so, disastrous for a singer with engagements lined up. "Now for God's sake keep still. It's all right, really. You'll be fine."

She tried, really hard, but her best proved to be not good enough. This time, at least he managed to avoid getting hurt.

"All right," he said wearily, "we'll just have to think of something else. Get up."

She climbed out of the box, feeling deeply ashamed. And then he punched her, and she went straight to sleep.

She woke up in a coach. It took her a split second to figure out how she'd got there, and then she was furiously angry. "You hit me," she said, without even looking to see if he was there.

He looked up from his book and marked the place with a feather. "You wouldn't go in the box."

"You *hit* me." She realised her voice sounded funny. She felt her lip. It was *huge*.

"Me too," he said, pointing to his face. True, his mouth was a little bit swollen as well. "It's all right for you. How I'm going to sing tomorrow night in this condition I have no idea."

"The way you sing, who'll notice?"

He did his pained expression, which was as irritating as ever. "You wanted me to rescue you," he said.

"I did *not*. For your information, I got out of the cell, I got past the guards and up on to the roof. I was doing just fine."

"Indeed." He sighed. "I shall just have to stick to instrumental stuff and hum. They won't like it. I'm supposed to be entertaining the troops."

She rubbed her jaw. It was aching. She hadn't realised he could punch so well. "What are you reading?"

He showed her the spine of the book. "Saloninus on human frailty."

Saloninus. She'd always assumed the books he read were mostly pictures. "You didn't have to hit me."

"Yes I did. You were kicking and thrashing about like a gaffed shark. You could've broken the box."

Through the window she could see flat salt marsh. Nowhere she recognised. "You could've got a rope and lowered me down off the wall."

"So I could," he said sourly. "I'll remember that for next time."

He put the book in the pocket of his coat. "You do realise, you haven't once thanked me. That's a bit—"

"Thank you? For what?"

"For saving a damsel in distress, you stupid cow." He closed his eyes and leaned back against the seat cushions. "We'll be at the border in an hour or so," he said. "You'll have to hide under the seat. I'll throw my rug over you. They won't search the carriage, I've got diplomatic status."

A map floated into her mind. "What border? Aren't we headed for the coast?"

"Alas, no. We're going to Blemya. Hope that's all right."

"I can't go to bloody Blemya, I'm due in Rasch the day after tomorrow."

He shook his head. "Sorry," he said. "Besides, they won't be expecting you in Rasch. They'll think you're dead."

She started violently. Of course, they would think that, wouldn't they? Intelligence would've picked up the news of her condemnation, attempted escape and miserable end. Then they'd write to her sister, who'd be devastated; and the landlord of her building, who'd sell all her things to cover the back rent and then relet her room; and the abbot, who'd grieve terribly for her and pray for her soul—

"How could you?" she said furiously. "How could anyone be so inconsiderate?"

He was frowning, genuinely mystified. "Oh, forget it," she said. "But as soon as we reach the border, you've got to write and say I'm not dead. It's vitally important."

He gave her a puzzled look. "Tel, we're going to *Blemya*. You haven't forgotten what happened last time you were there? I can't possibly write a letter naming you by name and then turn up with a female acolyte the same age, height, hair colour—"

Entirely valid point, which simply hadn't occurred to her; she'd completely forgotten about her last visit, when she'd murdered a cabinet minister in cold blood— "Don't be stupid," she said. "Your letters are diplomatic, they wouldn't dare read them."

He shook his head. "Not exactly. I have diplomatic *status*, but that's a courtesy thing: I'm not accredited or anything. Besides, what makes you think they don't read all the genuine diplomatic mail?"

She slumped back into her seat and rubbed her throbbing jaw. All her possessions, her books, everything, dispersed to the four winds; and her sister, crying her eyes out. And she hated being called Tel. "All right," she said. "How long are you staying for?"

"A month. Two at the most."

"Two *months*? Oh, for—"

"I didn't actually plan this to be difficult for you," he said. "I thought I was saving your life."

In the back of her mind she was doing geography. Assuming he'd come from Rasch or Choris, heading for Blemya – however you planned the route, it was still considerably more than a minor detour. If he'd heard of her arrest as soon as he'd landed and set off straight away; even so, he must've driven most of a day and through the night, on bad roads, in this rattletrap coach. More than just trivial inconvenience. "I suppose I could get a boat from Tryphola."

"With no papers? Please don't. I have some influence in Blemya, but I'd rather not have to fritter it away on rescuing you *again*."

He was right, it was a stupid idea. "Fine," she said. "So, what am I?"

He grinned at her. "I suppose mistress is out of the question?"

"Social secretary," she said. "Or accompanist. I can play the flute."

"I've heard you. No thanks. I'll just have to say *she's with me* and let them draw their own conclusions."

He'd heard her? When? She'd played in Temple a few times, that was all. "Do what you like. I'll try my best not to get under your feet."

"Oh, come on." He scowled at her, then grinned. "Don't be like that. Think about it. A month in Blemya, with tolerably good food, clean sheets and nothing to do but relax. When did you last have any time off? Well?"

"I don't like time off. I get bored."

"Don't be ridiculous." He turned his head and looked out of the window. If they were headed for Blemya, those must be the famous Aldocine Marshes. They looked grey and flat. "You can't keep on like this, straight from one gruelling job to another: you must be mentally and physically exhausted. Quite apart from anything else, that's how mistakes get made."

The coach passed over a rut; she felt like she'd been kicked. "So you're saying what happened back there was my fault? I screwed up, because I'm tired."

"No, of course not, it wasn't your fault." He sounded convincingly certain of that, and she wondered how he came to know operational details of something he'd had nothing to do with. "No, you handled it perfectly well, it was just rotten bad luck. But that's not the point. You need a rest. And now you're going to get one."

"Boring," she said. "And boredom makes me incredibly stressed. Give it two days and I'll be sharpening my claws on the furniture."

"I think anybody who knows you is used to that."

Just for a moment, she could think of nothing to say.

Oida managed to sing, in spite of his fat lip, and she heard the cheering from the balcony of her room. She had decided not to go – too many people, some of them quite possibly government officials who might've been in the capital when she was last in

Blemya; a good excuse for not watching him being worshipped by six thousand devoted followers. Remarkable, she mused, how often there's a good reason that masks the real reason. Very good-natured of Providence to arrange it that way.

She was asleep in her chair when he knocked on her door. She considered not hearing him, but that would only make him knock louder.

"What are you reading?" he asked, as she poured him tea.

"Your Saloninus," she replied. "I nipped down and borrowed it from you."

His door had been locked, with a guard outside, but his window overlooked the square, same as hers. He raised an eyebrow. "On the balance of probabilities I'd say he makes out his case. But some of the arguments strike me as a bit woolly."

She'd read three chapters and fallen asleep; and she hadn't exactly had a tiring day. "How did it go?"

"What? Oh, the show. All right, I suppose. Actually, I'm not sure the injury doesn't help a bit, in the lower register."

"Splendid. Next time you do a concert, ask me nicely and I'll hit you. I expect you're worn out after all that singing."

"Not really, no." He swilled the dregs round in his tea bowl. "Matter of fact, performing makes me all bouncy and full of energy. It's the morning after when I feel like death." He leaned forward and picked the book up off the floor, marked the place with the feather, closed it and put it on the table. "You know I told you we'd be here about a month."

"Two at the outside, yes."

He pursed his lips. "Well," he said, "it's possible there may be a slight change of plan. Apparently, the queen would like me to sing for her. I met some big-nose from the Chamberlain's department. Apparently, soon as they heard in the capital that I was coming, she sent for me. Rather flattering, actually, I'd sort of got the impression I wasn't highbrow enough for her."

She felt a great weight pressing down on her. "You're going to the capital."

"I don't think I can refuse. The Chamberlain's man did say it'd be all right to do the other two shows I've got scheduled first – entertaining the troops is top priority, which is just as well since they're both paying jobs, while I don't suppose a command performance for Her Majesty will involve any actual money." He looked at her steadily. "It'd probably mean another three weeks."

"Four at the outside," she said, before he could. "Bloody hell, Oida."

"I know, I know, it's a nuisance. Not to mention the risk involved in taking you to the capital, though I've been thinking about that. Trouble is," he went on, pouring himself more tea, "I can't really send you home on your own, the way things are at the moment. They've promised me an escort, but I don't think they'd spare a squadron of cavalry so my sidekicks and hangers-on can go home without me."

"The hell with that," she protested. "I can look after myself."

That made him grin. "No doubt," he said, "and, anyway, I think they're exaggerating this whole insurgency thing out of all proportion. If you were going south, maybe; but north to the coast, I'm sure you'd be fine. But that's not the point. If I sent you home and they didn't provide an escort, the relevant officials would lose face. You know how these things work. I really don't want to put anybody's back up."

A good reason; it made the palms of her hands itch. "So what am I supposed to do for three months? Sit about all day while you—?"

"As I said, I've been thinking." He beamed at her. "How would you like to be my niece?"

Something exploded inside her; she contained it as best she could. "Don't be ridiculous," she said. "You haven't even got a brother."

"Actually, I have." For some reason, that made him frown. "It's a matter of record, if you care to look me up in the Notitia."

"You're in the—"

He grinned. "Afraid so. Just enough Imperial blood in my veins to paint a butterfly's wings, but, yes, I qualify. And you can bet the Chamberlain's read up on me, so he'll know. Fortuitously, my brother's current status and activities are highly obscure, which is a way of saying they haven't caught him yet. For all I know, he might well have a daughter, scores of them, enough for a battalion of heavy dragoons. The point is, if I'm a purple-blood and you're my niece, then you're purple, too." He smiled. "Well, a sort of pale lilac. But it means they'd have to look after you."

She stared at him. "I could go home."

"I don't see why not." He sipped his tea and put the bowl down. "But I don't see us being able to arrange that until we actually reach the capital. It'd mean sweet-talking the higher-ups in the Chamberlain's office, which can only be done on the spot."

She frowned. "But I can't go to the capital," she pointed out. "Can I?"

"You can't be *seen* in the capital. There's a slight but effective difference."

She breathed out slowly through her nose. Oida a scion of the Imperial house. Well, he would be, wouldn't he? The same Providence that ensures that buttered bread always lands butter-side down would see to that. "Fine," she said. "We'll do that, then. Thank you, Uncle Oida."

He scowled at her. "My brother's much older than me," he said.

"Of course he is," she replied gravely. "Now, you get off to bed. Are you sure you can manage the stairs?"

*

Six days in the coach across the Great East Plains. They were using the military road, reckoned by experienced travellers to be one of the best in the world; it was flat, level and straight, free of ruts and potholes, and it seemed to go on for ever. The view from the window was always the same and mostly sky – blue, cloudless. It wasn't unbearably hot, and every twenty miles there was a way station, with clean water and stabling for the horses. They changed escorts every two days (there was a reason for this; Oida had explained it, but she hadn't been listening) but it was inconceivable that they should be attacked out here on the plains. The thought that anything could be alive out there, even savages, was simply grotesque. You'd have to rethink all your definitions of what constituted life.

As well as Saloninus on frailty, Oida had brought Eutolm's *Meditations on Darkness and Light*, a selection of Structuralist lyric poetry, *Achis and Sinuessa* (but no pictures) and *Notes on the Rituals and Protocols of the Imperial Court* by the Emperor Sarpitus II, the annotated edition with notes and commentaries. She read them all. Then they played chess – Oida had a travelling set; pegs on the base of each piece and holes in the middle of each square – but he got upset when he lost and they stopped. There was always sleep, but if she slept too much during the day she stayed awake all night, and the stone benches in the way stations were uncomfortable enough as it was. Oida was happy to talk; he was much better read than she thought he'd be, and tremendously well informed about every aspect of current affairs, but that just made her want to hit him.

"All right," she said one day, in desperation. "What do *you* do on long road journeys? When you're on your own, I mean?"

He frowned at her. "Actually, it's when I get a lot of work done."

For a moment she couldn't think what he meant. Then it occurred to her that by *work* he meant writing music. Somehow, she'd always assumed that it just came to him, fully formed and complete, in moments of enraptured inspiration, or else he bought it cheap from struggling young musicians and passed it off as his own. "Am I in the way?"

"Well, yes," he said. "I can't work when there's someone else there. I need to hum, and I'm self-conscious."

"Don't mind me."

"Yes, but I could. It's like peeing. You might not mind, but I would."

"I'm sorry."

He grinned. "Don't be," he said. "I'm pretty much up to date on commissions, and I never do anything on spec. Great art, I've always felt, is like a pearl; thousands of layers of creativity and sensibility built up around an inner core of money."

"Write that down before you forget it. Anyway, I'm sorry. I hate to think I'm depriving posterity of a masterpiece."

He looked at her carefully, as if assessing whether she'd bear his weight. "You don't like my stuff, do you?"

"Not a lot, no."

"Interesting. I know you like Procopius. Did I ever mention he's my cousin?"

"Oh, God."

"Don't be like that. Do you only go for the heavy stuff, or do you sometimes like something with a tune in it?"

She smiled. "I love tunes. I just don't like yours much."

"Fair enough." He nodded judicially. "I don't, either. I think they're trivial and derivative. But in one pan of the scales we've got you and me, and in the other about a million people who think they're wonderful. So I'd venture to suggest that you and I are probably wrong."

She shook her head. "I don't think so," she said. "But what I think about a whole lot of things doesn't really matter a damn, so that's all right."

"Quite. So, what do you do on long journeys?"

"I take plenty of books. For a trip like this, I'd bring at least thirty pounds, by weight."

He nodded again. "I think being bored is about the worst thing that can happen to you."

"Yes. Well, not quite. I've been raped three times and tortured twice, and once I was three days in a derelict barn with multiple stab wounds. But boredom is very bad, yes."

"I see." He pursed his lips. "In that case, I suggest we play Frame-of-Reference."

She blinked. "I don't know that one."

"Oh, it's great fun. I say three things, lines from poems or titles of books or characters from plays, and you say a fourth, which has got to be connected to the other three. Then I say a fifth, and you say a sixth, and so on. The trick is, when it's your turn, to change the frame of reference so I can't follow. Like, I say Diacritus, then Phemia on board ship, then Santor counting the stars; all arias from *The Wedding of Heaven and Hell*. But then you say Cinentia, which changes the frame of reference to Sanippo's *Eclogues*, and of course there's only four of them, so I can't follow. Get the idea?"

She looked straight back at him. "I don't think I'd enjoy that very much."

He looked disappointed. "Fair enough," he said. "In that case, how about a game of Shields?"

"You've got cards?"

"Of course I've got cards. I'd sooner go out without my trousers on."

There had been a time – one which she tried not to think about, because of other, unrelated issues – when she'd made a comfortable living playing Shields with men in coaches, or on ships, or in way stations and inns. Oida, she knew for a fact, had plenty of money, whereas she was uncomfortably aware of not having a single stuiver to her name until she got back to Rasch. She clicked her tongue. "Oh, go on, then," she said.

There was always the sickening possibility that he was letting her win, though she was fairly sure he wouldn't be capable of doing that. In any event, by the time they reached Mancio she could take comfort in the fact that money would be the least of her worries for quite some time. As the towers of the city resolved themselves out of the heat haze on the horizon, she thanked him for the games and said she'd be happy to take a letter of credit, if he was short of ready cash.

He frowned at her. "Hang on," he said. "We weren't playing for real money, were we?"

"I was."

"Yes, but—" She could see the battle going on inside his head. "I'll write you a note," he said sadly. "I don't carry huge sums like that on me. I'd need porters."

"That's perfectly all right."

He sighed, took out his writing set and a piece of parchment. He passed her the ink bottle and asked her to hold it while he wrote out the note, resting on the lid of the rosewood box. She checked to make sure he'd signed it, then thanked him politely.

"Of course, you won't be able to cash it," he said. "Not till we get back to Rasch. Well, you could cash it in Choris, I suppose, but I don't imagine you'll be going there."

"But I thought—"

He shook his head. "I don't have an account in Blemya," he said. "I'm with the Theudat brothers: they don't do business here. I suppose you could try and discount it, through the Knights or Ocnisant's or someone like that, but you'd be lucky to get three marks in the angel. Wait till you get home. It's not worth the aggravation."

"But—" She stopped herself. "I wanted to do some shopping

in Mancio," she said. "Get myself something to wear, for one thing. And something to read."

"Don't worry about that," he said cheerfully. "I can lend you enough for that, when we get there."

He lent her one angel thirty, which he claimed was all he could spare in cash money until they reached the capital. At five Blemyan hyperpyra to the angel (not so much an exchange rate, more an act of war; but what can you do?) she had enough for a couple of dresses, serviceable second-hand shoes and the complete set of Parrhasius' *Sermons*. She decided she could survive with that, but it wasn't going to be fun.

In return, he shamed her into coming to the show. She pulled faces and said that her shabby clothes would show him up; he told her she'd look good in anything, even an old sack, and he'd really like her to be there. He suffered, he told her, from nerves – a statement which, if true, was one of the most shocking things she'd heard in a long time.

True it proved to be. He was fine when they arrived at the camp gate and a select group of officers fawned over him as if he was the Annunciation, and he was cheerful enough to be insultingly condescending to the garrison commander, a seven-foot-tall mahogany Imperial twenty-year veteran who was struck dumb in his presence and could do nothing but mumble. But when they were alone in the officers' mess, the temporary green room, waiting for the start of the show, Oida started shaking, quite visibly, and pacing up and down. He could hear them, he explained; the audience outside, the hum of their voices. It set off a sort of buzzing noise in his ears, and he couldn't think straight or remember anything. That's just silly, she told him, he'd been on stage hundreds of times, thousands. He gave her a hopeless look. "I know," he said. "That just makes it worse."

"Pull yourself together, for crying out loud," she advised him helpfully. He grinned weakly at her and promised he'd do his best.

They'd saved her a seat in the front row, and a junior officer came to lead her to it. She felt awful leaving him in that state, but there didn't seem to be anything else she could do.

The man sitting next to her was some sort of political: white hair, beautiful fingernails. "I put in for a ticket as soon as I heard about it," he was saying, "but they said no, limited to military personnel only. So I applied to be logistics liaison officer, with the honorary rank of colonel. By the time that came through all the seats were taken, so I had to do a deal. It's cost the federal government forty tons of flaked barley, but I'm here."

"He's my uncle," she said.

"My God," he replied, and offered her a cinnamon biscuit.

When Oida walked on, there was sudden, total silence; she could hear his boots squeaking slightly as he crossed the stage. He was holding a five-string rebec in his left hand, the bow in his right; she knew for a fact that it wasn't his, because he'd been whining about having to leave his behind, afraid it would be broken or stolen. He didn't seem to have noticed that he wasn't alone. He tucked the rebec under his chin, and began to play.

It wasn't his usual sort of thing at all – a set of variations on a theme by Procopius (for her? Surely not). The first movement was slow, a complex melody rising like smoke on a windless day. Then, without warning, the key changed, the tempo quickened and the strange, lazy incantation became a reckless dance, wild and dangerous, swaying up and down the scale, swooping and staggering and abruptly stopping in mid-sequence. When it started again, the theme flashed in and out of a dark, malevolent fugue that made her hands clench and her eyes ache. Just when she thought she was about to drown in it, the fugue collapsed and the original theme soared up out of the wreckage, bright and harsh as winter sunlight, and quickly died away into stunned silence.

After a moment that seemed to last a very long time, the soldiers started to clap. There was a slightly grudging feel to the applause, as though they'd been tricked into agreeing to something they didn't hold with. Oida nodded the most perfunctory bow possible, tucked the rebec under his arm, and sang them "Dogs of War", which was what they'd come to hear. By the third verse, all six thousand of them had joined in. As the fifth verse ended, she realised she'd been singing, too – a mistake, as all who knew her well would testify, but luckily nobody could've heard her over the universal roaring.

After "Dogs" he gave them "The Longest Road", "Where My Heart Takes Me", all nine verses of "Grey Green Hills" and finally "My Life for Yours", perhaps her least favourite song in the whole world, at the end of which she found she was in floods of tears.

"There you go," he said abruptly (they'd been talking about different philosophies of salad dressing). "I think that's it, paid in full."

From somewhere he'd magically produced a big cloth bag, about the size of a bunch of grapes. His hand was clawed around it in a way that suggested it was heavy. "What?" she said.

"My gambling debt," he said. "Go on, take it, before I strain something."

The coach chose that moment to ride a particularly deep rut. The bag jarred out of his hand, fell on the coach floor and split open. Gold coins – the big, chunky Blemyan *tremisses*, each one roughly equivalent to ten angels Imperial. She looked at them, and then at him. "Where in God's name did you get—?"

"My fee." He smiled. "For the gig. That's nearly all of it."

All that money. He'd made all that money in *half an hour*. All she could think to say was, "They paid you in cash?"

He laughed. "Of course not. Government scrip. Which I

was able to change at ninety-nine *trachy* to the *hyperpyron* at the Knights, before we left. You do realise," he added gravely, "that now I'll be barely breaking even on this trip."

She stared at him. "Don't be silly."

"Two thousand angels," he reminded her, "for the spinet. Well, don't just sit there, that's your money on the floor. In case you hadn't noticed, there's a crack just below the doorframe."

She swooped like a hawk; unfortunately, so did he, at precisely the same moment, and their heads collided with a solid crack. He sat up sharply, moaning. She started picking up coins.

"They call it the Beautiful City," he observed, peering out of the window. "God knows why."

She was facing backwards, so she couldn't see. "It was all right," she said. "Mind you, we didn't get to see much of it last time."

"That's because we arrived from the north. Actually, it looks much better from that direction. All the good stuff, architecturally speaking, is crowded in around the Northgate." He sat back in his seat. "What we both need," he said solemnly, "is a bath."

"Yes."

"Don't get your hopes up," he said. "Because we're here by royal invitation, protocol demands that we're met by the Grand Logothete, the Grand Domestic, the Count of the Stables and/or the Chamberlain. There'll be a short religious service followed by an exchange of the Kiss of Peace, a thanksgiving offering to the Sea for our safe arrival, even though we've come overland, and a ritual meal of honeycakes and white bread. And that's before they've even checked our papers."

She looked up. "Papers?"

"It's all right, you're with me. I include you, for administrative purposes." He reached in his pocket for some raisins; she could have told him he'd finished them off an hour ago. "Then I expect we'll be escorted to the palace and shown our quarters, which will take up the rest of the afternoon, and then there's bound to be a reception, followed by a formal dinner. You may just get a shot at a bath sometime around midnight, assuming they keep the water hot all day and night." He gave her a sad smile. "You see what I've got to put up with."

She had a nasty feeling he knew what he was talking about. There had been all sorts of annoying ceremonies the last time, though she hadn't paid much attention to them, being preoccupied with the job she'd had to do. "How come you know so much about it?"

From his inside pocket he produced the Emperor Sarpitus on Protocol. "The Blemyans follow pre-Reform Imperial procedure," he said. "They're mad keen on it, because of their pretty notion that they're the last remnant of the true Empire, and the lads in Choris and Rasch are just jumped-up pretenders. It's quite interesting, actually, because they preserve certain archaic forms that died out in the empire proper a hundred years or more before Sarpitus wrote it all down."

"No, it's not," she said firmly. "Interesting, I mean."

He shrugged. "More fun to read about than to actually experience, I grant you. Oh, that reminds me." He leaned forward and fished something out from behind the seat cushion. "I got this for you. Well, the CO back at the army base gave it to me as a thank-you for doing the gig, but I don't want it, and I know you feel naked without one."

She unwrapped the narrow bundle of cloth, knowing what she'd find: a Blemyan officer's dirk, service issue but decorated with lots of fancy gilded engraving. She slid it an inch out of its scabbard, then put it back again. She felt guilty and ashamed but very grateful. "I agree," she said. "Not your style at all."

"Quite. Now put it away and don't play with it: they can get terribly stuffy about concealed weapons in this town."

She frowned. "I won't be going anywhere in public," she said. "That was part of the deal. You're going to get them to send me home, as quickly as possible."

He looked at her for a moment. "I think we may have to modify the plan a bit," he said.

"What? Hey, that's not—"

"I'm sorry," he said firmly. "It's annoying and maybe I should've anticipated it, but there it is. You've been invited to be presented to the queen. You can't not go, it'd be the most appalling breach of etiquette."

She remembered that there'd been a letter waiting for him at the last way station; but he hadn't said anything about it, and she'd assumed it was nothing. "You might've told me."

"And then it'd have been hanging over you all day yesterday, and you'd have been miserable and depressed. It's fine," he went on, "we'll get you out as quickly as we can, you've just got to do this one thing, and—"

"I can't meet the queen," she said. "She'll recognise me. Half the bloody Court—"

He smiled. "I think you overestimate your memorability," he said sweetly. "No offence. I'd remember you anywhere, naturally. But if you recall, it was a large delegation, and we stuck you at the back so people wouldn't notice you. It'll be all right."

"I'm wanted for *murder*."

He shook his head. "Suspected of, not wanted for," he said casually. "There's a difference. Besides, the woman they thought might just possibly have had something to do with that business was a priestess in government service. You're my niece. You're a lady of leisure and you've never been to Blemya before in your life. Just remember that and everything will be fine, you'll see."

"You must be out of your mind. Stop the coach, I'll walk from here."

"Where to?"

"I don't care. I'll find my own way home. I've got money. I can take care of myself. Whatever I do, it's got to be safer than—"

He shook his head. "Unfortunately, no," he said. "Not possible. They're expecting you now, and if you don't show up I don't think I'll be able to think of a convincing reason for you not being there. If I say you wandered off or got kidnapped by bandits, they'd insist on sending a regiment to find you. It's a nuisance," he added, raising his voice over hers, "but so long as we're sensible and we play it cool, there won't be a problem, I promise you. Come on, you're a professional. You can handle this."

There was something in the way he'd said it that made her skin tingle. Good reasons, she thought. "If I get caught, you'll be in trouble, too," she said. "You won't be able to smarm your way out of it: they'll know you knew and you lied. And then they'll guess you were mixed up in it the last time. It's your neck on the block as well as mine."

He looked at her, expressionless. "Yes," he said. "I had actually thought of that for myself, thank you. I'm risking my life as well as my career and my professional standing. Don't ask me why, because I'm not sure I know. But there it is."

She felt as if she'd been punched. Perfectly true; he had so much to lose, and he was risking it all, because of her, and it wasn't even a paying job . . . It made her feel angry, but other things as well, things best ignored. "Fine," she snapped. "This whole business has got completely out of control, so we'll just have to make the best of it we can."

He grinned. "That's the spirit," he said. "I love it when you're grateful."

"Oh, drop dead."

He thought of it at the last minute. She protested, told him it was a stupid idea and that it'd attract attention rather than deflecting it. He took out the book, found the place (bookmarked with a feather) and handed it to her without a word. She read it and handed it back.

It worked. As he'd anticipated, the Chamberlain knew all about the ordinance in Sarpitus that decreed that women who had recently recovered from various specifically female ailments were required to be veiled in public; the ordinance wasn't widely followed in Blemya, he said, because the rule was actually introduced sometime after the Blemyan code of etiquette crystallised into its present form ... However, the Court was always happy to recognise the younger tradition, particularly where a close relative of a distinguished visitor was concerned.

"You think you're so clever," she hissed at him, as the State coach drove them to the palace.

"Well, I am," he answered mildly.

"The sooner you can get me out of this horrible country, the better for both of us. I really can't face a whole week smothered in bloody cheesecloth. I can't breathe."

"We'll get you a proper veil," he reassured her. "Silk or something."

Their apartments in the palace were amazing. Oida's suite had been built as a council chamber, with seating for two hundred; they'd stripped out the benches and installed a bath, with hot water piped up from the huge thousand-gallon copper in the main kitchen, two floors below. The bath itself had once been the sarcophagus of a long-dead king; its sides were carved with graphic scenes of the Day of Judgement, the punishment of the damned and the enrapturement of the Elect. All four walls and the ceiling were covered with mosaics, mostly scenes of feasting and the hunt. The bed was the size of a large hay wagon, and the chamber pot was rose-pink alabaster. Her room was next door; half the size but still bewilderingly huge. The walls were decorated with tapestries and the ceiling was a fresco of a personified Blemya trampling on a nest of disturbingly realistic snakes, presumably representing the old Empire; there was, however, no bath.

"That's all right," Oida said. "You can use mine. Any time."

She glowered at him. "I'll send down for a big basin of hot water and a sponge."

"As you wish." He sat down on her bed. "A bit on the lumpy side compared to mine. Still, a damn sight better than what we've been used to lately. Now aren't you glad you came?"

"No."

"Ah well." He stood up, then knelt down and placed his hand palm-down on the marble floor. "Underfloor heating," he said. "They run hot water through bloody great copper pipes under the floor tiles."

"I thought it was a bit stuffy in here. Can you make it stop?"

"Not really. It'd mean putting out the fire in the big boiler down in the cellars, which supplies hot water to the whole palace complex. I don't think it's gone out any time in the last hundred and fifty years." He stood up. "You'll just have to grin and bear it," he said. "If it gets too much for you, I suggest taking a blanket and a pillow out on to the balcony."

She growled at him. "We didn't get anything like this the last time."

"True. But then we weren't guests of honour: we were part of a delegation they were being politely rude to, so we got stuck in the poky little rooms on the fifth floor. More protocol, see. They do love it so."

She took the makeshift veil off and wound it round a bed post. "Have you found out when we've got to do this presentation thing?"

"Not yet. You'd better get ready. We've got the reception next, followed by dinner."

She glanced down at the dress she was wearing. The other one was filthy with dust from the road. "I'm ready now."

He studied her for a moment. "No," he said, "you're not. Try and do something with your hair, for pity's sake. I don't know what to suggest about your nails. Make two fists, and lean forward when you eat."

Both the Eastern and Western ambassadors were at the reception, anxious to meet the celebrated Oida so that they could tell their friends about it when they got home. It was quite easy to tell them apart: the Westerner was short, bald and thin, the Easterner was tall and fat, with a mop of white hair. They both smiled very pleasantly at her, then ignored her completely.

There was also an ambassador, or something vaguely equivalent, from the Lodge, and she was sorely tempted to try and get a private word with him, in the hope that he could expedite her escape, or at the very least get a report back to her superiors, so they'd know she was still alive. But whenever she tried to get near him, he seemed to shy away and find some Blemyan to talk to. He couldn't be avoiding her, because how could he possibly know who she was; and if he did know, why wouldn't he want to talk to her? But it was rather strange, and made her feel nervous.

The dinner presented its own problems. She was hungry, and the food looked wonderful – escalopes of pork in a honey and mustard sauce, with chickpeas and anchovies and salad and thin strips of fried apple – but the thought of trying to eat in a veil melted her appetite like snow in sunshine, and she told the man sitting next to her that she was fasting, as part of the purification process. He turned out to be a junior minister in the Exchequer, so she asked him to explain Jotapian's Law of sound money to her, and was mildly amused when he got most of it wrong.

The man on the other side of her was a soldier, a senior staff officer just returned from patrolling in the desert. She asked him if he'd engaged the enemy: no, thank God, he replied with feeling, he'd been assigned the eastern side of the road, which had been dead quiet ever since Forza Belot slaughtered the enemy's main army. It was on the western side that they'd had all the trouble with the insurgents, who by all accounts had learned the lesson General Belot had taught them, and were concentrating on picking off villages and towns. There was something very different going on out there, he told her: you might almost call it a different attitude to war, a new way of defining victory – *sophisticated* was the only word he could think of, which was an odd way to describe hit-and-run attacks by savages, but there it was. So long as he wasn't called on to do anything about it, he was delighted to leave it to other, better strategists, who were welcome to slog up and down the sand dunes while he was back here, in civilisation, eating, listening to good music and maybe even meeting the legendary Oida—

She left as early as she could and went back to her room, to find that nobody had been in to light the lamps. She found the tinder-box by feel and discovered there was no tinder. So she sat in the dark for a while, then groped her way out on to the balcony; she misjudged the distances, bumped into the rail and nearly went over. A perfect end to a perfect day, in fact.

There was a seat on the balcony; cold, hard stone, but better than standing up (her feet were hurting; the incessant underfloor heat had made them swell, and her boots were uncomfortably small). It was a clear night and the moon was nearly full. She amused herself for a while by figuring out the geography of the courtyard below her, then fell asleep.

A prod on the shoulder woke her up, and there was Oida standing over her with a sort of cloth bundle in one hand and a lamp in the other. "Inside," he said. "Before you catch your death."

The bundle proved to be a linen antimacassar – there had been one on the back of every chair in the dining room – and when Oida unfolded it she saw that it contained bread rolls, five different sorts of cheese, apples, pears, honey and cinnamon cakes and six cubes of that amazing pink sweet soft stuff that was the only real justification for the existence of Blemya. "I thought you might be hungry," he said, "so I grabbed a few bits on the way out."

She gazed into his eyes for maybe two heartbeats, then lunged at the food like a jackal. He perched on the end of the bed while she ate, occasionally picking out something for himself. She ate solidly for quite some time. Then she looked at him again. "I don't suppose you thought to bring anything to drink," she said.

"Depends." From the baggy sleeve of his gown he produced a small stone bottle. "I know you don't usually touch the hard stuff," he said. "But there aren't any pockets in this rag, so I had to make do with what I could fit in."

She frowned at him. "There's water in the jug."

"Fine." He stood up, found the jug and brought it to her. "No cup, glass or beaker," he said. "Same in my room, oddly enough. I don't think the Blemyans drink in their rooms."

"Doesn't matter." She grabbed the jug and tried to drink from the side of the spout. Some of the water found its way into her mouth; the rest ran down her chin and then her neck. She pulled a face. "Tastes funny."

"I think it's for washing in," Oida said mildly. "My understanding is, drinking water comes from the well, or the rainwater tank on the roof. That stuff's probably been six times round the heating system, in lead pipes. Still, I don't suppose a few mouthfuls will kill you."

"I've had worse," she mumbled through a mouthful of bread.

"I know you have," he said mildly, and dabbed at his forehead with the hem of the antimacassar. "You're right, it gets quite stifling after a bit. I think I'll go out on the balcony and cool down."

She ate what was left, then went out to join him. "I wish there was some way of making it stop," she said.

"Ah." He smiled. "I asked one of the palace nobs about it, actually it's quite interesting. On the ground floor, the hot air from the furnace rises and passes through corridors of bitumen-coated brick under the flooring slabs. To get heat to the upper storeys, they run boiling water through miles of thick lead pipe laid alongside the rafters of the floors. They've got this system of pumps, with two dozen men working them all day and all night. Apparently, it takes five tons of charcoal—"

"In other words, you can't make it stop."

"No. Hell of an undertaking, though. The whole building is honeycombed with pipes and flues and hypocausts, which is why everything looks so chunky and solid. This chap was telling me, they had exactly the same system in the Old Palace in Rasch, except that it stopped working about ninety years ago, and now nobody remembers that it's there."

"Good," she said. "It's a menace. Did you bring the water jug?"

"No. Have a pull of this instead."

"What is it?"

"Local speciality. Distilled from peach stones."

"No, thank you." She started to get up but he was quicker than her; he came back a moment later with the jug. She held it awkwardly with the handle at the back and poured water into her mouth. "What kind of lunatic installs round-the-clock heating in a town built on the edge of the desert?"

"Ah." He grinned. "The empire had it, so the Blemyans had to have it, too." He cracked the wax round the spout of the bottle, drew the stopper and took a small swig. "Not bad," he said. "You can get it in Rasch occasionally, but it's not as good. Sure?"

She nodded. No way was she going to drink strong drink with Oida in her bedroom. "Have you found out any arrangements yet?"

"For the concert?"

"For getting me out of here."

"I'm working on it, I promise. Meanwhile, the concert's tomorrow evening, and then the presentation's the afternoon after that."

"I can't stay in this oven two whole days. I'll fry."

He nodded. "Do as I suggested and sleep out here," he said. "Apparently, that's what the locals do when they can't stand it any more. If you haven't got enough cushions, there's plenty in my room."

In the early hours of the morning, she had occasion to remember the first thing they tell you about the desert: boiling hot during the day, freezing cold at night. She went back inside, stayed there until the sweat was dripping off the end of her nose, went back outside and shivered. A bit like the fancy public baths in Rasch, with the difference that you could leave the baths if you wanted to.

"I want you to be honest with me," she said.

The sun was shining in the formal garden at the back of the Baths of Uxin, and Oida was drinking white wine flavoured with honey and mint. He had a straw hat tilted over his eyes. "I'm always honest with you," he said. "Nearly always."

The new veil was an improvement on the cheesecloth in that it didn't smell of cheese, but it made her want to scream. Through it she could see her big, strong hands folded demurely in her lap. Her mother had hated them, declared that she'd never get a husband with paws like that. Keep them behind your back, she used to say, or pull your sleeves down over them. "I want you to tell me why you were at the castle."

"To rescue you," Oida said. She couldn't see his face, because of the hat.

"There are good reasons, plausible reasons and the real reason," she said. "I want the real reason."

"You just had it."

She sighed. "There's a bit in one of my favourite books," she said. "A man is drowning. Someone pulls him out. The man starts to thank his rescuer, but then the rescuer's hood falls off and he sees his face. You're Death, the man says. That's right, says Death. Then why did you save me, asks the man, and Death says, for later." The veil was tickling her neck; she scratched. "Well?"

Oida yawned. "I liked his earlier stuff better," he said.

"That instrumental piece you played," she said, picking at a hangnail. "The Procopius variations. Yours?"

He nodded. "Something I threw together for a concert I did the time before last I was here. The garrison commander heard it the first time and asked me to do it again. It didn't go down very well, but what can you expect?"

He'd answered her question. "Real reason?"

"Good reason. Did you like it?"

"Actually, yes."

He nodded. "More your sort of thing. I know you don't think much of my songs."

"I wouldn't be a true friend if I wasn't savagely honest. No, I don't."

"Ah, well. Most people do."

"And most people pay more money, right. You know, you could write good music if you—"

He laughed. "Of course I could," he said. "You want to know a secret? Writing what you call good music is easy, piece of cake. You're writing for intelligent, educated people who are prepared to meet you halfway. It's the army songs and the romantic ballads that made me sweat blood."

"I don't believe you."

"Because they're simple and accessible? You don't know anything about writing music. Simple and accessible is the hardest thing there is. It's like designing a clock mechanism with only two moving parts. It's working with both hands tied behind your back. You're limited to a simple melodic line, which has to conform to strict form. You've got the voice and one instrument and that's it, no orchestra, no counterpoint, nothing. It's like explaining Saloninus' theory of the Eternal Recurrence to a six-year-old rather than a tenured professor of Ethics." He tilted the hat back and sat up a little. "And that's why I earn good money," he said. "Because I can give people what they want. Not just the smart ones. Everybody." Suddenly he grinned. "I do actually work for a living," he said.

"All right," she said grudgingly. "If money is all that matters—"

"It's the only reliable way of keeping score," he said. "A thousand cultured folk will tell you they love your symphony, but can you believe them? But if a hundred thousand poor people decide they can afford two stuivers to hear you sing, that probably means you're actually getting something right." He shrugged. "Not that I mind the money," he added. "One of these days I might get to spend some of it. Who knows?"

"Fine," she said. "But Procopius could write a symphony everybody would enjoy."

"Maybe. So why hasn't he?"

"Because he writes what he must. He's not desperate to please everybody on earth. And Procopius will still be listened to when your stuff's long forgotten. And I think that means that Procopius is the one who gets it right."

He smiled. "Listened to by whom? No, forget it, I'm sure you're right. I'm just a whore, selling my soul for money. Suits me. And, yes, I do like people to like me. It makes life so much easier." He tilted the hat back over his eyes and relaxed. "One thing I will say for Procopius," he said. "He's a hell of a card player."

When she got back to her room, she found a dress laid out on the bed. She spent a whole minute just staring at it. Then she tried it on.

There was a full-length mirror on the far wall; an amazing thing, Mezentine, probably five hundred years old, a few black clouds at the edges but the tone still absolutely perfect. She looked at herself and saw a thin, striking woman in a dress made for a fairy princess. It made her hands look like sides of pork. A sweet thought, she decided, but completely wrong. Therefore, Oida must have sent it.

She took it off and laid it out carefully so it wouldn't crease. He'd only done it so she'd have something respectable to wear to his concert, so she wouldn't show him up. Weird, though, that he'd imagined she'd look anything other than strange in a dress like that; as if he didn't see her the way the mirror did. She tried to remember just how long she'd known him, but couldn't. He'd always been there, somehow. Not that it mattered a damn.

The concert was held in what had once been a temple, though so long ago that nobody knew for sure who or what had been worshipped there; the old frescos had all been painted over (with Blemya receiving the tribute of all nations, in a rather garish Triumphalist style that made her teeth ache) but a few worn bas-reliefs could still be seen in the upper galleries if you craned your neck; whether they were meant to be human, animal, divine or abstract was anybody's guess. But the acoustic wasn't bad at all.

Oida was trembling so much before the show that she was sure he wouldn't be able to do it; ten minutes later he bounced on with a grin on his face and a violin, and began to play; a series of sonatas and fugues – Procopius, Alimbal, Lanaphe: if she'd chosen the programme it wouldn't have been much different. At first she was stunned, then enraptured, then angry. Their conversation that morning; was he making fun of her? Or had he engineered it, to make her feel small and stupid? Somehow the anger didn't spoil the music one bit.

There was a brief intermission, during which footmen brought round water and iced tea in silver jugs, which reminded her just how hot and thirsty she was (but the horrible veil meant she couldn't drink). Then Oida came back and sang; arias from *Truth* and *The Abdication of Rhixus*, the Invocation from *Luzir Soleth*, that sort of thing. She was sure he wasn't going to make the high notes in the Invocation, but he did, effortlessly. For an encore he gave them "Lord of Tempests", which he sang at breakneck speed, the way Saiva is reputed to have done, though nobody believes it. He did it perfectly, and when he'd finished she realised she was on her feet along with everyone else, and her hands were sore.

Mercifully, there was no reception afterwards. She waited patiently for the crush to file out, then headed for the grand staircase. To get there, she had to pass a colonnade. A hand appeared from behind a column, grabbed her by the elbow and hauled her into the shadows.

"Quiet," Oida said. He was still in his stage robe, but he had a small bundle wrapped in cloth. She recognised it. He pushed it into her hands. "Job for you."

She stared at him. "What?"

He drew her further into the colonnade, out of sight. "But first, a conjuring trick." His pack of cards appeared as if by magic in his hand. He fanned them (smooth as any professional) and held them under her nose. "Pick a card," he said. "Any card."

"Are you drunk?"

"Pick a fucking card."

She chose one. "Look at it." She turned it over and her heart stopped. Four of Swords.

There is no suit of Swords in an orthodox pack. And four was her next call sign; but only the abbot knew that.

"Listen carefully," Oida said. "Ten paces to your left, up against the wall, is a flagstone with a ring in it. Lift it up and you'll find steps going down. That puts you in the main hypocaust, which runs right across this floor. It'll be a bit of a squeeze and

I know you're not wild about confined spaces, but I'm sure you can cope if you try. Go precisely ninety-two yards – you'll have to count, it'll be dark as a bag down there, not to mention hot as hell – you'll find another slab with a ring in it, that'll let you down one level. There aren't any steps, you'll just have to drop, so for God's sake don't hurt yourself, because nobody can come and fish you out if you get into trouble. With me so far?"

She couldn't speak, so she nodded.

"Now I don't know the exact distance, so you'll have to feel for the hatches on the wall on your left-hand side. Hatch twenty-seven is the one you want; it opens inwards, so be careful. Crawl down that exactly eighty-seven yards, directly above you will be a trapdoor like the others, a slab you can lift. That's where it could be tricky, because you'll be coming up into a watch chamber, and there could well be a guard on duty. Deal with him if you have to, and pull the body down the hypocaust after you on your way back. Don't leave the knife behind, remember, it can be traced to me."

"Just a minute," she hissed.

Maybe he hadn't heard her. "In the chamber, you'll find a locked cabinet. You should be able to force the lock, or maybe you can pick it. I know you're good at that. What you want is a ring with five keys on it, one of them almost twice as long as the others. If there's more than one set answering that description, bring them all. Then it's back the way you came and meet me here in one hour. Got that?"

She opened her mouth to refuse, then closed it again. Four of Swords. The hand can't disobey the brain. Instead, she whispered, "So that's why you came to rescue me."

He gave her a look that stopped her in her tracks. "There are good reasons, plausible reasons and the real reason," he said. "A beautiful girl once told me that, but I don't think she loves me. Get moving, we're on the clock."

*

If there is a Hell, according to Saloninus in the *Third Eclogue*, it's probably the absence of light. Far be it from her to disagree, but he couldn't be more wrong. Hell, if there is one, is confined spaces.

That's why they bury people: because most people lead wicked lives, and the good are enraptured from the flesh at the moment of death; and putting someone in a tight-fitting box and covering her with tons of earth is the worst possible punishment any mind, mortal or immortal, could possibly devise.

At least there was no box. She could move; and if she kept moving it wasn't quite so bad; and if she kept counting, she couldn't think about it. But if she stopped or lost count, she knew she'd be finished – astray, off the beacon, no way back, she'd be there for ever and ever, unless you believe in a Day of Judgement and the end of the world, which she didn't.

She couldn't stand upright, but if she bent forward until her elbows were on her knees, she could just about get by – the top of her head brushed the roof, which was the home of many spiders, and the gentle drag of the gossamer on her hair made her flesh crawl – and she could accurately measure distance by the number of paces taken. There were columns of bricks on either side of her (she'd found that out by scraping her forearms against them) and they were accurately, regularly spaced, two feet between them. By counting them as well, she could cross-check on the distance. Ninety-two yards. Was that to the edge of the flagstone or the middle, where the ring was?

Just as well she wasn't relying on eyesight, because the sweat in her eyes would've made it impossible to see.

The dress, now; at least the dress had been explained to her satisfaction. It fitted. How Oida had got her measurements she didn't want to know, but it fitted and she could move in it, which was more than could be said for any of the other clothes at her disposal. The fabric had been well chosen, too. The hotter she got, the more it clung to her; the more it clung, the easier it was to move. Chosen by a man with a good working knowledge of women's bodies. A smart man, Oida, the sort who knows all kinds of things.

In the event, she overshot by a good yard, realised she'd come too far by the brick-pile count, had to shuffle backwards, groping on the floor for the ring. She found it; there simply wasn't room to straighten up enough to pull it. But it had to be possible, because the men who maintained the hypocausts could do it. Eventually, she got it figured: raise it a couple of inches and slide the knife in under it to keep it open, then get the other side of it, lie down and gradually lever it up until it slid away and clanged on the floor with a noise they must've been able to hear in Choris. She lay perfectly still and counted to a hundred, but she couldn't hear footsteps on the floor above her. Would the sound carry through the marble slabs? She had no idea.

On the clock, she reminded herself. Oh, and be careful of the drop.

It was just as well she'd slipped off her boots first. Her idea had been to brace herself in the hole with her arms, grab the sides of the hole, dangle, then drop the last few inches, feet, whatever. It didn't work like that. She slipped and caught herself from falling by her elbows, so that her full weight was supported by muscles that weren't usually called on to do that sort of work. They objected, and she felt their displeasure; meanwhile, she was stuck. She tried lifting up again, but she wasn't strong enough. All she could do was tuck her elbows in until she was free to fall.

For a moment or so after she landed, she was terrified that she'd broken something, just as Oida had said she would. But when she dared to wiggle her toes, she could feel them move, and she decided the pain in her ankles was just pain. A surge of relief left her too weak to move for a long time.

She tried to take a deep breath, but her lungs had got very small. But no matter. Onwards, as Oida would say.

The lower hypocaust was secondary and narrower. She could get along on her hands and knees, but she had to squeeze her way past every column of bricks. Remarkably, the fabric of the dress didn't tear, but her skin did. The floor slabs were almost too hot to bear, would've been intolerable without the sweat pouring off her. Twenty-seven hatches; she decided they were evenly spaced, but her progress was irregular, short paddles and long ones. She had to feel up past the bricks to feel for the hatch frames, and was scared stiff she might have missed one.

Twenty-seven, and she was panting like a dog, her heart was the size of a watermelon, she was dizzy and sick and her back was agony. The hatches open inwards, so be careful. Be careful? What the hell was that supposed to mean?

She found out. When opened, the hatch completely filled the hypocaust, airtight, a perfect fit, a gasket. She tried to close it again, because the opening was on the other side. It wouldn't budge: it was wedged, stuck. She bashed with the heels of her hands, shoulder-bumped it, no use. Only when she squirmed her way round and kicked it with both feet did it budge; then it slammed shut and she couldn't claw it open again. The tip of the knife levered it free eventually. She crawled past it, then swung it back, maybe a little too hard – it was stuck again, and there was no handle on the inside, and she'd have to come back this way. But, she told herself, I'm not going to survive much more of this, so I won't be coming back, so it doesn't matter. Through the hatch. Onwards.

Crawl exactly eighty-seven yards. How can you measure eighty-seven yards, exactly, in the dark on your hand and knees?

The new shaft was smaller still, but there weren't any piles of bricks. Instead, there was a pipe, dead centre on the floor, wide enough that she couldn't quite get her knees either side of it. Needless to say, it was scalding. She backed up to the open hatch and somehow managed to squirm out of the dress. It was sodden with sweat, as wet as if she'd been out in the rain. She draped it over the pipe and slid it along with her knees as she went.

The calibration problem turned out not to be a problem after all. Someone – the builders, maybe, or some extremely intelligent Clerk of Works – had cut marks in the brick on the right-hand wall at intervals of eighteen inches. She only realised what they were after she'd come a painfully long way. She established the interval by marking off in handspans. Then she backed up all the way to the hatch and started again.

One hundred and sixty-four notches. Directly overhead there should be a slab that lifted.

The knife, in its sheath, was gripped in her right hand. She'd almost forgotten what it was there for. Oh, that. Reaching up, she laid the flat of her left hand and the knuckles of her right on the underside of the roof, and pushed as hard as she possibly could. It lifted, a little. Not nearly enough. She gave it everything she had, but she couldn't move it any further.

Then, quite suddenly, it wasn't there any more, and she was drowning in unendurable light. Her still-upraised left hand was grabbed, and someone incredibly strong hauled her up an impossibly long way, then set her down lightly on a hard, smooth floor.

She blinked, but all she could see was a painfully bright blur, and all she could do was pant and whimper. A voice was talking to her. Unbelievably, it was saying, "Are you all right, miss?"

Later, she saw it from his point of view. A manhole opens; he hauls it up and there's a naked woman, trembling and squealing and sopping wet. The most extraordinary thing you've ever seen; but hardly a danger. What else would you do but pull her out, calm her down and try and find out how she got there?

It was pure, undeserved luck that she'd dropped the knife when he pulled her up, because if he'd seen it he might have formed a different view. As it was, she had no trouble at all drawing his sword and stabbing him in the pit of the stomach with it. Not a clean kill, but enough to shut him up; she pulled it out and stabbed him again, this time in the hollow between the collarbones. He rocked back, hit a wall and lay still. Onwards.

She stepped over him and located the cabinet Oida had told her about. Of course it was locked, and it was a great heavy thing, inch-thick oak boards with dovetailed joints. Her knife would've snapped if she'd tried to force it open with that, but the sentry's sword managed it, though she bent the blade. Like she cared; she was radiantly happy, because she was out of the hole, out of the grave, risen again from the dead, her heart had stopped pounding and she could breathe.

There were, of course, three sets of five keys with four short ones and one long one. Not her problem. She looped them round the middle finger of her left hand and closed her fist on them. She'd left wet footprints on the floor, as though she'd just got out of the bath; quite possibly a fatal mistake, but she simply didn't care any more.

Then she looked at the hole in the floor; the deep, black hole that led down to hell, where thieves and murderers go for all eternity. I can't, she thought. She backed away from it until she met the wall, then slid down it and crouched, not moving, as though it would pounce on her if it saw her.

She woke up with a start, because a voice in her ear had just said, *one hour, we're on the clock.* She looked round, but there was nobody there.

One hour, and she'd been asleep. She scrambled to her feet. The hole was still there, and it was going to eat her alive, but it didn't matter. She had a job to do, and she was late.

Pulling the guard down into the hole wasn't going to be easy; doing that and then closing the flagstone after her— Bloody Oida, she told herself, he just doesn't *think.*

She did the geometry. If she pitched the guard down the hole first, he'd fill the available space and she wouldn't be able to get past him. Would she? It was an assumption, but assumptions are there to be challenged. She considered the room available, her own size and shape, the alternative – go down into the hole, drag the guard down after her by the ankle, then somehow reach past and lower the flagstone – no, that wasn't possible. So, no alternative at all.

She dragged him by one foot and fed him down the hole legs first. Luckily he wasn't stiff yet; if she'd left it much longer, it could've made things interesting. It turned out that there was just enough of a gap for her to squeeze past him if she stamped on his head enough to pack him down and then pretended she was a liquid rather than a solid. She got stuck, her stomach pressed hard against the scalding pipe, and had to claw her way inch by inch, doing all the work with her hands because her legs had nothing to act against. She got through. As an afterthought, she hooked the scarf off his neck and wedged it between her skin and the pipe. It helped, a bit.

That was the hard part. All she had to do after that was drag him down a way – one hand hooked under his chin, the other with fingers hooked into one of the clever clerk's calibration grooves, the only handhold she could find – then scramble back up out of the hole, lift the flagstone, balance it with exquisite precision so that it'd topple down exactly into the hole when she nudged it from underneath; back down again, unseat the slab, then get her head out of the way before the slab came crashing down and smashed her skull like an egg.

And then, of course, it was dark again. She crawled over the dead man's face like a slug, then remembered the knife. She'd dropped it, she knew that, but where was it? She was guessing it was the presentation piece the garrison commander had given to Oida, and which he'd passed on to her; so of course it could be recognised and traced, and if they lifted the flagstone and shone a lantern down the shaft, there it would be. Turning round wasn't possible, so she had to backtrack, crawling feet first, back over the dead man again. It took a long time to locate the knife by feel, not really knowing where to search, since the slab had been replaced and it was pitch dark. She found it more or less by accident; also her dress, which she'd completely forgotten about. Lucky, because the scarf on its own wasn't really enough to protect her from the hot pipe.

When she passed from the pipe channel into the hypocaust it felt like coming home: just those extra few inches of space. There was, of course, the matter of the wedged-open hatch, jammed against the hypocaust wall. Nothing would shift it, and she felt the panic building up again; just in time before it swamped her, she thought of sticking the knife into the hatch frame as hard as she could, then looping the scarf round the handle and pulling on it. To her great surprise, that actually worked. She slithered through the hatch into the main hypocaust and burst out laughing.

Enough of that. She now had room enough to pull the dress back on – God only knew what state it was in, but at least the hot pipe had dried it out a bit, and it wasn't like wearing algae. She tried to stand up, but the soles of her feet had got burned on the pipe – she hadn't even noticed, at the time – and it took a substantial effort of will to put her weight on them, crushing the fat blisters and feeling the pus move as she bent her foot. But the keys were still looped round her finger, and she could walk again, instead of crawling. Onwards.

Forty careful paces, cross-referenced with the brick piles, and then she stopped. She couldn't remember. Was it ninety-two yards or ninety-six? For a moment, she panicked and lost her nerve, until she realised it didn't matter. Try both, and one of them will be right. And pull yourself together, for crying out loud.

Ninety-two, as it happened. She put the back of her head against the slab and heaved; it started to move, then disappeared;

light, brighter even than the last time, and Oida's voice, hissing, "Where the *hell* did you get to?"

"You've made it very difficult for us," he said, lifting her foot. She was flat on her back. "Getting yourself in that state. Just look at you, for crying out loud. We've got that presentation tomorrow."

She tried to tell him it hadn't been on purpose but her voice didn't seem to be working. He unhooked the brooch from his cloak, took a firm grip on her foot and burst the blisters with the brooch pin, one after another. "Right," he said. "Can you stand?"

Only one way to find out. Turned out she could.

Oida knelt down and unlaced his boots. "You'll have to wear these," he said, "and I'll just have to slop along in my bare feet, there's no time to get anything from the rooms. God, what a shambles."

Time was short, he explained, as they limped down the colonnade, because there was an incredibly small window of opportunity between the evening watch and the first night watch, most of which she'd dissipated by being late. Any moment now, the night watch would come on duty and the whole place would be swarming with guards.

"Where are we going?" she managed to ask.

"Work to do" was all he said. Then he tightened his grip on her elbow and made her walk faster. "Where's the knife?"

"Left it behind."

"Oh, you didn't." He sounded so disappointed in her. "It just keeps getting better. Well, if we run into trouble, you'll just have to rend our enemies with your teeth. Try and keep up, will you?"

She wanted to cry, but she knew she couldn't. Further or in the alternative she wanted to cut Oida's throat, but crying would be better. "Where are we going?" she repeated, but he didn't seem to have heard. He was getting ahead of her and she had to run to keep up.

"This is now all incredibly dangerous," Oida observed, opening a door at the far end of the colonnade. "If we aren't caught it'll be a miracle. For God's sake try and keep quiet, I don't want to have to slaughter half the garrison."

There was a long corridor, which came out in a small, dark courtyard which led into a narrow alley, at the end of which was an arch, past which was a gate with a small wicket set into it. Oida fumbled with the keys for a long time, until she heard a lock click. It was too dark to see his face, but he paused for a long time before opening the door very gently and peering through the crack. "Fool's luck," he whispered. "Come on."

It was too dark to see anything inside, but the floor under her feet felt like boards rather than slabs. "Carefully," Oida whispered, too softly for her to be able to place where he was or, by implication, which direction she should take to follow him. So she did the only thing she could, and stopped dead. "Keep *up*," she heard him hiss, loudly enough to give her a fix on his position; she hurried towards him and heard the floorboards creak slightly. She reached out on both sides and the fingertips of her right hand contacted what felt like unplastered brick. Now it made sense: he was following the wall. Reasonable enough, but he might have mentioned it.

She heard keys in another door, then he said, "Stairs". She shuffled forward, but in his boots, with blistered feet, she had real trouble feeling for the change between flat floor and stair. When it came she stumbled and was only just able to steady herself by clawing at the wall.

She counted sixty-five stairs, going down.

"Stop," she heard him say. She stopped. More keys. A click, and then he whispered, "Probably guards on the other side of this door." Then he opened it, and light hit her in the face.

Another gallery – it reminded her of mineshafts she'd been in, not her happiest memory; there were props every yard, supporting rafters, but the floor was paved with brick and there were lanterns hanging from hooks. The roof was rock, not earth. "We're in luck," he whispered. "There should be a guard here. Arrangement was he'd be paid to be somewhere else, but I didn't get a confirmation on that. Looks like Division got something right for once."

She counted a hundred and twenty-five paces, and then they came to another door. Oida had the key. He inserted it, then turned back to her.

"Look," he said, "I'm sorry for being a bastard. It's because I'm so scared I can hardly breathe. It makes me irritable. There may be a guard the other side of this door, or there may not. From now on, guards and fighting are your business, while I do the rescuing. All right?"

She nodded, too startled to speak. "Thanks," he said, and turned the key.

Just another corridor, also with a propped roof. "Oh, God, right or left?" he moaned, then turned left. Soon they were passing heavy oak doors, with small sliding panels at eye level; so, probably not the wine cellars. The doors were numbered, in chalk; some of the numbers had been rubbed out. "Sixty-two, we want," he whispered. "Trouble is, they're not in bloody order."

True: forty-one was next to twenty-seven was next to a hundred and sixty-six. The corridor was so narrow that if a cell door opened it would block and seal it, like the hatch in the hypocaust. She glanced up at the roof and tried to remember if Blemya had a history of earthquakes.

Sixty-two; he'd gone past it. She grabbed his elbow, pulled him back and pointed. "Shit," he said. "Just as well one of us has got a brain." He handed her the keys. "Right, you stay here, and when I say the word, unlock the door and pull it open. It's the longest key."

Now she understood the reason for the bizarre architecture.

It took two men to unlock a cell; one man couldn't do it on his own, he'd be blocked by the door and the prisoner could bolt. "Right," he said. She turned the key and hauled on the door, and was suddenly alone.

Presumably the door had a handle on the inside. It moved away from her, and she saw Oida. He had his elbow round the throat of an impossibly thin, bald young man – she assumed he was alive, but he could easily have been dead, the way he was propped up against Oida's body.

"He's completely out of it," Oida said sadly. "This is going to be no fun at all."

They ended up carrying him, because he couldn't or wouldn't move; she had his ankles, while Oida held him under the arms. They had to keep stopping so Oida could adjust his grip. The young man's feet galled the blisters on her ribs. "This is hopeless," Oida said, several times, and then they reached the first door.

Getting through it was complicated; they had to prop the young man up against the wall, and she kept him steady while Oida did the lock. Then it was Oida's turn at the feet end, and hers to do the heavy lifting. The young man wasn't exactly a burden. She realised, in the small, detached part of her mind that still gave a damn, that she was probably stronger than Oida, or at least better educated in managing heavy weights.

The stairs were all manner of fun and games. Oida seemed to have forgotten about the possibility of guards; he made a lot of unnecessary noise and barged through the door at the top of the stairs without looking. But the luck held, or the plan worked better than anticipated; surprisingly quickly, they made it out into the alley that led to the courtyard, and there Oida stopped.

"Got to get my bearings," he muttered, breathing heavily. "Fifth stable yard, it's where they keep the horses for the garbage carts. How's your sense of smell? I haven't really got one."

But she had, and it led them across the courtyard, through

an unlocked gate to the main palace midden. "Needless to say they work a night shift," Oida whispered, as they peered round a corner. "But it's dark as a bag, and they don't light lanterns, for fear of spoiling the sleep of the nobs on the upper floors. Just imagine you're the kitchen staff and we'll be fine."

Leaning against a wall were big stretchers, wide as doors, for carrying trash to the midden. They got the young man on one of these, carried him across the yard and dumped him in a heap of cabbage stalks and turnip peel. Then they put the stretcher back where they'd got it from and retraced their steps to the alley; from there to the colonnade. "What I should've done," Oida muttered, "is leave a change of clothes for us just inside the door here. I never thought we'd get this filthy." He went to the edge of the colonnade and peered out. "Coast is clear," he said. "We need to nip smartly across to that door there—" He pointed, but so briefly and vaguely she couldn't tell what at. "That's the servants' access to the state rooms on the fifth floor. From there we can take the kitchen stair down to the third floor and make a dash for it from there. Game?"

She nodded wearily. She hadn't had any strength left for a long time. "Fine," he said. "With me." Then he darted across the open hall, and she followed as best she could.

Many years earlier she'd watched a battle. It started at dawn and went on till sunset, and the thing she remembered most was watching the survivors of the shattered centre turning their backs and walking away from the enemy cavalry – walking, not running, because they were too exhausted to run and too drained to care. Now she knew how they felt. She followed him up and down various stairs, but she'd lost track of where she was and couldn't be bothered to try and figure it out. When they stopped outside a door, she didn't recognise it as her own.

"On second thoughts," Oida said, "you'd better come in mine. What you need is a bath."

While it was filling she stripped off the remains of the dress without a thought. Oida, however, was shocked. "For God's sake, look at you," he said. "How many guards did you have to fight?"

"One," she said, "and it wasn't a fight."

"You got in that state just strolling down a few passages?"

She didn't answer. Instead she got into the bath. It hurt like hell, but she was past caring.

He fetched clothes from her room. "The veil's a blessing," he said. "It'll cover those burns on your face, and you can wear gloves, so that's all right. What about shoes? Will you be able to get them on?"

She was wrapped in a towel but made no effort to dry herself. "I don't know."

He leaned back in his chair. He had a few smears of brick dust and cobweb on his cloak and robe, and a few swabs of her blood, and his hair needed brushing. "In a little while, all hell's going to break loose," he said. "But not officially, thank goodness."

She realised she was supposed to ask for amplification. "What?"

He smiled. "The man we rescued isn't supposed to be in prison," he said. "Officially, he's retired to his country estates. If the queen found out what they've been doing to him, there'd be blood on the floor. Division believes she's in love with him, but personally I think they're just friends; which is rather more significant, since he's the only friend she's got."

She pulled the towel round her. Unbelievably, she was starting to feel cold. "Who is he?"

Oida hesitated. "I'm not supposed to tell you, but what the hell. His name is Daxin, and he was the chief minister or grand vizier or whatever you want to call it. If you remember, he was the one who made such a muck-up of the first expeditionary force against the nomads, before Forza slaughtered their army. The ruling faction on the Council nabbed him and stuck him away down there – it's a sort of unofficial prison; nobody's supposed to know about it – and he's been there ever since, poor bastard. We're going to give him to the queen for a birthday present."

She forced herself to take an interest. "Will he be all right?"

Oida grinned. "At this moment he should be on a garbage cart underneath two tons of kitchen waste on its way to be sweated down into pigswill. The farmer will dig him out, brush him off and put him in a fast chaise to the coast, where a ship will whisk him far, far away. Her Majesty's birthday isn't for three months, so they'll have a chance to put some flesh back on him. Anyway," he went on, "it's all good for us, because the bad boys won't tear the place apart looking for him, since officially there's been no jail break and no crime committed." He paused and rubbed a mark off the back of his hand. "They'll know perfectly well we did it," he said. "But we're quite safe, at least until we've paid our respects to Her Majesty tomorrow evening, and after that I suggest we get out of town sharpish. But they won't do anything to us: I'm too high profile and besides, where's the point? It's done now, and killing us would just risk drawing attention. They'll be too busy packing small items of value in case they have to leave in a hurry."

She let her head loll forward. "Job done, then."

"I think so, more or less." A long silence, and then he said, "How are you feeling?"

"Not too bad."

"How are you feeling?"

She turned her head and looked at him. "You might have told me," she said.

He raised his eyebrows. "Told you what?"

"That you came to fetch me from the castle because you needed me for a job. There wasn't anything wrong with that. I'd have understood."

He looked steadily at her. "Would you believe me if I told you I didn't know there was a job until after we'd crossed the border?"

She closed her eyes. "Don't try my patience, Oida; there's not a lot of it left."

"A beautiful girl once told me—"

"Oh, for God's sake."

"—about the three categories of reason," he went on. "Good, specious and real. Would you believe me if I told you I was only allowed to rescue you because I said I needed you for the job, because in my opinion you were the only one on the payroll who could pull it off?"

"You'd be contradicting yourself," she said.

"Oh, this is all hypothetical. Well, would you?"

She shook her head, as if trying to dislodge something. "Allowed? Who by?"

"I'm under orders, same as you are, you know that. Rescuing Daxin was important. Sooner or later, someone was going to try and do it; the East, the West or us. If the East or the West did it, they'd have the queen and they'd have Blemya. More likely, given the quality of their personnel, they'd try and do it and fuck it up, Daxin would've been killed or there'd have been a revolution or a civil war, and Division doesn't want to speculate about what might happen then. So we had to do it, quickly; and now there'll be a new regime in Blemya that thinks we're wonderful and will do exactly what we tell them to. Joy in heaven?"

"If you say so," she said. "But you should've told me. Even if you didn't know right from the start, you should've told me earlier, not just out of the blue like that."

"Would you believe me if I told you I was specifically ordered not to?"

Yes, as it happened, because she knew how their minds worked. "Do you always obey orders?"

"Yes," he said. "Nearly always." He took a deep breath, then said, "Assuming, which is not admitted, that I've behaved really badly, will you forgive me?"

She shook her head. Too tired. "You haven't done anything wrong," she said. "So luckily the question doesn't arise."

"Ah," he said. "So that's all—"

"You've just done the right thing incredibly badly." She got up. "As usual. Goodnight, Oida, I'm going to bed."

She was very, very tired and went straight to sleep. In the circumstances, that was just as well.

The presentation ceremony was in the main audience chamber. She'd seen it before, on her previous visit, so it didn't come as a total shock. If this was Providence's way of making it up to her for all those confined spaces, she decided, Providence was overdoing it, yet again.

This time, however, she had to process down the endless central aisle, past the best part of a thousand men and women in gorgeous silks and gold tiaras, with only Oida for company. Every step was like trying to walk when you've got pins and needles, and brought her that bit closer to the extraordinary, grotesque golden throne, like an altar on which she was about to be sacrificed. For the first time she was truly grateful for the veil; it was something to hide behind, in a place with no natural cover whatsoever.

Twenty yards or so from the foot of the throne, Oida put his hand on her elbow and whispered, "Stay here." Then he went on alone. Some official intercepted him after he'd gone a few paces, and there was a muttered conference. Then the official walked up to her, tweaked aside the corner of the veil, looked at her face, nodded and went back to where Oida was waiting, then escorted him the rest of the way. He stopped about six feet short of the throne steps; if he'd gone any further, he wouldn't have been able to crane his neck back far enough to see the queen.

She could see her, a tiny, incongruous speck nestled in the extraordinary Royal regalia – chlamys, divitision, lorus, triple crown with pendetilia; a tiny human face peeping out over the upper hem of the lorus, like a monkey that's climbed the curtains. She thought she saw the lips move; an official on the upper tier of the scaffolding beside the throne scampered down six flights of steps, approached Oida's escort and whispered something to him. The escort then whispered to Oida, who turned toward the throne and said, in a loud voice, apparently to his feet, "Thank you, your Majesty." The upper-tier official scrambled back up the scaffolding; when he was back in position the tiny, faraway lips moved again. The official came down again and repeated the performance. Oida said, "Yes, indeed, your Majesty, it's a great honour." Then the whole colossal block that comprised the throne shot up in the air, until the little face was completely indistinguishable. Oida bowed to it three times, then turned smartly and marched back down the aisle towards her.

"Is that it?" she whispered.

"That's our lot," Oida hissed back. "Now then, easy does it."

There was a half-platoon of soldiers waiting for them at the door they'd come in by, and her legs went weak, but Oida muttered, "It's all right," and bustled her along with a hand on the small of her back. The soldiers parted to let them through, then closed in behind them and followed, all the way to Oida's door. Then they saluted and marched off.

"In here," Oida said, opening the door of his room.

"What the hell was all that about?"

"For our safety," Oida said with a grin. "I asked for them specially, but I think I was unduly concerned. While we've been lolling about all day, exciting things have been happening in Blemya. There's now a provisional Council, replacing the old one, all of whom have mysteriously disappeared. My bloke couldn't tell me if they'd hopped it or been rounded up or a bit of both;

anyway, the plan seems to be working just fine. I don't think we'll have much trouble, at any rate."

She sank into the chair and dragged the horrible shoes off her poor feet. "What was all that about stopping—?"

"Ah." Oida grinned. "Brainwave. Just came to me, as we were walking up the aisle. I told the Chamberlain's runner you're suffering from a mild form of leprosy – absolutely not contagious, I said, but better safe than sorry. Two birds with one stone, see. If you'd gone into the presence, you'd have had to unveil, and we couldn't have that, also explains the scars on your face, which I have to tell you are visible even through all that fishnet stuff." He poured two glasses of wine and put one down next to her. "Won't have fooled anybody, naturally, but it's plausible enough to be officially acceptable, if you see what I mean."

"So I'm a leper now. Thank you so much."

"Do you honestly give a damn what the Blemyans think of you? Well, then. This time tomorrow we'll be on a ship, and the hell with the lot of them."

Quite suddenly, the significance of something he'd said struck her, and she felt her insides twist. The scars on her face; like leprosy. She hadn't actually looked in her wonderful Mezentine mirror since she'd dressed for the concert. Not that she'd ever been beautiful, but—

"It's all right." Oida's voice made her start. "They'll heal up just fine."

"How would you know? You're not a doctor."

"Actually—" He shrugged. "They're superficial. There may be one or two small patches of shiny white skin, nothing a dab of powder now and then won't cover."

"I want a mirror. *Now.*"

At any other time, she'd have been amused by the speed with which he could produce one (and what a mirror; only just bigger than the palm of her hand, but also Mezentine, older and therefore with a better tone, and he carried it in the sleeve of his gown – well, of course he did). She grabbed it from him and looked. "There, see?" he said.

She didn't say anything. It doesn't matter, she told herself. Really, it doesn't matter.

"I do actually know a bit about burns," he was saying. "True, I never qualified, but I did do two years at the Studium in Choris, and there was this woman who'd been in a fire. Then I met her again, ten months later, and you'd never have known to look at her. Truly."

She handed the mirror back and said nothing. He sat down again, his head in his hands, then jumped up, left the room, came back with her best remaining dress. "Sorry," he said, "but I think you'd better go back to your room now. Try and get some sleep. We've got an early start."

For the first two hours he read a book: Cellec's *Confession of Faith*, which was supposed not to exist any more. She'd asked after it in half the libraries in the West, and they told her that all the manuscripts had been lost two hundred years ago. When she was sure he was engrossed in his reading, she studied him for a while. Of course, he was hard to see, because of his reputation. Oida the Great, who respected women the way the scythe respects the corn.

They stopped to water the horses; he stopped reading, marked his place with a feather and yawned. "Are you speaking to me?" he said.

She shrugged. "Why not? Who else is there?"

He grinned. "You can have the Cellec after I've finished with it," he said. "I always had this feeling that a copy might've survived in Blemya, and I was right. I have to say, though, it's a bit of a disappointment. Well, I guess it would be, after I've waited my whole life to read it."

She held out her hand. He hesitated, then gave her the book. She pulled out his feather and dropped it on the floor, then put the book down on the seat beside her.

"You're welcome," he said.

She lifted her aching feet and propped them up on the bag on the floor. In it, among other things, was the big fat bag of gold coins she'd won off him at cards. It wasn't quite enough to retire on, but she had a bit of her own put by. An image flashed through her mind – the tragic veiled woman living in seclusion in the big house on the hill; once, one of the local kids saw her without her veil and ran home screaming. Well; maybe she'd stick it out a few more years – assuming they could still use her, now that her face was instantly recognisable and profoundly memorable. A job in administration, maybe. And wouldn't that be fun.

The coach moved off. He opened his own bag and took out another book. *Calojan and Eioja*; her mother had read it to her when she was small. She reached over, took it from him and dropped it out of the window.

"Fair enough," he said. "All right, let's play cards."

"No. I don't need any more money."

He opened his right hand; it had been empty, now it was full of pistachios. She loved pistachios. "Play you for nuts?"

She allowed him a very wan smile. "I haven't got anything to bet with."

"Not a problem. Pistachios for absolution. If I win, you forgive me."

She looked at him, then suddenly smiled. Smiling hurt, so she stopped. "Why the hell not? You know you'll lose."

"Ah." He winked at her. "I cheat."

"So do I. Better than you can."

"You really believe that? How sweet."

They played for a long time. When he'd run out of pistachios, she took the pack from him and put it down beside the book on the seat. "Got anything else to bet?" she asked with her mouth full.

"Nothing you want."

She pulled her hair back behind her head, so it wouldn't tickle the burned places. "Oh, I'll have it anyway," she said, and picked up the cards. "My deal."

By the time they reached the coast, she owed him fifty-six angels.

"I could say, forget it, keep the money," he said, lifting the heavy purse and dropping it into his bag. "Or I could give you your revenge and let you win. But you wouldn't want me to do that."

She watched the bag close. "Actually."

"You wouldn't want that," he said firmly. "You don't take presents from strange men."

She was furiously angry with him, either for letting her win the first time or taking back his gift, she wasn't sure which; or maybe it was because she could have retired, with her scarred face, and now she couldn't, and he'd done it to make sure she didn't – or because she'd known in her heart that he'd let her win it in the first place, so she'd always known she couldn't keep it, so what was all that about, some kind of test? Good reasons, specious ones, the real one; and once they were back in Rasch he'd go off somewhere and she didn't know when she'd see him again. Bastard, she thought. And probably just as well.

"Job for you," he said.

She lifted her head so fast she hurt her neck. "Now what?"

He didn't answer straight away. "When we get to the coast, there should be a letter waiting for me telling me where they've parked young Daxin. I need someone utterly reliable to nurse-maid him and keep him out of trouble, for three months. Well?"

She felt a heavy weight on her chest. "It's not up to me," she said.

"Oh, I can swing it with Division," he said casually. "And you're the obvious choice. For one thing he knows you: you rescued him; he'll trust you. Also, if you've got him, I needn't give him another thought. Alternatively, another thing I could swing with Division is three months' expenses' paid leave anywhere you fancy." He smiled at her. "Sometimes it's nice being me," he said. "Well?"

She thought for a moment. "Will I have to fetch him back to bloody Blemya, or will someone collect him?"

"I think you'd better stay out of Blemya for a bit," Oida said. "Wish I could, I've had about enough of it. However, I don't have that luxury. I take it that means—"

"I get bored having fun," she said. "Are you doing this so I'll have three months' easy duty?"

"Yes," he said. "And because it's vitally important that Daxin is kept safe, and I wouldn't trust anyone else. And because wherever they put him is bound to have a good library."

"Of course," she said. "Tell me, have you ever just killed one bird with one stone?"

He blinked. "To the best of my knowledge I've never killed a bird. I have falcons to take care of that sort of thing."

She gave him a look that was meant to convey that this time he'd gone slightly too far. "Give me your writing set," she said.

"Sure." He took the rosewood box out of his bag and handed it to her. "What for?"

"So I can write you a letter for the fifty-six angels I owe you."

"Oops," he said, "well remembered. I'd forgotten about that. You'll be wanting some paper."

She scowled at him, picked what had once been his copy of Cellec's *Confessions* off the seat and tore out the flyleaf. He winced.

"You do realise," he said, "you just knocked twenty angels off the value."

"I wasn't planning to sell it." She balanced the ink bottle on her knee, unscrewed the cap and wrote out a letter of credit on the Knights, her only account with that much in it. He blew on it to dry the ink, folded it and put it in his book as a bookmark.

Their ship turned out to be a wine freighter, carrying six thousand barrels of sweet mistella to Axa Khora, to be watered down and blended with domestic red for the better-class taverns in Rasch. It was an open-hold freighter, with only the stern decked over, but the crew rigged up a sort of tent for them next to the galley, and they spent the next ten days kippering in the fumes of frying fish. The crew, who'd been paid in Blemya, asked Oida to sing for them, which he was happy to do; then he suggested a friendly game of cards and took all their money. They seemed to regard this as a great joke and something of an honour.

"If I ask you a question," she said, "will you give me a straight answer?"

Oida was sitting up with his back to the mast, a position which helped, a bit, when the sea was choppy. "Of course," he said. His face was very slightly green, and it was fortunate that the wind was carrying the frying smells in the opposite direction.

"You've got lots of money," she said, "and everybody adores you wherever you go and thinks you're bloody wonderful, everybody from trawlermen to emperors, and you can write good music when you try, and the less said about you and women the better—"

"All true," Oida said, and wiped his forehead with the back of his hand.

"Fine," she said. "So why do you do all this stuff? You know what I mean. For the Lodge."

He frowned. "I do it for the Lodge," he said. "Why do you do it?"

She thought she knew the answer to that. "Because the Lodge

doesn't give a damn that I'm a woman," she said. "I can go places and see things. I get important work to do, things that matter. If I wasn't a craftsman I'd be stuck in a farmhouse somewhere, making cheese."

He nodded. "I have a proposition for you. I represent a vast secret organisation dedicated to undermining civilisation, disseminating lies and false doctrine and spreading the plague to all major population centres. I'm looking for an operative to undertake interesting, demanding work, I'm a good employer, offering health care and a pension, and I have no silly prejudices against women. And whatever you're getting at the moment, I'll double it. What do you say?"

She sighed. "That's just silly," she said. She took a deep breath. "Yes, I believe that the Lodge is a force for good in a dark and dangerous world, and that's nice, yes, of course it is. And, no, I wouldn't take a job with the forces of evil, no matter what. But I work for the empire. I'd do proper work for them, if they wanted me, not just the silly stuff I do now."

He nodded. "Which one?"

"Either one."

"Both? Remember," he added. "That silly stuff nearly got you hanged."

She shrugged. "I can be myself in the Lodge. I guess that's what it means to me. What about you?"

"Indeed," he said. "When the enemy catapult a ball of burning pitch into your camp, catapult it back. What does the Lodge mean to me?" He closed his eyes. The ship lurched slightly; he sat up and groaned, and she laughed.

"It's not funny," he said. "What does the Lodge mean to me? I guess, everything."

She looked at him.

"All right, I'm being glib," he said. "But it happens to be true. I believe in it, in its vast, complicated, self-contradictory ocean of doctrine, in its overcooked mysticism and its ice-cold, rock-hard approach to politics. A man must believe in something greater than himself, and I look round and ask, what is greater than me? Bear in mind, this is me talking; the choice is somewhat limited. So I belong to the Lodge, heart and soul. I could not love thee, dear, so much, loved I not craftsmanship more. All right?"

She shrugged. "I take it that's the specious reason."

"No, actually it's the good reason. The specious reason is that everything else is too easy and I need real challenges to motivate me to carry on living. The real reason is, of course, it gives me a chance to spend time with you. Oh, God," he added, as the ship wallowed and lifted; he jumped up, staggered and sprinted to the rail.

As the ship coasted in to the jetty, she asked him, "Did you get your letter?"

He was repacking his bag for the fifteenth time. Everything had fitted in there when they left Blemya City, and since then he'd lost two books and a full bag of pistachios, but now it was overflowing. He stuffed the surplus in his pockets and stood up. "From the captain of this tub, yes. Congratulations. You're going north."

"Where north?"

"Somewhere up in the Rhus country. Theoretically it's still Western territory, but in practice I gather it more or less belongs to itself these days. I suggest you stock up on hardware first chance you get."

She lifted her own bag and slung it over her shoulder. "I don't suppose you've got an actual place name for me."

"Mere Barton," he said, and she frowned. "I know that name," she said.

"You'll know it a damn sight better before too long, I guarantee it. Going to be the most important place in the world some day, but I never told you that." He lifted his bag and things fell out of the top. "This is what comes of rushing about," he said. "They promised me faithfully they'd send on the rest of my stuff, but God knows when or if I'll ever see it again. From the map it looks like you draw a straight line up from Beloisa to Spire, then veer off about five degrees east; when the snow is over the tops of your boots, you're more or less there. I'd be amazed if that kid Daxin's ever seen snow. Break it to him gently if you can."

The ship nuzzled up to the jetty and bumped; he staggered, grabbed her shoulder then let go again. "I collected a specimen who said he was from there," she said. "But I don't suppose he's gone back. It sounded like the sort of place you don't go back to."

"But it has the merit of being a long way from the sea," Oida said firmly. "Who knows, I might just join you there. Anywhere the floor stays still seems good to me right now."

She hopped up on to the rail, jumped down and turned to help him lift his bag over. He landed heavily beside her. "In case you were wondering," he said, "this is the bulk cargo transit point at Asenbuth. Do you know it?"

"Never been here before." She looked round and saw a customs shed, the masts of a few fishing boats, a coach drawn up beside a narrow, rutted road. Three guesses who the coach was for. "Give me a lift?"

"Sorry, but I'm off to Rasch. There's bound to be a carter for hire in town. Oh, you'll need this." He put his bag down, pulled out most of the stuff he'd only just managed to cram in it, took out the heavy purse and handed it to her. "Expenses. There could be rather a lot. This isn't from me," he added, as she hesitated to take it: "from Division, so don't go splurging and bring back the change."

Now that it was just one more heavy thing to carry, she took it and put it in her bag. "Where to after Rasch?" she said.

He shrugged. "No idea. Back to horrible Blemya at some point, but not too soon, I sincerely hope. Look after yourself, Tel. The burns will heal, trust me."

She had parted from him at least two dozen times over the years, carelessly or gratefully or seething with irritation. "Do something for me?" she said quickly, before he could start to turn away.

"Of course. What?"

"In Rasch, if you've got a moment, go and tell my landlord I'm not dead and I'll be wanting my room when I get home. Would you?"

He looked at her. "I'm sure Division will have seen to it," he said, "but I'll check, I promise. I'll go there myself and count your spoons."

"You should be able to manage, I've only got one. Oh, and if you happen across the fifth book of Sensacuna, buy it and I'll pay you back."

"Sure," he said, and then there was no more reason for him to stay. Then he grabbed her by both shoulders, pecked her high up on the cheek (well clear of the burns), flashed her a smile and walked briskly away. She waved as he climbed into the coach, but he wasn't looking her way.

Four of Spears

As the coach pulled away, he made an effort and didn't look back. Instead, he opened his bag, took out a book and started to read. It was the sort of book that has pictures in it, and not much text.

At Strepsi Ochoe he got out and spent an hour in the inn, a small drab place he knew only too well. Then the military mail arrived, and he went out and introduced himself to the driver, who opened the coach door for him and offered him a rug.

There was another passenger, a stocky man in a grey travelling cloak with a hood. "Hello, Oida," he said. "I was beginning to wonder if you were all right."

"I'm fine," Oida said, tucking the rug round his knees. "I got a bit held up, that's all."

"Success?"

Oida considered his reply. "Not too bad," he said. "I made a mess of some aspects of it, but by and large it went well."

His companion grinned. "One theory is that you're a completist," he said: "you can't rest till you've had them all. I've got to tell you, that's not actually possible. They're being born and dying all the time, how could you possibly keep up?"

Oida clicked his tongue. "Do you want my report or not?"

"Don't bother, I know the basic facts. A good job well done, as always. You'll be pleased to hear the boy Daxin's safely on his way. Apparently her Majesty's beside herself with worry about him. Tell me, do you think it'd be a good idea to drop a hint or two, let her know he's safe? Or don't you want to spoil the surprise?"

"I think it might be nice if he writes her a letter," Oida said, after a moment's thought. "Nothing in it about where he is or who's looking after him, just I'm safe and well, having a nice time, wish you were here, that sort of thing. Otherwise, she's perfectly capable of starting a civil war, and that wouldn't help anybody."

"Good idea," the man in the hood said. "You know, I do believe you're a romantic at heart."

"With all due respect," Oida said, "go to hell."

"I imagine it comes from writing all those soupy ballads. You spend so much time putting yourself into the mind of the common man—"

"Have they found Forza Belot yet?"

The hooded man frowned at him. "Them as asks no questions," he said sharply. "Now, there's a little job we'd like you to do for us. If you can spare the time, of course. I know how busy you are."

Oida sighed. "You know perfectly well what my priorities are," he said. "Where to this time?"

From his sleeve the hooded man produced a little jar of preserved figs. He offered one to Oida, who refused, then ate one himself. When he'd quite finished, he said, "Have you ever heard of a place called Morzubith?"

"Actually, yes," Oida replied. "It's where Director Procopius is from, isn't it?"

"Very good. Do you know where it is?"

"No."

The hooded man inclined his head. "Not many people do," he said. "It's out on the Western moors, just before you go downhill and fetch up on the steppes. They tell me it's so remote, they haven't even sent any men to the war yet. Principal industries are sheep-rearing and logging. Climate—"

"Yes, fascinating. What have I got to do?"

The hooded man told him; he listened blank-faced. "That should be all right," he said. "What's the timetable?"

"Well, you need to be in Choris for the Remembrance Festival," the hooded man said. "You're the main attraction, or had you forgotten?"

Oida did some mental arithmetic. "I think I'd better cancel that," he said. "I don't think I'll have time."

"Nonsense. You can't not be at Remembrance: think how disappointed they'd all be. And directly after that it's the queen's birthday: you can't possibly miss that. No, you should have plenty of time, if you don't dawdle. Not a problem, particularly," he added with a smile, "since there'll be no distractions."

"Oh, don't start that again."

"Talking of which." The hooded man turned round in his seat and pulled out two brass tubes from behind the seat cushions. "Your friend. This one's a record of the personal information she's given us at various times – her initial interview, sundry reviews and interrogations. All about her background, family, early life. You've read it, of course."

"Some time ago," Oida admitted. "Look—"

"Just run your eye over it again, there's a good chap."

Oida glowered at him, took the tube, poked out the roll of parchment with his fingertip, unscrolled it and glanced down the page. "Yes, I know all that," he said. "But if you seriously think—"

The hooded man leaned forward and tweaked the page out of his hand. "The other roll," he said, "is what we've found out about her. You know, routine enquiries. Actually, most of it only came to light when you recommended her for promotion. We always do an investigation, as you know. Well," he added. "Read it."

There wasn't that much, about half a standard roll, written

in orthodox administrative minuscule. Oida read it, rolled it up and put it back in the tube. The hooded man took it from him. "Interesting?" he said.

Oida shrugged. "Not particularly."

"Aren't you just the tiniest bit interested? She lied on oath, for one thing. Repeatedly. Strictly speaking, I should cashier her from the Service, at the very least."

Oida looked up sharply. "You'll do no such thing."

That got him a big smile. "Now, then," the hooded man said. "And, no, I'm not inclined to take official notice of it, at this time. But ask yourself. Why would anyone risk their career and their life, lying about things like that?"

"Has it occurred to you she doesn't actually know about it herself?"

The hooded man shrugged. "It's possible," he said. "But unlikely, in my opinion. More to the point, did you know? Does that explain your interest?"

Oida's face didn't change. "I'll ignore that," he said. "Look, she's a superb operative, one of the best we've got. She does as she's told; she gets the job done—"

"She murdered a political officer at Beloisa."

"You say that like it's a bad thing. More to the point, I trust her. We work well together. One of the conditions of my working for you is, I choose my people. I thought that was understood."

The hooded man sighed. "The last thing I want to do is make problems or break up an eminently successful team. But when people lie, I want to know why. Most lies are easy to understand: it's when people lie for no apparent reason that I get concerned. You do see that, don't you?"

"I'm sure she doesn't know. If she knew, it's like you said: why would she lie about it?"

The hooded man thrust the two rolls into his sleeve. "How you conduct your affairs is your business," he said, "so long as it doesn't cause problems for Division. I'm just warning you, in the friendliest possible way; be aware of this, bear it in mind, and don't put me in a position where I have to do anything about it. Do you understand?"

"Perfectly."

"Of course you do, you're a smart fellow. Now, tell me about Blemya. Is it true that the Revisionists are poised to take over the Lower Chamber?"

He answered about a hundred questions as clearly and honestly as he could, glad of the respite. When the hooded man finally ran out of things to ask him about, he said, "You never answered my question."

"What question?"

"Forza Belot."

The hooded man was silent for a long time. "I don't know anything about that operation," he said at last. "I don't think anybody at Division does, either. As far as I can tell, it's being run entirely from Central, and you know them, they wouldn't tell you if your hair was on fire. My guess—" He paused and smiled. "Which is based on nothing but supposition, intuition and uncorroborated rumour—"

"Yes?"

"He's dead," the hooded man said. "He got a bad bump on the head, never came out of the coma. Which means Senza Belot has got to go. Don't ask me why the war's still going on; he should've had it wrapped up with a ribbon on it by now, even with no money and no men. I can only conclude he still believes his brother is alive, and he daren't do anything in case Forza swoops down on his neck with an incredibly smug grin on his face. But the fact that Senza's done nothing at all suggests to me that he can't be sure, therefore he doesn't know any more about it than we do. Less, probably. I hope so, anyway. That's beside the point. If Forza's dead, Senza has to be put down. Who'll get that job I simply don't know. I should think you're fairly safe, since your future's mapped out in great detail for at least the next three months, and I'm sure they'll want to act before then. That said, if you were thinking of having an accident and breaking a leg, this might well be a good time." He smiled. "Subject closed. What a lot of weather we've been having lately."

The hooded man dumped him at a way station in the middle of the Great Southern Marsh, in the early hours of the morning. Fortunately it was a clear night and the moon was almost full, so he managed to find the door. He bashed on it for a while, and the porter came and let him in. The next coach was due at noon the next day. Until then, he was welcome to use the hospitality suite—

Which turned out to be a redundant charcoal cellar, swept out (more or less) and fitted with a bedstead made from old rafters, a corn sack for a pillow and one blanket. The trumpet woke him two hours before dawn, and he slouched across the yard to the mess hall, where he was issued with military porridge and grey bread. Nobody spoke to him or seemed to realise who he was.

The mail arrived exactly on time, and he was pleased to see he had the coach to himself, at least as far as Malestan. He took the opportunity to plan ahead, with no danger of interruptions.

The military staging post at Malestan was one of the biggest supply depots in the West. The upland wheat arrived in gigantic wagons and was stored in towering stone silos. Cattle and hogs came in along the Military Droves. They were herded into the vast stockyards on the north side of the camp, where they stayed until they were driven to the slaughterhouse, reputedly the biggest in both empires. The salting and drying sheds alone covered eleven acres; the tannery was three miles upwind of the station perimeter, for obvious reasons. The textile factory, vehicle maintenance sheds and munitions plant were inside the wall, which was really a high bank topped with a palisade and surrounded by a deep flooded ditch. There was also a ceramics and glass works, said to be the most advanced in the world, barns, charcoal sheds, an acre of stables, three watermills, two enormous ponds (dug in the fond hope of farming carp; they all died, poisoned by the run-off from the slaughterhouse; the ponds were stagnant now, and nourished millions of mosquitos in the warm weather), the inevitable parade grounds and drill yards for the garrison, barracks for the soldiers, rather smaller quarters for the civilian workers, various administrative buildings and the Prefecture, a modest Third Kingdom manor house in the local stone which was the only building that was standing when the station was first built. The station had its own internal messenger relay – two dozen experienced riders mounted on fast ponies doing nothing but carry messages within the station precinct – as well as a temple, a lodge house and a theatre, used once a year for Empire Day.

That was Malestan when Oida saw it last, about four months ago.

The driver was as surprised as he was. They both got down from the coach, neither of them saying a word, and walked up to where the main gate had been. The bank was still there, but the palisade had mostly gone; firewood, and a litter of chunks of rock half buried in the ground – it was a moment or so before Oida made the logical connection. The foregate was a confused mess of wagon tracks; rainwater pooled in the ruts, and it hadn't rained the day before. The gate itself had been burned out, which was theoretically impossible. There was no smoke, and only a faint smell of burning.

They paused in the gateway, listening for any sound whatsoever, but the place was dead quiet.

"There ought to be crows," the driver said.

Oida pulled himself together. "Not if Ocnisant's been here," he said.

"Ah, right," the driver nodded, as if the clarification had somehow made it all better.

Oida's theory appeared to be borne out by what they found inside, which was more or less nothing. No dead bodies, for one thing, human or animal, but there were newly filled-in trenches across the main parade yard in the central square. Ocnisant prides himself on neatness – Just-So Ocnisant, they call him in the trade. The wooden sheds and barns were all gone, their footprints marked by black patches on the ground. The brick and stone structures were roofless shells. Oida stirred the cinders with his foot in several places, but couldn't find so much as a single fire-browned nail; all the metal fittings – hinges, pintles, latches, braces, brackets, hasps – had gone. Someone had even lifted the cabbages in the kitchen garden; there were rows of cut stalks, but not a single leaf remaining.

"He does a cracking job," the driver muttered, "I'll give him that."

Of more immediate concern, there was no hay (no hay barns, come to that) and no human food of any description. The driver made a fire from scraps of shattered palisade stakes, then wandered off with his bow in the forlorn hope of finding a deer. Oida sat down on a spent catapult stone and warmed his hands over the remains of the defences of Malestan. Interesting, he thought.

"It's that bloody Senza Belot," was the driver's theory. He'd managed to shoot a badger, which turned out to be surprisingly palatable. "If he's on the rampage, it'll all be over soon. Bastard," he added, without any particular malice.

"The East is bankrupt," Oida observed. "They can't afford to stage a sustained campaign, let alone a long-term occupation. I'm guessing this was just a raid, to show he could. Showing off."

The driver shrugged. "Nothing to stop him now, is there?"

Oida grinned. "Last I heard, the West had a quarter of a million men under arms. That's about fifty thousand more than the East."

"Then Senza'll kill them all," the driver said. "No big deal to him. We ought to pack it in now, save ourselves the grief. Should've done that back when Forza bought it. Bloody obvious back then we've got no chance."

Oida sighed and threw a slab of wood on the fire. "Ten years ago," he said, "I could've bought into Ocnisant's for a relatively trivial sum. But I thought, no, bad idea, the war'll be over by mid-summer. Ah well."

"Bet you wish you had."

"Indeed. I'd be retired by now, with an estate the size of Aelia."

"Now there's a man who's in the right business," the driver said. "If I had any sense, I'd see if he wants drivers. Must need a lot of 'em, in his line."

"You could do worse," Oida said. "You get your keep but no wages, and everyone gets a share in the net. They're not bad people to work for, if you don't mind hard graft. Stick at it long enough and you could put by a nice little stake for your old age: it's better than working for the government."

The driver grinned. "Don't reckon there'll be a government much longer."

"Oh, there's always a government," Oida said. "That's a rule of nature. But you'll be all right, you've got a trade. Come what may, people will always want stuff shifted from A to B."

"True," the driver said, "very true. What line of work are you in, then? You're not military."

For a moment or so, Oida couldn't speak. Then he said mildly, "I'm a musician."

"Is that right?" The driver was slightly impressed. "Well, there you are, then. That's another good trade. Always work for a good fiddler. Freelance?"

Now that was actually a very good question. "Yes."

"Best way," the driver said wisely. "You can go anywhere you like. Travel a lot, do you?"

"Quite a lot, yes. I've just come back from Blemya."

"Where's that, then?"

Oida told him; the driver looked blank. "Lot to be said for it, moving around," he said. "You've always got options, that's what I say. If it all goes tits up in one place, go somewhere else. All right if you've got no ties, of course. You married?"

"No."

The driver nodded his approval. "Best way, if you're on the move all the time," he said. "Take my old man, now. Freighterman, he was, never home more than three weeks a year. That's no way to bring up kids. No, love 'em and leave 'em is my motto. It's not like there's any shortage, specially these days, with all the men going to the war and getting killed."

"War does have that advantage," Oida said.

The driver grinned. "So," he said, "you reckon it'd be worth giving Ocnisant's a go?"

Oida looked at him. "I take it you think you might be out of a job sometime soon."

"I think the job'll still be there. It's whether I'll get paid I'm worried about."

"Talking of which," Oida said. "The thing is, I was supposed to change here and get the military mail to Rasch. I suspect that service isn't running any more."

The driver shrugged. "Might be," he said. "I mean, all this can't have happened very long ago or we'd have heard about it. Maybe they don't know about it in Rasch yet."

"That's possible," Oida conceded, "but I don't fancy camping out here in the ashes on the off chance the mail's still running. What about you? What's your schedule?"

The driver frowned. "I was meant to wait here two days, then take a service back to the coast. Don't see that happening."

"Tell you what." Oida's hand was in his pocket, identifying coins by feel. "I think that, in the circumstances, it's your duty to go to Rasch and report this, just in case they don't know about it yet, and then see where they want to assign you next. After all, they're going to have to draw up a whole new schedule now."

"That's true," the driver said thoughtfully; "hadn't thought about it like that. I mean, all the routes'll be buggered up now. They'll have to start from scratch, practically."

Oida casually opened his hand. Two little gold quarter-angels poked up from the furrows between his fingers, like the first crocuses. "I'd quite like to get to Rasch as quickly as possible," he said.

The driver looked at him. "There's money in fiddling, then?"

"I'm a good fiddler."

The coins chinked softly as they changed hands. "It's your patriotic duty," Oida said with a grin. "After all, someone's got to tell them."

The driver smiled at him and put the coins in his purse, a fancy thing with fiddly drawstrings. Maybe his mother had made it for him, or his sister. "Hell of a business, though," he said gravely. "I mean, just think of all the trouble it'll make for people. Main supply depot for the Western army."

"I think Senza may have had that in mind," Oida said.

"What the emperor ought to do," the driver said, after a moment's thought, "is offer Senza a shitload of money to come and work for us. I mean, he's only human, isn't he? And you know what they say: every man has his price."

"Good idea. The trouble is, the Eastern emperor has lots of money, too."

"Ah well." The driver got up. "There's blankets in the box under the driver's seat," he said. "Let's get some kip and then we can make an early start."

Next day, Oida rode on the box, next to the driver, who had a lot of questions to ask about the music trade. Must be interesting work, he felt; you must get to meet a lot of interesting people. Oida conceded that, yes, it was interesting. The driver confessed that he didn't go much on music, though he liked a good tune. That Oida, for example, he could write tunes. The driver had seen him once, when he sang for the troops at Ceulasia, or was it Nas Mocant? Hadn't actually seen very much of him, because he was stuck at the back behind a lot of tall bastards, but he'd heard most of it and it wasn't bad at all. Of course, he didn't make up his own tunes, but—

"How do you mean?" Oida interrupted.

"He doesn't do the tunes himself," the driver explained. "He takes the old tunes and messes them around a bit. But they all do that, don't they?"

Oida frowned. "Give me an example."

The driver thought for a moment. "Well, take that one about the man saying goodbye to his family before he goes off to the war. That's just 'The Miller's Grey Cat', turned on its head."

"I don't think I know that one."

"Of course you do. You know." The driver hummed a bit. "Probably they don't call it that where you come from."

"Hum me some more."

The driver did so, and Oida was forced to admit that it did sound horribly like "Loved I Not Honour More", transposed into the major key and speeded up a bit. "Does he do that a lot?" he asked. "Steal other people's tunes, I mean?"

The driver frowned. "I don't think you can really call it stealing," he said. "But take 'Four Donkeys and a Mule'. Know that one?"

"Not sure," Oida said. "How does it go?"

A little later he consoled himself with the thought that great minds think alike; well, no, not great ones. Procopius' symphonies and motets weren't shot through with unconscious echoes of folk music: anything so basic and naïve would be hopelessly out of place. But mediocre minds, like his own— That said; it occurred to him quite out of the blue that if you took "Soldiers' Joy", slowed it right down and shifted it into the minor key, you'd have a terrific theme for a fugue; and who would ever know?

The first stop on the way to Rasch, coming from Malestan on the military road, is Losjors. They found it in ashes.

"You've got to hand it to Ocnisant," Oida said, after they'd been staring for a while. "No job too big or too small." The same newly filled-in trenches, along what had once been the street of shops and taverns that intersected with the main road, and not a bent nail or a roof tile to be seen. "At this rate he'll definitely be taking on more staff. You should get in there."

The driver seemed preoccupied and didn't share Oida's enthusiasm at the opportunity. "You think the bastard's heading for Rasch?" he said.

"Looking that way," Oida agreed. "In fact, for all we know he's there already. I'm not sure what there is in the way to stop him."

The driver looked at him. "What about the Fifth Army?"

"I'd forgotten about them," Oida lied.

A few miles beyond Losjors they came down off the moor and into farmland. Oida saw livestock grazing the stubbles, but no people. They stopped for the night at a farmhouse, but it was shuttered and boarded up, and the hay barn was empty. That didn't matter too much, since there was grazing for the horses in the orchard. The driver found a crowbar in one of the barns and jemmied the farmhouse door. There was no fresh food, no hams or bacon, not even a jar of the dreaded fermented cabbage; but Oida found two sacks of barley at the back of the pantry. It was a bit black on top, but the grain underneath was sound. The driver ground a jugful in a hand mill in the dairy and made army porridge, slightly alleviated with a couple of windfall apples from the orchard.

"He could do it," the driver said: "he could bash his way right through to Rasch, if the Fifth don't stop him. But the city's safe. He hasn't got anything that'd put a dent in the walls."

Oida had taken a good look at the catapult stones at Malestan and wasn't so sure about that, but decided not to say anything. "He must be moving fast," he said instead. "Mind you, that's the Belot boys' trademark. Not sure you can carry much of a siege train, though, if you're travelling light."

The driver shook his head hopefully. "I've seen the limbers for those things," he said. "Bloody great big things, ox-drawn; horses aren't strong enough. Make ten miles a day if you're really lucky."

Oida didn't point out that whatever had pounded the palisade at Malestan into kindling must still be with the army, since they hadn't overtaken it on the way. "I think this calls for a change of plan," he said. "Suddenly, Rasch doesn't seem the most sensible place to be. What do you reckon?"

The driver looked at him, but said nothing.

"And besides," Oida went on, "my business isn't actually in Rasch itself. I'm headed west; I was planning on taking the military mail into town and then hiring a chaise, because that'd be quicker than the public stage. But if I branch off on to the Western Supply at Foliapar, I can get on to the Great West at Autet Cross and not have to go into Rasch at all."

"You could," agreed the driver.

"I was thinking." Oida's hand was in his pocket again. "Looks like there's an unhealthy amount of war going on at the moment. At times like these, all sorts of military equipment and personnel go missing, presumed lost or destroyed, and nobody gives it any thought." He paused again. "I wonder what that coach of yours would cost, to buy, I mean."

"Don't know," the driver said. "Never given it any thought."

"Must be two angels. A man could set himself up in business with a coach like that. Quite a good living to be made, I should imagine. And even if you decide you do want to go work for Ocnisant, it won't do you any harm if you've got your own rig."

The driver looked at him. "What, just go off with it, you mean?"

Oida shrugged. "Why not? Like I said, when there's lunatics fighting huge battles all over the place, and there's supply columns being cut up by the cavalry every day, and whole stations burned to the ground, who's going to miss one little cart? Also, if anyone stops you, all you say is you found it abandoned and it's lawful salvage." He grinned. "Bear in mind it's highly unlikely you're going to get paid any time soon. Me, I'd consider it's payment in kind in lieu of wages."

"I don't know," the driver said. "I could get in all sorts of trouble."

"And so could I," Oida said, "if I don't get to my appointment on time. A ride as far as the Great West is worth an angel forty to me." The driver looked up sharply. "If you're interested."

"I don't know," the driver repeated. "Doesn't seem right to me, somehow. We ought to be doing something, for the empire." Oida put his closed hand on the table and opened his fingers. There was a little gleam as the candlelight caught on something. "Still, you're right," he said, "what can we do? A carter and a fiddler."

"Quite," Oida said. "And the answer is, the best we can, in the circumstances. This could be your big chance. In five years, who knows, you could have a fleet of coaches."

The driver thought about that for a moment. "It's an ill wind," he said brightly. "Where did you say you wanted to go?"

They still had thirty miles to cover before they could turn off the Military Trunk on to the Western Supply. The whole of the next morning they drove through wheatfields.

"This lot should've been cut weeks ago," the driver commented. "It'll all be spoilt by now."

Oida didn't reply. The country they were passing through was one of the principal growing areas for Rasch. It would be interesting to know what they were doing for bread in the big city.

They stopped at noon for a bowl of disgusting porridge, then picked up the pace on the long straight down into the Necua Valley.

Then the road turned sharply. As they rounded the corner, a huge flock of rooks got up out of the standing corn and flew away shrieking.

"Bloody things," the driver commented. "Once you get a few patches where the wind's laid the corn flat, they go in and strip it bare. And what they don't eat, they trample and shit on."

Except that they weren't rooks: too big and black, and they didn't fly right for rooks. "You know what," Oida said. "I think we should stop here a minute."

They climbed down and walked into the wheat crop. A few yards in, Oida nearly tripped over a dead man. He wore Western-issue armour, minus the helmet, and the back of his head had been smashed in.

"What've you found?" the driver called out to him.

"I think it could be the Fifth Army," Oida said. "No, don't come any closer." He knelt down and took another look at the dead man. He was cold and stiff, but the crows hadn't been at him much. Therefore not more than a day and a half. The armour was the standard lamellar, as favoured by both empires; these days, usually supplied by Ocnisant or one of his competitors. But the neck scarf was the green and blue of the Western Fifth. He'd sung for them, not six months ago. They'd made him do three encores of "Eyes of the Eagles". He stood up, and walked back the way he'd just come. "I'm guessing they were stragglers," he said, "or running from the main action and got run down by cavalry. The battle proper would be somewhere over there." He pointed north-east. "Of course, there's no way of telling. Could be this was just one wing of the army that got caved in or routed. There's lots of battles where a bit of one army got wiped out, even though their side won." He looked round. There was nothing as far as the eye could see but standing corn. But the last time he'd seen that many crows was the day after Lucis Operna. "I think we'll be all right back on the road," he said. "If we lost, they'll be headed for Rasch, and if we won there's nothing to worry about."

The driver had a terrified look on his face; he nodded, and walked quickly back to the coach. When they were both aboard, he said, "Shouldn't we do something for them?"

Oida shook his head. "Ocnisant'll be along directly," he said. "My guess is, his carts were all full, so he's gone to his big depot just this side of Rasch to unload, and then he'll come back and clear up this lot. No hurry, after all. Those poor buggers aren't going anywhere."

The driver looked at him. "You could be all wrong about this," he said. "I mean, you didn't actually go and look."

"Quite so," Oida replied. "But it's none of our business, is it? We're going the other way."

The driver looked unhappy. "That's a bit hard, isn't it?"

Oida shrugged. "I'm just a musician," he said. "I don't do politics."

The road started to climb again. They were passing through the celebrated vineyards of Amportat, reckoned to be the most valuable real estate outside of the cities in the whole Western empire. There should have been men everywhere, harvesting the grapes. Instead, all they saw were vast flocks of starlings.

"I don't like this," the driver said. "It's like there's nobody left."

"Well, what would you do if the war moved into your neighbourhood?" Oida said. "You'd clear out till it was gone. Common sense."

"You don't think they're all dead, do you?"

Oida turned his head and looked at him. "No," he said. "And I'll tell you for why. I don't think this is one of those campaigns where the invaders go through the countryside killing everything that moves. I've seen what that looks like. So far we haven't come across burned-out farmhouses or deliberately spoiled crops, or stray livestock on the road, or dead bodies thrown in the hedges. It's not that sort of campaign. I think Senza's moving very fast; he hasn't got time for scorched-earth stuff. My guess is, his whole army is on horseback, cavalry, mounted infantry, horse artillery. It's the only way he could move so damned fast, and it's just the sort of crazy, brilliant idea he'd come up with. I think he's making a hell-for-leather charge straight at Rasch, hoping to get there before they can gather enough supplies to stand a siege, with a view to taking the city before the Western armies can get back home. I think the countryside is deserted because we're following exactly the same route as he did, and if we turned off and went inland a few miles, we'd find people and cattle and life going on more or less as usual. I think that this time next week, the people who ran away when they saw Senza coming will start drifting back – stands to reason, surely. Either he wins, in which case he'll stay in Rasch and fortify it, or he loses, and the crows will get a treat. In any event, he won't be coming back this way any time soon. This is probably the safest place in the empire right now."

The driver looked petrified. "You think he could win?"

Oida considered his answer. "It's possible, yes. If anybody could do it, Senza could. People are so scared of him, as soon as he's visible from the city walls, the army commanders could figure they've got no chance, change sides, kill the emperor's guards and hand over the emperor and the keys of the city. Things like that have happened; it's not impossible. A lot would depend on how much food they've got in store. A city like Rasch is too big to stand a siege for very long, unless they drive out the civilians to fend for themselves. If they did that, assuming the garrison is anything like up to strength, they could probably hold out indefinitely, certainly long enough for the Second and the Fourth and the Eighth to get here and relieve the siege. Of course, that could be what Senza wants, to bring them to battle. If he can wipe all three of them out at a stroke, basically he's won the war."

The driver looked at him oddly. "You know a lot about this stuff," he said, "for a fiddle player."

Oida grinned. "I play a lot in grand houses," he said; "you can pick up all sorts of things, eavesdropping." He put his hands behind his head and yawned. "The point I'm making is this. It may look a whole lot like the end of the world, but I don't think it is, not this time. I mean, take a really extreme case; let's suppose Senza wins, the West surrenders, the emperor's strung up and the streets of the capital run with blood. So what? Big deal. In a year's time there'll be a new government, pretty much the same as the old one, except the capital will now be in Choris, six hundred miles away, instead of here on the doorstep. Won't change anything that matters. The only real difference will be, the war will be over and things can start getting better again. And you'll be taking on men to drive your fleet of carts, and building yourself a big house somewhere."

They pressed on until it was quite dark, hoping to reach the turning before nightfall. But eventually it was too dark to see, and the driver refused to go on, in case they missed the crossroads. In the morning, they woke up to find that they'd spent the night in the middle of a battlefield.

The dead were all Western light cavalry; they'd been shot, and the arrows were still in the bodies, which strongly suggested haste, since no sensible archer leaves a good arrow behind if he can possibly retrieve it. Once again, they'd beaten the crows to it, though none of the bodies they examined was warm.

"I wish I could make out tracks," Oida said with feeling. "But they built these bloody roads so well you can't see a damn thing. I want to know if they came down the road or up, and which direction they left in."

The driver was badly shaken, and Oida guessed he hadn't had much experience with battlefields; he neglected to point out the implications for a possible career with Ocnisant. "What about if they come back?" he kept saying, and Oida grew tired of pointing out that one coach, carrying one civilian, was unlikely to be seen as a threat or a military prize worth stopping for, and that in any event they'd hear them coming even if they didn't see them, in plenty of time to ditch the coach and hide among the vine rows. It bothered him a little that he hadn't been able to calm the driver down and soothe his nerves; the man was getting as jumpy as a cat and was clearly worrying himself to death – with good reason, sure enough, but it was Oida's job as a communicator to mislead him into thinking there was nothing to be scared of.

"Don't worry," he said, as they scrambled back aboard the coach. "Once we find that turning and get on the Western Supply, we won't be seeing any more of that sort of thing. There's absolutely no reason why Senza should go a single yard further west than he has to. He's headed for Rasch, remember."

A burned-out way station didn't help matters, and it was just as well they reached the turning without stumbling on anything else. They stopped at the crossroads and looked down the Western Supply, a straight grey line running downhill for as far as they could see. "We made it," the driver said. "Thank God for that. All that death and gore was starting to do my head in."

"I suggest we try and make up speed on the downhill section," Oida said. "I expect we'll both feel better if we can get a few miles behind us."

Maybe he shouldn't have said that. The driver went fast; too fast, as it turned out. They'd been on the road about an hour when they heard a loud thump and the coach began to judder and weave and then to track wildly to the left. The driver swore and hauled on the reins. When the coach stopped, it was listing over.

"You know what," Oida said. "This trip is starting to get on my nerves."

It wasn't the axle, as Oida had thought; it was the wheel itself.

A spoke must've broken, and taken all the others with it. All that remained was the hub, with smashed stubs sticking out of it, like a badly laid hedge. The driver walked back down the road, found the rim and brought it back, rolling it like a hoop.

"Can you fix it?" Oida asked. The driver looked at him. "Sorry," Oida said, "stupid question. Right, so what do we do?"

The driver shook his head. "God knows," he said. "We aren't going very far on that. It needs new spokes fitting, and that's a wheelwright's job. I reckon we're going to have to footslog it as far as the way station." He stopped. No need to say what had just passed through his mind. He sat down on the ground and stared at the coach, as if he'd never seen one before.

"Well, obviously," Oida said quickly. "And even if there's nobody there, I don't imagine they'll have cleared out all the tools and the spoke blanks. If needs be, we can whittle something up ourselves: it doesn't have to be pretty. Come to think of it," he went on – the driver was still staring blankly into space – "isn't the whole point about these mail coaches that they're all built to a pattern, so if something breaks you can just grab a spare off the rack and slot it in? Bet you anything you like they've got spare wheels there, stacks of them. Your tax money at work. Where's the map?"

The driver shook his head. "No map."

Oh. "All right. So where's the next way station?"

"Don't ask me. I don't do this route."

Oida took a deep breath and let it out slowly. "Well, it can't be far," he said. "Twenty miles at the very most, and maybe they'll lend us mules so we won't have to walk back carrying a bloody wheel." He looked up the road, running dead straight up into the hills. It would have to be uphill, he said to himself, I hate bloody up. Still, downhill on the way back, something to look forward to. "Wonder what made the spoke suddenly go like that," he said. "I thought they built these things to take any sort of punishment."

"It was me," the driver said, "going too damn fast. It's a judgement on me, for deserting."

"Right," Oida said. "Because if you'd done your duty and gone scampering after the enemy and actually managed to find them and got yourself killed about two seconds later, what a difference that would've made." He picked up the rim of the wrecked wheel and rested it on his shoulder; he reckoned it'd be less of a pain to carry than the spokes. "Come on," he said. "Sooner we start, sooner we get there."

The vineyard country stopped at the top of the rise. Beyond that was moorland; a shallow dip, and then the road rose steeply. There was nothing to see but heather, starting to go over, and couch grass and bog cotton, with the occasional island of startlingly yellow gorse. The driver had brought his bow as an afterthought, but there was absolutely no point; the deer would see them coming three miles away, the birds flew too high or got up too quick, there should have been sheep but there wasn't a single one to be seen. Whatever had happened here, Oida was at a loss to understand, and it was fortunate, in a way, that there was no point trying; if he managed to figure it out, he'd only upset himself, and what would that achieve? He concentrated on trying to remember once-glimpsed maps. Logic demanded that there should be at least one way station on the link between the Military and the Great West. He could just about visualise a straight line marked in blue, drawn with a ruler by a clerk who'd never been outside the city but who believed unshakably in the straightness of military roads; his handwriting, the rather affected cursive government minuscule – looks crystal clear from a distance, but up close you have to look really close to read it – Boa Cyruos or Bos Cypua, something like that? Not that the name mattered a damn, except that if it had a name on a map, it had to be there. It'd be on lists and schedules, and Supply would send it shipments of food, tools, footwear, forage, stationery, horseshoes and copies of Imperial decrees; if the driver got there and found nothing but heather and bog cotton, he'd report it when he got back and they'd inform the Survey, and the Survey would send someone out to look— You had to believe in the way stations, because the alternative was mental and spiritual anarchy.

Faith is traditionally tested in the wilderness; according to the best philosophers, it's what the wilderness is for. (It was at times like this that Oida reverted to thinking in essay titles; In a Created universe, account for the existence of deserts; 25 marks. Instinctively he began to marshal his arguments, then remembered he wasn't nineteen any more.) It was hard to believe in way stations, or anything human. There was the road, of course, but it was so perfectly straight, so unyieldingly regular, that it seemed improbable that fallible mortals had had anything much to do with it – the gods built it, presumably, or the giants, on one of their better days. For a giant, twenty-five yards in one stride, the road would be useful, manageable. Just too damn big for humans. Imagine ants trying to use the cities of Men.

The driver had gone quiet, which wasn't a good sign. He was probably one of those people who need time for things to sink in. Jollying him along wasn't working, and neither was plausibly argued optimism; probably best to leave him alone and let him sweat it out, and if he did decide to sit down on the verge and die, it wouldn't be the end of the world. There had to be coaches or horses or mules or donkeys still, somewhere on earth, it was just a matter of plodding on until he found them, and then getting a real move on to make up the time he'd lost, which was another thing he didn't particularly want to think about.

He remembered the name of the way station, Bes Cyroia, just as it came in sight on the top of the rise, as they trudged up out of the dip that had hidden it. All the stations west of Rasch look the same – square, flat-roofed red-brick boxes, with three rectangular sheds out back. He quickened his pace, which reminded him of how much the calves of his legs hurt. The driver lagged behind, the hub of the broken wheel cradled in his arms like a refugee's baby.

The door was open and there was nobody home. The inside was neat, tidy and clean, as though the station crew weren't sure whether it was an invasion or a proctors' inspection. They'd taken the food, but not much else. Oida was in and out before the driver caught up; he shook his head, then hurried across the paved yard to the furthest shed: forge, wheelwright's shop and stores. There was a big military-issue padlock on the door – a good sign, but military padlocks and hasps are the best that taxpayers' money can buy.

"We need a sledgehammer," Oida said. "And an axe."

A way station ought to have plenty of both. They'd be in the stores.

So; no hammer and no axe. What they did have was time, and the driver's muscle and Oida's patient ingenuity. After various experiments with stone slabs, crowbars and a bit and brace they found in the stables, Oida hit on the idea of clambering up on the roof and smashing their way in through the slates. There was no rope anywhere, but they found six pairs of decommissioned reins in the stables, dismantled them and knotted them together. Oida volunteered to be lowered down through the hole. The improvised rope was almost long enough.

Once inside, Oida had the pleasure of being vindicated. There were rows and rows of coach wheels, new and brightly painted, racked up between rails, the iron tres still clammy with grease. They tried hauling one up through the hole in the roof, which broke the improvised rope; so Oida passed up a cold chisel and a big hammer, then sat down for a much-needed rest while the driver took out his feelings on the padlock. He used the time to reflect on the pattern of dereliction and abandonment he'd observed along the road; he had the feeling of a shape, which wasn't the shape he'd expected but which had a sort of internal logic of its own. If his hypothesis proved to be right, the West was in even deeper trouble than he'd assumed it to be: they hadn't been taken by surprise by Senza's onslaught; they'd seen it coming and abandoned huge swathes of the inner empire as indefensible – a strategy of defence in depth based on letting Senza reach the capital unopposed, in the hope of mauling him a bit on his way back. It was a strategy they taught in military academies, suitable for situations where you can't possibly hope to win, but there's still an outside chance that the enemy might be induced to lose. It was also the equivalent of cutting twelve-foot letters into a chalk hillside reading FORZA IS DEAD. He thought about that, but couldn't make up his mind.

Once they'd got the wheel outside, they offered it up against the remains they'd brought with them and were pleased to find it was an exact match. That was good; not so good was the weight of the thing. The driver could lift it and stagger a few yards before he had to put it down again, but that was about as much as he could do. They tried rolling it along the road, but it kept veering off and falling over. Then Oida hit on the idea of passing a long pole through the axle hole and carrying it like a stretcher, or the spoils of the hunt. By then it was pitch dark outside. They broke a lantern and a jar of lamp oil out of the stores, but they didn't need it; they were asleep within minutes.

Oida woke up the next morning with agonising cramp in his hips and calves, to find the driver roasting something on a spit over a fire of broken door planks. It was about the size of a small dog and tasted foul, and Oida knew better than to ask.

The driver was fretting about his horses. He'd left them hobbled rather than tethered, and there was probably enough grazing for them, and they'd probably have smelt the bog pool twenty yards from the coach by now and had the sense to drink without getting stuck in the bog, but he couldn't be sure; and they needed those horses, and, besides, a man gets attached to his team. Oida pointed out that worrying about it wouldn't help them and made him less efficient, but he got the impression the driver couldn't quite grasp the logic behind that.

There was a rainwater barrel under the eaves of the shed. The water in it was a dark brown colour, but Oida decided to risk it; he loathed being dirty. He washed as thoroughly as he could and climbed back into his clothes, which stuck to his skin, as on a particularly hot day. His razor, face powder, hair oil, nail clippers and other basic necessities of life were in his luggage, supposedly on its way back from Blemya – God only knew where it was now, or who it belonged to – so he spent a long time putting the best edge he could manage on the tiny silver-handled penknife he carried in his sleeve, and had a go at shaving. He stopped when he saw blood on his hands, and hoped he hadn't scarred himself for life.

"What happened to you?" the driver asked.

"Tried to shave."

"Is that right? I guessed you'd been fighting."

Oida grinned. "It was a bit like that, and I lost. I suppose we'd better be on our way."

The driver looked at him. "I was thinking. Maybe we could just hang on here till they come back."

"Better not," Oida said, as gently as he could. "We might be waiting some time."

So they started to walk, with the wheel on a pole and the pole on their shoulders. Oida had doubled over his scarf as a pad, but it wasn't enough to keep the pole from chafing on his collarbone. He tried shifting it, but sooner or later it always managed to work its way back on to the most painful spot. He could feel the torn skin move under his lapel and the scarf. He tried to think of something else, the war, politics, the things they'd need to do as a matter of urgency once the coach was fixed, theological doctrine, music, the exact dimensions of his student room at the Studium, rivers in Permia beginning with the letter Y, but the pain got into everything, like sand at a beach picnic. He called out, "Do you think we could stop for a bit?" but the driver didn't seem to have heard him. He thought about torture, about various men and women who'd ended up in the hands of torturers through his direct and indirect agency. He felt sick.

"You should've said something," the driver told him, when eventually they did stop and Oida tried to improvise a dressing of some sort for the mess. "You shouldn't have let it get in this state."

The driver had come up with a dressing for it; pads of bog cotton splodged with mashed-up dock leaves and two other plants he didn't recognise. To begin with it stung like hell; then the pain faded into a hot glow, and then his whole shoulder went completely numb. It was the most wonderful feeling he'd ever had in his life. He kept saying "thank you" over and over again, until the driver gave him a funny look and told him to shut up about it. "It'll be stiff as buggery in a few hours," he warned; "you won't be able to move that arm at all. Fat lot of good to me you'll be when we're fitting the stupid wheel."

Oida apologised, several times. "This stuff is amazing," he said. "Where'd you learn about it?"

The driver looked blank. "I thought everybody knew," he said.

He made the driver show him the plants he'd used and tell him their names; but they just looked like weeds to him, and the names were obviously what those plants were called within five miles of the driver's birthplace and nowhere else. Still, he committed them lovingly to memory: blue marwort and shepherd's sandal. If ever I get out of this alive, he promised himself, I'll get seeds and plant five acres of them and make enough money to retire on.

What he should have done, the driver explained to him as to a small child, was cut the soles out of three pairs of military boots from the stores, wrap them in cloth and pad them underneath with a double handful of sheep's wool twisted into a ball. Since he'd neglected to do that, he'd have to make do with his shirt, folded into ever-decreasing rectangles. It wasn't nearly as good as doing it properly, but it protected his other shoulder quite adequately the rest of the way, which was nearly all downhill.

They saw the coach in the distance, and immediately the driver slithered out from under his end of the pole and broke into a run. Oida lowered his end slowly and pushed it away so it wouldn't smack him on the way down. From the top of the rise he could see for miles. There was no sign of the horses.

Oida was one of those men who does cry, but not for sorrow. Beauty moved him to tears, and acts and stories of great courage and endurance; certain passages of music had him in floods, no matter how many times he heard them. He often cried for joy, relief and gratitude; but mostly for anger. It was a weakness he was aware and ashamed of, but he couldn't help it, and there it was.

The driver came back at some point and stood looking at him. "For God's sake," he said, "pull yourself together."

Oida sniffed hard, swallowed and dabbed at his eyes. It was a good time to say something, but he couldn't.

"It's all right," the driver was saying scornfully, "they won't have gone far. I found their tracks; the ground's good and soft. I'm used to catching them up. There's nothing to get in a state about."

Oida looked at him through a salty blur. He read confidence in his face, the all-in-a-day's-work look he'd seen at various critical times on the faces of doctors and lawyers; you think you're screwed, but I know about these things and it'll be fine. He took a deep breath, considered apologising and decided that would only make things worse. "You stay there," the driver said. "Do some deep breathing or something. I'll be back directly."

He walked away briskly, and Oida saw him pick up the trail and follow it out on to the moor. When he was too small to see, Oida got up, pulled the pole out of the axle hole, hauled the wheel upright on its rim and slowly and carefully began to roll it down the hill. It took a long time, but he had time to burn. He propped the wheel against the side of the coach, got down on his hands and knees and examined the end of the axle. It would redeem matters slightly, he decided, if by the time the driver came back with the horses, he'd managed to get the wheel on all by himself.

After a bit, he got up again, went back and retrieved the pole. Leverage: Lodge doctrine has a lot to say about leverage, though mostly in terms of metaphor and mysticism. But Oida knew what a fulcrum was, and he'd read about how they built the Single Span Bridge at Exesti. He looked around and found a dozen big stones, which he eventually managed to scrabble out of the peat with a lot of effort. The flattest stone became his fulcrum; if he sat on the end of the pole, he could lift the cart so that the axle was level with the hole in the propped-up wheel. Problem was, he couldn't reach the wheel to slide it on to the axle without standing up and taking his weight off the lever. It was fortunate that patience and concentration were special virtues of his; also fortunate that he was alone, with nobody to see the contortions he went through, trying to sit down and reach out at the same time, or offer advice, which he hated beyond measure when he was trying to think. He eventually cracked it when he found he could stand with one foot on the lever and get his elbows on the ground, which gave him enough strength and purchase to lift the wheel. He had a couple of nasty spills, when the lever moved under his foot, got away from him and flipped him over like a pancake. At maybe the fiftieth attempt, he felt the axle slide into the hole and take the weight. Very carefully he lifted his foot off the lever and was overjoyed to see that the wheel didn't move and the cart stayed perfectly still. The wheel was now jammed on the very end of the axle, blocking the hole for the cotter pin. He had to bash it down the axle with a rock, an eighth of an inch at a time. Finally, however, he managed to drive the pin home with a stone, and the job was done. He stood up (his back was so stiff he was afraid he'd snap it when he tried to straighten it), looked at what he'd managed to achieve and felt wonderful. Then it occurred to him that he'd been playing with the stupid wheel for a very long time, and the driver wasn't back yet.

It was getting dark. He knew plenty of stories about men who'd gone wandering about in the dark on the moors, unable to see the bogs and sinkholes. Typically, either they vanished without trace or all that was ever found was a hat, or a single boot. He decided that the driver knew the same stories and had settled down with the horses in a known dry place for the night. So he made himself as comfortable as he could on the seat of the coach, dragged the blankets over him, and had no trouble at all going to sleep.

In the morning, he set out to follow the driver's trail. He didn't know very much about tracking, but it was mostly common sense, and footprints and hoofprints in the soft patches of black peat were easy to follow. They petered out among the tussocks of couch grass and heather, so he held on as straight a line as he could. The landscape was open, with little in the way of dips and dead ground. Six horses would stand out like a temple spire.

He found the driver purely by chance; it would have been so easy to miss him. He was lying face down in a dark brown pool, his left ankle lodged in a tangle of exposed heather roots. The slimy black mud was barely churned up at all, so at least the poor devil drowned quickly.

No tears. Instead, he debated whether to head back to the road or keep on looking for the horses; at which point he realised that he'd got himself turned round and had completely lost his bearings, with not a clue as to which direction the road was in. But there were hoofprints, unequivocally clear, leading away from the pool. He conjectured that the horses had come to the pool to drink (presumably the driver had come to the same conclusion). He knelt down and studied the hoofprints, wishing he'd read a book about tracking so he'd know what he was looking at. Well; the prints were sharp and clear and there wasn't any water in them, whereas other prints he'd seen earlier had been partially flooded with water seeping up through the peat. Therefore (logic suggested) these prints weren't all that old, and the horses – hobbled, so they'd be walking slower than a man – couldn't be all that far away.

He stood up and looked round, and noted that the mist was starting to come down. The stories had been eloquent about mist on the moors. A sensible man would stay put until it lifted, but that could be hours, or days. But horses aren't sensible. Are they? He realised he didn't know. Nor did he have any idea how long the approaching mist would take to reach him. Could he outpace it by walking fast, or would it be all round him in ten minutes? No data. He shrugged, and followed the hoofprints.

Horses, it turned out, were very sensible indeed. They'd found a little shelf in the peat, worn away by the backs of generations of itching sheep and just tall enough to provide a little shelter from wind and rain, almost high enough for a man searching for them in bad light to mistake them for dead gorse or a granite outcrop.

Tears were dribbling down his cheeks as he walked up on the closest horse, taking care to avoid eye contact (which makes horses wary), not going straight up to it, standing beside it for a count of twenty to let it get used to him before reaching out and grabbing a handful of mane; then a slow, patient ritual of greeting, patting, rubbing between the ears, before squatting down to cut the hobbles with his sadly inadequate toy penknife. The peat shelf made a marvellously convenient mounting block. No bridle or saddle, of course, and the wretched thing's back was as broad as a highway; just as well that, when he was twelve years old, his father had insisted that he learn to ride bareback without a bridle, controlling the horse with just the pressure of his legs and feet. He felt bad about the other horses, but he couldn't risk dismounting again just to cut their hobbles.

All that, he decided, had been the easy bit. Now he had to find the road again.

Easy enough for a man with a good memory who'd once looked at a map, provided that he could see the sun. But instead he could see mist, and not much else. Well; he'd already established that horses are sensible, therefore unlikely to stumble into bogs. He nudged the horse into a slow, easy stroll, direction irrelevant, for now the priority was building a relationship with the horse so it'd do as it was told.

When the mist lifted some hours later, it turned out he'd been heading due east – not ideal, but not too disastrous, either. He made the necessary adjustment and rode on until it started to get dark. By this point he reckoned he and the horse understood each other well enough for him to risk dismounting. He knotted the ends of the severed hobbles together as best he could, lay down in the heather and closed his eyes.

Cramp woke him four times in the night, thirst twice and horrible-sounding animal noises once. The last item didn't bother him; he knew from his experience as a traveller that the more bloodcurdling the cry, the smaller and dopier the animal or bird. When he awoke the fifth time, the sun was high in the sky and he was being stared down at by a dozen armed men. He blinked at them. Unlike the infantry, the cavalry of the two empires looked nothing like each other. These were Easterners: Imperials, swathed in woollens and furs over their mail shirts and shivering with cold. They wore the distinctive pillbox off-duty felt hats of the Seventeenth Lancers, a skirmishing and reconnaissance unit particularly favoured by Senza Belot.

One of them wore a twisted golden collar, identifying him as a squadron commander. He cleared his throat, took a deep breath and said, "You're him, aren't you?"

"My name's Oida. Do we know each other?"

"I saw you in Choris. You did a concert in the hippodrome." The officer pursed his lips. "Sorry, I've got to ask. What the hell are you doing out here?"

*

They made him tea, on a dear little portable stove, and gave him oatcakes, and dressed his blistered shoulder, and lent him a fur cloak that must've weighed ten pounds, and scraped the caked mud off his boots and gave them a good rub-down with dry bracken and sheep's-wool grease. "This is amazing," said the officer (his name was Timao). "They're never going to believe me back home; we all absolutely love your stuff, my whole family, especially my sister; she plays the flute and the bass viol; she's always playing your tunes. They're going to be so jealous."

Of course he could ride with them; they would be delighted to lend him a horse – they had a couple of remounts with them, standard procedure, but if neither of them suited Timao would be honoured to lend him his mare – and where was it he was going exactly? Ah. Unfortunately they couldn't escort him all the way there, on account of it being hostile territory in the middle of a major campaign, they hoped he understood, orders are orders and so forth; in point of fact he was highly unlikely to run into any soldiers, since the Seventeenth had wiped out the last remnants of General Sallaco's forces and was heading back to rejoin the main force for the big push against Rasch, so nothing to worry about there. The war? Oh, yes, going swimmingly. Nothing between Senza and Rasch except a few hayfoot local levies and the stub end of the Western Twelfth, and then the war would be over and everybody could go home. Meanwhile, it was an awful imposition, naturally, but could Oida possibly see his way to scribbling just a few words to his sister Hilditunn?

Oida smiled graciously and jotted down a tune that had been running through his head at various times over the last few days. He added, for Hilditunn, the sister of the man who saved my life, signed it with his usual squashed-crane-fly squiggle and handed it to Timao, who stared at it open-mouthed for a moment, then stuffed it into the lining of his helmet.

*

They were supposed to be hunting down stragglers from the recent battle (in which Senza had been outnumbered six to one, and had smashed the Western centre with a lightning charge before enveloping the bewildered wings and slaughtering them like sheep; same old Senza), but instead they escorted him as far as Epoi Esen, three days along the Great West Road. There they caught sight of a substantial body of horsemen in the distance, which Timao reckoned had to be the advance guard of the Western Eleventh Army, hurrying to the relief of Rasch. Oida assured him he'd be fine, thanked him profusely for his help, and urged him to be on his way before the Eleventh noticed him. Timao insisted that he should keep the horse and gave him food for four days, his personal silver cup and bowl and the portable stove. "My sister will be so pleased," he said for the fifteenth time, then dressed his troop into column and galloped away.

Oida rode into Epoi, which was deserted apart from a small garrison posted in the Prefecture. The town had been evacuated, the garrison commander told him; he had no idea where the townspeople had gone, north maybe. Meanwhile, he'd be honoured if Oida could join him for dinner, and if afterwards he felt like singing a few numbers, the men would appreciate it very much.

The Eleventh, Oida learned, was heading for Rasch by way of Celeuthoe. The garrison commander didn't know why, it seemed an odd decision to him, but of course he didn't know all the facts and couldn't see the bigger picture. Yes, the situation was pretty bad. Senza had smashed up every force sent to oppose him; the policy now seemed to be to keep what assets remained out of his way and let him go straight to Rasch, where he could cool his heels in the shadow of the impregnable walls until hunger, dysentery and mountain fever decimated his army and sent him creeping home; at which point the Eleventh, the First, the Seventh and about a million local levies would come down on him like a ton of bricks and the war would be over by Ascension Day. Which might just work, the garrison commander added, though personally he was inclined to doubt it.

Oida exchanged his horse for a hot bath, a razor and a seat on the internal mail to brigade headquarters at Estin; the journey took three days and was blissfully dull. He spent the time working up the tune he'd given to Timao's sister into a ballad, which he was fairly sure would pay for his expenses and lost luggage and show a tidy profit on top. He decided to call it "The Soldier's Homecoming", and made a mental note to get some words written for it as soon as he had the chance.

Estin, to his great relief, seemed to be normal and in full working order. He got out at the Eastgate, thanked the driver and walked down to the Flower Market. The bath-house was still there, and he paid extra for a full massage, haircut and manicure. The barber-surgeon told him his shoulder was healing up just fine – there would be a scar, but interesting rather than off-putting – and the aches and pains in his chest and back were just pulled muscles and nothing serious. After his bath he walked up Empire Way to Tailors' Row. The outfit he ended up with was solidly classic, if a bit provincial, and he managed to pick up a fine pair of plum-coloured boots with a small silver buckle. After a light lunch in a tea house on the Square, he visited the stationer's and a couple of bookshops, and finally the cutler's on the corner of Victory Row and Old Temple.

There were other customers in the shop, so he browsed quietly until they'd gone. Then he took the things he'd chosen – a chess set and writing kit to replace the ones he'd lost and a rather hand-some bone-handled knife with silver mounts in the Mezentine style, though almost certainly modern – to the shopkeeper, who looked at him, scowled and said, "Where the hell did you get to?"

Oida smiled apologetically. "I got held up on the road. Sorry."

The shopkeeper bolted the shop door. "In the back," he said. "Leave all that."

Oida dumped the chess set and the rest of the stuff on a chair and followed him through a curtain into a small, dark room that smelt strongly of cats. There was a lamp, a small charcoal stove, two chairs and an officer's folding table, with one leg broken and mended with rawhide. The shopkeeper banged down an old-fashioned brass kettle on the stove, sat down in the comfortable looking chair and pointed at the other one. Oida sat.

"Of course, everything's gone to hell," the shopkeeper said. "Absolute chaos everywhere you look. I've had nothing from Division in three days and meanwhile I'm supposed to sort it all out and wipe everybody's arses for them." He glowered at Oida and added, "And now I've got you. Lucky me."

"I'm sorry," Oida repeated. "What exactly is happening? I've been out of touch for several—"

"Good question," the shopkeeper said bitterly, "bloody good question. The first we knew about anything was bloody Senza Belot appearing out of nowhere like a djinn in a fairy story. Best guess is he came over the bay from Blemya: what he was doing there I would very much like to know—" He paused and gave Oida a foul look. "I was under the impression you were handling Blemya, but perhaps there was a change of plan and nobody bothered to tell me. Anyway," he went on, before Oida could say anything, "Senza made pudding out of everything they threw at him, it's practically certain he's heading straight for Rasch, so all existing plans and projects are on indefinite hold, and it's up to me to decide what the hell we do next." He paused and massaged his forehead. "Now, then," he said. "On the face of it you've had a wasted journey. Still, since you're here, I take it you won't object to making yourself useful."

"Of course," Oida said quickly. "If there's anything I can do—"

The kettle started to steam. The shopkeeper got up and poured boiling water into a red porcelain teapot. "Let's see if you're as smart as they say you are," he said. "Right. What's wrong with this picture?"

Oida thought for a moment, then said, "Senza Belot is making an all-out attack on Rasch. His army is entirely cavalry. He's got some good-quality horse artillery with him, but obviously nothing that's going to make a dent in the walls of Rasch. He's moved very fast, but still left enough time for the City Prefect to lay in stores." He looked up. "It's pointless," he said. "There's no way he can take Rasch."

"Very good." The shopkeeper nodded. "Unless—?"

"Unless," Oida said, "he knows that when he gets there, someone will be waiting with a key to let him in."

"Good boy." The shopkeeper nodded again. "Of course, we don't know anything because nothing's getting in or out of Rasch, even for us, so we can't be sure. But it stands to reason, Senza's done a deal with one of the factions and they're going to hand the city to him on a plate. You don't need me to tell you—" He scowled again. "It's a disaster. I've written to Division – and Central – but the way the roads are at the moment, I have no idea when they'll get it, if they get it at all, or how long it'll take them to reply. Nobody can tell me where Senza is right now, not even Ocnisant – he's been warned off, would you believe – so there's no way of knowing how long we've got. I mean, for all we know, Senza could be in Rasch right now, barbecuing the emperor over an open fire, in which case—" He broke off again, wiped his forehead on his sleeve and poured tea into two tiny blue bowls. "Why me, is what I want to know. Why the hell does absolutely everything have to be my fault?" He handed Oida a bowl, then dropped heavily into his chair. "All right," he said. "Let's just assume that Senza hasn't taken Rasch yet. Is there anything – anything at all – we can do to make it better?"

Oida put the bowl carefully on the floor; his hand was shaking and he didn't want to spill tea on the rug, which was Aelian and quite valuable. "We can kill Senza," he said.

"That's right. Take him out of the situation and the traitors in Rasch will forget about it and melt quietly away, the Easterners will go back home and everything will be just fine. Trouble is—" he lifted his cup, looked at it, picked out a dead fly "—easier said than done."

Oida nodded. "We haven't got anybody in close?"

"I don't know," the shopkeeper said irritably. "It was ordained that I didn't need to know that. I'm guessing yes, because it'd be the most appalling dereliction of duty on someone's part if we didn't, but of course I've got no way of getting orders to him, if he exists, even if I knew who he is. You see the problem? Nobody's going to be able to get close enough to Senza to kill him except an insider, but even if we've got one we can't use him, or I can't, anyway, and I'm the poor sod who's got to give the order." He turned his head and looked straight at Oida; his eyes were small and deep soft brown. "Can you think of anything?"

Oida felt a lump in his throat, and it was hard to speak naturally. "Sorry, no."

"I think you can," the shopkeeper said quietly. "Providential, really, you turning up like this. Name me one other craftsman in the whole of both empires who could roll up at Senza's camp unannounced and be shown straight into the presence, no questions asked. Well?"

Oida's mouth was bone-dry. "I see your point," he said. "But if I stroll into Senza's camp and kill him, how am I going to get out of there in one piece?"

The shopkeeper didn't speak for a long time, until it wasn't necessary to say anything. "It's the only solution I can come up with," he said. "Unless you can think of something. I'm open to suggestions."

"Not really, no."

"Well, then." The shopkeeper looked away. "Hell of a thing to have to ask of anybody, but there it is; we didn't make this mess, damn bloody shame we've got to sort it out. I know for a fact they were relying on you for this Blemyan thing, so you'll have to tell me who you think would be best to take that one over when you're—" He stopped, picked up his teacup, put it down again. "Any recommendations?"

Oida heard himself propose a couple of names.

"Yes, they'll do, I suppose," the shopkeeper said gloomily. "Anyway, that one's not my problem, thank God. While we're on the subject, are there any arrangements—?" He tailed off and looked at the toes of his slippers.

Oida cleared his throat. "I never got round to making a will," he said.

"What? Oh, well, that's easy enough, just let me have a note of the names and I'll get it done straight away."

"I can tell you now," Oida said. "There's a woman in operations, Telamon. Did you ever come across her?"

"No. Name rings a bell."

"She might as well have the lot," Oida said. "Apart from that—" He shrugged. "I can't say I care terribly much. I suppose my brother Axio had better have our father's sword, assuming he's still alive. Oh, and I'd like Director Procopius of the Music School to have my score of his Third Symphony. It's the original manuscript, so he'd probably like it back. It's at the White Cross Temple in Choris under my name. If you could see to that, it'd be appreciated."

The shopkeeper was making a note on a wax tablet with his fingernail. "Procopius, Third Symphony, got that." He put the tablet on the table. "Anything you think you might need for the job itself?"

"I don't think so. As I understand it, the plan is, I walk up to him and stick him in the side of the neck. I wouldn't have thought that called for specialist equipment."

"Keep it simple, I always say," the shopkeeper said vaguely. He was writing something down on his wax tablet. "Now, as far as the timetable's concerned—"

"I suppose I'd better be going," Oida said. "I'd have liked a good night's sleep, but I guess that's out of the question."

"Catch a nap in the coach," the shopkeeper said. "You may as well take my chaise," he added mournfully. "It's quick and it doesn't look military, which is an advantage in the circumstances. Cost me two angels fifteen, but I suppose that's neither here nor there. I'll get Aisimon's boy to drive for you."

Oida grinned. "He's expendable, too, I take it."

"He's a good, reliable driver and he doesn't charge stupid money." For the first time, something like sympathy flitted into the shopkeeper's face, though not for long. "I'm afraid we won't be able to go shouting anything from the rooftops," he said, "but the people who matter will know, I can promise you that."

"Screw them," Oida said. "If they'd been doing their jobs properly, this wouldn't be necessary." He shrugged. "It's all Forza Belot's fault," he said. "Thoughtlessly getting himself killed. I'll give him a piece of my mind when I see him."

Clearly the shopkeeper didn't think that was funny. "You'd better go," he said. "I don't want to be seen with you; you know how it is."

Oida understood. He got to his feet – he was surprised at how steady his legs were – and walked out into the shop. "I need to pay you for this stuff," he said.

"What? Oh, right." The shopkeeper picked up the knife and looked at it. "I think we can do better than that," he said, and pulled a dagger in a silver-chased sheath off a hook on the wall. Oida glanced at it; it was a good choice. "That's on the house," the shopkeeper said. "Least I can do."

Oida felt in his pocket for coins. "No, really," he said, "I insist. I think money's the least of my worries now."

The shopkeeper looked unhappy but held out his hand; Oida tipped coins into it without looking at them. "Be at the stables round the back of the Poverty and Patience in an hour," the shop-keeper said. "I'll have the will ready for you to sign."

An hour; the last hour of free time in a civilised place he'd ever have. He considered various conventional ways of passing it, but decided he wasn't in the mood. Instead he sat down on a low wall under a tree, opened his beautiful new writing set, unfolded a half-sheet of new milk-white parchment and unscrewed the top of the ink bottle.

Oida to Telamon, greetings –

He sat looking at what he'd written for a while, then crossed it out and turned the page over.

Oida to Director Procopius, greetings;

When I say that I have always valued your friendship more than your music, I would not wish you to imply—

He pulled a face, screwed the page into a ball and dropped it on the ground. Then he put the writing things back in their box and closed it, stuck his hand in his pocket, pulled out all the rest of his money and counted it. Twenty-seven angels seventy.

He went into the Poverty and Patience and ordered a beer with a brandy chaser, found a seat in the corner next to the fire, took out Bardiya's Garden of Entrancing Images and started to read. A little later, one of the kitchen maids walked past carrying a brace of white ducks, their heads swinging and bumping against her knees. Oida smiled at her. "May I?" he asked, and pulled out a wing feather to use as a bookmark.

*

The driver was maybe seventeen years old, with a tuft of fluff on his upper lip and chin and an Eastern army mail shirt. "You'd better not let them catch you wearing that when we're on the road," Oida advised him; he looked worried, stopped the chaise and wriggled out of it, like an unhooked fish escaping from the angler's fingers.

"Are you that singer?" the boy asked, when they'd been driving for an hour or so.

"No," Oida said.

He finished the Garden at noon the next day and asked the boy if he wanted it. The boy said thanks, but he couldn't read; Oida pointed out that he didn't need to, he could just look at the pictures. The boy gave him a horrified look and accepted gratefully.

On the morning of the fourth day they started to come across dead bodies lying in the road; soldiers mostly, but not exclusively. The boy didn't seem unduly concerned about them. His ambition, he said, was to join Ocnisant's; it was a really good way to get ahead, so he'd heard, and he didn't want to stay a carter all his life, thank you very much. A couple of the kids from his neighbourhood had got in with Ocnisant and when they came home to visit they always had plenty of money. Oida looked away and asked him if he thought the war would last that long. The boy laughed, and asked him if he'd ever been to Rasch. A few times, Oida said. It's great there, isn't it, the boy said, there's always so much going on, and of course there's nowhere like it for making money. It was his dream to live there one day, he said, and Oida replied gravely that he hoped he'd get the chance.

"Strictly speaking," Oida told the boy, "as far as they're concerned, you're the enemy. Now, because you're with me and I've got dual citizenship, in theory you ought to be all right. Depends how well up the soldiers are in international law."

The boy lowered the reins. "They wouldn't do anything, would they?"

"Physical violence?" Oida shook his head. "On balance, I'd say no. But they'd be within their rights to requisition the horses, and the food. I suggest you stop here and let me walk the rest of the way."

The boy hesitated. "Are you sure? Macrobius told me to take you right up to the camp gates."

I bet he did, Oida thought. "Like I said, I'm sure you'll be all right. But is it worth taking the risk, for the sake of saving me half an hour's walk? Up to you."

The chaise came to a gentle halt. "Thanks," the boy said.

Oida jumped down, winced as his stiff ankles took his weight. "No problem," he said, and hauled down his bag. "Here." He dug his hand in his pocket and scooped out the remaining money, clamped his fist tight around it. "Cup your hands," he ordered. The boy did as he was told. Oida poured the money into them, then crimped the boy's hands tight around it, so he couldn't see what he'd been given. "So long," he called out, as he walked quickly away. "Safe journey back."

He heard the boy call out after him but didn't turn round.

The first thing you see, when you approach Rasch from the east, is the spire of the Red Temple. It's easily the tallest building in the city, and some people love it and some people think it's an eyesore and an affront to the Deity and should be pulled down. Your first glimpse of it will probably be through the gap in the hills just past the fifth Government milestone, about halfway between the Sun in Splendour and the Grace and Austerity; you only get to see it as more than a vaguely unnatural spike when the road takes you round the lower slopes of the Four Sisters; and that was where Oida got out and began to walk.

Cavalry moving along roads in inhabited areas can be hard to track. They shouldn't be. But it's remarkable how, even in time of war, people can't seem to resist the sight of steaming pyramids of horseshit on a metalled road. As soon as the soldiers disappear over the horizon, out the people come, with their buckets and pails, and before long there's nothing left to show that the military have ever been there.

The road to Rasch, however, was no place to walk in new, expensive boots. The only consolation, from Oida's perspective, was proof positive that Senza's army was entirely made up of cavalry. There were no human footprints in the dung piles; which told him, among other things, that Senza wasn't impeding his own mobility with prisoners.

Needless to say, Oida knew all the approaches to Rasch like the back of his hand. It was bizarre, therefore, to have the road entirely to himself, at noon on a bright, clear day. He passed the Five Pillars of Faith and saw that the door was shut – he hadn't ever seen its door before, didn't know it had one; he was tempted to sneak inside and see if there was anything left to eat, but decided against it.

Beyond the Five Pillars is salad country, the market gardens and orchards that supply the city. Being heavy loam on top of clay, the ground is firm, and Senza had let his column leave the road and spread out without fear of getting bogged down. It looked to Oida for all the world like spoiled paper, as though someone had written a landscape, thought better of it and scratched it out until the nib broke. Purely as a mental exercise he tried to calculate the cost of the damage and came up with a figure of two million angels.

The patrol captain recognised him at once, so that was all right. He quickly ran through the story he'd prepared – on his way here to do a concert, heard about the forthcoming change of management, decided to do the gig anyway (pause for laugh); the kid driving the coach got scared and refused to bring him any closer, so he'd had to footslog it all the way from the Grace: any chance of a beer and just possibly something to eat?

The captain swallowed it whole and said he'd send ahead and let the general know he was here. Please, don't bother him, he's got far more important things to do. No, really, he'll want to see you, more than my commission's worth if he finds out Oida was here and nobody told him. Oh, all right then. Easy as that.

Senza had pitched his camp on the Ascension Flats race track. It was a logical choice – flat, more than enough grazing, water from two rivers, excellent visibility, and the covered stands offered plenty of seasoned timber, just what you need when you're about to embark on a siege. By the time Oida got there, they'd already torn up the rails and were halfway through dismantling the Imperial Stand; a pity, Oida thought, and where will the ruler of the newly united Restored Empire sit when he's opening the End of Year Games? It was at that point that he remembered something the shopkeeper had said; it hit him like the low branch whose height you guess wrong when you're out riding, and for quite some time he felt too stupid to think.

Someone in a gilded breastplate and a red cloak came bustling out to meet him. Fortunately he had plenty to say, so Oida didn't have to make conversation. He followed the red and gold gleam to the guest tent, where there was water and a clean towel, and then to the officers' mess, where they brought him a rather good sweet white wine and a big plate of honeycakes, Eastern-style, with syrup.

"This is all rather sudden," he heard himself say. "I'm here to give a recital in the Victory Hall. I'm guessing that won't be possible."

The man in the pretty breastplate grinned at him. "We'll give you a safe passage through the lines, if that's what you want. But I'm guessing they won't be in the mood right now. Why don't you stay out here and sing for our troops instead? They'd love it."

"I'd be glad to," Oida replied. "So, how long have you been here?"

"Four days," the breastplate replied. "Just long enough to dig the latrines and organise the sittings in the mess tent, the really important stuff. Storming the city comes later, when we can get round to it."

They were very good honeycakes. "You brought a good cook with you."

"Senza's own personal man," the breastplate said. "Earns more than I do, and you can see why."

Oida smiled. "You expect to be here some time, then."

"Who can say?" the breastplate said with his mouth full. "Not too long, I hope, but there's no sense in pigging it if you don't have to." He swallowed and went on, "I know what you're getting at. Where's the food coming from to feed all this lot?"

"Military secret?"

"Oh, I don't mind telling you. All right, how many men do you think Senza's got? To the nearest thousand."

Oida hadn't given it any thought. "Sixty?"

"Thirty. All the rest is baggage train, mostly supplies."

Not what he'd been expecting to hear. "What about the artillery? I'd assumed—"

"No." The breastplate smiled. "We've got a bit, but only enough to bash down the odd cowshed. No, we brought everything with us, like a picnic."

Oida nodded slowly. "Forza's still alive, isn't he?" he said.

The breastplate gave him a blank stare for a moment, then suddenly grinned. "Not for long, we hope. But, yes, he is."

"And all this is just—"

"To winkle him out, yes." The breastplate poured them both more wine. "You know, it's a real privilege working for Senza; you don't know how exciting it is for a military man, actually being here on the spot and watching it happen. It's all about risks, you see; that's how it's always been between them, ever since they were kids. How far dare you go in order to beat the other one? Will you fight me if I have one hand tied behind my back? One hand behind my back and blindfold? All right then, if I have one hand behind my back, blindfold and unarmed, will you fight me then? Really, it's all just the three-card trick. When do you reach the point where the other man can't resist having a go at you, even though he knows in his heart of hearts that he's bound to lose? That's where Senza's so brilliant. I think it's because he's the younger brother. It's all about self-confidence, really. Senza knows he's the best, therefore he is. It's a sort of metaphysical thing, if you know what I mean."

Oida wanted to laugh out loud. "You really shouldn't be telling me all this," he said.

"Oh, why not? Everybody knows you're neutral. You know, you really ought to stick around, and then you can sing at the victory celebrations. The biggest party in the history of the world – you wouldn't want to miss that, now, would you?"

"Certainly not," Oida said, "and, yes, I'd love to, if I won't be under your feet. I won't ask how long you expect to be here for, because obviously—"

"Quite," the breastplate said firmly. "But actually we can make you quite comfortable, if you don't mind tents. There's plenty of the good stuff left. This came from the old Grace and Austerity, out on the west road. Know it?"

Oida smiled. "I thought it tasted familiar. You didn't happen to find their private stock of Aelian red, did you? From memory, it was right at the back of the cellar, under a pile of old coats."

"I'll save you a bottle," the breastplate said gravely. "My word as an officer."

The shopkeeper had seemed confident that the Lodge had someone close to Senza, and Oida was prepared to share that confidence. Figuring out who it could be and establishing contact, however, wouldn't be easy. Logical; if Oida the musician could work out who it was, so could Senza's intelligence people. It had to be someone unlikely – and once you started playing that game, you were simply begging to make catastrophic mistakes. It was infuriating to think that there was someone close at hand he could report to, get a message out by, hand responsibility over to, and no way to get at him; but life is full of intense frustrations and painful ironies, and yet here the human race still is, clinging grimly on and managing somehow.

His meeting with Senza was brief and rather uncomfortable. At first he wondered if Senza somehow knew that, right up to that dramatic last-minute reprieve, Oida had intended to kill him – no, surely not, Senza was smart and had almost superhuman intuition, especially where anything to do with violence was concerned, but the fact that Oida was still alive strongly suggested that the thought had never crossed Senza's mind. Then he realised what it was, and the revelation struck him like a bolt of lightning; Senza simply didn't like him very much. Oida hadn't been expecting that. It wasn't the first time they'd met, and as far as he could gather Senza hadn't manifested any antipathy at any of their previous meetings; but on those occasions Senza hadn't been quite so preoccupied with other things, and had therefore presumably made more of an effort to mask his feelings. This time he wasn't actively rude or hostile or anything like that; on the contrary, he welcomed Oida to the camp, thanked him for agreeing to entertain the troops and told him he was welcome to stay as long as he liked: anything he wanted, just ask. But anyone with any degree of sensitivity can tell. Senza didn't like him. Why not, for God's sake? Everybody likes Oida: what's not to like? But there it was; and what can't be explained must be accepted.

So he filled his time with making himself useful, something he was good at. He sang ballads for the troops (and the garrison inside Rasch must've wondered what all that cheering was about) and scurrilous topical songs for the junior officers and arias from the classics for the senior officers and the general staff; he made himself generally available at certain specified times so that men could come up and tell him how wonderful he was and how much their female relatives adored him; he hung around the officers' mess so that captains and majors could write home saying how they'd spent a whole half-hour talking to the celebrated Oida, and, actually he was a really nice man, quite ordinary, once you got to know him. He signed things and added sentences to the ends of letters home, assessed the merits of cherished musical instruments and played a bar or two on them, then wrote his name on the back, thereby rendering them exquisitely saleable. It was the sort of thing he was used to doing wherever he went and he did it particularly well, but he found himself feeling increasingly depressed. For one thing, there was the possibility that Senza was wrong and Forza really was dead, in which case— He tried not to think about that.

"Oh, he's alive all right," his friend the breastplate (his real name was Frontizo) assured him over a bowl of tea in the mess. "I can't tell you how we know, but we know. He's just biding his time. It doesn't matter. We've got foraging parties out all over the place fetching in supplies, so we won't starve, and you simply don't get camp fever and dysentery and all that nonsense in one of Senza's camps. We can stay here practically indefinitely and wait the bugger out. He'll blink first, you can bet on it."

Oida nodded. "What if he's out there raising armies?" he said. "Have we got reinforcements on the way?"

Frontizo shook his head. "Don't need them," he said. "Senza's got it all worked out. The more troops Forza brings, the more trouble he'll find himself in. We're counting on seventy thousand: any more would be a bonus. If they come to us, we won't have to go out and find them. It's been one of the great ambitions of Senza's life to fight a battle here at Rasch; he reckons there's a unique combination of landscape features that make this the perfect killing bottle."

Oida didn't try and hide his shudder; he was the sensitive artist, after all.

"It's for the best," Frontizo reassured him. "The more of them we kill, the sooner the war will be over. I know it's hard, but buying peace is like buying anything. You've got to pay through the nose for quality. The main thing is to make sure the other chap ends up getting stuck with the bill."

Oida usually made a point of not staying too long in one place. He recognised that there was something about him (he had no idea what it was) that got on people's nerves after three days. Under normal circumstances this wasn't a problem, since his schedule was so hectic that three days in one place didn't happen very often. For those occasions where he found himself stranded for longer periods, he'd worked out various ways of being elusive without any risk of giving offence. The best excuse was work; he could claim to be in the throes of composition, and everyone was perfectly happy to give him a wide berth. Further or in the alternative he could be ill; as a result of long and diligent practice, he could make himself sneeze for extended periods more or less at will, and he knew the symptoms of half a dozen minor but tiresome ailments better than most doctors.

After eight days in Senza's camp, he was both ill and working. It was vitally important, he realised, not to get on these people's nerves. In particular, he couldn't do anything that might possibly alienate Senza himself.

So far, the highly efficient and far-ranging scout network had seen no sign at all of an approaching army. Fair enough; if Forza was coming, he'd make an effort not to be seen, and he was as good at that sort of thing as his brother, if not better. But time was passing; if Forza was out there, why hadn't he come to the defence of Rasch? He'd discussed this topic endlessly with Frontizo, whom he'd identified as a high-ranking nonentity, someone he could irritate with complete immunity; in fact, it appeared that Frontizo genuinely liked him and looked forward to their conversations.

Frontizo's hypothesis was that Forza was calling Senza's bluff. He'd figured out that Senza didn't have the manpower or the heavy plant to pose a real threat to Rasch, and could therefore be ignored. Oida told him he was missing the point. Forza wouldn't be lured into the trap by the danger to Rasch. He was wise enough and icy-hearted enough to let Rasch be taken and burned, if he thought there was any risk of losing a battle against his brother if he tried to relieve it. No, the lure had to be the relatively small size of the Eastern army and the distance Senza had put between himself and any source of resupply or reinforcement. On which score, Oida reckoned, he'd done more than enough – he had a tiny army, he was surrounded and hopelessly exposed. So where was Forza?

Frontizo replied that Forza was far too smart to go for something that was so obviously too good to be true. It had TRAP written all over it in letters of burnished bronze, and Forza could read. No, what Forza was doing was really quite subtle. Instead of taking the bait when he was supposed to, namely right away, before Senza got smart and changed his mind, he was deliberately biding his time. He'd guessed or learned that Senza had brought all his provisions with him, instead of depending on a traditional line of supply; he was waiting till Senza had eaten his very last biscuit and had no option but to give up and go home, and then he'd strike.

"Which is where he's gone wrong, of course," Frontizo went on. "Thanks to everybody in the West being scared stiff of us, the countryside's deserted for miles around: we can send out our foragers and help ourselves to the standing corn. We've got two thousand men out right now, harvesting wheat. Also, the local peasantry bolted so quick, they neglected to empty their larders first. We can sit here in comfort till Forza's realised he's made a mistake, and by then Rasch will be starving and he'll have to do something; or else we actually take Rasch, and then Forza won't be a general any more."

Oida looked at him. "You don't suppose Forza really is dead, do you?"

Frontizo shook his head. "He's alive," he said. "Trust me." He yawned, and lifted the lid off the teapot. "That's enough shop talk for one day," he said. "How about a game of cards?"

"If you like."

"Do you know a game called Cartwheels?"

Oida thought quickly. Ever since he'd given away all his money, only to find he probably wasn't going to die after all, he'd been wondering how to raise his travelling expenses back to civilisation without having to beg or steal. The way Frontizo dressed when off duty had tagged him as a viable mark, but Oida hadn't wanted to make the suggestion himself for fear of looking predatory. "I used to play it when I was a kid," he said truthfully. "But that was many years ago."

"It'll come back to you," Frontizo said cheerfully, producing a worn-looking pack painted on thin lime board. "Basically it's just Catch-Me, but prides beat straights and sevens are wild."

Oida did his apologetic smile. "I'm afraid I haven't got any money," he said. "But we can play for olives or something."

"I think I can risk taking your marker," Frontizo said. "I'll deal, shall I?"

Oida played it classical, losing the first four hands and exhibiting a weakness for over-cautious bidding. Frontizo, he observed, was a twitcher, but it seemed certain he hadn't realised. Oida did a quick calculation of how much a senior staff officer could afford to lose without feeling aggrieved.

Frontizo dealt the fifth hand, and Oida frowned. Almost too good to be true. He played cautiously to start with, until all four sevens were accounted for and there remained nothing at all that could beat his pride of red kings and jacks. "Double that," he said. "It is all right to double now, isn't it?"

Frontizo laughed. "You can if you like," he said. "I'm sure you're good for the money."

Oida was enormously tempted to enjoy himself for a bit, but

decided not to. "In that case," he said, "I'll double and raise ten."

"Fifty."

Twitch, twitch. Much more of this and the fool would wipe himself out, which could lead to bad feeling. "I think I'll see you," he said, and turned over his last covered card. "King of Spears."

But Frontizo nodded, as though they'd rehearsed all this before, and flipped his card over.

It was the Seven of Swords.

There is no suit of Swords in the regulation pack.

Frontizo grinned. "And sevens are wild, so that's my trick, making five, so I win. You owe me one hundred and sixty-one angels."

Oida stared at the card, then at the fool sitting opposite. "You're Lodge," he said.

Frontizo flipped the seven face downwards, then tucked it up his sleeve. "Don't want to leave something like that lying about," he said, "just in case. Yes, I am."

"You bastard. Why didn't you—?"

Frontizo frowned. "Oh come on," he said. "Actually, I was fairly sure you were Lodge from the start, but I couldn't be certain. So I figured, if he's Lodge I bet I know what he's here for; in which case, he's had a wasted trip and he could probably do with some money to go home on. Hence the game."

Oida looked at him. "You knew about me?"

"Oh, I'm not supposed to, obviously," he said. "But I happened to meet your brother a while back, and he sort of hinted. Don't pull faces," he added. "I know he's the skeleton in your cupboard. But I'm good at keeping my mouth shut, believe it or not."

Oida breathed out slowly. "And you reckon you know why I'm here."

"I don't think you'd have to be Saloninus to work that one out," Frontizo said gravely. "Anyway, you don't need to worry about that any more. If it turns out that Senza needs killing, I'll do it myself. Tastefully," he added, "without undue fuss. Poison, or maybe an accident, even. I can get away with it: you can't. In fact, I've got a choice of personal enemies lined up to take the blame, if it becomes necessary, which it won't, I'm morally certain. So you can stop fretting yourself to death and relax."

Oida grinned weakly. "How did you—?"

"One of these days, buy a mirror and take a look at yourself. Ever since you got here, you've been as jumpy as a rat in a kennel. People have been commenting on it. I tell them it's because you're a damn sight closer to the front lines than you're used to being. You really ought to get a grip, though. You're about as inscrutable as an inn sign."

Oida was deeply shocked by that, but this wasn't the time or the place. "Well, that's a relief," he said. "I'd have done it if I had to, but I'm ever so glad to be let off the hook."

"Of course you are," Frontizo said. "Show me a man walking calmly and resolutely towards certain death and I'll show you an idiot. Though I'm guessing you had something up your sleeve, a clever boy like you."

"Actually, no."

"Really? I'm disappointed. Assuming you're telling the truth. Still, it's all academic now, the burden's been lifted off your shoulders and you can breathe again." He smiled warmly and poured the last of the tea. "Did you really not guess who I was?"

"Absolutely not. I thought you were a loyal officer of the Eastern army."

That got him a dirty look. "I am," Frontizo said, "none more so, except where there's a conflict of interests with the Lodge. Anyway, you surprise me. Didn't it occur to you to wonder what an inveterate low-flier like me is doing attached to Senza's elite strike force?"

Oida shrugged. "I assumed you're someone's brother-in-law."

"As a matter of fact, I am." Frontizo laughed. "That's why Senza thinks he's saddled with me. At least, I don't think he suspects, but you never know with that one. It's not a comfortable posting, believe me. There are thousands of acres across two empires fertilised with the remains of people who thought they knew what Senza Belot was thinking. Still, that's not your worry. I imagine you'll be buggering off now. Nothing to keep you here."

Oida looked startled. "I can leave?"

"No offence, but we'd be glad to see you go. Not that it hasn't been a privilege and a pleasure, but you know what they say about guests and fish. I'll file a favourable report about you with Division if I live that long. Now then, would you like a pen and some paper? You've got some writing to do."

Oida wrote him a note for a hundred and sixty-one angels. Frontizo glanced at it and handed it back. "Better make that three hundred," he said: "you'll need some travelling money. Must be nice to be able to afford to troll round the place like the King of Permia, dining at all the best places."

Oida took another sheet of parchment. "Are you sure it's all right for me to go? After what I've seen and heard, I mean."

Frontizo shook his head. "What you think you've seen," he said. "We aren't quite as stupid as you think we are. And what you've heard from me, and if anyone asks, all we talked about was the truth behind your reputation as the empire's premier sex pest. Once you'd got started, I shall tell them, the problem was getting you to shut up. So, no, don't worry about that, it'll be fine."

Oida stood up. The tea had gone cold and he felt like he'd been in a fight. "One thing," he said. "Do you know Forza's not dead? I mean, has someone actually seen him?"

"I'll have the money for you in an hour." Frontizo tapped the side of his nose. "Stick to singing your songs and running errands," he said. "It's what you're good at. No offence."

*

The money was in an old sock, military-issue, carefully darned. "You sure you can spare it?" Oida asked.

"It's not like I'll have anything to spend it on any time soon."

"I meant the sock."

That got him a smile. "Where to now, then?"

Oida put the sock in his pocket and folded down the flap. "Actually," he said, "for the first time in a long while, I don't really know. Never thought I'd get out of here alive, so—" He shrugged. "I think I can safely assume my tour of the Western home provinces is cancelled."

"Yes. Sorry about that."

"Oh, don't be," Oida said. He checked the horse's girth, then shortened the stirrup leathers. "Saves me having to sing the same ten songs another fifteen times. I'll head back to Division, I guess, assuming I can get there, see if they've got anything for me. I was supposed to be going to Blemya at some point, but for all I know that's off, too. I suppose I could wander up to Central and see a few old friends."

Frontizo held the stirrup for him while he mounted. "I'll say this for you," he said: "you're a brave man, in your own way. Did you really not have a back-up plan for getting out?"

Oida shook his head. "How could I? I didn't know anything about the setup here when I arrived."

Frontizo frowned, then grinned. "I'm an idiot," he said. "Of course. You were going to pin it on me."

"I didn't know you properly then," Oida said, gathering the reins. "And anyway, by that stage I was fairly sure I wasn't going to have to do it myself. Nothing personal."

"Indeed. While I think of it, I don't like your music very much. All froth and no substance." Frontizo looked at him for a moment. "Giving your life for the Cause," he said. "I guess it depends on the quality of the life. In your case, I can see how you'd be prepared to do it. Not sure I could. Have a good trip."

Oida hesitated. The camp gate was open, and the sentries on the gate said there was nothing on the road as far as the eye could see. "My brother."

"What? Oh, yes. What about him?"

"When you saw him, was he all right?"

Frontizo shrugged. "Seemed to be. Nice chap, under all the swagger and bluster. I guess they run in the family."

"On my mother's side," Oida said, nudging the horse with his heels. "Thanks for everything you've done for me."

"It wasn't for you," Frontizo said. "Safe journey."

When Oida was out of sight, Frontizo went back to his tent, sat down at the low pile of boxes he used as a writing desk, pushed aside a mound of paperwork until he found a return-of-requisitions form he'd neglected for so long that it no longer mattered. He trimmed off the lower margin, the width of his thumb, then put an impossibly fine nib on his pen. Next he picked up a leather satchel off the floor; on the flap it had the insignia of the military mail, in thick paint just beginning to crack. He studied the strap for a moment: whoever had made the satchels for the mail had thoughtfully inserted a bit of cotton waste between the two halves of the strap before they were stitched together, as padding for the despatch rider's neck. With the tip of his penknife, he slit the stitches and prised the seam open, just enough so that he could tease out the cotton. Then he went back to his scrap of salvaged parchment, and began to write.

Four of Stars

Frontizo to Axio, greetings.

You'll never guess who I've just had the pleasure of entertaining. Your idiot brother showed up here. I've only just this minute managed to get rid of him. You'll be relieved to hear that he's safe and well, and Providence in its unfathomable wisdom seems to be taking special care of him. Well, make that one part Providence and three parts me. You never told me what a terrible card player he is. Special love to our special friends. Wrap up warm and don't forget you owe me six angels thirty.

Axio shrugged, screwed up the scrap of parchment into a ball and went to throw it on the fire, only to find it had gone out. He sighed, stood up and grabbed two handfuls of kindling from the sack by the hearth, then felt in his pocket for his tinderbox. Then he scowled.

"Musen," he shouted. "Get in here."

A few moments later an impossibly tall, flat-faced young man pushed aside the sacking curtain. "What?"

Axio held out his hand. "Give it back. My tinderbox."

"I haven't got it."

"Oh, come on." Axio gave him a grim smile. "I'll say this for you, you're getting better. The first time you stole it, I felt you. For crying out loud, son, it's freezing in here."

"I haven't got it."

Axio nodded and turned away, immediately turned back. Musen saw him coming and took a long step to the rear but not quickly enough; Axio was behind him, and trod down hard on the inside of his knee. Musen dropped to the ground. Axio stooped and put his hand round his windpipe, bearable but firm pressure from thumb and forefinger. "Pockets," he said.

Musen turned out his pockets; then, unasked, took off his boots and shook them out. Axio sighed. "You've sold it," he said. "Marvellous. So now we both sit here and freeze."

"I can light a fire."

Axio let go of him. "The point about tinderboxes is," he said, "they make lighting a fire *easier*. That's why it'd be nice if one or the other of us had got one." He sat down again, while Musen squatted by the hearth and picked through the kindling. "Who'd you sell it to?"

No answer. Musen broke a piece of dry bark off a log, gathered some withered moss from another.

"Presumably that horrible old woman who hangs round the stables," Axio said. "I think I'll have her arrested and strung up. Then I might get to keep some of my stuff."

"It wasn't—" Musen checked himself. "She hasn't done anything wrong."

"Ah." Axio nodded. "In that case it was that fat groom on the night shift. If he tries to *sell* it back to me, I'll break his arm." Musen was twirling a bit of stick. That'll never work, Axio thought, then saw a tiny feather of smoke. "That tinderbox happened to be a present from my brother."

"I thought you couldn't stand him."

"I can't." Axio closed his eyes and tried to get comfortable in his chair. Physically impossible. "How do you do that, exactly? Whenever I try, it doesn't work."

"I don't know," Musen said. "I've always done it this way, and it always works for me."

He blew on the dry moss and it glowed red. He tipped it into the grate and started laying kindling over it, rafters-fashion. Axio got up, unhooked the remains of a side of bacon from the wall, took out his folding knife and cut four thick, ragged slices, which he stuck on the tines of a home-made toasting fork, four strands of the heavy-grade fence wire twisted together. Musen tipped charcoal from the bucket on to the fire, crouched down on his hands and knees and blew on it until the first tentative flames appeared.

"It's dumb stealing things from people you live with," Axio said. "Doesn't matter how well you cover your tracks: they know it's you because they know stuff's missing and you're a thief. True, there's not a shred of evidence, but who needs evidence when you *know*? Like the Craft, really, I can't prove the Transmutation by Fire, but I know it happens. I'm surprised you do it, actually, because in other respects you're not completely stupid."

Musen took the toasting fork from him and held it in front of the fire. After a while, drops of fat dripped into the flames and ignited in a brief yellow flare.

"Some of them reckon you can't help it," Axio went on, yawning. "They say you're ill, it's something loose up here. I don't think so." He paused. "Out of interest, why do you do it? I'm interested, that's all."

Musen didn't turn round. "It's my gift."

"Mphm." Axio closed his eyes. "The Great Smith made you a thief, and it's the Lodge's duty to find a good use for you. I know that's what they taught you at Beal Defoir. Do you believe it?"

"Yes."

"Fair enough. But if I catch you perfecting your gift around my stuff ever again, I'll break all your fingers. Understood?"

He knew he'd phrased that wrong, since he wouldn't catch Musen, not now. But it was too late to rephrase: that would just be weak. Besides, they both knew it was an empty threat. Thou shalt not damage the property of the Lodge. Ribs were different, though. Musen didn't use his ribs to steal.

"I don't know why you annoy me so much," he said, almost as an admission of his error. "My guess is that you're smart and you act stupid. Growing up with my brother, I'm used to the other way round, so you confuse me. Tell you what," he went on, "stop doing it and I'll stop giving you a hard time. How about it?"

Musen went on toasting the bacon. Axio rather admired him for that. It takes a degree of integrity, as well as intelligence, not to give in to an offer of friendship. He was beginning to see why Beal Defoir had thought so highly of the boy. Even so. It was irksome, not being able to talk. The prospect of the job he was about to do was making him nervous, and the sound of his own voice soothed him like nothing else.

They had no special privilege on the southbound mail, which was crowded, and ending up riding on the roof, squashed in between two merchants' couriers and a government official. Axio wedged his back against the rail, closed his eyes and eavesdropped.

It was all going really badly, the government man said; he was on his way to take up his new appointment as Clerk of Tolls at Saphes, but whether there'd be a job for him when he got there he simply didn't know. Everything was done through Rasch, and it was quite possible that the letter confirming his appointment hadn't got out before the siege started, in which case he'd get to Saphes and nobody would have the faintest idea who he was. Furthermore, even if there was a job for him there, it was anybody's guess how he was supposed to do it. The main function of the Clerk of Tolls at a provincial capital is to send the returns compiled by the sheriffs to Rasch, and then receive a reply and pass it on to the governor's office, who passed it on to the sheriffs, who did whatever they did. With Rasch cut off, what was he supposed to do all day?

The merchants' couriers weren't impressed. Their employers had tens of thousands of angels' worth of scrip signed off against deposits with the Knights and the Temple Trustees and a dozen or so private banks; they'd handed out hard cash against this paper, to the point where they had nothing left but a few boxes of old green copper change, and now nobody was interested in taking their notes, because everybody knew their money was the wrong side of Senza Belot's army and quite possibly only a few days away from a cart ride to Choris. Meanwhile, honest, hard-working couriers were expected to rush around the countryside with letters of credit and bills of exchange that were probably only good for mending shoes and wiping arses. It wouldn't be so bad (one of the couriers added) if Rasch would only get a move on and surrender. Then the war would be over, and presumably some sort of arrangement could be made with the new administration to overwrite existing deposits at so many stuivers in the angel – life would go on, after all, once the war was over, and whoever won they'd need banks and merchant venturers, and all that money couldn't simply evaporate, like rainwater on a sunny day—

"How about you?" Axio realised the government man was talking to him. "You heard anything?"

Axio shook his head. "We've been up in Rhus, the boy and me," he said. "Last I knew about it, the siege was still on and nothing much was happening."

"You mean you haven't heard about the battle?"

Axio caught his breath but covered it. "What battle?"

The battle. Apparently, four of the remaining Western field armies, comprising at least a hundred thousand men, had converged on Rasch. Senza Belot, with thirty thousand cavalry, had met them in a wheatfield to the north of the city. Casualties – well, the rumours flying around were obviously nonsense, there was no way they could be that high, but apparently a big man with the Gasca brothers, who were joint-venturing with Ocnisant on a strictly one-off basis for this job, reckoned they'd buried forty thousand, at least, and precious few of them had been cavalrymen. Where what was left of the Western army had got to and what sort of state it was in, nobody knew. What was certain was that Senza was back standing guard outside Rasch, with the plunder from the Western supply trains to keep his men happy; and it was simple arithmetic, say ninety-five thousand civilians in Rasch plus the garrison, eating a pint and a half of flour a day.

"Rasch can't *fall*," said one of the couriers. "It's the capital city of half the world. They'll just have to raise more armies, that's all."

"It's time the Blemyans did something," the government man said. "Everybody knows they're on our side. They're civilised people; they're not just going to stand by and see the West go to hell. If it wasn't for the bloody diplomats—"

"What about Forza Belot?" Axio asked.

All three of them looked at him. Hadn't you heard, one of the couriers said. Forza's dead. Been dead for months.

Iden Astea was originally built by refugees from the Third Political War. They chose the site well, or were extremely lucky to stumble across it. The old town occupies a substantial island in the middle of the lake formed by the run-off from the mountains that surround it on three sides. The suburbs crowd the eastern and southern shores of the lake; you can get to the island by an artificial causeway (which can be breached in the middle in half an hour, if needs be) or by boat; the regional myth that the Identines are born web-footed is untrue, but they are beyond question the best fresh-water boatmen in both empires. There are submerged rocks and shoals in Lake Iden that you can't begin to understand unless you were born there, they say, and navigating the narrow lanes between the rows of buoys is a mystery not lightly revealed to outsiders.

Iden was, therefore, a natural choice for the Western emperor, as soon as the threat to Rasch was fully appreciated. He arrived in a two-wheeled chaise in the middle of the night, escorted by five captains of the Household Guard; the rest of the Inner Court arrived over the course of the next few days, accompanying a long train of sturdy wagons carrying the Imperial treasury. Two days after that, two battalions of the Ninth Army arrived to form a garrison. The extent to which the Identines appreciated the honour of entertaining the Brother of the Sun and his entourage for an unspecified length of time is not recorded. They were probably quite philosophical about it. Iden has a massive granary, cut from solid rock in the side of the mountain that dominates the island, and the alluvial plain is enormously fertile; the arrival of a thousand noblemen and their accumulated movable wealth was probably seen as an opportunity, or at the very least a challenge, rather than an unmitigated imposition.

The arrival of the Court had the effect of rekindling the dormant Relocation Debate, which had been quietly seething under the surface of Imperial politics ever since the schism. Rasch, the relocators were now saying, has been proven to be hopelessly vulnerable; at the first sign of trouble, what does our eminently sensible emperor do? He jumps in a chaise and heads for Iden. Is there any good reason why he should ever go back? Iden is not only far more defensible, it's also closer to the geographical centre of the Western empire, it backs on to an unlimited food supply, it's healthier and the view is better. To which the conservatives replied: Rasch is a city, everywhere else is just villages, and it's blasphemy to ask the Co-Regent of the Firmament to make his official residence in the provinces. To which the relocators replied: if Rasch falls, does that have to mean that the war is over, and we've lost?

*

Axio and Musen arrived in Iden to find the road closed. They were stopping all traffic at Barys; there were barricades manned by guardsmen in gilded armour. Axio put on his best parade-ground face, marched up to the checkpoint and asked the sergeant what was going on.

Riots, apparently. Late the previous evening, a snaking column of wagons, carriages and carts had arrived at the head of the causeway, carrying the Imperial kennels, which had evacuated from Rasch shortly after the Court, and had only just got here; two hundred dogs and four hundred men, together with ancillary equipment – each dog its own special bed and favourite cushions, its dedicated cook, the cook's specialist pots, pans, trivets and spits, five wagons filled with Blemyan corn, from which was baked the only sort of bread the dogs would eat, seventy cages of pedigree chickens and other necessary items too numerous to particularise. The City prefect arrived and told the convoy commander that there was no room on the island, which was exclusively reserved for people. The commander appealed over his head to the Chamberlain, who decreed that the dogs would have to rough it in Prosc Docian, the largest of the suburbs on the southern shore of the lake. The guard commander was given the job of evacuating the residents of Prosc to the nameless shanty town on the edge of the western marshes. The residents had objected, the guards had driven them out at spear point, and now they were occupying both ends of the causeway, tearing up paving stones and throwing them at the Watch. The guards couldn't simply wade in and slaughter them, since the people of Prosc Docian did most of the actual work in the City – ground the flour, chopped the vegetables, made the beds, waited at tables, none of which they'd be available to do if they were dead. The emperor, for his part, was still white with anger at being told he couldn't have his dogs with him on the island, and refused point-blank to allow the kennels to be relocated yet again. A committee had been formed to consider possible resolutions; rumour had it that the favourite was currently the construction of a temporary floating barracks for the providers of essential services, to be moored off the City dock during the day and cast adrift to float on the lake by night. Meanwhile, nothing was going in or out until the situation had been dealt with.

Axio thanked the sergeant politely, the sergeant saluted and Axio walked slowly back to the mail coach in the middle of the glacier of halted traffic. "Get the bags," he told Musen. "Can you swim?"

"No."

Axio shrugged. "Guess I'll have to be resourceful, then," he said. "I hate being resourceful; it gives me a headache."

A few enquiries along the waterfront revealed that all boats had been requisitioned by the Prefect for the duration of the emergency. Since the Prefect paid half as much again as the usual tariff, the watermen were grimly resigned to doing their patriotic duty, which meant the cost of an unofficial ride across the lake was now more than Axio was prepared to spend out of the limited war chest at his disposal.

"We steal a boat," Musen said.

"*You* steal a boat. I'm a brigand, not a thief. Tell me when you've got one. I'll be under that tree, sleeping."

In fact, although his hat was pulled down over his eyes and his feet were propped up on the luggage, Axio was wide awake. He'd learned quite a lot from his conversation with the sergeant, much of it reassuring. The City was clearly a shambles, with the military and the civil authority getting under each other's feet, mostly on purpose. Reasonable to assume, therefore, that nobody knew who anybody was, and the usual security protocols surrounding the emperor's person were probably coming apart at the seams. Between those parted seams a clever man could insert a sharp instrument and press down hard. What they could really do with, of course, was a dog.

*

"Yes," Axio explained, when Musen came back, "but not just any old dog. It's got to look plausible. Some tripehound you find hanging round the back door of the butcher's shop won't fool anybody."

"Fine," Musen said. "What sort do you want?"

Axio looked blank. "I don't know, do I? There were always hundreds of the wretched things around the place when I was a boy, my father was mad keen on them, but I could never be bothered to take an interest. I know there's one called an alaunt, and there's lymers and brachets and grazehounds. They're all hunting dogs, of course, and I don't think that's the sort His Majesty goes for. Little tubby things like overgrown rats are more in his line, so I gather. Just use your common sense, all right? So long as it's neat and tidy and you can't see its ribs. I don't suppose the Watch know any more about it than I do."

A surprisingly short time later, Musen came back leading a small, skinny fawn and white object on a bit of string. It had a face like a very small mule and ears that folded down like the corner of a page in a favourite book; if memory served, it was a kennet, the go-to dog for persecuting hares. Ideal. "Is that the best you could do?"

Musen shrugged. "You want me to find something else?"

Axio shook his head. "Life's too short. Where's this boat of yours? And did you remember the cheese?"

Musen had hidden the boat under the sprays of a trailing willow. It must've been a smart piece of work taking it, and not in Musen's usual line; you can't just tuck a twelve-foot tender under your coat and stroll away looking gormless. They waited till dark. Fortunately the dog curled up and went to sleep, while Musen went back to steal it a collar.

"I don't suppose you know how to row a boat."

Musen shrugged.

Axio climbed in carefully, then held out his arms for the dog. "It's been a while," he said, "and I was never very good at it. Still, we weren't expecting to win any prizes."

Musen didn't like getting in the boat; he staggered badly when it shifted, and sat down heavily on the oars. "Shift," Axio said, "I need them to make it go. You sit at that end and steer."

"I don't know how to."

"Fine. Grab hold of the dog and keep it quiet."

There were lanterns burning all along the quay; but Axio had made out other mooring places on the east side of the island, used by sawmills, tanneries and the like, where he reckoned they could put in without attracting undue attention. The one he chose was the landing stage of a foundry, working a night shift. Inside the sheds was a blaze of white light, which would dazzle anyone looking out, and the noise of the drop-hammers would mask any sound they made, even if the dog decided to bark.

"Have you been here before?" Musen asked, once they were safely on dry land.

"Once," Axio replied. He gave the boat a shove and it drifted out of the light. "Nice place if you've got money, a bit grim if you haven't. Like most places, really."

Musen nodded towards where the boat had been. "Won't we be needing that?"

"It would've been nice," Axio replied. "But we can't rely on it staying there. Chances are some evil bugger would've stolen it before we got back. There's a lot of thieving goes on in this town. I don't know if you've noticed." He wrapped the dog's lead twice around his hand. "I plan to walk back, across the causeway. Unless we can hitch a lift, of course. I don't believe in walking if you can ride."

Finding a soldier was easy. They walked towards the noise; at first a gentle hum, almost soothing, like distant bees on a hot afternoon; then jagged with unintelligible shouting, banging and breaking sounds. There was a cordon of the Household Guard around the head of the causeway, their gilded armour flashing in the disturbingly bright light of burning shops.

It had been a while since Axio had actually commanded regular official troops. Some things, though, you don't forget.

"You," he snapped, as soon as he was in earshot. "Yes, you, soldier. Get the duty officer, quick as you like."

Some people can do it with horses and dogs; it's all to do with confidence, knowing you're a superior form of life. "Sir," barked the nearest guardsman, and turned and ran.

The duty officer – praise be! – was tall, thin, painfully young, transparent down on his upper lip like the hair on a girl's forearm. He came striding up, struggling with the straps of his helmet (they can be a bitch, Axio sympathised, until you get used to them). Before he could open his mouth, Axio snapped, "Let's see your commission."

The young officer stopped as if he'd put his foot in a rabbit hole. "I'm sorry," he said, "I don't carry it with—"

Axio allowed himself a tiny but eloquent gesture. Crammed into it was the certainty that he'd have seen to it that the officer was broken to the ranks and sent to guard convicts, if only the business in hand wasn't so urgent. "All right, what's your name?"

"Ethizo, sir. Second lieutenant—"

"See this?" Axio gave the bit of string a fierce jerk, and the dog stumbled forward into the light. "Well?"

Lieutenant Ethizo looked at the dog, desperately trying to understand what was wrong and why it was his fault. "Sir?"

"I found it roaming the streets out on the dark side," Axio said, his voice heavy with quiet, suppressed rage. "And I want to know who's responsible."

A look of utter helplessness on the lieutenant's face; then a tiny ray of illumination, to spotlight his peril. "Is that one of the emperor's—?"

"For God's sake, man, pull yourself together," Axio snapped. "This is a seal-point sand kennet: these buggers were gods in Blemya when your ancestors were still running around in goat-skins. Don't you know anything?"

Maybe he'd overdone it slightly there. The lieutenant frowned. "I don't think I've heard of—"

"Your ignorance isn't at issue here, lieutenant." (There, that was better.) "The point is, what do you think will happen if His Majesty finds out one of his precious dogs has got out and was found roaming the streets? Well? Answer: he'll overrule the Prefect and send us in to clear out the protesters, there'll be a massacre and then a proper riot, not this peely-wally stone-throwing, and come morning we won't need Senza Belot, we'll have done it all ourselves. Well?"

Mirrored in the lieutenant's eyes he caught a fleeting glimpse of himself, fifteen years earlier, surrounded on all four sides by Major Blepharo concerning the matter of an illegal still in the harness sheds. He felt a pang of remorse and crushed it. He was, after all, about to save this young idiot from the disastrous consequences of his negligence. "What we need to do," he said, lowering his voice to strained calm, "is get this wretched animal where it's meant to be, out of harm's way and off our slop chit." He paused to let the significance of the first person plural sink in; the lieutenant wasn't going to have to face this crisis alone; this godlike stranger would help him, and everything would be fine. "Agreed?"

"Sir."

"Splendid." Axio glanced down at the dog, which was scratching its ear with its hind leg. "Now obviously we can't get it back across the causeway, and we haven't got a hope in hell of finding a boat." No explanation, just a statement of fact. "So our only option, would you agree, is to get the dog inside the State Apartments without anybody seeing, dump it in an anteroom somewhere and fuck off out of it quick before anyone asks what we're doing there. Questions?"

The lieutenant looked petrified. "Won't they wonder how it got there, when all the rest of the—"

"Of course they will," Axio snapped. "There'll be an almighty row about it: some poor sod will take the blame and probably end up with his head on a spike, but it won't be us and there won't be a massacre. Have you got a better idea?"

"No, sir."

"Sorted, then. Oh, and one other thing. If you ever mention my name in connection with this, I'll have you court-martialled. 'Got that?"

"Sir."

"Splendid." Axio handed the dog's lead to Ethizo, who swallowed hard and took it. "Right then," he said. "What we need is a back way into the Capitol. Lead on, lieutenant."

They had to pass four sentries, all of whom snapped to attention like components in a machine as soon as they caught sight of the nodding red crest of the duty officer's helmet. Ethizo didn't like that one bit, but Axio told him to get a grip and look like he was supposed to be there. He felt bad about that, too, but it served the lieutenant right for being stupid, as he himself had once been, and look where it had got him.

They found an empty bedroom on the third floor of the east wing of the Inner Capitol. Axio untied the string from the dog's collar; it jumped up on the bed, curled itself into a ball and went to sleep. They backed quietly out of the room and closed the door.

"Right." Axio grabbed the lieutenant by the wrist and squeezed till it hurt. "I've never seen you before in my life, got that? None of this ever happened, you never left your post all night, and your men will back you up on that. Understood?"

"Sir. Thank you, sir."

"Get lost," Axio said. "Come on, Sergeant," he snapped to Musen, and strode off down the corridor without looking round.

*

"Well, we're in," Axio whispered. They'd ducked into some sort of dressing room off the main passageway. Probably a woman's room, but with the Court you just couldn't tell. Axio sat down on the spindly legged chair, which probably wouldn't have taken Musen's weight. "Pause, catch our breath and regroup. You might as well know, I haven't got a plan for the next bit."

Musen accepted that in silence. Axio looked at him. "Put that back," he said.

A slight hesitation; then Musen took a silver-backed hairbrush out of the front of his shirt and put it on the dressing table.

"When I say I haven't got a plan," Axio went on, as though nothing had happened, "I mean I don't know where we are or where the stuff is likely to be. That's not as much of a disaster as it sounds. We've got plenty of time; no need to rush. We just search this place from top to bottom. If we meet anyone, just keep your face tight shut. You're good at that, it shouldn't be a problem. All right." He stood up. "Onwards."

On the way out, once Musen was through the door, he grabbed the hairbrush and slipped it into his coat pocket. Well, why not?

They wandered about for a while, but there seemed to be no obvious logic to the place. Axio vaguely remembered that before it was an Imperial residence the Capitol had been a monastery, built by a large and affluent order, long since disbanded. That helped. "We should be going up, not down," he muttered to himself. "If this was a Sky monastery, there ought to be a Dawn chapel, east and central and very high up. Logic dictates—" He stopped and frowned. "This is no good. We need camouflage. We won't get very far just hitting people." He thought for a moment, creating stories, doing the geometry. Then he punched Musen in the face, as hard as he could.

"Sorry," he said, helping him up and inspecting his lip, which was bleeding well. "Now, here's the idea. I just caught you snooping around, I have reason to believe you're a thief, after the Imperial regalia. I've been wandering around for hours looking for a guard to hand you in to, but there's never one about when you need one. Got that?"

Musen scowled at him and nodded. A bright boy, just as he'd always thought. Axio glanced down at his knuckles and was pleased to see he'd skinned them. "Teeth all right?"

"Mphm."

"Good, no harm done, then. On we go."

They climbed stairs whenever they encountered them and tried to keep bearing east. They met people, but only footmen and chambermaids; no need to explain, just stay in character. "Remember," Axio muttered in Musen's ear as he frogmarched him down a long, wide gallery, "if we meet anyone, you're the desperado, I'm the peace officer. Got a knife on you?"

"Yes."

"Give it here. I don't want you getting carried away."

Axio recognised the knife. It had been his once, and he'd been sure he'd dropped it. "Do you ever steal from anyone else apart from me? Just out of interest."

"Yes."

With a pang of regret he dumped it on a window ledge. "Next good knife you steal is mine, all right?"

"All right."

"Deal. The thing is, I'm a very materialistic person. I like my things. Rather more than I like people, as it happens. You might want to bear that in mind."

Round the next bend they ran into a pair of sentries, flanking a closed door. There was no time to say anything to each other; nothing but mutual trust would save them now, the sort of faith Axio generally reserved for the Great Smith. "I caught this one sneaking about in the—" he began to say, and then Musen hit him.

It worked because he really hadn't been expecting it. No time or capacity for acting his part; the world went soft around him, he tried to breathe but couldn't, and sank to his knees. By the time he could breathe again it all appeared to be over; Musen was bending over him helping him to his feet.

"Sorry," Musen said with a grin.

"That's fine," Axio whispered. "Oh, hell, you didn't kill them, did you?"

Musen shook his head. Axio looked for himself. They seemed secure enough. "Did they teach you to punch at Beal Defoir?"

"No, I'm just strong."

Fair enough. "You'd better put them away tidily," Axio said. He didn't like the way one of them was lying, but it could just be a broken leg. But how do you break a man's leg by punching him on the jaw? "I think we passed a laundry room a little way back." He searched them for keys, found none. "Dump them in there and cover them with sheets or something."

The lock was actually quite simple: four massive great wards that turned back easily, a credit to the locksmith for the quality of his filing and stoning, if not his imagination. Axio turned the handle and opened the door a crack, slipped the lock pick back in between the seams of his boot top and waited for Musen to return. He was gratified by the brief look of surprise on Musen's face. "Teach you to do that one day, if you're good," he said.

"Thanks, I'd like that."

"I bet." He put three fingertips against the door and gently wafted it open. There was light on the other side of it. "Here goes," he whispered, and walked through.

He was at the foot of a staircase. There were two chairs and a brazier, but no guards. Bless the Household regiment for its self-confidence.

It was a long staircase, but Axio knew they hadn't gone high enough to be there yet. At the top was another of those damned wide galleries, with tapestries on the walls and rush matting (thank you, someone) on the floor. Whoever used this part of the building believed in being snug. His throat was sore from reflux and his knees were still weak, but he'd felt worse. "My guess is there's a priest's cell of some kind, and the stairs to the chapel are in there. Our tough luck if someone's sleeping in there."

There were nine rooms leading off the corridor, all unoccupied. At the back of the ninth was a door that had no rational explanation. It opened on to more stairs.

"How did you know?" Musen asked.

"Every Dualist monastery had a Dawn Chapel." Axio was breathless on the stairs, but he told himself it was just the after-effect of Musen's punch. "The abbot went there every morning to greet the rising sun. They kept all their best stuff in there, so it had to be tight as a drum. Logical place for a temporary strongroom."

The staircase ended in a steel door. The only light came from a lantern Musen had thought to bring with him from the gallery. "Hold it still, for pity's sake," Axio said, scrabbling around the lock plate with his lock pick. "I need to see what I'm doing."

"I thought it was all by feel."

"It helps if you can actually see the keyhole."

Five wards: four flipped easily; the fifth was stiff and nearly bent the pick. "That was so easy, you could've done it," Axio said, as the door moved under his hand. "Cover the lantern, you idiot. We're not in the lighthouse business."

They blanked off the windows as best they could with Axio's coat and Musen's cloak and hood. When Musen unmasked the lantern, they saw a stack of steel strongboxes, floor to ceiling, each one with at least one padlock. Axio groaned. "How long does a man stay put out when you thump him?"

"I don't know."

"Well, it varies." Axio fished in his other boot for his spare pick. "Now pay attention. I'm going to teach you how to pick locks."

To Axio's delight, Musen was a quick learner. It helped that the padlocks were deplorably old-fashioned and simple, but the fact remained, the boy had a natural aptitude, a gift. "Fine," Axio said. "Now, you take that stack and I'll do this one. Don't hang about and don't steal anything."

Musen, of course, was the one who knew what they were looking for. Luckily, it was him who found it, in the sixth box he opened. Axio only realised when he noticed how still and quiet the boy had suddenly become.

"You've got it?" he whispered. "Is that it?"

Musen didn't answer. On the stone floor beside where he was kneeling lay a silver box, its lid hinged open. Musen was staring at something cupped protectively in his hands, the way you might hold an injured bird. "I said, is that it?"

"Yes. I think so."

"Thank God for that. Here, let me see."

Musen hesitated, then opened his hands. Axio saw a pile of thin silver wafers – longer and wider than any playing cards he'd ever seen, embossed with figures he couldn't make out in the poor light. "You're sure?" he said. "Come on, it's important. Every human life in Rasch depends on this."

"I think so," Musen said. "They're like the ones back in the village. Yes," he said, his voice suddenly confident, "it's them."

"Give them here."

For a moment, Axio was sure Musen would refuse, and that would have been extremely awkward. But then he looked away and held out his hand. Axio snatched the cards, and scrabbled on the floor for the box. The cards wouldn't go back in; he tried to straighten them up so they'd fit, and dropped two. Musen took the cards back from him, dropped them neatly in the box, added the two strays and handed the box back.

"You're absolutely positive," Axio said. "We can't come back again, you know that. It's got to be right."

"It's them."

Well, Musen was the expert; which was to say, he was the only specialist thief available who knew what the wretched things were supposed to look like. Damn all rush jobs and emergencies. "If they're not, I'll kill you."

"I told you, it's them."

"Good enough for me." Axio reached to put the box in his coat pocket, then remembered that his coat was serving as a blackout. "Kill the lantern," he said. "Come on, quickly."

The two guards were still dead to the world in the laundry room. "We need a new story," Axio muttered, dragging dirty washing out of a big wicker basket. "All this making stuff up is incredibly stressful for me. I'm basically a very truthful person." He held up a long black priest's robe, then saw the vomit stains on the lower skirt. "This is no good, it's mostly women's clothes. What we want is a couple of those beige sack things the clerks wear."

"Like these?"

Axio swung round, then sighed. "They're the wrong colour, and they're *frocks*. God preserve me from provincials. Just a moment, though." He shoved Musen out of the way and rummaged. "In the gold," he said, "score ten", and held up a pale blue scholar's robe. There were wine stains on the bottom hem. "How would you like to be drunk?"

"I don't think so. I don't drink."

Axio thought for a moment. "It's a very hard thing to pretend to be," he said. "All right, I'm the drunk and you're a servant taking me to sleep it off." He reached inside his shirt and pulled out a gold star on a fine silver chain. "This is actually mine," he said. "I'm entitled to it. Order of Academic Merit, second class. They don't give these things away at weddings." He stripped off his coat, retrieved the silver box and put it down on the laundry basket, then slipped and wriggled into the gown. It was slightly too long for him, but not to worry. He hung the gold star round his neck, then tucked the silver box safely in the deep sleeve of the gown. "Watch and learn," he said. "I'm good at this."

A noisy, aggressive drunk who also happens to be a high-ranking scholar is the sort of bad news a sentry can do without. "Would you mind keeping it down, sir?" he asked, ever so politely; in response, the drunk took a swing at him, and only prompt action by the drunk's enormous servant stopped him from making contact, which would have obliged the sentry to report the incident and made trouble for everyone. The servant rolled his eyes apologetically; the sentry nodded. "Get him out of here," the sentry said imploringly. "And for God's sake stop him singing."

No such luck. For an intellectual, the drunk had fairly basic taste in music: mostly romantic and scurrilous ballads by Oida, with a few old army favourites thrown in. People came out of their rooms to look, saw the blue gown and the servant's split lip and closed their doors quickly. A captain of the guard came bustling up as the dreadful pair weaved their way across the inner cloister, caught sight of the gold star and ducked behind a column. The drunk started to sing "Soldier's Joy" in a loud, clear voice that would have been quite attractive if not for the tendency to roar.

Their luck stuttered at one point when they found themselves face to face with another blue gown, draped over a short, stocky man with a long white beard. "Name and college," he roared; the drunk lunged at him, but the servant tripped him neatly and he went sprawling. The short man took a step back. "I don't recognise him," he said to the servant. "Who is he?"

The servant gave him a weak grin. "Just arrived, sir. With the dogs. Doctor of Natural Philosophy."

The short man grunted disgustedly. "Get him to bed before anyone sees him," he said, and stalked back the way he'd just come.

The riot petered out just before dawn, when it started raining heavily and the Prefect and the mayor of Prosc worked out a compromise, the details of which have not been recorded. By noon, wheeled traffic was crossing the causeway once again, and Axio (who'd slept in a coal bunker, with Musen curled up at his feet like a dog) decided it would be safe to leave the city. He dumped the blue gown, which by then was filthy with coal dust, and sent Musen to steal him a coat. Musen protested that he was covered in coal dust, too, but Axio pointed out that the rain would wash most of it off, so that was fine.

Carts and coaches were streaming into the city; not much was going the other way. They tried to hitch a lift on a farm cart, but the driver told them to go to hell, so they walked. Axio's ankle was playing up; he couldn't remember damaging it, but it's easy to tweak something and not notice when your life gets exciting for a while. Musen's lip had scabbed over. "Don't pick at it," Axio advised him.

"I must confess I didn't give a lot of thought to how we get home," Axio said, as they sheltered from the rain under a chestnut tree on the edge of the northern marshes. "Never thought we'd get this far, to be honest. Still, fool's luck."

Musen had taken off his left boot and was wringing out a wet sock. "Can't we just walk?"

Axio gave him a sour look. "Theoretically, I suppose we could. I hate walking. It's boring and I get blisters."

Musen shrugged. "Where I come from, we walk everywhere."

"Oh, well, then, in that case." Axio craned his neck to look up at the sky. "Bloody rain," he said. "Come on, we've done the difficult bit, surely. The rest should be easy."

Musen dragged his boot back on. "Did you really think we wouldn't make it?"

"I was convinced of it. Our continued existence is a complete but agreeable surprise to me."

"You seemed so sure of yourself. Like it was all a prank or something."

Axio shrugged. "I appease the Great Smith by playing the clown. One of these days he won't find me funny any more."

Musen turned his head away.

"You don't like me saying things like that," Axio said, "making jokes, taking His name in vain."

"Not much, no."

"Provincial." Axio wriggled back up against the trunk of the tree. "Hasn't it ever occurred to you that the greatest blasphemy of all is implying that He can't take a joke?"

Musen frowned, then suddenly grinned. "I never thought of it like that."

"Course you didn't, you're a provincial. I imagine you think of Him as an old man with a white beard and a leather apron. Well?"

"I suppose so, yes."

"Fair enough." Axio pulled two apples from his coat pocket, offered one to Musen, who took it. "It's a valid interpretation. Me, I see Him as a vast, extraordinarily complex concatenation of circumstances." He bit into the apple. "Which, taken together, admit of no other possible explanation other than intelligent design and conscious purpose. All as broad as it's long, of course. I from the evidence, you from intuitive revelation, we both arrive at the same point. Which is all that matters, really."

Musen looked at him. "I've always believed," he said. "Ever since I was a kid. Nobody else in our village did, so I had to keep it to myself."

Axio nodded. "Like the thieving."

"I guess so, yes."

"Your special gifts." Axio yawned. "I used to wonder about that," he said. "Why would He do that? I guess it's easy to see why He would call someone to be a saint, a healer of the sick, a champion of the poor and oppressed, or even a great artist or musician. But why did He call you to be a thief and me to be an enormously talented leader of irregular troops? It seems unlikely."

"He needs thieves sometimes."

Axio clapped his hands and pointed. "Exactly. As we've just demonstrated, in fact. He made us as we are, therefore by implication we must be good for something: our duty is to find out what it is. It's a bit crazy, though. I mean, take me and my brother. You ever come across him?"

"Once."

"Once is enough. He was always so jealous of me when we were kids. And quite right, too, because I was always smarter, stronger, better looking, better singing voice. It was quite pathetic sometimes. He was always trying to find something he could be good at, and as soon as he did, I took it up, too, and got better at it than him, just to put him in his place. Drove him crazy. I never let him keep a girl for more than five minutes, either. I guess I'm partly responsible for the mess he's turned himself into, but what the hell. I never liked him very much. I think the day I joined the army was the happiest day of his life."

Musen grinned. "I can see why."

"Well, quite. But the point is, here you have me, a man with all the talents, all the graces, I could've been a great musician or a poet, I could've been a wise statesman, definitely an outstanding general. And what does He decide to use me for? Robbing people and leading bandits." He shrugged. "His will be done, I guess, but I can't help thinking it's a waste."

Musen looked at him sideways. "You sure that was Him and not you?"

"Oh, yes." Axio scowled. "That was Him all right. He put me in a position where I had no choice but to throw it all away and become the sorry object you see before you. I don't actually care if you believe this or not, but you'll never ever meet anyone who's given up more for his faith than I have." He smiled. "Just as well He and I both have such a strong sense of humour," he said. "Otherwise we wouldn't be nearly such good friends."

He waited for Musen to ask, but he didn't. So he said, "You don't approve of me, do you?"

Musen pulled off his other boot. "Have we got any money left?" he said.

"Not much," Axio replied, "apart from what you filched out of the strongboxes, in spite of what I told you." He held out his hand. Musen tapped the heel of the boot he'd just taken off, and coins tumbled out. "Just as well you don't obey orders," Axio said, and picked them up. Twelve angels; old coins, pre-schism, but still current, the few that were left. Most of them had been melted down long ago, because the gold content was higher. "Not bad," he went on. "We can buy a coach and horses to take us home and still have enough left for a small farm."

Musen gave him a look that wasn't a scowl but did just as well.

But the sad reality is that it doesn't matter how much money you've got if there's nobody around to sell you things. That morning they passed four substantial farms, all boarded up, the stables empty. Musen climbed a roof, dug down through the thatch and came out again with half a cheese and a slab of dusty bacon, or they'd have gone hungry.

Mail coaches passed them once or twice; but all going to the city, none coming back the other way. Axio didn't like that at all.

"For all we know," he complained, "Rasch has already fallen, Senza's on his way up here and this has all been a complete waste of time." He covered his pocket with his hand, just to make sure it was still there. "You're definite that was the right pack?" he added.

"Yes. You keep asking me that. I'm sure."

"It's ironic, the fate of a great city depending on the antiquarian knowledge of the likes of you. Don't they have horses in Rhus? Is that why you walk everywhere?"

"Horses cost money."

"That was never a problem when I was growing up," Axio said

gravely. "Everything else, but not money, we were fine for that. All gone now, of course. I was the eldest, so when I had my bit of difficulty it was all forfeited to the Exchequer. Oida's never forgiven me for that. Actually, he's never forgiven me for anything. Do you have brothers?"

"No."

"Figures. That sullen introversion is typical of an only child. Did you know only children are three times more likely to take to thieving than kids with brothers and sisters? Whereas siblings are twice as likely to be murderers or arsonists. I don't know where they get the numbers from, but it's interesting, don't you think?"

They slept in a semi-derelict linhay. Axio woke up at first light and immediately checked his pocket. The box was gone, and so was Musen.

So, come to that, were the twelve gold angels, which was where Musen had made his mistake. Even so, it took Axio four days to find him.

He got lucky at an inn, miles off the main road, where there were still people. At the time he was the aggrieved master of a runaway servant. Ungrateful bastard cleaned me out, he explained to a sympathetic innkeeper, money, my horse, even took my best boots, left me tied up in my own root cellar, if he wasn't so useless at tying knots I'd have starved to death. And all because I caught him fooling with the dairymaid and gave him a fat lip.

The innkeeper looked up. "Man came in here with a split lip the day before yesterday," he said.

"Tall man?"

"Like a tree. Had a meal and a night's sleep, tried to pay me with a bloody great gold coin, size of a cartwheel. I said to him, where's an honest man like me supposed to get change for that? He was on about hacksawing a bit off it, but I told him to forget it and get lost. Bloody joker. I knew he was no good."

Naturally the innkeeper had no map, but he gave a clear enough account of the local geography that Axio was reasonably sure in his own mind where Musen would go next. Sure enough, late the next afternoon he met a farmer who'd sold a tall man a donkey for a gold angel.

"That was my money," Axio said. "Didn't you think there was something wrong?"

The farmer shrugged. "I didn't ask to sell it him. He kept on and on about it, and I just wanted shot of him."

A very tall man riding a donkey gets himself noticed. "Kids dragged me out of the house and made me look," a farmer's wife said the next day. "Daftest thing I've seen all year. Tried to buy a loaf off me but all he had was some big brass buttons."

"You might want to count your chickens," Axio said. The woman turned white as a sheet and ran off across the yard.

Having established a likely speed and direction, Axio considered what the innkeeper had told him about the layout of the countryside and decided on a suitable point for interception. The donkey proved to be a stroke of luck; a heavy man on a donkey would take the slow, easy road up the hills on to the moor, whereas a man on foot in a hurry could scramble up the shale outcrops and get there ahead of him. On the moor, of course, neither of them could hide from the other; but that's why the Great Smith made the night dark.

The donkey nearly ruined everything, braying and kicking up a fuss; but by then he was close enough, and he'd come prepared. As Musen sat up, he threw the heavy stone he'd picked out earlier and caught him on the side of the head. He went straight down, and a moment later Axio was sitting on Musen's chest, with his thumbs digging into his windpipe.

"The point is," he said (he was panting slightly, which spoilt the effect), "I don't need you any more. You've done your part of the job, and it only takes one of us to fetch the stuff home. Do you see what I'm getting at?"

Musen opened his mouth but of course he couldn't speak. Axio maintained the pressure but didn't increase it.

"Put yourself in my place," Axio said. "If I think there's the slightest chance of you doing anything like that again, I've got to kill you now, it's my duty. I can't jeopardise ninety thousand lives just for sentiment." Musen's face was dark red and he'd stopped struggling. "God knows I've done enough stupid things in my life. I can't afford any more." He let go with both hands. Musen started choking and spluttering. Axio got to his feet, kicked him hard in the ribs once, then reached down and hauled him to his feet; Musen staggered and dropped back on to his knees, wheezing helplessly. Axio dragged him back up again, just long enough to find the box in the pocket of his coat, then let him drop. "Just because I crack jokes sometimes doesn't mean I'm a clown," Axio said. "I'm sticking my neck out for you, letting you live. I don't think a tiny bit of gratitude is too much to ask."

He tied Musen up with the donkey's bridle, then sat down and took out the box. He stared at it for several minutes before tucking it down the front of his trousers – not an ideal arrangement by any means, but he defied Musen to get it out of there without him knowing.

When he woke up, the moment his eyes were open, he ran the checklist. He was still alive. His hands and feet were free. The box was still where he'd put it. Musen was lying where he'd left him, tethered by the reins to the donkey's hind leg. He flexed his hands, which were stiff and sore from all that throttling. "Good morning," he called out. "What's for breakfast?"

Musen was in better shape than he had any right to be. The bruises came right up to his chin and he rasped and rattled when he breathed, and there was a lump the size of half an apple where the stone had hit him, but there didn't seem to be any evidence of concussion or a broken rib. Axio leaned over him and smiled. "If I untie you, are you going to make trouble?"

Musen didn't answer. "Oh, come on," Axio said, and kicked him on the thigh, hard but not hard enough to hurt anything. "Either we make up and we're friends again or I'll leave you here for the crows. But I won't have you sulking at me the rest of the way home, and that's final. I've had about enough of this job."

Musen blinked at him; weary, dying cow eyes. "I promise," he said. "No trouble."

"I hope you're telling the truth," Axio said, stooping to untie the knots. "For your sake. I don't think you can take much more persuasion."

Musen had damaged his knee in the fight and could barely hobble, so Axio put him on the donkey. He could see why the sight had amused the farmer's wife's children so much. "Why'd you do it?" Axio asked, after they'd travelled in dead silence for a couple of hours. "You must've known I'd find you."

Musen closed his eyes. "What do they want it for?" he asked.

"What's that got to do with it?"

"Tell me."

"All right," Axio said. "You're not supposed to know, but I guess you have the right. Actually, I'd sort of assumed you'd figured it out for yourself. After all, it was you who brought the Sleeping Dog pack to Mere Barton in the first place."

Musen looked at him. "They're going to sell it to the Eastern emperor."

"Sort of." Axio reckoned he understood now. "You don't think he should have it."

"He just locks them up in cabinets," Musen said. "He's not a craftsman; he doesn't understand what they mean."

"Better him than the Western emperor, surely. The only reason he valued it was because his uncle wanted it so badly. That's no reason at all."

"Oh, he shouldn't have had it either. It should go to the Lodge."

Axio grinned. "That's exactly where it's headed."

"Yes, to sell it. That's not right." Musen massaged his throat; talking must be very painful for him. "It wasn't right for either of them to have it. Disrespectful."

"Actually," Axio said, "I don't entirely disagree with you. I read about these silver packs: apparently there's every reason to believe they go right back to the very beginnings of the Lodge, so if you believe in relics and icons and sacred images and all that sort of thing, I guess they're about as fundamental as you can get."

"Well, then."

"Oh, quite. On the other hand, this little trinket is probably the only remaining hope for saving ninety thousand civilians in Rasch Cuiber. A substantial number of whom, don't let's forget, are craftsmen."

"You keep saying that," Musen said. "I don't understand. What's a pack of cards got to do with Rasch?"

"Isn't it obvious? You know about Glauca. Of course, I keep forgetting, you've actually met him. You know what he's like. A straight swap. The pack for Rasch."

Musen looked stunned for a moment. Then he said, "He'll never go for that."

"Don't you believe it. Did you know, he made a formal offer: the silver pack for Beloisa and the mines? When that got turned down, he said he'd throw in two provinces on top, his nephew's choice. And he meant it. He was furious when the West wouldn't play ball, said they were only doing it out of spite. Which was true, of course. No, this little silver box can achieve what forty thousand soldiers have died failing to do. And, yes, I know it's insane, but that's absolute monarchy for you. The worst possible form of government, apart from all the others." He paused, then said, "So, how about it? If it saves all those lives, does that make it all right for Glauca to get the pack?"

Musen didn't answer. It was a stupid question anyway.

*

All twelve angels, the donkey and the silver-backed hairbrush bought them a pony and trap from three elderly sisters who kept geese and who claimed not to have heard there was a war on. They also said that the nearest village was Poitin, which Axio remembered as being about as far from a military road as you could get in the Western empire; but two miles south of Poitin ran the Green River, which meandered in the general direction they wanted to go, and had broad grassy banks used by carters trading south. Musen made no further attempt to steal the box; partly because Axio tied him to the back wheel of the trap every night and slept a dozen yards away – but that wouldn't have stopped him, Axio was sure, if he'd really wanted the thing.

Four days along the riverbank they came to a bridge. On the other side of it, the level bank continued; on their side, the ground rose steeply and was covered in heather, gorse and granite boulders. They got down from the cart and inspected the bridge, which gave way in the middle under Musen's weight. That answered that question. They abandoned the trap, shooed the pony away as far as it was prepared to go and continued on foot.

"Fifteen thousand angels," Axio said. "That's what it costs to keep an infantry regiment in the field for a month, and that's just pay, supplies and materiel. I mean, you can do the arithmetic for yourself. Ten regiments in an army, fifteen armies on each side, minimum, that's four and a half *million* angels this war is costing, every month, excluding cavalry, fortifications, siege operations, maintenance of roads, communications and other infrastructure, death-in-service gratuities, pensions and central command. Fifty-four million a year, at a woefully conservative estimate. Now, you look back to the last general census before the schism, and it's worth bearing in mind just how much more prosperous the empire was back then; the total combined revenue of the entire empire, that's East and West, guess what it came to. Go on, guess."

"I don't know."

"Thirty-seven million angels," Axio said. "Mind you, that's the pre-schism angel, sixty grains weight at nine twenty-six fine. For your information, the Eastern angel is now fifty-eight grains at seven forty-six, and the poor bloody Western angel is fifty-*two* grains at a miserable seven oh-three. So at current values, the pre-schism revenues would be something in the order of sixty million, but let's not forget the additional expense of two Imperial courts, two Imperial secretariats, not to mention the collapse of east–west trade and the loss of what should've been Imperial revenue to foreign trading partners, not forgetting that one angel in twenty presently in circulation is a low-weight counterfeit; that knocks a good ten million off, so even allowing for currency debasements you're looking at a theoretical total of fifty million, to cover *everything*, as against military expenditure of fifty-four million *plus*. So, again being hopelessly conservative, let's assume an annual deficit of four million, multiplied by twenty-six, that's a hole in the Imperial economy of one hundred and four *million* angels, more than two years' total revenues, which I'm given to believe is rather more gold than has been dug out of the ground in the history of the world. Now, let's assume that a hundred million is being financed at four per cent compound per annum. Even supposing the war ended tomorrow, that's an ongoing yearly interest charge of—" He paused. Musen had stopped dead, bent over, hands on knees. "What's the matter? Not feeling too good?"

"I've got this pain in my stomach," Musen said. "And I feel sick."

Axio frowned, then put his hand on Musen's forehead. It was hot and clammy. "Where does it hurt?"

Musen pointed to his right side. "There."

Axio prodded him with his forefinger, and Musen howled with pain. "Here, sit down," Axio said. "Gently," he added, as Musen stumbled and nearly collapsed; he grabbed his arm and guided him as best he could, to keep him from jarring his back on the ground. "Look, has this been coming on gradually or was it just suddenly there?"

"Sudden," Musen said. His face was twisted up. "What is it? Is it bad?"

"I don't think so," Axio lied. "Listen, is it more a sort of stabbing pain, or a dull—?"

Musen hit him and he fell down. The sky started to fold in around him, as Musen bent over him and hauled the box out of his pocket; the corner must have snagged, because he heard cloth tearing. Then he was alone for a while, in the dark.

He came round, and his head was splitting, as though he'd been drinking for a week. He felt empty and incredibly weary, but he dragged himself on to his knees; everything went blurry and runny and he threw up. His jaw ached, like bad toothache. "Idiot," he tried to say, but all that came out was mumbles.

So he thought it instead. Idiot, fool, moron. How could anyone be so stupid and still know how to breathe? He managed to sit up, and noticed a big red stone about a yard away. He closed his eyes and opened them again. It hadn't been there a moment ago, not when Musen did his ridiculously obvious fake illness that would only have fooled a really, really stupid person—

He was going to kill me, Axio thought. And then he changed his mind.

That makes two stupid people, he decided. He stood up, nearly went over, straightened his back. The fog was clearing and his head was worse than ever. His mouth was dry and full of something like mud but rather worse. He limped to the riverbank, got slowly down on his hands and knees and cupped water into his mouth. It made him feel very slightly better.

It was all so much effort. He wanted to lie down and go to sleep, more than anything in the whole world; instead, he tottered backwards and forwards until he found footprints in the soft ground, a big foot, the print of the toe deeper than the heel; that's someone running. Well, of course. Bet you anything you like he's a marvellous runner, the sort that can run all morning. Miles away by now. Too much effort. He'd be starving hungry if he didn't feel so sick. He put one foot in front of the other and started to walk.

The Thief

Musen propped himself up on the rail of the bridge and tried to catch his breath. Stupid, to keep running until he was completely worn out. Now he'd have to sit and rest, and that would lose more time than if he'd walked the last mile. He groped at his pocket to make sure the box was still there, then sat down with his back to the rail, looking back the way he'd come.

He remembered – what was his name? Thin man with a turkey neck, lived outside Lower Town. He ran away with the wife of Rensa the wheelwright, many years ago. They went up on the moors, everybody reckoned he must've had some half-baked idea of heading for Spire Cross, but of course Rensa and his brothers caught up with them both and they ended up dead in a bog pool. A bit fairy tale, the doomed lovers running through the heather with Rensa's hounds at their heels, but when you thought about it clearly, just stupid. They must've known they'd never get away with it, but they went ahead anyway. For love. Stupid.

He pulled off his right boot and shook it out, dislodging a few coins and a small silver brooch. The brooch pin had ripped open his sock and lacerated the front of his big toe. He stuffed the coins and the brooch in his pocket, then eased the boot back on. His foot appeared to have grown in the minute or so it had been exposed to the air; it was now far too big for the boot and he couldn't get his toes all the way down. He stood up; his shins protested furiously and he sat down again.

The pony cart, he noticed, was gone. It was only just over a day since they'd abandoned it, but it wasn't there. Not that it mattered particularly. Even if the cart had still been there, the pony would be long gone by now; and even if he'd found them both exactly where they'd been left, even if he then traded the pony trap for a coach and eight and galloped without stopping all the way to Permia or Sashan or the Blemyan desert, it wouldn't make any difference. Sooner or later he'd be woken up by those fingers round his neck. The longer he postponed it, the angrier Axio would be, the more unpleasant the reckoning. Pointless, the whole thing, just like the wheelwright's wife and her stupid lover whose name he couldn't even remember. All for love.

Even so. He remembered the first time he'd ever killed a chicken. He'd squeezed and squeezed, pinching his thumb and forefinger together on the little thin pipe under the feathers; he'd counted to ten, but the bird just looked at him, opened and closed its beak. He'd squeezed again, counted to twenty-five, and the chicken blinked and screamed without sound and scrabbled with her claws, giving him a scratch that had gone bad and needed a poultice. Life isn't so easily got rid of, even when the enemy is ten times your size and the hands round your throat are very strong. He'd dropped it in fear and disgust; it lay for a moment then tried to get up, wobbled a few determined steps and then flopped in a heap; and then his mother came and finished it off with a small, quick upward flick of the wrist, like God answering a prayer. Maybe there are people who have the gift of being able to give up and give in when it's obvious what the outcome must be, but Musen knew he wasn't one of them. And certainly not while he still had the pack.

He realised he hadn't actually looked at them yet, not beyond a brief glimpse or two by lamplight in that weird tower with the painted walls. He reached for the box, stopped, patted his pocket to make sure it was still there. Why in God's name hadn't he killed Axio while he had the chance? You may not kill a fellow craftsman – that, of course, but stealing from the Lodge was ten times worse, and that in effect was what he'd done, and he hadn't thought twice about it. (Oh God, he thought, I've stolen from the Lodge: that's so bad. How could I possibly have done that? Only at the time it didn't feel like stealing; it was rescuing ...) The Great Smith will forgive you, he remembered, but not in this form; you will be softened in the fire and hammered out until all your shape and memory is gone, and then He will make you again into something new; there is no fault in the material, only in the form into which it is shaped, which is transitory, inconsequential; there is no death, only change of form, there is no evil, only poor workmanship, which can be corrected. He always found that bit comforting, except that it seemed to contradict itself.

He tried to think like Axio. I come to the bridge, and I see the cart isn't there, and the footprints stop. So I assume— He frowned. I assume the stupid little thief has taken his boots and socks off and waded twenty yards upstream, fondly imagining I'd be fooled by the oldest trick in the book. So I walk up and down the bank until I find where he got out again—

A sound in the distance made him freeze; a voice, and another answering it. He pulled himself together, jumped up, looked round. A stab of pain from his foot reminded him of the stupidity of running with something sharp in your boot toe. He hobbled a few yards on to the bridge, then stopped. Hiding wasn't a practical proposition, he wasn't sure he was flexible enough to get across the broken place in the planking, and running was out of the question. He heard the voices again; at least one of them was female. He went back to where he'd been and sat down again.

Before very long he saw a small, neat wagon, drawn by two

horses. The driver and the passenger sitting beside her on the box were both women: one about forty-five (he wasn't good at women's ages), the other somewhere around seventy. The older one was driving. Both of them were wrapped up in enormous honey-coloured fur capes. Behind them in the bed of the cart were eight large barrels.

They must have seen him, because the cart stopped. He stayed where he was. So did the cart. The hell with it, he thought. He got up and walked slowly toward the women. When he was about ten yards away, the younger woman reached down and picked up an axe; call it an axe, it was a little hatchet, for splitting little logs into kindling. He stopped again, smiled and raised his hands, palms outwards.

"Who the hell are you?" the younger woman called out.

"My name's Musen. Look, if you were planning on crossing at the bridge, I'm afraid you can't. It's all broken up in the middle."

"What?" The older woman scowled at him. "You're joking."

"Come and see for yourself, if you like. But you won't be able to get that rig across, not unless you've got tools and about a dozen twelve-foot planks."

The younger woman climbed down; not an easy process, there was a lot of her under the cape. "You keep away from the cart," she said, walking round him. Her heels clopped on the bridge. "Shit," she said. "He's right. It's completely shot."

"Well, that's just perfect," the older woman said. "We'll have to turn round and go back to bloody Shant, or straight on to Cusavant and double back to Stert Ford. Either way, we can forget the fair. Might as well go home."

The younger woman was staring through the hole into the river. "You," she said. "Can't you do something?"

"Me? Sorry, no. I'm not a carpenter, and, anyway, there's no tools or materials."

"You could cut down a tree or something. There's one, look."

She pointed to a frail willow sapling growing out of the bank on the far side. "Chop it down, split it into planks, lay 'em over the gap. You can use our axe if you like." She held it out to him. He raised his hand politely.

"I don't think that'd work," he said. "I guess we could break up one of your barrels and use the staves, but like I said, I'm not a—"

"Don't even think about it," the older woman said. "Tell him, Gorna, that's six-year-old mead, it's worth more money than he's ever seen in his life. And don't give him the axe; he might be dangerous."

"It's all right, Mother." The younger woman rolled her eyes. "Don't mind her," she said. "She doesn't like strangers. You're sure you can't do anything? Maybe if you could carry the barrels across, we could go downstream to that shallow place and swim the horses across."

"How big are those barrels?"

"What? Oh, forty-five gallons. Why?"

"That means they weigh close on a third of a ton," Musen said. "Sorry."

"Oh, well." She looked at him. "What's the matter with you? Been fighting?"

Musen gave her a weak grin. "Bit of a one-sided fight," he said. "I work for this man, and he's got a nasty temper. When he gave me this, I thought, the hell with it. I'm sort of between jobs now."

"Mphm. Caught you stealing things, did he?"

"Maybe there was a bit of that," Musen said. "Anyway, sorry I can't help you."

"Gorna," the older woman called out. "Come here."

There was a brief whispered conversation; it looked like the younger woman was trying to get her case across, but she lost. Then she came back.

"My mother seems to think," she said, "that if you come with us as far as Hart Ferry, you can unload the barrels, take them over, then bring the boat back and fetch over the cart. I told her, those things weigh half a ton, but she wouldn't listen. Well?"

"We could do it, if we had a couple of planks. Where's this ferry?"

"Five miles upstream, give or take. What do you care? You aren't doing anything." She hesitated, then added, "Mother says you can have thirty stuivers."

"Where did you say you were going?"

The woman frowned. "I didn't," she said, "but if you must know, we're going to Malfet fair." She paused, then added. "It's a hiring fair: you could come with us and look for a new job. But that would be instead of the thirty stuivers."

"Gorna, what's he saying?" the older woman called out.

The younger woman sighed. "Come on," she said. "She gets impatient. Well? Do you want to come with us or not?"

"How fast does this cart go?" The words came out before he could stop them. The woman looked at him. "You said there was a hiring fair," he said. "I wouldn't want to miss that."

The woman frowned, then shook her head; there was a mystery, but it wasn't worth solving. "You'll have to ride in the back with the barrels. I expect you can find somewhere to sit."

The younger woman was Gorna, and her mother was Elaim, and the family had been carters for six generations, until the war came and took all the men away. It would be all right, the soldiers said; nobody was expecting them to fight or anything like that. All they were expected to do was drive their own carts along the military roads, for which they'd be paid their usual rates plus a third, in government scrip, guaranteed by the emperor himself. This war's a wonderful opportunity for people like you, they said. That was eight years ago.

So Gorna and her mother fixed up the last remaining cart, which the soldiers had declared unfit for service, and taught themselves how to drive it; and now they had a flourishing business, pretty much a monopoly, because the soldiers had taken all the other carts in the county, along with the wainwrights and the wheelwrights and all the good lumber. There wasn't much actual cash money, of course, because the taxmen had had all that long ago, but they were happy to be paid in kind: it's surprising how well you can get along without money. It was only men who couldn't run a business or a farm without money and tallies and chequerboards and ledgers, and you can get along pretty well without men, too.

"However," Gorna said, her eyes on the road ahead, because craning round hurt her neck, "I'm not saying we couldn't use a strong pair of hands about the place. I mean, it's amazing how much lifting and loading you can do once you've learned all the tricks and dodges, but Mother's not getting any younger, are you, dear, and I hurt my back about ten months ago and it's never really been right since. Of course we couldn't pay you in money, there simply isn't any, like I said, but there's plenty to eat and you can have a house of your own to sleep in, there's all those buildings empty and just falling down, it wouldn't take you hardly any time at all to fix one up and you'd be quite cosy and snug, if you used the slates off the old trap-house roof. Of course it's entirely up to you, but you might think about it. I mean, it's not like you've got anywhere else to go, and I'd have thought someone in your position would be glad of a roof over his head and two square meals a day, and who knows, I mean, when Mother and I get too old for the business, someone might as well take it over, there's no point the cart just mouldering away in a shed. No hurry, of course: you take all the time you want, and if you don't want to you can take your chances at Malfet fair and see if anybody'll have you. They're always looking for men for the stone quarries, though I gather they don't last very long there, because of the dust. Still, it's up to you entirely."

The ferry was an old charcoal barge, little more than a raft, hauled along on a double chain that spanned the river. All you had to do was haul on a lever, which opened an ingate and allowed water to run down a channel, which filled a dam. You then pulled another lever which opened the dam, and the water poured out and turned a waterwheel which drove the chain; when the dam was empty the chain stopped, but by then the ferry was across to the other side, where there was an identical arrangement. The ferry was rated at two tons – if you put any more load on it than that, you'd break something and be stuck in the middle of the river. There used to be ferries like it every ten miles, but none of the others worked any more; they'd been broken up for scrap metal, which was so much in demand because of the war.

There was also a derelict shed, where the ferry keeper used to live. Musen demolished the door and came away with two strong inch-thick planks. Rolling the barrels down off the cart wasn't easy, and one of them nearly got away from him into the river, but Gorna managed to head it off and between them they wrenched it on to the barge and got it standing upright. Mother operated the levers – anything mechanical or that needed manipulation seemed to be her province – and Musen and Gorna rode over to unload the barrels. Gorna had Musen operate the levers on the far side. "I'm hopeless with machinery," she said, with what sounded like pride. "My father and my husband always did that sort of thing, and the boys, when they were old enough. Of course, Mother does her best, bless her."

The horses didn't want to get on the barge. Gorna had to talk to them quite sharply. There wasn't any trouble after that.

Musen half killed himself getting the barrels back into the cart. He'd thought to bring a couple of rafters from the fallen-down shed to use as levers; Mother and Gorna sat on the ends, while he heaped stones up under the barrels to raise them a foot; then more levering, more sitting, more stones, until eventually the barrel could be tipped and wrestled over the lip of the bed, forced upright and walked into position. By the time the last barrel was loaded he was shaking, and his arms felt as light as air. After that, it turned out that there was enough room for three on the box, if Musen didn't mind sitting on the end and hanging on to the rail.

It had been a good road once, but the frost had got into it, followed by the grass and then the briars. But Mother was a single-minded driver and the cart had good springs; just as well the soldiers didn't want it, of course, but, really, it was a very good cart; they knew how to build them back then, of course you could get the materials then, before the war. At this rate, they'd be in Malfet by noon tomorrow, which would mean missing the first morning of the fair, but that couldn't be helped, and mostly the first morning was just the village people coming in to town to gawp: the serious people didn't do any real buying or hiring till the second day. The owners of the six barrels of mead might be a bit upset about missing a morning's trade, but they'd just have to understand, it's not easy moving stuff about these days. Take the bridge, there was a very good example: ten years ago the village would've come out and fixed it straight away, but nowadays—

In fact, they were making such good time that Gorna agreed to a brief stop, near the first substantial copse they'd passed in some time; she hurried away and walked back a little later, and suggested a bite to eat before they carried on. She flipped up the hinged lid of the box and came up with wheat bread, dried ham, sausage, apples, honeycakes and a stone gallon bottle of beer: just a snack, she said, to keep them going. She offered Musen some of the beer; he said thank you, but he'd rather have water. Later he washed the jar out carefully in a stream beside the road and filled it up, for later.

The cart had two lamps, very good quality, imported, so they were able to keep going through the evening and well into the night, until they came to a stretch of road that Mother declared wasn't fit to drive in the dark. The women slept sitting up, on the box; Musen crawled under the cart and tried to sleep, but every time he started to drift off he seemed to feel the presence of someone close to him, breathing without making a sound. He was glad when the sun rose and they could get going again.

"I think it was a government road originally," Gorna was saying. "It's not straight like an army road, but look at the way they've cut through the hill rather than going round. It's amazing to think there was a time when they could do that sort of thing, though of course it was all other people's money."

Musen didn't like the cutting. The embankments were steep on both sides, and thorns and ash saplings had taken root in them and grown into dense clumps, big enough to hide an archer. Gorna laughed at him. "There used to be bandits on this road at one time, about five years ago," she said. "But hardly anybody comes this way any more, and those that do haven't got anything. If you hung about here waiting for someone to rob, you'd starve."

Musen didn't tell her it wasn't bandits he was worried about. But they passed through the cutting without any trouble, and beyond it the countryside was flat and open; all the way, Gorna assured him, to Malfet.

"All this was marshes once, of course," she told him. "And then they dug the rines and drained it, but the land's too sour, apparently, so it's only fit for sheep. Of course nobody clears the rines out any more so it's getting soft again."

There were no sheep: nothing living except for a distant hovering buzzard. Musen tried to remember the last time he'd seen anybody out working on the land – not the sort of thing you notice, until you realise it's not there. Still, there was a positive side. Axio would stick out a mile; he'd see him coming, at least by daylight. He wriggled his toes in his boot, wondering if he was fit to run yet.

*

"See that plume of smoke? That's Malfet." Gorna was pointing; he tried to follow the line of her finger, but the cart was bouncing up and down. He couldn't see any smoke. "Should be there just after noon, assuming Mother doesn't run us into one of those damned potholes and crack the axle."

Mother scowled at her and flicked the whip; the horses shied forward and carried on at their former pace. A town, Musen thought; a town where there'd be people, a normal place where there was buying and selling, buildings, windows with shutters and doors with locks. And a hiring fair. If half of what Gorna had said was true, he'd have his choice of work – remote farms in the hills where nobody ever went, or in some busy town where nobody remembered faces. Or perhaps it would be better to stick with the women, who were always on the move, at least for now, until he could think straight again and find out about faraway places and how you got there.

"You wouldn't have thought anybody had the money to buy fancy mead these days," Gorna continued, "but apparently they have, because Frassa – that's the beekeeper – he reckons he could've shifted twice as much if we could've carried it. Of course, if we could find a bigger cart, maybe something that needs a bit of work doing to it – did I mention we've got six horses, though don't go telling anybody, the last time the soldiers came round we sent them all up to the shieling on the moor and said they'd been stolen. I think the soldiers suspected something but they couldn't prove it, of course—"

There was a loud noise, like a crack, but also like a heavy stone falling into mud. Gorna had stopped in mid-sentence; her eyes and mouth were wide open and there was something in the middle of her forehead – like a walnut, only grey. Then she fell back off the box, hit her head against a barrel and slid forward, so Musen had to grab her to keep her from sliding off the box and under the wheels. Mother saw him and turned her head, and there was another noise, slightly different, solid, like a hammer on a wooden wedge, and she dropped off the edge of the box, the reins still in her hands. The cart lurched sideways and something hit Musen in the ribs, like a punch from an invisible fist. He grabbed the rail to steady himself but it snapped off in his hand and he fell and the ground rushed up to meet him.

"See that?" A boy's voice. "Did you see, Grandad? I got them both. Two in two shots. Is that good or what?"

Musen opened his eyes. A boy, maybe thirteen years old, in clothes he recognised as Western army fatigues, sleeves and trouser legs rolled up into ludicrous ruffs; he had a cloth bag over his shoulder, and the thing like a long sock in his right hand was a slingshot.

"Keep your voice down, for crying out loud. And come down off of there. You don't know who's watching."

An old man, maybe sixty, sixty-five, and another boy, say fifteen and also with a cloth bag and a sling; both of them in the same fatigues. The old man's limp suggested a badly set fracture many years ago, and two of the fingers of his right hand were missing. Didn't General Moisa, Senza's predecessor, use to cut off two fingers of any Western archer he caught?

"Look at those barrels, Grandad. Wonder what's in them. Do you want me to go and look?"

"Shut up and get up on the box. Pileo, you, too, while I see to these reins. No, leave it, for God's sake, we don't have time."

But the older boy was tugging at Mother's hand for a ring; he put his foot on her neck to hold her steady. That couldn't be right, Musen thought; and then his left hand felt a stone, and before he knew what he was doing, his fingers had closed around it and he was sitting up.

"Grandad," the younger boy called out. Musen guessed the range and threw his stone. It hit the older boy on the ear; he rocked, and dropped. The old man stood up on the box; the other boy was scrabbling in his cloth bag. It was a simple case of time and distance. Musen jumped to his feet and ran towards the cart. The old man must've seen the little axe; he stooped for it, but he didn't have time. Musen grabbed his ankle and pulled his feet out from under him, and he went down, cracking his head against a barrel. The boy was still fumbling in his bag; Musen vaulted on to the box and kicked his head like a ball, then bent down, snatched the axe and sank it into the old man's skull, like you do with a stump in the woods, so you can find your axe again.

He looked round. The older boy was trying to get up. Musen leapt down, dragging the axe free as he landed. The boy saw him coming and raised his arm. Musen swept low and chopped into his shin; then, as he dropped, he pulled a draw-cut along the side of his neck, skipping sideways to keep from getting spattered.

The boy he'd kicked was out cold. He chopped into the top of his head and left the axe sticking there.

There was no shovel or pickaxe on the cart. There were iron hoops driven into the timbers of the bed, for stowing a shovel and a pickaxe in, but the tools themselves were long gone; the war, probably, like everything else. He briefly considered trying to hack a hole in the turf with the axe, or scooping one with a barrel-stave, but both the women were large, you'd have to dig a long way down, and the ground looked like a thin layer of peat over limestone; the hell with it. He scrambled back up on to the box, grabbed the old man by the scruff of the neck and pitched him on to the ground, then sat down. He was exhausted, and his rib hurt like hell, so he could barely breathe. He prodded it gently with his fingers and reckoned it was just bruised, not broken. Just as well he was wearing a heavy coat and that it had been a slingshot, not a bow. But bows cost money; a sling is just a bit of old cloth, you can make them out of scraps and leftovers.

He closed his eyes and forced himself to breathe, in spite of the

discomfort. There was something in the liturgy about not killing – or was that just fellow craftsmen? – but he was pretty sure
it was in the same section as not stealing, and he knew the Great
Smith had made him to be thief, so maybe He needed killers,
too. His father had killed all the time, and not just for the table;
there was the time they dug a run-off from the stream to flood
the rats' nests under the barn, and Dad reckoned they'd probably
drowned a thousand rats that day, and bloody good riddance. His
foot hurt like hell where he'd kicked the boy. He wondered if he'd
broken his toe.

Look at it this way, he told himself. If He hadn't wanted me to
do it, He wouldn't have rewarded me with a cart of my very own.
And there was the pack to consider, of course. If he'd died and the
boy had searched his pockets, the boy would've found the pack and
sold it to some heathen, and He wouldn't have countenanced that.
He wouldn't even let it go to save a whole city.

It wasn't a good place to be, Musen could see that, but finding
the strength to get moving again was another matter entirely.
Deserters, presumably; he'd heard they were calling up young boys
for rear-echelon duties, or maybe they'd scavenged the uniforms.
It was all as broad as it was long, as Axio would say.

Sitting upright to drive was particularly painful, but he
couldn't help that. At least the horses were all right, though he
fancied the right-side horse might have a shoe coming loose. He'd
have to check that some time. Not now. He called to them softly
to walk on.

Malfet fair turned out to be smaller than he'd anticipated. There
were maybe two dozen stalls, fitted comfortably into the market
square, with possibly a couple of hundred people milling round
them; clean, neatly dressed. He hadn't seen anything like it since
he left Mere Barton.

He found a watering trough and a rail to tie up to, then gently lowered himself to the ground and put his weight on his bad foot. It held up better than he had any right to expect. All he could do was choose a stall at random.

"I've got six big barrels of mead," he explained, "ordered in from up-country. I don't actually know who they're for. I'm new with the firm; the women who fixed up the deal couldn't make it." The stallkeeper thought for a moment, then referred him down the line; inaccurately, as it turned out, but the woman there put him right and sent him across the square to a stall with a great rack of barrels on solid-looking trestles. "This is a bloody fine time to show up," the stallholder said irritably. "We'd almost given up on you. What kept you?"

Musen explained about the bridge being down, though he wasn't sure the stallholder believed him. But what the hell, better late than never, and the stallholder's sons would unload the barrels if he'd point out the cart. And presumably he wanted paying? Three angels.

Musen walked away, turning the coins over in his hand. He stopped by a stall selling fancy metalwork, and pointed to a dear little three-legged stand for a teapot.

"That's nice," he said to the woman.

"Mezentine," the woman replied. "If you turn it over, you can see the mark. Twenty stuivers."

Musen grinned. "I haven't got a teapot. What about that?"

"The knife?" The woman picked it up and put it in his hand. "That's Blemyan work, very rare. Pre-war, that is. Fifty stuivers."

Musen gave her an angel. She raised both eyebrows, then scrabbled frantically for change. "Where's Blemya?" he asked.

"What? Oh, way down south somewhere, other side of the sea. Bloody hot, so they say, which wouldn't suit me." She gave him a full handful of coins, which he stuffed in his pocket without counting. The woman leaned forward a little. "They do say," she said, "Blemya's going to come in on our side in the war, any day now. It's all settled, apparently. And then we'll show that bastard Senza what he can do."

It was a very good knife, in fact, and he felt sure that if ever he got a chance to draw it he'd be able to put up quite a fight. But against the man who crept up on him and cut his throat in his sleep, he couldn't see how it would be any use at all.

For one angel eighty-five he bought eight big jars of flour, a side of bacon, six strings of smoked sausages, a sack of carrots, four sacks of oats, four jars of dried fruit, five honeycombs, four good coats, two hats, three pairs of boots, two linen shirts, four pairs of trousers, two iron pots, a ladle, two wooden bowls and four matching cups, a shovel, an axe, a pick, a sledgehammer, a carpenter's cross-pein hammer, a frame saw, four chisels, a dozen five-foot oak floorboards, two blankets, a tinderbox, a coil of rope, three iron splitting wedges, a small oilskin tent and a pair of stockman's gloves. He arranged them in the back of the cart so he'd be able to find what he was looking for, covered them over with the tent and took the right-side horse to the smith to have its shoe seen to. It was dark by then, and the usual crowd of old men, boys and hardened drinkers had wandered away. The smith was a young man, not much older than Musen; he worked quickly and well, but the effort he had to put into striking suggested that his hammers were too heavy for him.

"I don't think I've seen you here before," Musen hazarded.

"Only been here six months," the smith replied, working the bellows. "Got this." He pointed to his foot; it looked perfectly normal to Musen. "Which got me my demob, praise be, and I got on my donkey and rode west till my money ran out, and here's where I ended up. This place was all boarded up, so I had a word with the old smith's widow and got the whole lot for fifty stuivers a month, tools and fixtures included." He grinned, and splashed water all round the edges of the fire from a copper can on a long handle. "I lit the fire the first day and it hasn't gone out since."

"You were a smith in the Service, then."

"Farrier." He pulled the shoe out of the fire with the long tongs, inspected it, shoved it back under the coals, worked the bellows a few times. "But if you can make horseshoes you can make pretty much anything. Mostly round here it seems to be gate fittings, nails, busted tires and general mending. You can't get coal, but charcoal's quite cheap."

"My uncle's a smith," Musen said.

Out came the horseshoe, cherry-red and almost translucent. The smith draped it over the horn of the anvil and gave it a few smart taps. "Is that right?"

"Yes. He lives in Mere Barton, in the second street. The fifth house, on the third floor. He keeps his hammers and his anvil at our house."

The smith held the horseshoe up to inspect it, turned it over, put it back in the fire. "If you're looking for a discount, forget it," he said. "Otherwise, I'm Glabria, pleased to meet you. Don't get many craftsmen out here in the sticks."

"I'm Musen."

The smith looked at him for a moment. "You ought to be in the army," he said.

"I was, for a bit. Didn't suit."

"Ah well. Nobody's going to give you any trouble round here, and the draft doesn't bother coming here any more. Cleaned this whole district out years ago. You could try walking with a limp, though. You don't get asked questions if you limp."

"Actually, I don't need to fake it. But thanks for the tip."

"Right." Out the horseshoe came again; many light taps, until the iron turned grey. "Let's have her foot up and we'll see if it fits."

It fitted; Glabria tapped in the nails and cut off the ends, and Musen thanked him. "How much do I—?"

Glabria grinned. "Get out with you, I was just kidding. Keep your money." He tipped charcoal from the bucket on to the fire, heaped it up evenly with the rake, then doused all round with the copper can. "You in a tearing hurry, or have you got time for a drink?"

The cabin next to the forge was what you'd expect of a hard-working man living alone. There was one chair and a stool, and the table was thick with black dust. Glabria lifted a stone bottle off the floor, pulled the stopper and sat on the stool. "So," he said. "You stopping here or passing through?"

Musen hesitated, then sat down. "Depends," he said.

"Really? What on?"

He put his hand in his pocket. "Been a craftsman long?"

"Born to it. We're all Lodge in our family."

Musen took out the silver box and put it on the table. "Go on," he said. "Take a look."

Glabria opened the box, took out the cards and laid them on the table one by one. "There's a pretty thing," he said. "What is it?"

Musen felt a wave of disappointment. "Lodge property," he said. "It's very rare and worth a lot of money, and I need to keep it safe. There's a man trying to steal it from me. He'll kill me if he catches me. He's very dangerous."

The look on Glabria's face would have melted a heart of stone. "What do you expect me to do? I'm not anybody. I'm just a blacksmith."

"And I grew up on a farm, it doesn't matter. This belongs to the Lodge, it's really old and special. You're a craftsman, you've got to help me, it's what the Lodge is all about, helping each other."

"What do you want me to do?"

"I don't know." Musen started putting the cards back in the box. "I can't make up my mind. If I stay here, he'll find me. If I go—"

"If you wanted to keep from being noticed, you've gone the

wrong way about it," Glabria said. "You've been going round buying up enough stuff to found a colony. Even I heard about it, and I wasn't interested. Your man's only got to ask a few people: he'll know you've been here and the direction you left in." He shook his head. "That wasn't smart."

"All right," Musen said, "maybe it wasn't. So what do I do now?"

Glabria thought for a while. "You reckon this man of yours is a hard case. Just how bad is he?"

"He'd kill either of us without a second thought, if he reckoned it'd help."

"That's not encouraging," Glabria said. "What I was going to suggest was, you find someone else to drive your cart full of stuff out of town. He follows the cart, by the time he figures out he's been tricked, you're miles away in the other direction. But who'd be prepared to do that for you if it meant getting his throat cut?"

"He wouldn't do that," Musen said quickly. "He's not crazy or spiteful or anything. He'd kill you for a reason, but not just because you pissed him off."

Glabria looked doubtful. "I don't think I want to take that chance," he said. "Anyway, you're a head taller than me, and everyone round here knows me, so I couldn't do it." He thought for a moment. "Of course, it's the hiring fair. You hire a carter, big tall chap your size and build." He grinned. "So maybe he decides to rip you off, take the cart and keep on going. Like you care. Yes, that's what I'd do."

"Will you hire someone for me?" Musen asked eagerly. "Only, if he catches this carter and asks him, who hired you?"

Glabria shrugged. "Sure, I can do that. Then, if your man comes looking for me, I can send him the wrong way, buy you a bit more time. You need to figure where you actually want to go, mind. Just wandering about aimlessly won't do you any good."

"Blemya," Musen said.

"What? Where the hell's that?"

"South, across the sea. Oh, he'll follow me there, if he knows that's where I've gone. But maybe by then I'll have thought of a way of making it safe, somewhere I can hide it away where he won't find it. That's all that matters, after all."

Glabria seemed bothered by something. "If it's Lodge property," he said, "why don't you take it to the authorities? I bet you they can look after it far better than you can."

"I can't do that," Musen said quickly. "It's complicated, I can't tell you why, but I can't. It's up to me, and I've got to take care of it. You don't think I want this, do you? I've lost everything because of this—" He stopped, as if a door had just closed. "We'll do what you said. It sounds like a good idea."

Outside, someone was calling Glabria's name. "Stay there," he said. "I know who it is, just a customer. I won't be long."

Shortly afterwards, Musen heard a hammer ringing on an anvil, and cheerful voices. He leaned back in the chair and suddenly realised how exhausted he was, and how many bits of him hurt, and how filthy his clothes were. He looked down at his hands and noticed grains of flaked dried blood lodged in the webs between his fingers, and had no idea if that blood was his own or somebody else's.

Glabria woke him with a slight nudge against his foot.

"I took a look in your cart," he said. "That's a lot of stuff you've got in there. Worth quite a bit of money. Are you sure you—?"

Musen shook his head. "I couldn't give a damn. No good to me if he kills me."

"No, I suppose not. Look, while you've been asleep, I've been busy. I found you a carter."

"That's marvellous. Thank you."

Glabria sat down on the stool and unstoppered the bottle. "I spun him this load of rubbish about supplies for a gang of men up on the moors mending a wall. I suppose he believed it, not that it matters; I don't think for a moment he's going to be heading the way I told him. My guess is, he'll run up the north road and take the east fork, over to Sleucis or somewhere like that, sell the rig and the gear and move on quick. If he gets that far." Glabria shrugged. "He's not from around here, so he doesn't know me, I told him a made-up name, and I washed my face and took the apron off, so he may not even have figured me for a smith. I don't think he was listening too carefully. Anyway, I told him to come round first thing, at sunrise, so he should be here any minute." Glabria paused. "You sure you want to go through with this?"

"What? Yes, of course I do."

"Fine. Listen, I've put two loaves and a skin of water in a bag. I reckon, if you're smart, you'll hike down the south road till you come to the river, then look out for one of the big charcoal barges. They'll give you a lift as far as you like for twenty stuivers, and you don't leave footprints floating down a river. If you're serious about wanting to get to the coast, you ought to be able to find barges that'll take you the whole way, and you won't have to set foot on land once, just hop from one boat to another. If anything'll make you hard to find, that will. Boats move on, see: by the time your man's figured out you're on such and such a boat, it'll be twenty miles downstream; he'll be chasing about all over the shop." He frowned. "Look, I can't give you any money. I haven't got any to spare right now. If you hadn't been quite so—"

"That's all right," Musen said. "Money isn't a problem."

Glabria sighed, and gazed at him. "Never thought I'd meet anybody who could say that with a straight face," he said. "And when I do, he's one step ahead of the Devil. Nothing's ever perfect, is it?"

Musen didn't watch the cart leave, though he heard its wheels on the stones of the yard. He took a while rubbing sheep's-wool grease into his boots; it was all he could do by way of preparing for the journey, so he did it as well as he possibly could. He had the Blemyan knife, the decent coat he'd bought at the fair, the cloth bag with the bread and water and a hundred and fifteen stuivers in small change. He felt like he was wearing armour, safe and strong.

Glabria let him out of the side gate, with directions for finding the south road. "Good luck," the blacksmith hissed, then shut the gate firmly behind him, and then bolts shot home, top and bottom; it was a pleasure meeting you, and please, please don't come back. Well; he could see Glabria's point. He hoped the smith had been human enough to steal something from the cart, to make it worth his while.

It was a good time of day to be starting out. There were a few people about, but not too many. Musen guessed they'd finished their business early at the fair and were starting home. He walked for a while behind two men, close enough to eavesdrop on what they were saying – actually, it was one man talking and the other presumably listening; the duties of a newly hired brickmaker, followed by a long list of offences that would earn instant dismissal. Musen quickened up and overtook them as soon as he could. A bit further on, he came up behind an old man, an old woman and a girl: similar situation, except that the woman was telling the girl what she'd do to her if she caught her fooling around with the man, who didn't utter a word all the time Musen was trailing them. It was just as well Musen had long legs and could outpace people without having to run.

At noon he passed an inn – door open, windows not boarded up, four men sitting outside sharing a jug of something. But the men were old, and there were no horses tied to the rail. Apart from Glabria, he hadn't seen a man under fifty for a long time.

He guessed most of his fellow travellers must've stopped at the inn, because from then on until sunset he had the road to himself. He managed not to let that bother him. The fields on either side of the road were flat stubbles, with broad headlands and only the occasional maiden willow, so he could see a long way and be sure he wasn't being followed. He realised he was walking fast, setting a pace that hurt his calves and ankles. He tried to slow down, but it didn't feel right. Glabria had told him he wouldn't reach the river before nightfall, but maybe he could; there would be barges tied up for the night, and he'd have a far better chance of finding one that would take him. Plenty of time to rest and take it easy once he was safely on board, floating down the middle of a wide river.

He reached the river quite some time after the sun had set, walking toward lights which he assumed to be the boatmen's campfires. In fact they turned out to be lamps, hung on the side rails of the barges, which loomed like a street of houses out of the shadows. He walked a short distance down the towpath listening for voices, and found himself face to face with a girl, in a big coarse blue coat, carrying a bucket of water. She stared at him, then called out, "Nula, come here. Right now."

He took a step back, out of the lamplight, so the girl couldn't see his face. He heard boot heels on a wooden deck, then a thump as someone jumped from the boat on to the path. A lantern glared at him, and a girl's voice said, "Dear God, it's a—"

"Shut up, Maza," said a third girl's voice behind him. "Here, you. What are you snooping round for?"

He turned, into the light of another lantern. Behind it he caught a flash of golden hair, under a dark hood. "I'm sorry," he said. "I was wondering—"

"Maza, Frez, on the boat, now." The lantern lifted up; the girl behind it was inspecting him. "On the *boat*, I said."

"Nula—"

"*Now.*" He heard unhappy noises behind him, but didn't turn. "Now listen, you," the girl went on. "You're very tall and pretty but I'm afraid we can't have you; we don't know where you've been. Obviously you're a deserter—"

"You don't know that," said a voice behind him. "Nula, it's been *years.*"

"And you know as well as I do what happens to people who harbour deserters," the girl in front of him went on: "we could lose this boat and, frankly, I don't care, you're not worth it. Now please go away before I start screaming."

Musen started to back away, then remembered he was hemmed in. "I just want a lift to the coast," he said. "I'm not a deserter. I got my discharge. I won't be any bother."

"I see. Got your papers?"

"No, but—"

"Fine. I'm going to count to five. One."

Musen took a long step back, collided with something, sidestepped, turned and ran. Behind him he heard a piercing voice – "Nula, how *could* you?" – and decided he hadn't run far enough. He didn't stop till he'd reached the end of the line of barges; then he dropped to his knees and crouched for a moment, until the lanterns left the towpath and went back on the barge.

"Hey, you down there." A man's voice. "Yes, you. I'm talking to you."

Musen stood up. "Excuse me—"

"Quiet. Let me look at you." Another artificial yellow sunrise blazed in his face. "What was all that racket about back there?"

Musen took a deep breath. "I'm looking for someone who'll give me a lift downstream," he said. "I asked some women, but I think I must've scared them or upset them or something, so I—"

"Ran away. Very wise. Wish I'd had the sense when I was your age. Still." The lantern lifted, and he saw an old man, big head, bald, stubby white beard. "Trouble is, no matter how hard you run, they catch you in the end. This is my wife, Altea. I'm Cusen. Come aboard."

The lantern swayed, and he saw an old woman, with long white hair tied back in a ponytail, and a ladder. "Don't just stand there," the woman said. "Come on, we won't eat you. And don't listen to him," she added: "he's an idiot. Where did you say you were headed?"

The barge must've been a grand affair once; it had a cabin, with three bunks and a table. The old man put the lantern down, sat on the edge of the bunk and said, "Now then, let's have a look at you."

"I'm not a deserter," Musen said. "I just want to go south."

"Course you do," the woman said. "What's in the bag?"

"Bread."

"Good, we're hungry. Got any money?"

"Give the boy a chance," the man said. "Let him sit down, take the weight off."

"Thirty stuivers," the woman said. "Just passage, no board."

"That's fine," Musen said. He dug his hand in his pocket and showed them the money. "And I can help out, if you want me to."

The old man shook his head. "No need," he said. "It's no sweat working a barge: if it was, we couldn't do it." He got up, took the coins, gave them to the old woman, who put them in her mouth. "If you wouldn't mind sharing," he went on, nodding at the bag. "What with one thing and another, we ran out of food. Make it up to you at the lock."

"That's fine," Musen said, and took a loaf from his bag. The old woman hopped up, pounced on it like a cat and took it to the table. "You don't want to pay any mind to those stupid girls," she said, tearing into the loaf with her fingers. "They'd have eaten you alive, and that's a fact."

"Truth is," the old man said, "nobody gives a shit who you are on the river. That Nula, she didn't want the other two scratching each other to death, that's all. Got some sense, that one, more than the other two, though that's not saying a great deal. You stick with us, son; we'll take you where you want to go."

Cusen hadn't always been a waterman, oh no; his father had been one of the original Ocnisant gang – that was Piemo Ocnisant, the old man, not young Siama who was running things now. This was back before the war, mind – well, this war, anyhow: there's always a war, isn't there, but people don't notice unless it's right under their noses. No, they were high old times growing up with Piemo's bunch, good money to be made and never in the same place twice, except when the gang blew into town with money in their pockets. But his father made him promise: son, this is no life for an old man; put a bit by when you can; get yourself a stake and go into some other line of business. Poor old devil didn't take his own advice, mind, he loved the life too much, moving about, always the chance of the big score; caught a fever and died when he was forty-seven. But the Ocnisants look after their own, famous for it, and a lad who was willing to work was fine by them. But then Cusen had got married, kid on the way, and there was a big score – start of this war, matter of fact, hell of a big battle and they all reckoned it'd be over by midsummer. So he sold out his share – God only knows what it'd be worth now, of course, didn't bear thinking about – and sold off the various bits and pieces he'd put by, and bought this bloody old boat. Not that it was a bad life, the three of them working together: that was before the boy got called up, of course. Different now, just the two of them slogging away, and not getting any younger. Made you think, really; what's going to happen when all the old folk get too old, and then there'll be nobody at all left to do the work, and God only knew what'd happen then. It'd be just girls, like that mad Nula and her sisters, and a few cripples with only one arm.

He woke up because he couldn't breathe. Axio was standing over him. He smiled, lifted his heel and stamped on Musen's ribs.

"Hello," he said. "You bloody idiot."

The lamps were still lit, and Musen could see the old man and his wife, sitting on a bunk, watching. The Blemyan knife was on the deck beside him. He moved his hand, and Axio stamped on that, too; then he shuffled it away with the side of his foot and kicked it across the cabin.

"That's him, then?" Musen heard the old woman say.

"Oh, yes," Axio replied. "That's my boy."

Musen tried to breathe, but the weight on his chest – there was nothing there – was too great for his muscles to lift. He managed about a cupful of air, and choked.

"You're not going to kill him here, are you?"

"I promised, didn't I?" Axio reached down, caught hold of Musen's wrist and hauled him up; doubled the hand behind his back and applied pressure. Musen's own weight was on the joint, pulling it apart, but Axio's grip was the only thing holding him up. "Thanks ever so much. We'll be going now."

"We know our duty," the old man said. "I'm an old soldier, me."

Axio wheeled him round, like a heavy barrel or a crate, then lifted him by the agonising elbow joint and kicked his heels forward to get him walking. "Course you are," he said, and his free hand opened, and four gold angels landed on the table, rolled and fell off.

"Deserters," the old woman said. "String 'em up, I say. Nothing but cowards, that's what they are."

Axio solved the problem of getting Musen off the boat by jamming him against the rail and shoving him in the chest. Musen toppled backwards and landed on his shoulder on the towpath; a moment later, Axio vaulted down after him and dragged him up again. "Onwards," he said briskly. "We haven't got far to go."

About a hundred yards down the towpath, well clear of the lights from the boats. Axio let go of him and he dropped, and then he felt Axio's boot on his neck.

"You might like to know the blacksmith told me," Axio said. "Of course, the forge was the first place I asked: have you seen a tall man, split lip nearly healed? He couldn't have been more helpful, once I told him who I was." The boot was slowly crushing his windpipe. "He guessed the pack was something really important, and that you'd stolen it. But you looked so desperate, and you had a knife." He laughed. "I told him you were soft as butter."

Musen couldn't keep his eyes open any longer. He tried to think of the cards: Poverty, the Chariot, the Angel, the Drowned Woman (no, not her), the Cherry Tree, Destiny, Hope. There is always grace, he told himself, grace in life, grace in death, the one grain of grace that cures the flesh, grace disregarded in the mud and trodden on, but harder than diamonds. Death doesn't matter, the fire and the hammer. Grace will draw us up and make us clean—

The pressure had stopped. Using every last scrap of his strength, he breathed in, dragging the air past all the creases and the pain, like a man hauling a heavy sack up into a loft.

"You clown, Musen," Axio said. "What the hell am I going to do with you?"

"You really want to pack it in," Axio was saying, as he built the kindling up round the thin, guttering flame. "For one thing, all this getting beaten up and having the shit kicked out of you, it's not good for you: first thing you know, it'll ruin your health. I mean, you're young now, you heal quickly; in six months or a year you'll be up and charging about good as new, should you manage to live that long. But sooner or later it'll be one boot in the kidneys too many, and you'll be pissing every five minutes for the rest of your days. I ask you, is it worth it?"

Axio was heating up some chicken broth. He had three horses tied up in a barn, about half a mile from where the boats were moored. Two of the horses had saddles and bridles; the third was a packhorse, for carrying the supplies.

"I don't know how anyone could be so damned inconsiderate," Axio went on. "You do realise, if anyone ever finds out what you've done, and I let you live, not once but twice, that's me finished. Out on my ear: lucky if they don't string me up too. Yes, I know, sparing a fellow craftsman's life – well, sparing, saving, all the same thing, really. But I have to point out, I'm not a saint; there's a limit to the level of risk I'm prepared to expose myself to, even for a comrade in arms, even for a friend. I really mean it, Musen. One more stunt like that and you'll leave me no choice." He filled the ladle and sipped from it. "Just as well you're in no shape to run any more."

Axio had had to carry him the last couple of hundred yards; over his shoulder, like a sack. He'd brought bandages with him, for binding up the cracked ribs and the crushed hand, splints for the broken fingers. "You'll never play the violin," he'd observed. "Just as well you're not musical. You aren't, are you?"

Axio had taken the cards. Musen had watched him stow them away in a pocket, with a flap that buttoned down. It was his right hand Axio had stamped on. He didn't have nearly the same dexterity in his left.

"Here," Axio said, and held out the handle of the ladle. "Careful, it's hot."

Musen reached for it with his left hand, then hesitated. "Not hungry," he said.

"What? Don't be so bloody stupid, eat the damned soup."

"I'm not hungry."

"Fuck you, Musen. What are you, six years old? You do realise, don't you, that thanks to your stupid, idiotic behaviour, Rasch Cuiber might fall before we can get these cards to the emperor. In which case, tens of thousands of people will die, and it'll all be our fault, yours and mine." He put the ladle back in the pot. "And after all the misery and pain and effort I've been to keeping you alive, you've got the ingratitude, the sheer *bad manners* to pull some sort of childish hunger strike and starve yourself to death. What does it take to get through to you, Musen? You won't bloody listen and I'm just too bone weary to hit you any more. You won't even tell me why you want the stupid thing."

"If I did, would you listen?"

Axio groaned. "Of course I'll listen. Dear God, why must everything be so *difficult*?"

"All right," Musen said quietly. "You remember I asked you what we were stealing the cards for. You told me, it was to trade them for Rasch."

"Yes, that's right."

Musen took a deep breath. "I met him, remember," he said. "The emperor. It was when he wanted to buy the Sleeping Dog. I know how he thinks. About the cards, I mean."

Axio frowned. "Go on."

"He'd never just swap ending the war for a pack of cards," Musen said, "not even the pack he wants most of all, in the whole world. He wouldn't do that, not if he knew they were safe somewhere, and you all know it. But if you went to him and showed him one card, and told him, if Rasch falls, you'll destroy the rest of the pack—" He paused and looked at Axio, who looked away. "I think he'd go for that, but I can't be sure. And if he said no, you'd send him the cards, cut and mangled, one by one, until he gives in or they're all spoiled. And I couldn't let you do that."

Axio sat quite still for a moment. Then he turned and met Musen's eye. "You're a bright boy," he said. "I keep telling everyone, but they all think you're stupid, just because you're from Rhus and you act like a fool." He sighed. "I'm sorry," he said. "I've got my orders. And you know you can't beat me."

"No," Musen said. "But I can keep trying till Rasch falls and the cards are safe." He shrugged. "Or I thought I could."

"Maybe you have." Axio poked the fire with a stick; it was going out, and there was no wood left. "God, I hope not. If all those people die—"

"They'll die anyway," Musen said shrilly. "This time, or the next time, or they'll just starve because there's no more food. But the silver packs, once they're gone, they're gone, for ever." He shook his head. "I knew you wouldn't understand."

"Oh, I understand," Axio said sharply. "I've seen it, the Sleeping Dog, the pack we sold to build Central. I was so angry—"

He took a deep breath, then went on. "You know what? If I'd been a bit braver, a bit less of a chickenshit, I'd have stolen the Sleeping Dog myself, so they couldn't sell it. I planned it all out. I had a plan, it would probably have worked, but I couldn't be sure, and I lost my nerve, and now it's gone. Probably I'll never see it again. Oh, I understand all right. But building Central was a stupid reason, it was just *vanity*, it was obscene. I had to make a choice, Rasch or—" He looked up, and Musen saw his eyes were wet. "You know what?" he said. "It could so easily be me with the busted hand and the busted rib. I understand you: that's why you're still alive." Then, quite suddenly, he laughed. "My idiot brother," he said. "He's got a saying. There's always three reasons: the good reason, the plausible reason and the real one. And they're all true. Oh, screw this for a game of knucklebones, now you've made me quote my brother, and that always riles me. You can't have it, Musen, I'm sorry, but that's final. Do you get that? *Capisce?*"

Musen slowly let go the breath he'd been holding. "Actually," he said, "that can't be your brother. It's Saloninus."

Axio stared at him. "You what?"

"That thing you said. It's from Saloninus. You know, the great writer, hundreds of years ago. They taught us that at Beal Defoir."

"They'll want to send you to Choris," Axio said. "After all, you've met the man: it'd make sense."

Riding hurt. Every movement the horse made twisted the broken rib and stretched the bruised one, and the pressure of the stirrup iron on the ball of his foot made his crushed toes ache. "They'd send a diplomat, surely. I mean, you'd need somebody trained, who could do all that."

"Indeed." Axio grinned at him. "Like me."

"You."

"Yes, as a matter of fact, like me. I'm perfect for the job, I'm used to dealing with the nobs and I've got a great deal of relevant experience in extortion. Actually, I'm something like his fourth cousin four times removed. I wouldn't be surprised if he knew that. He's a terror for stockpiling useless information, my cousin Glauca."

"They can't make me go, can they?"

It was starting to spit with rain. Axio pulled his collar up round his neck. "Well, they can't make you do anything, strictly speaking. But they can give you a direct order, and if you don't obey, you'll be excommunicated. So, in your terms, yes they can. Which is awkward, right?"

Musen took a deep breath, in spite of the pain. "Maybe you should tell them."

"Are you mad? No, that's got to be our little secret. Bloody awkward, really. I mean, you're the best man for the job and the worst possible man for the job, both at the same time." He grinned. "Test for you. What logical form does this situation represent?"

"Paradox," Musen said.

"Correct, five marks. What else did they teach you at Beal, apart from logic?"

"Oh, loads of stuff. Theology, doctrine and moral philosophy. I liked the theology."

Axio frowned. "Yes, I imagine you did. Personally, I found it got in the way. It sort of tests your faith when you realise just how much rubbish your fellow believers are capable of believing. But I survived, which is all that matters. Did they make you read Saloninus?"

"I went to the lectures."

Axio laughed. "Quite," he said. "Me, too, actually, I'm not a great reader, unlike my dear brother. Always had his nose stuck in a book, when we were kids. No, I got through the exams by sticking to the Method, and it never let me down."

"The what?"

"The Method," Axio replied. "Don't you—? Oh well. Its

proper name is scholarship by intuitive revelation, and let me tell you, it really works. What you do is, you spend the whole term not reading the set texts and going out drinking instead, and then, the night before the exam, you sit up with the books and open them at random, and allow Him to guide you to the bits that are going to come up next day. You have to have faith, of course, but I did, so it worked a charm. I came third in my year, out of two hundred and forty. It's just simple logic, really. If He wants you to serve Him, He can be relied on to see to the formalities."

Musen smiled. "I wish I'd known," he said. "I got a blistered finger, reading all that stuff." He shifted the reins into his damaged hand, just for a moment, while he flexed the other one to ease the cramp. "If I have to go to Choris, will you come too? Promise?"

"Promise," Axio replied. "I think I'll have to. After all, you're now my fault, God help me." He wiped rain out of his eyes. "Don't worry, I'll see you through. I have so far, haven't I?"

Musen didn't answer that. "Will it be just us two, do you think? Or will they send someone else as well?"

"Well now, that depends," Axio said. "Which would you rather?"

Musen didn't answer that either.

They rode for three days. Musen's ribs ached and he heard a lot about Axio's brother, not all of which he believed. At one point, after a long, rambling anecdote that didn't seem to have a point to it, Musen said, "I can see why you hate him so much." Axio seemed shocked.

"I don't hate him; he's my brother. Whatever gave you that idea?"

"But you said— I mean, you keep going on about what's wrong with him. Surely that means—"

"God, no." Axio shook his head, just in case there was any doubt. "Just because he's hopeless and a mess, I don't *hate* him. If

I went around hating people just because they're not perfect, I'd loathe the whole human race and die of bile."

Musen thought about that. "So his good points outweigh his bad points."

"He hasn't got any good points. No, I'm being unfair; he can whistle quite well. And he's punctual. What you're doing is confusing not liking very much with hating. I don't like my brother, but I don't hate him. I don't go around thinking, the world will never be whole again until Oida is dead. But if he was sick and someone had to ride ten days each way across the desert to get medicine, I'd be off like a shot. He's my brother, after all. That's special. Never stopped me kicking his arse every chance I got, of course."

"But you hate that he's rich and famous, don't you?"

Axio nodded. "But only because it's so bad for him. My fault, I guess, for being born first. If he'd been the eldest he'd have stayed home, learned to manage the estates, organise haymaking and the harvest and the sheep-shearing: he'd have been good at that. He likes people, gets on well with them; he'd have been good with the tenants and kind to servants. But instead he had to go off and make something of himself. Bricks without straw, in his case. And I blame myself for not bringing him up right. Still, there you go. You any good with a slingshot?"

"Me? No, not really. What's that got to do with—?"

Axio nodded. "Then I'm guessing that you were hitching a ride with the two women and the deserters attacked you. That's right, isn't it?"

Musen had to wait a moment before he could answer. "Yes, that's right."

"Thought so." Axio took something from his sleeve. It was a lead sling-bolt, about the size of a wild plum. "It's got the Tinzain arsenal stamp on it," he said. "Western military-issue. Of course, there must be millions of the things floating about, thanks to

Ocnisant and his pals." He put it back in his sleeve. "I didn't think you'd be capable of cold-blooded murder."

"I killed the old man. And the two boys."

"Yes, I know. But that was fighting: even the best of us tends to get a bit carried away. I was fairly sure you didn't kill the women or I wouldn't have mentioned it."

The next day they reached the crossroads. There was a way station there. It looked deserted, but when they got close they saw a single horse tethered to a broken-down rail. For some reason that made Axio grin.

"Keep your face shut and leave the talking to me," he said. "I think our luck may just have turned."

Inside the station house someone had lit a fire; unfortunate, since the chimney was obviously blocked. A man was sitting beside the hearth, wrapped in several blankets. He peered up out of them at Axio and scowled. "Oh," he said, "it's you. Where the hell—?"

"Sorry," Axio sang out merrily. "We got held up, this and that, you know how it is. Anyway, we're here now. Musen, this is Corason. He and I go way back."

"Half of bloody Central's out looking for you," Corason grumbled. "For crying out loud shut the door; you're letting the cold air in."

Axio coughed loudly, then sat down beside him. Musen looked round, saw a stool and took it as far away from the smoke as he could go. "Did you get it?"

"Of course we did," Axio said. "It's right here, in my pocket. What's the news?"

"Last I heard." Corason paused, and gave Axio a nasty look, which he ignored. "Last I heard, Rasch was still holding out. Senza's just sat there, and nobody can figure out why. Nor have there been any significant troop movements in the east. They're all just staying where they are, like they're waiting for something.

So, as far as I know, the plan's still on. Which is just as well. How can it take two grown men all this time just to ride a few miles along a road?"

"Musen's not been well," Axio said. "It slowed us up."

"It takes both of you to carry one small box." Corason shrugged. "Well, you're here now. Obviously, time is now of the essence. You two are to proceed directly to Choris, best speed possible, and do the deal." He scowled some more. "I have to say, you weren't the first choice for this mission. You'll just have to do the best you can."

"Of course," Axio said. "Are you coming with us?"

"What do you think?" Corason said bitterly. "And you know how I feel about travel. Still, there's got to be two of us to dispose of Lodge property or it's not valid." He stopped, made a gasping noise and sneezed. "Right, then," he went on. "You'd better give it to me."

Musen felt his heart stop, but Axio said quickly, "No, I think I'll hang on to it, if that's all right."

"It's not all right," Corason said. "I've got seniority, you know that."

"Quite true." Axio sounded himself again. "But you're a bloody awful swimmer. Well, aren't you?"

"So?"

"So," Axio said, "I heard on the way up that the Green River's in flood and all the bridges are down, right out as far as the Great West. Therefore there's a good chance we're going to have to take our shoes and socks off and paddle. And you're a shit swimmer and I'm not."

"Bloody hell." Corason sounded deeply unhappy. "Can't we go east and round?"

"Of course we can, and it'd only add a week."

"Hell. In that case, you're right: you'd better hang on to the bloody thing."

"Broad as it's long," Axio said. "Of course, you'll do all the talking when we get there."

"You bet I will," Corason assured him. "After last time."

The road south wasn't military specification, but it had at some point been made up with a mixture of crushed sandstone and field flints. Corason led the way, buried in a huge riding coat with a fur collar, and a military pillbox fur hat with earflaps. Musen trailed behind; after a while, Axio dropped back to join him.

"Who is this prick?" Musen asked.

Axio smiled. "It's amazing how few people like him on first acquaintance," he said. "Actually, he's one of my oldest friends. It's all right," he added. "Nobody else likes him, and I have to try really hard."

"Yes," Musen said, "but who is he?"

"One of the ten High Commissioners for Ways and Means," Axio said gravely. "Which makes him a very important man indeed in the Lodge, and don't forget it. That's why we have to have him along. The Lodge can't part with a valuable or significant asset unless two commissioners are present to witness and approve the transfer."

Musen knew about the High Commissioners; he looked at Axio but said nothing.

"I know," Axio said, "it's a pain in the bum, but what can you do? Please don't get any ideas; and *please* don't let's have any more of the nonsense, because Corason isn't an old sweetheart like me, so either I'd have to kill you, or him. And, like I said, he's an old friend. I'd hate to lose him."

Musen thought about that for a moment. "You never said you're a commissioner."

"You didn't ask." Axio wiped rain off his forehead. "Corason isn't so bad once you get to know him. He's always worse when he's feeling the cold. Unfortunately for ordinary mortals like us, he feels the cold at any temperature lower than the melting point of copper."

Musen's lip twitched. "I bet he hates it at Mere Barton."

"Oh, he does. In fact, there's a theory going the rounds that that's why they chose it as the site for Central. Not the main reason, of course."

"The good reason?"

"One of the three. It helped sway my vote, I have to confess."

Whenever they stopped where there were people, Axio or Corason seemed to know somebody to ask; the reply was always the same. Nothing had happened. Senza was still sitting under the walls of Rasch. Nothing was going in or out, but he seemed to be making no effort to prosecute the siege; no mining operations, no diverting of watercourses, no bombardment. Neither were the Western forces making any attempt to relieve the city, or even to gather a force large enough to stand a chance of doing so. In fact, it was almost as if the war had come to an end; the refugees on the outer edges of Senza's wake were starting to creep back to their homes, in some cases bringing their flocks and herds with them, and a few brave souls were out in the fields, ploughing for the spring wheat. There had been something of a washing of the spears at the Imperial court at Iden Astea, following some undisclosed lapse in security; various well-known heads were rotting quietly on spikes outside the main gate and there were new men in charge of the guards and the city patrols. Also, the garrison had nearly doubled, and they were building a wall all round the lake, a monstrous undertaking which the military regarded as pointless and the local civilians had to pay for.

"Can either of you two remember who Beloisa belongs to these days?" Corason called back, as they climbed over a ridge and saw the sea. "Last I heard it was the West, but I may have missed something."

"I haven't heard anything since Senza burned it out and sabotaged the mine workings," Axio replied, unwinding his scarf and stuffing it in his pocket. The sun was out for the first time in days. "I sort of gathered it was a ruin and nobody wanted it."

"There's ships in the bay," Corason pointed out.

Axio shook his head. "Could be pirates."

"Then we're in luck," Corason said. "Probably friends of yours."

Musen stood up in his stirrups to look, but couldn't see anything. "It's possible," Axio said. "Though I'm a bit out of touch. Still, it's worth a try." He nudged his horse into a brisk canter, as Corason yelled after him, "I was joking."

Musen started to follow; Corason reached out and grabbed his bridle. "Just a moment," he said. "I want to talk to you."

"All right."

Corason pushed back his hood. "About Axio," he said. "I've known him a long time. That." He levelled his riding crop at Musen's ribs. "He do that to you?"

"No."

"No," Corason said, "and I don't suppose he crushed your hand, either." He let go of the reins. "My old mother had a cat," he went on. "Vicious bloody thing, scratch half your face off soon as look at you. It used to sink its teeth in my hand and not let go, I could lift it off the ground and it'd hang by its teeth. I told her, that thing's got to go; it's evil. And do you know what she told me? She said, it means she likes you. It's her way of showing affection." He sniffed, then stifled a sneeze. "You wouldn't be the first tall, muscular young man Axio's taken a liking to. They tend to come to a bad end, I have to say; mostly alone, in a room bolted on the inside. We don't say suicide, because suicide is a mortal sin, but there's been some really freaky accidents over the years." He wiped his nose on his wrist. "The other nasty thing my mother's cat did, it played with mice. Got really upset when they broke and stopped working, and she had to get off her fat arse and catch another one."

Musen looked at him. "He thinks you're his friend."

"I am." Corason smiled. "No angel myself, as it happens. It's as much for his sake as yours. A true friend helps you stay out of trouble. Watch yourself, that's all." Then he gave his horse a savage kick and followed down over the hill.

Yes, they were pirates, and, yes, Axio knew them; or at least they knew Axio, and welcomed him with open arms. It turned out he'd done a favour for a son-in-law's uncle at some point in his career, which was the sort of thing they took very seriously. A trip across the bay? No problem. No payment required. They were going that way anyhow.

Musen rather liked the pirates. They reminded him of home – not necessarily a good thing; but there was a sort of naïve cheerfulness in the way they did their work, everyone knowing exactly what he had to do without being told, everyone an expert in his own limited field of endeavour, that put him in mind of days and nights with the shepherds on the high summer pastures. They were mostly young, invariably cheerful and friendly, not sullen or scornful around strangers like so many people, and the way they left their personal possessions lying about suggested a strong feeling of community and mutual trust. Under other circumstances he'd have seriously considered asking if he could join them, and it was a pity they cut throats for a living.

Their ship was smaller than the one he'd been on the first time he crossed from Beloisa, but it wasn't nearly so crowded, and it didn't wallow about in the same horrible, terrifying way. He spent the first day cautiously sitting still, but after that he had no trouble at all. Unlike the sailors on the other ship, the pirates seemed capable of working round him as he walked about, so he wasn't forever conscious of being under people's feet. Corason spent most of his time huddled in his blankets in the galley, where there was a small charcoal stove, and Axio and the captain were apparently inseparable; Musen realised how much he'd missed being on his own and made the most of it. Nice to have friendly people around him, of course, but nice also that they kept it down to a smile and a wave as they got on with their work. He didn't think any of them were craftsmen, though he made no effort to find out. But one of them had a pack of cards, the ordinary lime-board sort with brightly coloured pictures. Musen put it back where he'd found it, identified the owner and offered him forty stuivers for it, so that he could use it openly rather than have to hide away in the scuppers with the rats.

"You tell fortunes, then?" one of the pirates asked him, as he sat turning the cards over one day.

"I can do," Musen replied.

The pirate was one of the older men, in his mid-thirties, a short, lean man with long white-blond hair in braids. "How much?"

"No charge," Musen said. "When are you off duty?"

The pirate sat down beside him. "Now's as good a time as any," he said. "Sure you don't want paying?"

"I don't really hold with using the cards to make money," Musen said. "It's like pimping for your sister."

The pirate thought that was hilarious. "Never had to bother," he said: "my sister's got a much better head for business than me. Right, what do we do?"

Musen collected up the cards, shuffled them quickly, handed them to the pirate and told him to shuffle them again. "Now lay out nine cards face down," he said, "going from right to left."

"I thought they were meant to be face up."

"Not the way I do it," Musen said gravely. "There's all sorts of different ways you can do it, but this is the only one that works. Now, starting from the left, turn them face up."

Poverty. Four of Spears. Four of Stars, reversed. The Thief, reversed. Musen shivered. The Scholar. Nine of Wheels. Hope, reversed. The Angel, reversed. The Cherry Tree.

"It's like this," Musen said, and his mouth was dry. "You're going to have six months of sheer misery and lose everything, and then you're going to die. Sorry."

The pirate was staring at him. Musen forced a grin. "Only kidding," he said. "Right, Poverty. Poverty doesn't actually mean poverty, it means a change in your fortunes. Four of Spears is someone you're going to meet, or someone you know already who's going to make a difference to you. In this case, he's a sort of big, noisy know-it-all who'll probably make trouble for you, but the card's not reversed so it'll be fine. Four of Stars is another man you'll have dealings with; he's a tricky one, a good friend and a bad enemy; again, not reversed, so it'll be all right. The Thief means you're going to do something clever; reversed means it'll be bad news, but not necessarily for you. The Scholar, that generally means money, nice things, good stuff generally. Nine of Wheels—" He paused. He was running out of ways of twisting the meanings while still not actually lying.

"That's another important bloke I meet, right?"

"You're getting the hang of this," Musen said. "Nine of Wheels is someone really important – at least, important to you. Could be the captain of this ship, could be the emperor, could be the girl you fall in love with. Actually, following on from the Scholar, it could well be something like that."

The pirate was frowning. "The next one's upside down. That means it's bad, right."

"Not always. It just means the opposite of what it means when it's the right way up. Now Hope's another tricky one, it can be the good news that keeps you going when you're right down, or it could be the crazy notion that gets you in all sorts of trouble. Reversed – I really couldn't say, until a bit more of this stuff's actually happened. Sorry to be vague, but there it is. Now, the Angel reversed, that can actually be quite good. Like, if I was reading for you and you were in the condemned cell, the Angel reversed would mean you'd get a reprieve at the last minute."

"Well, that's a comfort," the pirate said, frowning. "How about the last one? At least it's the right way up."

"Oh, that." Musen shrugged. "That means the end of the world."

The pirate didn't like that. "Oh, marvellous."

Musen laughed, and it came out sounding convincing. "Well, that can mean all sorts of things. In your line of work, it could mean a long journey – that's what the card stands for; there's supposed to be a cherry tree growing at the very edge of the world, and when you see it, it means you can't go any further. Or it could mean the end of your old life and a new one about to start; like if you got married, or suddenly came into money."

"Or it could mean I'm going to die."

"Yes, it could. Or someone else is going to die, possibly your worst enemy. Or it could mean the end of the war." He gathered the cards up in a fast, slick movement and put them back on top of the pack. "You've got to take all the cards together," he said. "And I'd say, that's a pretty good spread."

The pirate looked at him. "You would?"

"Oh, yes." Musen nodded confidently. "I can't be definite about details, mind, but broadly speaking, I'd guess it's something like, you get one or maybe two new crew members, you have a big score, you all decide to break up the crew and retire, there's a bit of aggravation about dividing up the money but it comes out all right in the end, and you go off with a nice stake and maybe just possibly the girl of your dreams. But that last bit's just a guess," he added with a grin. "I'm not guaranteeing that."

The pirate looked as though the noose had just been lifted off his neck and he'd been told it was all an unfortunate mix-up. "I'll settle for that, thanks very much. If I get the money, I don't suppose the girl'll be a problem. Thanks."

"Don't mention it," Musen said, tucking the pack away. "Only, do me a favour, will you? Don't go telling everyone I do fortunes. I don't mind occasionally, but—"

"Sure." The pirate looked puzzled, but smiled. "You don't want the whole crew hassling you for readings all the time, I can see that. Hope I didn't—"

"No, that's fine," Musen said brightly, hoping the man would go away; which he did, which was just as well. Once he'd gone, Musen took the pack out again and put it down in front of him on the deck. Served him right, he told himself, for telling fortunes. You ask a question, you're at grave risk of getting an answer, and if you do, you've got nobody to blame but yourself.

He shuffled the pack, to clear it, then went through picking out the picture cards, which he then put in order, starting with the Crown Prince and ending with the Cherry Tree. Then he went through the homily of the City, starting with the prince in exile, ending with the avenging armies seeing the tree that marked the end of the world and turning back. He wasn't sure it was the right homily for the circumstances; it reminded him of the war (there was a homily for that, too, but they didn't teach it at Beal Defoir; you had to have a lot of seniority to learn it, and he'd even heard that it needed the special pack, with the extra cards) and he wanted to forget about that, because of Rasch Cuiber and the silver pack that was less than thirty yards away from him, and which he was having to try very hard not to think about, all the time. So he shuffled and sorted the pack again, and started over with the Faithful Son ("Once there was a merchant's son who was sent on a long journey . . . "); first with the cards orthodox, for the happy story, and then with them reversed, for the sad one. Then he shuffled the picture cards and cut, which got him the Angel; so he laid them out again and told the stories, orthodox and reversed, from the Angel's point of view, reflecting at each stage on what he would have done in her position, and what that told him about himself. Then he laid them out in order descending, starting with the Cherry Tree and ending with the Crown Prince, and said the homily of the Leper, orthodox; at the end of the world there grows a magic cherry tree, and all who touch its leaves are cured of their diseases. He got as far as the Thief; and then the cook rang the galley bell, and it was time for lunch.

For some reason, the pirates didn't want to bring their ship into the main harbour and tie up among the naval galleys and the revenue sloops, so they dropped anchor off a secluded cove, in the middle of the night, and rowed them ashore in a little boat. It struck Musen as a ludicrously dangerous enterprise, but apparently the pirates had had a certain degree of practice.

"You'll have to hoof it into town from here," said the pirate captain, who'd come along to wish Axio Godspeed. "Just climb up to the top and follow your nose across the downs till you get there. The inn's called the Diligence: just keep kicking the door till they answer. Say I sent you; they'll see you right."

Needless to say they did no such thing, but the innkeeper saw them right anyway, as soon as Corason flashed a handful of silver fifty stuivers under his nose. Nothing was too much trouble, apparently, not even for strangers who walked in over the fields in the dead of night.

In the morning, Corason asked if he could buy three horses. The innkeeper didn't laugh, because that would've been rude; instead, he hazarded a guess that they might just possibly find something at the Wheel Star, where from time to time they sold off pit ponies that were too old and feeble to pull a cart; but that was thirty miles away in the other direction, so maybe the gentlemen might prefer to wait for the stage.

While Corason conducted the negotiations, Axio had wandered off; he came back with the news that there were four very fine geldings in the stable – remounts for the Imperial couriers, in all probability, but the emperor already had far more horses than was good for him, as witness the appalling mischief Senza was getting up to with all that cavalry, whereas three good horses and a fourth to carry a few supplies would get them to Choris quickly and in relative comfort. "Now if only," Axio said, looking straight past Musen as if he wasn't there, "we knew a good horse thief—"

Musen was rather inclined to resent being given the job, since stealing horses doesn't call for a skilled and talented thief, just a dishonest groom. Walk across the yard, look round to see nobody's watching, go inside, saddles and bridles, lead the horses out into the yard and ride like hell; where's the technique or the finesse in that?

At least once they'd got clean away there was no danger of being pursued; not when they'd stolen the only four horses in the county.

They had to get rid of them, of course, before they reached the main road, where horses with the Imperial brand but ridden by obvious civilians might excite comment. They tied them to a rail outside a farmhouse, then trudged up a long hill to the road, four miles shy of a way station, where they caught the stage. But they'd cut off forty miles and saved a day and a half. The stage was due into the suburbs of Choris by nightfall. The journey was nearly over.

"Of course, you've been here before," Corason said as they stood in the queue for the checkpoint outside the South Gate. "I keep forgetting that. For Axio and me, of course, this is practically home from home. I suggest we spend this morning catching up on the news, meet up again at midday and decide on what we're going to do. Axio?"

"Fine," Axio replied. He seemed preoccupied. "The usual place?"

"If it's still there," Corason said. "It's been five years since I was in Choris. If not, I'll see you outside the Prefecture. That'll still be there, you can be sure."

The news was, there was no news. Senza was still languidly besieging Rasch, the Western army was still lurking in funk holes, nobody knew what was going on and everybody had a theory. Musen and Axio heard this about a dozen times in various different tea houses, taverns and barbers' shops, then headed into town to find Corason.

Musen was disconcerted, to say the least, when he saw the sign over the tea-house door.

"What, the Cherry Tree? Been here for ever." Axio sat down at a table in front of the main door and put his feet up on an empty chair. "Everyone who comes to Choris has to visit this place, it's the law." He yawned. "Can't say I see much to it myself, but I like a bit more atmosphere, if you know what I mean."

The sign was a painting, in rather fine style, though the paint was beginning to flake. Musen thought it was almost obscene, that particular picture, the size of a gate, stuck up in the air for everyone to see. A bored looking girl in a long yellow silk gown brought them tea and a plate of honeycakes. They were ever so slightly stale.

"I've found us a clerk," Corason said, "in the Chamberlain's office. He'll get us in to see the Grand Domestic of the Wardrobe, who I know for a fact is a craftsman, and he'll arrange for a message to go in through either the barber or the food taster, I don't know which, who's also Lodge. By this time tomorrow, we'll have our audience with His Nibs."

"Why don't I just go and see him?" Musen said. "He told me himself, if I ever heard anything about another silver pack—"

"Bless the child," Corason said. "Listen, you wouldn't get ten yards. We've only got this incredibly straight line right through Imperial protocol as the result of years and years of slow, careful infiltration. The whole majestic bulk of the Imperial civil service serves one overriding imperative: stopping people from getting to see the emperor."

"But they can't just turn me away. The emperor said—"

"They can do what they like so long as the emperor never finds out. And how does he find out about things? They tell him." Axio smiled. "You can play a sort of game," he said. "It's called breaking into the palace. If you can sneak past the guards, you reach the emperor and he agrees to speak to you. If the guards catch you, they kill you and bury your body in a dungheap, and nobody ever knows what became of you. Or we can do it Corason's way."

"I broke in once."

"Yes, you did, and it was one of the best-planned operations in the history of Division," Corason said irritably. "To get you there, so the emperor could believe he'd caught you. And the trouble is, we used up so many one-time-only resources on that job that now we've got hardly anything left. So we do it my way."

"Fine," Musen said. "I'm not bothered."

The tea was stone-cold. Axio had asked for some more, but that was a long time ago. Musen liked cold tea, so that was all right. "My brother really likes this place," Axio said. "Well, he would. Apparently they keep a table empty all the time, just in case he should happen to drop in."

Axio, Musen knew, was a light sleeper. Just for once, however, he'd hung his coat on the back of the chair next to his bed. Musen knelt beside it and let his fingertips drift up the cloth until they encountered the flap of the pocket. He prised the pocket apart with his thumb and little finger, then slipped his hand down inside, until his fingertips came up against something straight and square. He let them follow the line; and then there was a click, and blinding pain—

"Well done for not screaming," Axio said. "It's a small mechanical device for catching rats. One hell of a spring on it."

Musen dragged his hand out, catching it on the edge of the pocket. The thing was still crushing his fingernails; he couldn't think while all that was going on.

"Here, let me." Axio was beside him, grabbing his wrist; then the pressure stopped, though the pain continued. "Your left hand," he said. "Oh, well. You'll probably lose two of those nails, when the quicks swell up."

Musen tried to back away, stumbled and banged against a wall. He knew his chances of getting away were draining fast, but the pain had taken all his strength. He could feel tears running down his cheeks, and something else running down the inside of his leg.

A familiar whirring noise, and a flare of light that grew steadily. He turned his head and saw Axio, in his shirt, trimming the lamp. "Corason's got it," Axio said without looking round. "I gave it to him earlier. The rat-catching thing cost me fifty stuivers, by the way. It's the very latest thing in vermin control."

On the other side of the bed was a small square single-leg table and on it was a pack of cards, a tall brown pottery jug and two tiny porcelain bowls. Smashed, one of those bowls would have an edge like a razor. But you'd need to be able to use your hands.

Axio got up, walked to the door and turned a key in the lock. Then he crossed to the window and threw the key out. "Bear in mind we're three floors up," he said. "I asked for the attics specially. I can pick that lock, but you can't, not with your hands like that." He sighed. "It's a shame. I could really have done with a good night's sleep. But I suppose that's out of the question."

Axio lifted the pillow; under it was another rat-trap. He prodded the back end of it gingerly until the spring triggered and the bar came down with a snap that made Musen's heart stop for a moment. A surge of pain swept up his arm into his chest. "I got a good deal on half a dozen," Axio said. "The other four are in Corason's room. I told him it was just in case. Apparently there's been a lot of thieving in this district lately. I hope he remembers where I set them."

Musen looked at him. "What are you going to do?"

"I thought we might play cards," Axio replied, pulling out the chair and lifting it over the bed. "There's a stool over there in the corner: you can sit on that."

A sudden wild thought crossed Musen's mind; but the cards on the table were just cards, a conventional cheap lime-board pack. His pack, in fact. He patted his coat pocket with his right hand: empty.

"Have a drink," Axio said. "It's pretty foul stuff, but it might help with the pain. It won't stop it hurting, but after a bit you just won't care."

Musen shook his head. Axio shrugged and filled one bowl from the jug. "Been a change of plan," he said. "Corason sent up one card – Four of Spears, I think it was – for the old man to look at. I gather he damn near wet himself. But he's learned some sense, by the look of it. He'll see just one of us, alone, at dawn, up in his tower. Corason pulled rank, so he's it. You and I just wait here till he gets back. Or until the kettlehats come and march us off to the dungeons; we'll just have to wait and see."

Musen looked at him. "You mean, he's going to see the emperor alone, and he's taken them with him?"

Axio laughed. "Oh, come on," he said. "He's not that stupid. Well, actually he is, but I'm not. I told you, we've got someone inside – the food taster, turns out he's a very big fish indeed, though of course I've never heard of him. Anyway, he'll hold on to it for us while Corason's in with the old man. Even if all three of us are arrested and he beats it out of one of us, the food taster won't let him have it." He paused. "I'm sorry," he said. "But it's not up to me. Come on, let's play cards."

Musen stayed where he was. Axio sat down, shuffled the pack and started to deal. "Think about it," he said. "By the time your hands have healed up, the emperor will have the pack. He'll keep it safe, and you'll know exactly where it is. If you choose to take a month's leave and come back here, that's entirely your own business. I'd strongly advise you not to, of course, but I promise faithfully I won't try and stop you."

Musen got up. His knees were weak and the pain was still very bad. He sat down on the stool.

"I've taken the liberty of dealing," Axio said, "for obvious reasons. Can you cut for trumps? Or shall I do it for you?"

Musen tried, but even with his right hand he couldn't. Axio took the pack from him. "Spears it is," he said, and picked up his cards. "Oh, God in heaven, what a load of old rubbish."

Musen pulled his cards down into his lap and spread them out as best he could with the sides and heels of his hands. He'd drawn four high Wheels and the rest were picture cards. "I haven't got any money."

"Not true, as it happens." Axio dumped a handful of coins on the table. "That's yours," he said. "I figured you wouldn't get far with no money." He grinned. "I've learned a lot from watching you," he said. "Which is fair enough. I taught you to pick locks."

Musen looked at him, then swept the coins over to his side of the table with the inside of his wrist. Then he glanced down at the cards in his lap. There was no way a hand like that could lose. "I'll bet the lot," he said.

"You sure?"

Musen nodded. Axio dropped a gold angel on to the pile. "Read 'em and weep," he said, and turned over his cards. All pictures; the highest, counting back from the Cherry Tree. He gathered the money and swept it to his side of the table. "Nominally your deal, but I'll do it for you. Now, since you're broke, we'll have to think of something else you can bet with."

"I haven't got anything else."

"Don't you believe it. For a start, you've got all those teeth. I'll be generous, twenty stuivers against each tooth. And after that we can play for fingers."

Musen thought about the window. He'd break his neck. "Corason told me you like hurting people," he said.

"Did he now?" Axio frowned. "That's a gross oversimplification, as he well knows. I like doing things – to people, for people – that sometimes involve pain. But pain isn't the reason. It's *involved*, but it's not the reason." He leaned back in his chair. "We don't have to play cards," he said. "I just thought it'd help pass the time, that's all." He gathered the pack and put it in his pocket, then did the same with the money. "Did Corason tell you about the time he was a junior captain commanding a half-squadron of light cavalry, and orders came down to intercept an enemy raiding party? Turned out when he got there he was outnumbered eight to one, he didn't have a hope in hell. But the enemy took over this village, it was in the marshes somewhere, out back of Bresc; village was on an island, with a palisade all round it, and great big wooden gates, I think about five hundred people lived there. So Corason sent his men out to set fire to the reeds. The village burned down; there was no way off the island; the few that made it past the flames went down in the marshes, soldiers and villagers alike. And Corason didn't see anything wrong with that. He'd been given a job to do, and the orders didn't mention civilians at all, so he left them out of the equation. Of course, the purpose of the exercise was to stop the raiders hurting the local population, but he couldn't see that." He shrugged. "There's doing things that might have certain side effects which aren't pleasant, and there's doing things that utterly defeat the object of the exercise. I'm sure you can see the difference, but I don't think he can." He closed his eyes and folded his hands on his chest. "What I'd really like to do is get a couple of hours' sleep," he said. "Will you promise me you won't do anything annoying if I close my eyes for a bit? Bearing in mind your hands are all bunged up and I'm a light sleeper?"

"I promise."

"Thanks," Axio said, and yawned. "You're a pal." He breathed in deeply and immediately went to sleep.

*

Musen lifted his head. Light was streaming through the window, the door was open and Axio was gone. He started to get up, pressed his hands to the floor to lever himself up, winced and remembered. He looked at his left hand and saw three black, swollen fingernails.

He found Axio outside, on his hands and knees in the gravel of the yard. "Bloody key," Axio explained. "That's my window there, look. Got to find the key and hand it back in, or they won't let me stay here again."

Musen took a step back and trod on something. "Here," he said. "Sorry, I can't pick it up for you."

Axio crawled towards him like a dog, then stopped, just out of kicking range. "Thanks," he said. "I obviously couldn't see for looking." Musen took two long steps back; Axio retrieved the key, stood up and brushed gravel off the knees of his trousers. "I've seen Corason," he said. "It all went off like a charm. One very pissed-off emperor, but Corason said there was never any doubt. He stood over him while he wrote out the orders for Senza, and our man the food taster confirmed they reached the courier." He turned the key over in his hand. "Nothing can catch those boys once they get going," he said, "but just to be on the safe side, Corason told him we've kept back one card." He produced it from his sleeve, like a conjuror; it flashed dazzling white in the morning sun, and then Axio put it away again. "He gets that the day after tomorrow, assuming no further couriers get sent to the Front. Not from us, though, thank God. We're free to go, once I've made the arrangements for this little beauty."

Musen took a deep breath. "Can I see it?" he said. "Just a quick look. Please."

Axio shook his head. "Better not," he said. "Kinder if you don't, if you see what I mean. Right, I'd better hand this key in, and then I've got to meet this man. Corason's out on the stoop if you want company."

Musen watched him go, then followed him back into the tea

house and out on to the covered porch. There he saw Corason sitting alone at a small table, with a teapot and an empty plate.

"There you are," Corason said. "Sleep well?" Then he frowned. He'd caught sight of Musen's left hand. "Been playing rough games, have you?"

"I caught it in a door."

"Of course you did. I thought Axio seemed bright and cheerful this morning, I should've guessed." He nodded at a spare chair; Musen sat down. "He's told you, I take it."

Musen inclined his head.

"Job done," Corason said. "Rasch Cuiber saved from annihilation; everyone breathes again. I watched him write it out; withdraw to the frontier by the shortest possible route, regroup and await further orders. I guess you could say we've won. Well, someone has, anyway." He grinned. "Excuse me if I babble, this is the most amazing weight off my mind. I never thought we'd do it, it was such a bloody stupid idea." He shivered, and pulled his heavy cloak up round his face. "To be honest with you, I never expected to survive this one. When you two showed up in that horrible shack, I said to myself, this is it: this is the end of the line. Ah well." He grinned and sipped his tea. "I've got to hang around here a day or so, then I'm off to make sure Senza's pulled out like he's supposed to." He put the teacup down. "Fancy a trip to Rasch? Two capital cities in one month, can't be bad."

Musen stared at him. "What do you need me for?"

"Absolutely nothing," Corason replied. "But it occurred to me you might like a break from Axio. Particularly since he appears to have taken a shine to you." He waited for a moment or so, then clicked his tongue sharply. "Up to you entirely: you think about it, tell me what you want to do. Otherwise, I imagine, you two'll be heading back to Central. Just you and him. What fun."

Musen stood up and walked away, not looking back.

*

Axio didn't come back to the tea house that morning, or in the afternoon. Corason wasn't worried to begin with – he had various theories about what Axio might be up to – but around mid-afternoon he put on a heavy scarf and a thick hood and went out. He came back after dark, when Musen was eating in the dining room.

"Well," he said, "there's been no couriers at all sent today, which is unusual in itself, but I think we can take that as meaning they haven't got the missing card, at any rate. Nobody's seen him anywhere." He sat down at Musen's table and lowered his voice. "Our man in the kettlehats reckons he'd know if Axio had been brought in, and I believe him. Far as he's aware, they haven't even been looking. The idea was to keep both of you out of it, hence the last-minute change of plan, so there's no reason to suppose they've got either of you linked to me. In which case, whatever's happened to him, it's not because of this business. My guess, based on knowing him most of my life, is that he's either sleeping it off on a trash heap somewhere, or he ran into one of the hundreds of thousands of people who don't like him. Ah well. Life goes on."

Musen looked at him. "What was the bad thing he did?" he asked. "When he was younger, in the army."

"Oh, that." Corason looked down at his hands. "Let's say he tells that story much better than I do, and leave it at that. Neither of us came out of it exactly smelling of roses."

Musen sat up in Axio's room all night, but he didn't come back. Corason looked in just before dawn. "You're here," he said. "No sign, I take it."

"No."

"Mphm. Look, if he's not back by the time I leave, you'd better come with me. All right?"

"Is that an order?"

"Yes, I think so." Corason hesitated, half in and half out of the doorway. "I don't know your file very well, but I gather you steal things. Is that right?"

Musen nodded.

"Well, not while you're with me, you don't. Not unless I tell you to. Got that?"

"Yes."

"Fine." He lifted his hand to his mouth and bit off a hangnail. "I guess I'll be the one who has to write to his damned brother," he said. "It's just one gloriously wonderful thing after another in the Service."

News. A drunk staggered out of a wine shop, tripped over the cobbles, grabbed at Musen's arm, missed, crashed into Corason, flung his arms round his neck to keep from going over, and whispered in his ear that the courier known to be carrying Senza's recall orders had passed through way station 26, paused only to change horses, ridden off at a hell of a lick, no sign of anybody following him.

Corason spent most of the day writing letters, which he stuffed into hollowed-out bones he'd got from a butcher. Musen's job was to dump the bones on the trash heap out back of the Nine Cardinal Virtues, which led to a misunderstanding with an overconscientious dog, during the course of which he damaged his right hand still further climbing a fence in a hurry.

No sign of Axio. Contacts and contacts of contacts in the kettlehats, the Watch, the prefecture and the subsection of the Works Office responsible for pulling dead bodies out of the river all confirmed that nobody answering that description had been seen, dead or alive – and Axio would be hard to miss. Musen clearly remembered thinking, the first time he saw him, that here was the most handsome man he'd ever seen – not particularly tall; strongly built but perfectly proportioned; beautiful hands with long fingers; dark hair just shy of shoulder length; high cheek bones, quite a long face ending in a square chin, straight nose, clean-shaven, clear grey eyes, a strong mouth, that typical smile of mild amusement. True, he'd shown that he had the knack of making himself nondescript, practically invisible, but he only did that when he had to; he plainly enjoyed the slightly stunned look on people's faces when they met him. It was a terrible burden, he used to protest, a real handicap for a man wanted by the authorities in sixty-seven provinces. But it should have made him easy to find, and they hadn't found him.

"I want to stay here," Musen said. "Just in case he comes back. Then I'll catch you up."

Corason burst out laughing. "You, all alone in the big city? Sorry, I don't think so. Anyway, it's not up to you: you're under orders. You'll do as you're told."

"I'm staying here," Musen said. "Just till he turns up again. Sorry."

Corason rolled his eyes. "Another one," he said. "Fine. The only reason I'm going to let you stay is, I'm quite sure he's not coming back – he's dead, or arrested, or defected, or he's been taken up to heaven in a fiery chariot, what-bloody-ever. What are you proposing to do for money, by the way? I can't fund you, I'm short enough for myself as it is."

"I'll manage."

"Yes, well. If you get caught managing, you're not a craftsman and the Lodge has never heard of you, *capisce*? I'll pass the word around before I go."

"I won't get caught," Musen said.

"You realise, this'll have to go in your file. It won't do you any good."

Musen didn't bother to react to that. It broke his heart to disobey the Lodge; but the Lodge had sold the silver pack to Glauca the emperor, and he wasn't sure he could ever forgive something like that.

Choris is the last place on earth where you'd expect it to snow;

but it does happen, very occasionally, when cold winds from the north meet wet winds from the east in the corridor between the mountains. It's fine, powdery, gritty stuff and it never settles, but the locals act as though the sky was hurling down brimstone; the streets are deserted, and the few desperate souls who venture out in it run from doorway to doorway, cocooned in multiple layers of woolly clothing.

"Marvellous," Corason growled, as he lengthened his stirrup leathers. "I'll be riding west in a blizzard. Exactly what I need to make this whole trip perfect."

He was wearing his thick fur hood over a military flowerpot fur hat, and the tip of his nose poked out over his scarf. His fingers were bright red. Musen reached inside his shirt and produced a pair of sheepskin mittens. "I got you these," he said solemnly.

Corason stared at them, then grabbed them and stuffed his hands into them. "God bless you," he said hoarsely. "I went all over town and everywhere said there wasn't a pair to be had." He frowned. "Should I ask if these were honestly come by?"

"No."

"Fine, I won't." He stuck his foot in the stirrup and hoisted himself into the saddle; not an easy thing to do in all those bulky clothes. "Now then," he said, gathering the reins. "Change of plan, as far as you're concerned. Your orders to accompany me to Rasch are cancelled. Instead, I need you to stick around here, keep an eye on the situation, in particular try and find out what you can about the whereabouts of Commissioner Axio. If he shows up, use regular channels to inform Central, and tell him I strongly urge him to return there. Got that?"

"Yes."

"Good lad. I've always said that, given enough patience, Rhus can be trained to carry out simple tasks. Now, since you're here officially, I can authorise a subsistence allowance out of Lodge funds. You'll find it on the bed in my room."

Musen nodded. He'd found it already. Most of it had gone to buy the gloves from the hall porter.

"Your room here's paid up six weeks in advance," Corason went on; "that wasn't a problem, since they take Lodge paper." The horse was getting impatient, tossing its head and backing up. "Listen," Corason said. "If Axio does turn up, you watch yourself, you hear me? And give him my love. All right, you stupid bloody animal, that's quite enough of that. Onwards." He turned the horse's head and gave it a gentle nudge with his heels; it broke into a trot, which Corason tried to sit out; but by the time Musen lost sight of him under the arch, he'd given in and was rising to it, a huge furry shape shrouded in falling snowflakes.

Nine of Wheels

Musen wasn't the only one to see him off. He noticed her out of the corner of his eye as he rode down Victory Row, saw her again as he cleared the city gate, knew she was following him as soon as he turned left and headed up Foregate. Just for a split second he considered turning off and trying to lose her in the tangle of yards and alleys by the Tanneries, but it was quite possible she knew the streets of Choris better than he did. Well, he thought, why not? He managed to confine the stupid horse to a brisk walk and waited for her to catch him up.

"I thought you had people for this sort of thing," he called out, when he was sure she could hear him. "Don't tell me, they've cut your budget again."

He heard a brisk clatter of hooves on the road behind him, and she drew level and pulled aside her veil so that he could see her face. "Commissioner," she said.

He winced. "This isn't what was agreed," he said.

"On the contrary." Her voice was deeper than he'd imagined it would be, but rather pleasant. "We've stuck to the agreement in every particular, and now it's completed."

"Quite. All done and dusted. So why are you following me?"

"To find out where you're going and what you do next."

"Ah." He nudged his horse into a trot. She kept perfect station with him, shoulder to shoulder. He slowed down again. "Surely now I know about you, there's no point."

"Maybe."

It wasn't a good time for him to get one of his headaches, but he could feel it gathering, just behind his eyes. "All right," he said. "I'll tell you where I'm going and what I'm about to do. I'm going to see for myself that Senza Belot's army is pulling out. There, I've saved you a long and uncomfortable ride. In the snow."

"Thank you," she said. "That's what we'd assumed."

They rode on for a while. "You're not turning back, then."

"No."

He sneaked a sideways look at her. It was hard to tell – she was almost as heavily wrapped up as he was – but he got the impression of a severe-looking woman, about his age or maybe a few years older, in an expensive but well-used riding cloak with a dark fur hood that probably wasn't issue; apart from that, he could see the toe of her boot, which was dark and slightly gleaming with sheep's-wool grease. She sat the horse well, back straight, hands low, weight in her heels; not cavalry-style, or the farmer's lolling crouch, or the lazy-centaur look of the government courier or the horse archer. Someone had taught her to ride, and she'd been a good pupil. "You do realise," he said, "you're about as conspicuous as a forest fire. Women just don't go riding about the place on their own, it's unnatural."

"I'm not on my own," she said. "I'm with you."

He sighed. "Who are you?"

"My name's Eufro."

"That's not what I meant."

"Mphm."

He rode on for a while, trying to pretend she wasn't there. Too difficult. "I can only assume," he said, "that the object of the exercise is for me to know I'm being watched."

"Every move you make, yes. Well done."

"And you think that because you're a woman, when we're out in the wild somewhere and I finally lose patience, I won't bash your head in and leave you for the crows. That's so naïve it's rather sweet."

"You can try."

"Ah." He nodded. "A tough girl. A warrior maid, a chick in chain mail. I've read about your sort."

"Have you now?"

"Oh, yes. And I've read even more about dragons, and they don't exist either. Women are rubbish at fighting: they've got more sense. Go home. Before your mother starts worrying about you."

"You'll have to do better than that, I'm afraid."

"Trust me, I've barely started." His head was hurting quite a lot now. "You'll find this hard to credit, but I can be quite obnoxious when I try."

"Do what you like. I'm under orders."

Corason sighed loudly and kicked his horse into a gallop. The road wasn't really suited to it, and he slowed down again before the horse cast a shoe or broke a leg or something equally tiresome. She was, needless to say, still there.

"Of course there's the reasonably well-documented case of the Emperor Hyastes' bodyguard," he said. "Six hundred virgins, trained from birth in the warrior arts, head to toe in shimmering mail like a load of fish. Only I seem to recall that most of them were over fifty and stank like goats, and wasn't Hyastes assassinated in his bath?"

"Before my time, I'm afraid. I dare say you're right."

No luck so far. He kept at it. "Well," he said, "you're a bit on the young side and I can't smell you from here. Virgin?"

"You meet so few attractive men in this line of work."

"From what I gather, Hyastes' amazons weren't all that interested in men. I gather it's good for *esprit de corps*, though there's not enough reliable data to draw any firm conclusions. In any case, I don't need a bodyguard, thanks all the same."

She didn't reply straight away. Then she said, "I gather your Lodge uses women as field agents. Quite highly thought of, some of them. Are you offensive to them, too?"

"Dear God, no." A terrible thought struck him. "You're not—"

"Lodge? No. For what it's worth, I regard your organisation as sinister, disloyal, parasitical and a threat to Imperial security. I think you hide a rather unpleasant political agenda behind a smokescreen of superstition and garbage-grade mysticism, and if I had my way you'd be rooted out and dealt with once and for all. But that's just my personal opinion, which does not necessarily reflect the views of my superiors."

"Ah," Corason said. "I'm glad we got that straight." He turned and looked at her. "What are you doing here? Real reason."

She smiled at him. It wasn't meant to be friendly. "Would you believe me if I told you I had pressing business somewhere between here and Rasch Cuiber, and a woman riding on her own wouldn't be safe and would attract too much attention? Like those little fish who hitch rides on sharks."

"Surely you've got people for that."

"Nobody was available. This is an elegant use of opportunity. An eye is kept on you, and I get to where I need to be."

"Plausible," Corason admitted. "Tell me, was I right about the chain mail? What *have* you got on under that cloak?"

She gave him a very slight frown. "If you must know, I'm a political officer attached to the Directorate of Archives and Observances; which is, as I assume you know, one of the few branches of the Service that employs women. I'm a widow, my husband died in the war, and I have a nine-year-old son who lives with my mother-in-law. Nominally, I'm a deaconess in holy orders, which is why I'm allowed out on my own, and it means I can earn money in my own right, instead of it being paid to my nearest male relative. If needs be, I'm under orders to cross the border into hostile territory, which is another reason for tagging along with a man, particularly one with a safe conduct order personally signed by the emperor. I'm assuming you've got similar papers for the West. Now, will that do you, or are you going to carry on acting like a pig all the way to Rasch?"

Corason was quiet for a long time. Then he said, "So it's true. They really are ordaining women in the East."

She nodded. "Not enough men, because of the war. I take it you don't approve."

"Whatever gives you that idea?" He pushed back his hood and loosened the scarf a little; he was starting to feel uncomfortably warm. "Is your name really Eufro?"

"Actually it's Eudaemonia Frontizoriastes, I'm Aelian. I don't like being called by a shortening, it makes me feel like I'm somebody's pet. But I'm a realist."

"I've never met an Aelian before," Corason said. "What brings you all the way up here?"

"Bad luck," Eufro replied. "Where are you from?"

"Leuctria. Down past Blemya, turn left, keep going until you get your feet wet."

"No wonder you feel the cold."

"Tell me about it. I haven't been really warm since I was seven."

She nodded gravely. "If you don't mind my asking," she said. "You're a known associate of Axio Scephantis, the highwayman and armed robber. Does that explain your antipathy to women?"

Ouch. "I have no antipathy to women," Corason said. "Just political officers."

She grinned. "Me, too. A complete waste of space, most of them. There now: we do have something in common, after all."

But Corason wasn't ready to declare peace quite yet, even though he had a feeling he was outnumbered and surrounded. "You ride very well," he said, "for a clerk."

"My father taught me. Women hunt in Aelia, and they ride in the horse races. And we beat off the empire when they tried to invade us. And we grow the best apples anywhere. Who was the boy?"

"Excuse me?"

"The tall Rhus boy you had with you. You know, the sneak-thief. Some sort of lackey, or Axio's packed lunch?"

Corason breathed out through his nose. "Let me guess," he said. "Archives and Observances is where you hide your spies."

"The civil side," she said. "Military intelligence is separate."

"But you're genuinely a deaconess?"

"Genuinely. I can say a prayer for you, if you like."

Well. It's always nice to have company, as the man said when he discovered he had fleas. It was nice to have someone to talk to on the road, someone he didn't have to be polite to, someone who understood the references; someone he could be as rude as he liked to, a rare indulgence. If she really was wearing chain mail, she had exceptional self-discipline. You can't help slumping in the saddle, because of the weight on your shoulders. Obviously he'd have to think of some way of shaking her off, because being marked like this all the time was intolerable; but at least he could take his time, wait for the right opportunity and do it properly, rather than rushing at it and making a botch of it.

"Out of interest," she said, after a rare silence, "which empire do you belong to? East or West?"

He realised he didn't know offhand. "East," he said.

"Really? Why?"

"Well." He thought quickly. "I was only a kid when my family came here from Leuctria, it was before the war. When the war started, we were in the East. Therefore, presumably, I'm an Easterner."

She nodded. "You're not down on the census rolls as a citizen," she said. "Therefore, you aren't an Easterner. Which makes you a Westerner or an enemy alien. I only mention it because it means you have no rights whatsoever and no protection under the law." She smiled. "I thought you might like to know that."

"You're making that up," he said. "There's no way you could've found that out so quickly."

She shrugged. "The central records are in the Green Stone temple in Choris," she said. "The rolls are definitive: if you aren't on them, you don't exist. And my department has charge of the rolls, we know where to look things up. How old are you?"

"Thirty-six."

"Ah. We guessed you were forty. But we checked six years on either side, just to be sure."

"Really."

"Yes, indeed. Naturally we make allowances for records being incomplete once the war started. But since you're pre-war, the records are reliable, and you aren't in them. Not," she added pleasantly, "that it matters very much. All I'm saying is, I could cut your throat while you sleep and the courts wouldn't be interested."

"What courts?"

"Oh, indeed. Still, I thought I'd mention it, out of interest."

He tried to think of a reply, but there wasn't one. So he asked, "Who else did you look up?"

She laughed. "Oh, we know all about Axio, so we didn't need to. And the boy's a Rhus, so he's a definite enemy. If it's any consolation, I'm not on there either. But Aelia's neutral, so I'm all right."

It wasn't something he'd ever given any thought to. However— "Are you serious?" he said. "No rights at all?"

"Oh, well," she said, "it's not like any of that sort of thing counts for anything these days, not in the middle of a war. If the war ever ends you might want to do something about it, though."

He frowned. "Such as what?"

"That's a good question," she said. "You've got no standing to apply for citizenship, you haven't served in the Eastern military and you aren't rich enough for mercantile status. You could always marry a citizen's daughter, of course; that'd do it."

"That's allowed?"

"In the East," she said. "In the West you'd be restricted by property class. Of course, in the West you'd be a friendly alien, and you did serve in their army. If I were you, I'd be a Westerner. Much less hassle, and no poor unfortunate girl would have to marry you."

"I'm not sure I want to be a Westerner," he said, "not if they're going to lose the war. Didn't you say you're a widow?"

"Hm. No, thank you."

"I'll pay you. Twenty angels."

Her face went blank. "You've got twenty angels."

"Yes. Wrapped up in an old sock in the vaults of the treasury of the Shining Path temple in Aia Propontis. It's supposed to be for my old age, but the way things are going I don't suppose I'll have one."

"Twenty angels. Are you serious?"

"I imagine your kid could use twenty angels, even if you couldn't."

She looked away. "Maybe you weren't listening," she said. "I'm Aelian. Not on the register."

"No. But you did say your husband died in the war. Therefore, he was in the Eastern military. Therefore, you have a valid claim for citizenship. True, there'd be paperwork involved, but it's still an easy way to earn twenty angels."

She turned and looked at him. "I hardly know you."

"You know more about me than I do, apparently. Besides, it'd be a purely commercial transaction."

"Quite. Like all your relationships with women, I would imagine." She looked thoughtful. "It's a long way to Aia Propontis," she said. "And I'd need to see the money first."

"Naturally."

"This is just bizarre," she said. "Anyway, couldn't your precious Lodge take care of it for you? I thought they had their claws in everywhere. I'm sure they could fake you a few records if you asked them nicely."

That made him laugh. "You really don't like us, do you?"

"I don't, no. I think you're poisonous."

He shrugged. "That's so perverse," he said. "Still, if that's what you choose to believe. The offer stays open as far as the border, by the way. Think about it. Twenty angels, pre-war. You'll never get a chance like it again."

She snored.

Not just ordinary snoring. It was like some monstrous industrial activity – a sawmill or a foundry, where the roof and the floor shake, but you put up with it because you have to. Out in the open it was bad enough; what it would be like in a confined space, he couldn't bear to imagine. Her poor husband. The man was a saint.

But you couldn't fake a noise like that; therefore she was asleep, profoundly so. Fortunately it was a clear night with a bright, helpful moon. He got up slowly, watching her as he did so, stepped gently over to the horses, took great pains over saddling and bridling, because one clink or creak could spoil everything. When his horse was ready, he crept back, picked up her bridle, wrapped it carefully in his scarf and tucked it away in his saddlebag. A bit hard on her, he reflected, but much kinder than cutting her throat or hamstringing her horse.

He could still hear that terrible noise a hundred yards away.

She caught him up just after noon the next day.

He was impressed. He wouldn't have thought you could jury-rig a functional bridle out of a few bits of rope, a stick and strips of plaited cloth. And she must've ridden like the wind to make up the time.

"You can't have imagined you'd get away with it," she said. "So I can only assume it was spite. Really rather petty, don't you think? But, then, you're a spiteful man."

"I never said I wasn't," Corason replied.

"Who likes playing nasty tricks on people."

"Yes."

"Then I've had a lucky escape, haven't I? Just think, I might have married you. Can I have my bridle back now, please?"

Corason fished it out of his saddlebag. It only took her a minute or so to change over; good with horses, no doubt about it. "Thank you so much for waiting," she said, as she swung lightly into the saddle and gathered the reins. "I'd hate to think I'd inconvenienced you in any way."

Later, after a period of stony silence, he said, "If it makes you feel any better, I really was trying to get rid of you."

"Not really, no. It means you were prepared to leave me to walk back to Choris, which for a woman on her own probably constitutes attempted murder. Also, you thought I was too stupid to improvise a bridle. On balance, I'd prefer it if it was just a mean-hearted prank."

"Ah. In that case, it was."

More silence; during which he concluded that she probably wasn't wearing armour, because nobody could spring into the saddle like that carrying an extra thirty pounds dead weight, not even if they were used to it. Nor, in all likelihood, was there a sword under that cloak; he'd have seen it stick out when she bent her knee. Not that any of that meant he could downgrade the threat level. Was it really likely that she'd been sent to kill him? If so, when, or conditional on what event? It all seemed wildly improbable in the daylight; but, then, so did his way of earning a living, if he thought about it long enough.

From the Cascanis plateau to the Horns is thirty-seven miles, and nobody enjoys that section of the road, not even in summer, when the sky is blue and the strange white flowers bloom in the shale. Before the war, elegant young ladies and artistic young men used to go as far as Laxas-in-Cascana to sketch the dramatic basalt outcrops; only professional silk-painters ventured beyond Laxas, to capture the majestic canyons, which look so well on those great long wall-hangings that drape all round a room. Eremite priests and cenobite monks occasionally set up cells in the strange egg-shaped caves in the rocks or on top of the inexplicable chimneys; mostly they never came back, which was probably just as well. There's water, if you know exactly where to look for it, and from time to time desperate men have raised sheep and goats there; occasionally, travellers driven off the road by thirst have come across their homes in the honeycomb caves, perfectly preserved, as though the occupiers had just stepped out for a moment. It's one of the few places in the Western empire where you never see crows. Instead, you quickly get sick to death of the sight of the red-collared kites; big, noisy, clumsy, slow, living on snakes and lizards when they can't get carrion. They aren't afraid of humans, even when you throw rocks at them; they can judge range to perfection, and tend to gather, in groups of four or five, just over a stone's throw away, waiting patiently for you to die of heatstroke.

Imperial couriers, trained and mounted at public expense, cover this section of the road in one gruelling, breakneck day. Lesser mortals are strongly urged not to: don't feed the kites, it only encourages them.

"You can't still be cold," she said. "You just can't."

She'd long since taken off her cloak, revealing no armour, just a sensible riding outfit, the sleeves of which she'd rolled up to the elbow. She'd tied a scarf round her head to keep the sun off, and kept shading her eyes with her hand.

"I don't know," Corason replied. "There's a bit of a nip in the air, don't you think?"

"You're mad."

"It gets very cold at night."

In truth, he was starting to feel a trifle close; but the sight of his multiple layers seemed to irritate her beyond measure, so it was worth it. A drink of water wouldn't be unwelcome, however. If he wasn't mistaken, there was a freshwater spring just round the next bend, about four hundred yards up the slope. She could probably do with one, too; no water bottle, he'd observed, which showed how much she knew about the road east.

"Won't be long," he said, dismounting briskly and handing her his reins.

"What? Where are you going?"

"For a shit in the rocks."

Some springs dry up unpredictably; others are infallible. This was one of the latter. It was somewhere between a drip and a trickle, but you could bet your life on it, as generations of travellers had. He was thirstier than he'd thought, and it took him a while to catch enough in his cupped hands. Then he began to fill his pewter pint flask, eagerly anticipating the grateful, angry look on her face when he produced water out of nowhere when she was truly desperate.

"What are you *doing* up there?" came a voice from below. He grinned. Then he caught a glimpse of movement in the valley on the far side of the ridge, and forgot all about water for a while.

"Corason? Where are you?" The sound of her voice made him wince; he'd forgotten her, too, and now she'd come to look for him. He craned his neck round and saw her, clambering unsteadily up through the loose rocks towards the top of the ridge. He leapt like a lion, grabbed the backs of her knees and sent her toppling; then he grabbed her face and pressed the palm of his hand into her mouth.

"Never," he hissed, "never *ever* stand on a skyline. Got that?"

A frantic mumble implied that she'd got it just fine. He let go, then shushed her. Then, keeping his arm bent and using only one finger, he pointed.

"I can't see anything," she whispered. "It's just – oh."

Well, she could be forgiven for that. It was only movement that had caught his eye. Whoever they were, they knew what they were doing; no flash of sunlight on spear blades or armour, presumably they'd painted them or allowed them to rust. It was only once you'd noticed them that you realised how many of them there were; the whole mountainside was moving, crawling with them. The closest thing he'd ever seen to it was a flow of lava.

"Who are they?"

"Well," he said quietly, "they aren't Senza's lot, so they've got to be the West. Other than that, I haven't got the faintest idea."

"There's so many of them."

A tiny shake of the head. "You're just not used to seeing armies," he said. "That's probably only four or five thousand. My guess is, though, that that's just a vanguard. See how they're picking their way? They're light troops, well ahead of the main body. If the usual ratios apply, you multiply them by twenty."

She tried to wriggle away; he clamped a hand on the back of her neck, and she stopped still.

"We stay here till they've gone," he said. "Doesn't matter how long it takes. They're well down the slope; we're on the bloody skyline. If they see us, they'll have to catch us. Do you understand?"

He felt her head nod, and let go. "Now then," he said. "A question for you. Apart from Senza Belot, who do we know who's mad enough to bring a hundred thousand men through this appalling place, and brilliant enough to actually be able to do it?"

She turned her head and stared at him. "He's dead," she said.

He remembered the flask, groped for it with his left hand, found it. Empty, of course. "The spring's just behind you," he said, handing her the flask. "Very carefully, squirm your way round and fill this. Don't raise your hand or any part of you more than fifteen degrees above the horizontal."

That kept her busy while he thought. She would, of course, insist on trying to tell Senza. Did he have a problem with that? Not really. Except – he had no idea why, he just *knew*. Senza wouldn't need telling. Senza Belot, sprawling in atypical idleness under the walls of Rasch. He'd never intended to take the city. He'd known this army was coming. He'd been waiting for it. And now, thanks to Commissioner Axio and Commissioner Corason of the Lodge, he'd be meeting it at a place he hadn't chosen, outnumbered five to one, with no prepared resources, no diabolically ingenious strategy. And all for a stupid pack of playing cards.

"Change of plan," he said.

"What?"

He kept his eyes fixed on the stream of movement. "We need to get off this ridge," he said. "We need to get our horses, get back on the road and ride like lunatics till we meet Senza. Agreed?"

"You want to warn him?"

"Don't sound so surprised. Well? Are you coming or not?"

Only Imperial couriers and lunatics venture beyond a cautious trot on the steep climb up from the Crossed Hands to the Horns. Corason had never been so scared in his life. He didn't spare a single thought for his companion until he saw the crumbling rock-carvings of Horn Gate and knew the worst of it was over; downhill, and a straight, flat road. Then he looked over his shoulder. She was still there, about seventy yards behind him, going well.

They reckon the winged gods of Horn Gate were put there to commemorate some battle or other. It's exactly the place where you'd expect a battle to have been fought; five hundred men holding off a million, or something of the sort. If so, it would follow that the commander of the million was an idiot, to have brought so many men to a place with no water or shade, where the road crawls between two soaring mountains. Two thousand men could beat five hundred there; a million wouldn't stand a chance.

He waited for her. She drew up beside him and gasped, "What's the matter? Why've you stopped?"

"He's not here," Corason said. "I was sure he would be. It's what—" He laughed; it came out as a snorting noise. "It's what I'd have done, so of course Senza wouldn't, because he's a genius, et cetera." He breathed out slowly. "In that case, we don't have to kill ourselves hurrying," he said. "Beyond the Horns, the road ceases to matter. It's irrelevant. There's another way round, quicker, it cuts a great fat dog-leg off the road."

"Not on the map."

"You believe in the map, how sweet. It's there all right, as seventy thousand Esjauzida found out the hard way about six hundred years ago, when they tried to invade the empire."

"Who?"

"Precisely. Things did not go well with them, and all because they didn't know about the back road. Senza knows about it, you can bet your life, and so he'll stop short. Which means they, that lot, the lot we've just seen, will get there before we can, no matter how fast we go." She was staring at him, which annoyed him. "We've failed," he said. "We can't warn Senza. Our chance at a place in history – gone. Oh, well, never mind." Suddenly he realised what was eating him, and he tore off his heavy coat and threw it on the ground. "God, I'm hot. Let's stop and let the horses catch their breath. No point being cruel to dumb animals."

"We can't just—"

"I can." He dropped his feet out of the stirrups, stretched his legs and more or less fell out of the saddle. "You go on if you like; you'll be wasting your time." He peeled off a jerkin and an arming coat; they were soaked in sweat. "I'll say this for failure: I feel wonderfully relaxed." He tucked the end of the reins under a heavy stone and sat down on the ground. "Takes all the pressure off you."

She stayed where she was for a while, then got down and sat next to him. "Aren't you boiled in all that lot?" he asked.

She was staring at her toes. "Do you really think that could be Forza Belot?"

"Can't be, he's dead." There were a few grey lines in her hair, he noticed. Well, he had that to look forward to, if he lived that long. "So, presumably that's another general of equal brilliance and daring that Central neglected to brief me about. Come on, who else could it be?"

She shrugged. "I don't know. I haven't got a clue about war stuff. I'm only here to stop you sending news of Senza's withdrawal to the West. I think I've had a wasted trip."

He stared at her. "You're kidding," he said. "That's what they sent you for?"

She nodded. "They think your lot are on the West's side," she said. "That's why you stopped Senza from taking Rasch. They think you're spying for the West, and your job was to report about troop movements. And I've come all this way for nothing. And Senza's going to walk straight into a trap and be slaughtered, and we'll lose and there's nothing I can do about it. Not that I care all that much, except those bastards killed my husband." She sighed, and stretched out her legs. "I don't suppose you've got anything to eat, have you?"

"No."

"I don't believe you, but it's all right. I have absolutely no idea what I'm supposed to do next."

Corason yawned. "It's not like we're awash with options," he said. "We can't turn round and go back to Choris; the horses would starve even if we don't. Therefore—"

"We?"

"Sorry, I'm being presumptuous. *I'm* going to carry on, at a gentle ambling pace, until I reach either Senza Belot or the huge flock of kites feeding off his dead army. In the former instance, I shall cadge food, water and possibly a fresh horse; in the latter, I guess I could sit around and wait for Ocnisant to show up. Or I could follow Forza and try my luck with him." He paused. There was no reason why he should add anything. "If you want, you can come with me."

"Tag along with Senza's army and get slaughtered. No thanks."

"Cadge what you need to get home, then make an excuse and leave. That's what I intend to do, I just told you. We can go together."

"Really. Where, exactly?"

"It's not going to matter terribly much, is it?" He hadn't meant to shout. "If Senza's army gets wiped out, the war will be over and your side will have lost. Unless my people can work another miracle, Choris will be rubble and ash, and you won't have a home or a life to go back to. Just for once, try listening to what I'm telling you, instead of scoring points all the time. There's a fair chance that the world is about to change out of all recognition. We're lucky: we can see it coming. If we're very, very lucky we might just be able to get out of the way before the sky falls on our heads." He hesitated; he no longer seemed to be in control of the words tumbling out of his mouth. "Come with me to Lodge Central. They can find work for you there: you can pretend to be a craftsman. No, listen. If you're with the Lodge, you might stand a chance of finding out if your family's made it through. We might be able to reach them, bring them out. We can do that sort of thing. Looking after our own is what we're there for. I know you've got a whole bunch of silly prejudices about us, but if everything collapses in ruins, we're your best chance of seeing your son again. Well? Or are you just going to wander around here among the rocks and give the kites indigestion?"

She was quiet for a very long time. Then she said, "Is that what they are, kites? I thought they were some kind of buzzard." She stood up and brushed dust off her skirt. "It's a very kind offer and you may possibly mean it, but I think I may have other options you haven't mentioned. No, don't get up." She walked past him, then half turned and kicked him hard just above his ear. And that was that, for an indefinite period.

When he woke up, he was stone deaf. He could see blinding light, and his head hurt unbearably, and he couldn't hear anything. Maybe there wasn't anything to hear. He raised his boot and banged his heel on the ground. Nothing.

He dragged himself on to his hands and knees and loomed round. No horses – no, not as bad as that. His horse was gone, but hers was about fifty yards away, nibbling a tiny clump of grass sticking out of a crack in the rocks. Had she really kicked him in the head? It made no sense. Could it possibly have been, well, an *accident*?

He considered the memory, which was quite clear and sharp: no, not really. *I may have other options*, she'd said, and then, wham.

He tried to stand up, but that made him dizzy and sick. He squatted down on a stone until the world stopped spinning, and tried to think; not easy, in a bobbing, silent world where he'd just been kicked stupid by a lady clerk.

His horse was gone; therefore, she'd taken it in preference to her own; also the saddlebags, containing two and a bit days' rations of dried fruit and biscuit and a three-quarters-full leather bottle of water. Nice of her to leave him her horse; a delicate, graceful thing whose legs might well snap off under his weight. Was there a spring near here? He couldn't remember.

The headache was getting worse. I'm maimed for life, he thought; I'm useless, nobody will want me for anything if I can't hear what they're saying. He filled his lungs and yelled as loud as he could; he felt the breath leave him, but heard nothing at all. The effort made him feel sick again, and his mouth filled with acid. Just as well there wasn't anything in there to come out.

He closed his eyes, which was worse, so he opened them again, and looked at the horse. Probably a good idea to grab hold of it as soon as possible; if anything spooked it and it bolted, that wouldn't be good. He stood up, and this time managed to stay up, though the pounding in his skull made him want to cry. Even if there was a spring nearby, he had nothing to carry water in. He took a step, and his knees buckled. God, what a state to be in. At times like this, you can see the real advantages of death; so much less pain and misery than the other thing.

Maybe the horse was sorry for him. It held still – a mare, he noted, maybe nine, ten years old; well, it had got this far, so maybe it was tougher than it looked. His hands had somehow turned stupid while he'd been asleep, and it took him a long time to lengthen the stirrup leathers. He saw something he recognised, but couldn't understand what it was doing there. He hoisted himself into the saddle and felt the mare wince and sag. And why not? Misery isn't something you hoard, it's something you share.

Actually, it was better in the saddle than on his inadequate, swaying feet. He waited for his head to stop pumping, then looked up and down the road. Which way? He couldn't remember. Did we come up the road or down it?

Up; because there behind him were the Horns, definitely past those; therefore this way. Onwards. He nudged the mare with his heels. She stayed where she was. Women.

The familiar thing he'd seen was a maker's mark. Where was it, now? Oh, yes, on the girth. A curious sigil, embossed into the leather. But it was just a plain old ordinary maker's mark, that was all. Seen dozens like it.

Down this road somewhere was Senza Belot's army. They'd have doctors, you could bet your life. They could tell him about his injuries; yes, and he wouldn't be able to hear a word they said.

The sun was low in the sky by the time he reached the bottom of the dip, and there wasn't much point in staring at the ground for hoofmarks or the scrapes of wheels. In front of him the road climbed steeply. Right at the top, he knew for a fact, there was a stream that ran down the side of the rock face and under the road; it came out again about forty yards on the other side, and there was a soft patch, plainly marked with reeds. He decided it would keep till morning. A good night's sleep, that was what he needed. While there was still light enough to see, he scouted round for enough cover to hide himself and the horse; deaf, he was easy prey. But he found just the thing, a place where a large boulder had rolled down the slope and split in two; the crack was just wide enough for a man and a horse to lodge in comfortably, and there was even a patch of grass, about the size of a spread-out cloak, to take the horse's mind off her misery for a while. He wrapped the reins round his ankle and double-knotted them to make sure, then lay down with his rolled-up coat as a pillow. He was freezing cold again, and thirsty, and painfully hungry, but at least he couldn't hear the kites laughing at him.

The horse woke him up, tugging at his ankle. For a moment he couldn't remember anything: why something was trying to yank his foot off; why it was so damn quiet. Then it all came back to him, infinitely depressing. He opened his eyes and saw clear blue sky. His forehead was faintly damp with dew. He ran the back of his hand over his brow, then licked it.

The horse gave him a look that would have touched a heart of stone; he swore at it, disentangled the reins from his leg and levered himself upright by bracing his arms on the sides of the split boulder. A kite got up suddenly a few feet away in a silent explosion of wings. He tried to lead the horse on, but she dug her heels in. At least his head had stopped hurting. Another glorious day in the arsehole of the universe.

When he reached the road, he saw that it had changed. Loose stones had been split or ground to powder; the verges were shredded with hoofprints; apple cores and a hat monstrously squashed. He stared for a whole minute, then burst out into silent laughter. Senza's army had passed him in the night, and he hadn't heard a damn thing.

At least he knew which way they'd gone, by the direction of the hooves: back the way he'd just come. Incredible; it must have taken them hours to file past the place where he'd been sleeping, and he'd missed the whole thing; like that man who came all the way from North Permia just to hear Oida sing at the Old and New Festival at Choris, got slightly delayed and arrived just as the audience were filing out of the amphitheatre.

The horse didn't want to let him get on her back. She wouldn't keep still, walking on when he had one foot in the stirrup and one on the ground. At one point, he seriously considered leading her all the way back up the damn hill, but eventually he made it into the saddle, using a stone as a mounting block and leaping through the air.

They couldn't be that far ahead of him, surely. He tried to kick the mare into trotting up the hill, but she preferred being booted in the ribs to killing herself.

Halfway up the rise, he realised he knew something important, but he couldn't remember what it was. Definitely there was something, he knew it for sure. Quite possibly it had come to him during the night, the solution to a problem gradually working its way up to the surface, like an arrowhead in too deep for surgery. He wondered if it was something to do with the bang on the head; perhaps, as well as being deaf for the rest of his life, he'd have great big holes in his memory and not be able to concentrate. Perhaps something significant had happened, but he'd forgotten it completely, because of the concussion; he'd been through something similar once before, except that on that occasion it had been strong drink rather than a boot to the temple. He tried to distract his mind by thinking of what he'd do to that bloody woman if ever he caught up with her, but that didn't work at all. The stupid thing was, he was more worried about her than anything else. If Forza's scouts got her, and she had anything in the way of official papers on her, they might well lynch her as a spy.

Something appeared on the skyline, and he couldn't make out what it was; the sun was behind it and it was shrouded in dust. He stopped the mare and gazed at it, and made out a man, on foot, running faster than he'd ever seen a man run before. That was all the more remarkable because the runner was wearing full armour, forty pounds of small rectangular steel plates from knee to collarbone and a six-pound crested helmet. A moment later, two horsemen came up over the rise, also going ridiculously fast. They were horse-archers, slim, long-haired young men on ponies, no stirrups, their toes almost trailing on the ground. The armoured runner wasn't looking round. It was incredible how he could run so fast on an imperfect surface without stumbling, but he was managing it. But the horsemen overtook him, parting so as to come up on either side of him. They passed him, and he was lying on his face, two arrows sticking out of him, like withies growing out of the trunk of a fallen willow. The horsemen crossed each other, miraculously not colliding, wheeled and turned back; a moment later they'd vanished, as though they'd never been there.

The armoured man was moving, a slow, irregular crawl, dragging himself along with his elbows. He stopped about ten yards from where Corason was sitting. He'd left a furrow behind him in the dust you could've sown artichokes in.

Maybe it was the silence that made it seem so unreal. Corason sat staring for a long time, then nudged the mare into a slow walk. He looked down at the dead man, but didn't stop. Part of him really didn't want to see what was going on on the other side of the rise, but he knew he couldn't stop and go back. He was being drawn, like filings by a magnet.

As he reached the top and looked down, he remembered what it was that he'd forgotten.

If the Great Smith had chosen to sell tickets to the battle, Corason knew he could never have afforded to be where he was: best seat in the house. Below him he could see the whole thing, the greatest show on earth, staged in a natural amphitheatre to delight the discerning student of history. The bigger, faster moving specks were cavalry – Senza Belot, ambushing the ambush; so obvious, he'd chosen practically the only square mile in the two empires where the plan could work, he must've set the whole thing up months ago, all leading up to this; the smaller specks, scurrying in terrified swarms, were the last concentration of the forces of the West, rounded up, chivvied and worried and funnelled into killing zones. Horse-archers were the key, of course; he must have got them from Blemya, or the savages in the southern desert who'd been giving the Blemyans a hard time; captured them, maybe, when he and Forza had cooperated for the one and only time.

It wasn't real, of course. It was a vision, hallucinations induced by concussion or possibly a prophetic insight, the sort that sages and ascetics came to this place to find. He knew it had to be something of the sort because there was no sound, not even his own heartbeat or the incessant nagging of the kites.

And he knew exactly what it was that he'd noticed yesterday, when he was fooling with the mare's stirrups. A maker's mark on the girth: two crossed hammers over a horseshoe. Of course it was familiar, because he'd seen it so many times; because it was the mark of the Lagriana brothers, that well-respected and old-established family firm of saddlers and harness-makers whose workshop was just outside the main gate at Division and who worked exclusively for the higher echelons of the Lodge. She wasn't a Western spy, or an Eastern spy pretending to be a Western spy; she didn't work for either empire, of course not, neither of the Imperial governments employs women in any capacity that doesn't consist of cooking or cleaning or folding laundry. Only the Lodge, enlightened, all-accepting, recognises that there are some important jobs that a woman can do just as well as a man, and sometimes better. Only the Lodge.

He watched the battle; it would have been churlish not to, since he'd been granted the unique privilege of this vision. But his mind wasn't on it. All he could think about was the terrifying, unbearably true fact that the Lodge had sent someone to spy on him, kick his ears out and leave him for dead in the wilderness. Which was impossible. It was an abomination so horrible he couldn't stand it; he wanted to crawl into a hole and drag a rock over his head, get away from it where it couldn't follow.

Something was happening. He realised he hadn't been following; like when you're preoccupied and you read the words of a book without taking them in. Another mob of cavalry, a substantial one, had popped up out of nowhere and was driving a straight line down the middle of the battlefield, cutting it in half. No doubt Senza had his reasons, but they seemed to be getting in the way. He saw them collide with a much smaller unit; a mess; were any of Senza's officers capable of making a mistake like that? Then the small unit was swept out of the way, squashed up against the side of the mountain; it stopped moving, like it was dead. Suddenly all the cavalry was pulling back, breaking on the newcomers like small, ineffectual waves against a breakwater, and Corason realised that the new arrivals weren't part of Senza's plan, or his army.

That would be Forza Belot.

It was a bit like that puzzle; where you stare at the silhouette of two wineglasses, and suddenly realise you're looking at a human face. It was a trap all right, but not a trap for the Westerners. Whoever was commanding them (it couldn't be Forza; he was dead) had sacrificed his entire infantry strength to spring it, but it was a deliberate trap and a deadly one. Senza's cavalry was being rounded up, kettled and confined in surrounded circles or wedged up against sheer mountainsides; horse-archers, no armour, most of them didn't bother carrying a weapon apart from the bow, and they were being ground like wheat.

Whoever that man is, Corason thought, remind me never to play cards with him.

To sacrifice a hundred thousand just to kill twenty thousand didn't make sense. He looked for the Western infantry, but he could see no sign of them. They weren't reforming or regrouping, or even running away. They just weren't. Made no sense.

To sacrifice a hundred thousand just to kill one man. Now that made sense.

Something on the edge of his vision caught his attention. He looked round and saw a boy on a pony. He was young, and he wore his long hair in braids down his back; a loose-fitting white shirt with effeminate sleeves; and a bow.

The boy looked at Corason for some time, frowning, as though he was a badly placed ornament that spoilt the symmetry. Then he nocked an arrow on his bowstring – no hurry, might as well have been practising at the range – drew smoothly and took careful aim.

"It's all right," Corason said. "I'm not—"

Then the boy shot him.

Hope, reversed

The horse-archer, whose name was Chantat mi Chanso, considered the shot and figured he must have pulled it at the last moment; a snatch in the release, sending the arrow low right, into the fleshy part of the thigh rather than the heart. He was annoyed with himself. He'd have to watch that before it turned into a bad habit.

The enemy had fallen off his horse – quite a pretty little mare, carried its head well, rounded nicely on to the bit; but too much trouble to lead back through the battle, and who was buying women's horses these days, anyway? He considered shooting the man again, but he discovered he only had five arrows left. Slovenly, to leave a wounded target, but that really only applied to animals, not people. He wondered why a big man had been riding such a small horse, but it was none of his business.

Talking of which – he really ought to be getting back, he knew. Down in the valley the big battle was slipping away without him. What did you do in the big battle, Daddy? Oh, I wandered off and shot stragglers, while your Uncle Garsio and your Uncle Razo captured the enemy standard, killed the emperor and looted his golden treasury. No, that wouldn't do at all.

He rode past the mare and over the brow of the hill, looking for his squadron. Last he'd seen of them they'd been out on the far east wing, cutting up Ironcoats. But they didn't seem to be there any more. He looked again, more carefully; the Dream of Bright Water was easy to spot, because their dragon was the only one with a real gold head; it caught the sun and sparkled, you could always tell it was them. And now he couldn't see it, and that was worrying.

Best to get back down there and find them. He nudged Firebird into a gentle canter, keeping her over on the soft verge. He wondered how Garsio had got on; he'd been plugging away shooting Ironcoats from a standstill (did they count if you weren't moving? They'd never actually clarified that point) but he'd soon have run out of arrows doing that, so he'd have had to go back to the packhorses for some more. Had they brought enough? Fifty sheaves had seemed plenty when they set out that morning, but who could have anticipated a day like this?

Nothing to be seen on the road except dead Ironcoats. He glanced at the fletchings of the arrows that had killed them, but they were all reds and greens, no sign of the yellow and white of the Bright Water. Maybe it hadn't been such a good idea to go hurtling off after the men in the red cloaks. It'd be embarrassing if he couldn't find the Bright Water and had to muck in with another squadron until they got back to the wagons. And if you piggybacked on another squad, didn't you have to pay for your arrows?

Something caught his eye and he pulled Firebird up short. Under an overhanging rock beside the road he saw dead men and dead horses; no Vei, not Ironcoats. He jumped down, looped the reins round his wrist and came closer.

It was horrible. At least fifty or sixty; he didn't recognise any of them, but there was their dragon, crushed almost flat, its pole snapped. A whole squadron, near enough. None of them had been shot. They were cut about and stabbed, there was blood everywhere.

One of them was looking at him.

He wasn't sure at first. Dead men with their eyes open can look so very intense; yes, you, I'm talking to you. But this one blinked. He let go of the reins and edged over, stepping over dead bodies. The man licked his lips and said, "I can't feel my legs."

"I'm sorry," Chanso said. "How can I help? I don't know what to do."

The man just looked at him. He wasn't cut up like the others, but the way he was lying wasn't right at all. "Horse threw me," the man said. "Think my back's broken. I can't move."

What Chanso really wanted to say was: I'm sorry, but don't look at me like that, it's not my *fault*. Two kites swooped down over his head, turned into the wind and pitched on the rocks above him. He looked at them; they looked back. In your own time, they were saying. We don't want to hurry you, but we've got work to do. He waved his arm and yelled, but they didn't move.

"Please," the man said.

Please what, for crying out loud? Please lift me up and carry me back to the wagons, or please shoot me? "I'll get help," Chanso heard himself say; then he raced back to the horse, scrambled up on her back and got out as fast as he could.

He followed the road, simply because it was better going than trying to pick a way through the stones. He'd gone a few hundred yards when he heard shouting. He reined in and looked round and saw horsemen coming at him from three sides. They were riding big, heavy horses. They were Ironshirts.

Which made no sense, as the enemy had no cavalry in this battle, that was the whole point. But there they were; spearmen, therefore most likely the notorious Dragons' Teeth lancers – don't go tangling with them, sunshine, they eat little boys like you. He reached round for an arrow, realised just how stupid that would be, wrenched Firebird's head right round and galloped back the way he'd just come.

Was it just conceivably possible that while he'd been away,

in the half-hour or so his back had been turned, some fool had contrived to lose the battle? Impossible. There weren't any enemy left; we killed them all. Whoever these lunatics were, they couldn't have anything to do with the real outcome of the day. That had been settled long ago. They could only be some purely local anomaly, a minor incident out on the edge of the main action. It would be stupid to get himself killed by an irrelevancy. He gave poor Firebird a vicious kick and felt her accelerate. Then he glanced over his shoulder. They were closer now; much closer. It was as though he could already feel them, cutting his skin. He flapped his legs wildly, hammering Firebird's ribs, but she couldn't go any faster.

And then he was in the air, watching the road coming toward him. And then—

"Wake up, for crying out loud." There was a hand gripping his jaw, waggling it from side to side. He grabbed at its wrist and it let go. "You're all right, you're fine. All over. Time to go."

The man crouching over him was no Vei; too old to be on the raid, properly speaking, his hair was streaked with grey and his face was deeply lined. The pattern of fine scars on his forehead was Glorious Destiny. "What happened?"

"Tell you later. Right now, we've got to go. Come on."

"Just a minute. What *happened*? Where's my horse?"

"Forget the bloody horse, we've got a spare. Come *on*, will you? Or we'll leave you here for the shitehawks."

An arm clamped to his elbow yanked him upright; he tottered and caught his balance. He tried to pull away but the older man was much stronger, dragging him along with one hand, shoving him between the shoulders with the other, so that he had to go forward or fall over. He heard the sleeve of his shirt rip. Another voice called out, "Get a move on, will you? They're turning."

"Oh, shit," said the older man, and Chanso realised he was terrified. "Look, pick it up, can't you? Or they'll kill us all."

He was being hustled towards a line of boulders along the verge, where a rockfall had been cleared out of the road. As he got closer he could see men behind it, three, no, four, all no Vei, and, behind them, six horses. They were watching something behind him, as anxiously as heavy betters at a horse race. The strong man grabbed a handful of the back of his shirt and boosted him over the boulders.

"Now can we get out of here?" pleaded one of the men angrily.

A moment later, Chanso was on a horse – he wanted to explain, I've already got a horse, I don't need one; then it occurred to him that maybe he didn't any more. He twisted round to look for Firebird, but someone grabbed his reins and he had to catch a handful of mane to stay in the saddle as the stranger's horse broke into a gallop. As soon as he was secure in his seat he craned his neck round and saw a grey line sweeping towards him. More of the terrible Ironshirt lancers. Fear flooded his mind, drowning everything else. He had no control over anything. He clung on tight, like a little boy.

After a very long time, the pace slowed and eventually he came to a halt. He looked up, realised his face was wet with tears. The strong man threw him back his reins; he muffed the catch and had to gather them handspan by handspan.

"I think they've given us up," someone said. "Conselh, what do you reckon? Are they still following?"

The strong man took another long look before answering. "I believe so," he said. "Looks like they've found some other poor buggers to play with." He swung one leg over his pommel and dropped lightly to the ground, then flopped in a heap, sliding his back down against a bank. "Don't know about you boys but I'm about done. If you want to keep going, I'll catch you up."

"The hell with that," someone else said. Then he nodded at Chanso. The strong man sighed, nodded back. "Right," he said. "What's your name, son?"

"Chanso. Chantat, Bright Water."

The strong man shrugged. "Can't say I've heard of you. I'm Conselh, this is Trahidour, Folha, Verjan and Clar: we're all Celquel, Glorious Destiny. Did you see us?"

"What?"

Folha, a skinny young man with a small chin and a huge Adam's apple, grinned. "Guess he didn't."

"Fine," Conselh said. "Anyway, we were hiding, hoping those Ironshirts wouldn't see us, and you led the fuckers straight at us. We used our last eight arrows fixing them; also, your horse, sorry about that, I never was much of a shot. Still, you can have that one, Dolor won't be needing it any more, poor bugger." He stopped. Something about Chanso's face was confusing him. "You do know we lost the battle, don't you?"

"I—" He was all choked up and could barely speak. "No, I didn't. I got drawn off, and—"

A slight frown told him that Conselh didn't want to know. "Well, we did. Buggered if I know how. One minute we were shooting Ironshirts like a pig hunt, next thing we knew there were Dragons' Teeth right up us. They smeared us all over the hillside like cheese on bread. We'd used up all our arrows, so we were empty-handed, and those monster horses of theirs can outrun us easy. It's like someone set it up like that, but it makes no sense. I mean, we killed thousands of them before the lancers showed." He closed his eyes for a moment and leaned forward, as if he had stomach cramps.

"Get a grip," advised one of the others. "Time for all that later. Let's get moving."

"No," Conselh said. "We're out of sight here: we stay put till those bastard Teeth have pulled back and then we move on. I don't know what it takes to get it into your thick skull, but they're faster than us." He grinned. "My kid brother," he said. "You'll get used to him." The man who'd been speaking shot Conselh a foul look, but he didn't see it. "Now then," Conselh went on, "time we started thinking. We need to get back to the wagons, that's if the Teeth haven't got there first—"

"For crying out loud, Conselh," Folha said. Conselh ignored him.

"Now if the boys back at the wagons have got any sense," he went on, "they won't be where we left them, that's for sure. You got any arrows?"

Chanso reached round to his quiver and pulled them out. All of them were broken.

"Figures," Conselh said, after a long silence. "The way our luck's going. Five bows, no arrows. Probably a good thing, saves us from thinking we could make a fight of it, which I don't suppose we could, with those Teeth. Better off without."

"I don't think they're taking prisoners," Verjan said; he was the short one, broad-chested, with a beard and no moustache.

"Why should they?" Conselh shook his head. "Our best chance lies in being more bother than we're worth. Same goes for the wagons, I guess. What've we got that the Ironshirts could possibly want?"

"Lives. And horses," Folha replied. "And carts."

"Well, yes, there's that. No use us trying to figure it out, anyhow: we haven't got the brainpower." He got up and peered cautiously over the bank. "Looking good at the moment," he said. "Let's make a move. Don't know about you boys, but I'm sick of this place."

Conselh and Folha were both wrong about the wagons. They were still there, and the Ironshirts hadn't wanted them, or the horses, or any of the gear; not even the arrows, which they'd used as kindling. Another thing they'd got wrong was the assumption that Ironshirts didn't know anything about the no Vei. Apparently they knew that if a no Vei's body is burned, his soul finds no peace, because they'd filled the carts with dead bodies before setting light to them.

It was a long time before anybody spoke. Then Folha said, "Do you reckon we're all that's left?"

Conselh didn't answer. Verjan said, "There must be more than just us. But I'd have thought they'd have headed back this way and we'd have seen them."

Trahidour, the tall, slim young one, was rootling about among the ashes. "Leave that," Conselh snapped at him; he turned round and held out eight arrows, intact and undamaged. "I take that back," Conselh said. "Any more?"

Just one more, which they found after a long, disgusting search, making a total of nine between the six of them. "Makes no sense having one each," Conselh said. "You. Any kind of a shot?"

Chanso remembered his last effort. "No."

"Folha, you're elected Minister of Defence. Sorry, make that Secretary of State for Supply. I don't want you shooting at any Ironshirts; that'll just piss them off. Deer only, and for crying out loud make sure you don't miss. Got that?"

Folha nodded and dropped the arrows into his quiver. Eight of them were red and black, the ninth was white and red. Chanso hadn't seen any yellow and white, not even among the ashes. "Now where?" he said.

Nobody wanted to answer that. Then quite suddenly Conselh grinned. "Home, of course. Where else?"

"Talk sense," Verjan snapped. "We're on the wrong side of the sea, for one thing. Or had you forgotten?"

"So we get a boat. Don't look at me like that, we get to the sea, we'll find a boat."

"Fine. Which direction is the sea in?" Conselh opened his mouth, then closed it again. "You don't know, do you? You haven't got a clue."

"It's that way," Folha said quietly, pointing. "Look at the sun," he explained. "But Verjan's got a point, hasn't he? We don't know this country, and we're going to stick out a mile. What we want to do is get back to Choris Anthropou. We know where that is: follow the road, you can't miss it."

"If that's what you want," Conselh said. "If you really think you can just stroll past the Ironshirts, go ahead. Suit yourselves. I'm going home."

"What do you think?" Trahidour said, and Chanso realised he was looking at him. "Well? You want to head south or make for Choris?"

Chanso knew what his answer would be without having to think. "South," he said. "I'll stick with Conselh. If that's all right," he added quickly.

Conselh laughed. "You can if you want," he said. "Any more?"

There was an awkward silence. Then Folha said, "I think it's a stupid idea, but splitting up's even worse. You do realise, we haven't got any food, or water. Do you know how far it is to the sea? Three days? Three weeks? Months?"

"You shoot it, I'll eat it," Conselh replied. "And, no, I don't know how far it is, but it can't be that far."

"It's a hell of a way with only nine arrows," Verjan said.

"Which is a damn good reason for staying clear of the Ironshirts. Come on, nobody's asking you to walk. And once we get down off these mountains it's all grassland, right down to the sea, everybody knows that. It's a soft, fat country, full of soft, fat people. It'll be a stroll, you'll see."

There was no road south. Instead, there was a mountain. Conselh reckoned they could probably lead the horses up it, but nobody agreed with him; the only alternative was to go round it. Conselh refused to take the road east, so they went west, the way they'd come.

"Leave it to the horses," Conselh said: "they can smell water."

Maybe there wasn't any water to smell. Nor was there any end to the mountain; beyond what they'd seen was a second range, hidden by the first. "We'll be back to Rasch Cuiber at this rate," Verjan said, and nobody laughed. To the north, however, the mountains subsided into moorland. "You don't want to go up there," Conselh advised. "It's bloody cold: we'll freeze." To Chanso, wiping sweat out of his eyes, that didn't sound so bad.

But it was cold at night, of course. There was nothing to burn, so they took the saddle blankets off the horses and tried to wrap up in them. Not much help.

Folha shot a kite. "There's not much meat on the buggers but it's better than nothing," he declared. A long, thirsty search found them a withered thorn bush, over which they roasted the kite. Its flesh was hard, bitter and stringy. Conselh declared that he'd had worse, and they'd grow to like it.

"For all we know we're practically at the end," Conselh said, surveying the southern mountains, stretching from one horizon to the other. "If we go on just a bit further, there we'll be. I don't remember there being mountains all the way from Rasch Cuiber."

The trouble was, none of them had been paying much attention on the way from Rasch to the big battle. They all had a vague recollection of mountains away to the south, but where they'd started and whether there were gaps in them, nobody could say for sure. Conselh said he could picture it clear as anything in his mind. There was a huge great gap, rolling green downs as far as the eye could see. Verjan remembered it as a solid wall of rock. Chanso was fairly sure Conselh was right; he'd seen grasslands at some point, and he was fairly sure they'd been on the lower side of the road, but the image in his mind was uncertain; at times, it looked disconcertingly like the summer pastures back home, and at others he was sure there had been mountains on the other side. But maybe not; perhaps he was confusing the second day with the fifth, or something like that. He couldn't actually remember how long they'd taken to get from Rasch Cuiber to the battle. He'd been riding with the wagons, in any case, and had spent most of his time chatting with the drivers.

"Why the hell did we come this way?" Verjan said loudly to the back of Conselh's neck. "What we should be doing is heading back to Choris Anthropou. Instead, we're going in the opposite direction, deeper into enemy territory. Anyone want to explain that to me?"

Nobody seemed to want to answer. Conselh had gone quiet, ever since Verjan started moaning. Whether he was just angry or whether he had no good answer, Chanso couldn't tell; half and half, he guessed. He didn't want to go south any more; he wasn't sure it was even possible. It was pretty obvious that Folha and Verjan had been right all along. But Conselh couldn't be wrong, could he? He seemed so wise and so strong, and how stupid it'd be to turn back now, if they were only a short way from the gap, which Conselh was absolutely sure he'd seen.

They found one little spring; they had to lie on their stomachs and lap like dogs. Folha shot off all nine arrows at kites, and they only found eight of them.

That night, while Conselh was on watch, the others huddled round a tiny fire they'd built out of tussocks of dry grass. When Chanso came over to join them, they went quiet.

"You're going to leave him," Chanso said.

They scowled at him; then Verjan said, "He's lost his grip. He knows he's wrong but he can't bear to say so. He'll keep going till we die of thirst or starve, or we run into Ironshirts. Fine. I don't want to do that. I'll survive this, if it kills me."

"Verjan doesn't like him much," Folha explained with a grin. "But he's right. Soon as his watch is over and he's asleep, we're off. He can follow us or he can do what he wants, up to him. It's stupid going any further."

Chanso hesitated for a moment, then said, "Can I come with you?"

Awkward pause; then Folha said, "I don't see why not. So long as you don't make trouble."

"Sure."

"All right, then. Go and lie down, pretend to be asleep. We'll tell you when we're ready to go."

Chanso lay down on his side, his eyes closed. Conselh would do the sensible thing, he was sure; as soon as he realised what had happened, he'd turn round and follow. Folha seemed a sensible sort of man; he'd taken charge now, and everything would be fine. All they had to do was retrace their steps, follow the road. It had been two days since the battle, so the Ironshirts would be long gone by now; who'd hang about in this horrible place if they didn't have to? Going south had been a terrible idea, but wasting the two days had served some purpose. It was all going to be fine.

Unless they left without him—

He sat up and looked round. The others were all there, lying quite still, and beyond them he could just make out Conselh's back. He lay down again, facing the others, eyes open. They weren't moving at all. Maybe they'd frozen to death.

Conselh came back and crouched down beside him. "You awake?"

He considered not answering, but said, "Yes."

"Take the next watch." Chanso stood up. Conselh went on a yard or so, then lay down on his back, hands folded on his chest, looking straight up at the stars. He didn't seem sleepy. Too much on his mind, probably.

It would be broad daylight at this rate. Conselh didn't move, but from time to time Chanso caught the glitter of his open eyes in the dying glow of the fire. He was supposed to be keeping watch; what if Ironshirts crept up on them while he was looking the other way? He turned round, but there was nothing to see. The pale moonlight made him think of mist, early morning on the summer pastures at home. His fingers and toes were aching from the cold and he was thirsty again.

Some time later Folha got up. Conselh raised his head to look at him. "My watch," Folha murmured; Conselh nodded. "You should get some sleep," Folha said.

"Fat chance."

Folha relieved him at watch; then it was Verjan's turn. What if Verjan got tired of waiting and tried to stab Conselh with an arrow? Stupid idea? Couldn't happen? Chanso wasn't so sure. They were all so wound up, so quiet; and Verjan struck him as just the sort of man who'd do stuff like that, though Chanso had never actually met a murderer. But people act differently when they're at the end of their rope. Conselh could handle Verjan, no question, but would the others feel obliged to pitch in? What if they all ended up bashed up and cut about? That would really make things bad.

Trahidour took the next watch, and then it was dawn. You could tell by the way they moved that nobody had got any sleep at all. Had Conselh figured out what was going on, overheard them maybe and stayed awake on purpose?

Halfway through the morning they came to the gap in the mountains. Below them lay a wide, flat, grassy plain, through which flowed a broad river. "You know what," Conselh announced, "I think I can see the sea."

Nobody said anything, and they turned off the road, heading straight for the river. They reached it not long after noon and lay on the grass while the horses drank. Verjan got up after a while and sat next to Chanso.

"He's still wrong, you know."

"He was right about this gap, wasn't he?"

"Meaning nothing. Maybe he's got a slightly better memory than me: so what? He's wrong about going south, and you know it."

Chanso thought for a moment. "There's plenty of water now,"

he said. "And you can bet there's deer and waterfowl and plenty other game along the river. Should be cooler in the day and warmer at night. In fact, it reminds me a lot of home."

"I'm not saying you're wrong. But we're going deeper and deeper into hostile territory."

Chanso shrugged. "Why would there be Ironshirts here?" he said. "I figure, if they haven't caught up to us by now, they're not going to. I think we've seen the last of them. They've got to have better things to do than tracking a few stragglers."

"Oh, sure. And the moment the country people see us—"

"So we won't be seen. Don't know about you, I haven't set eyes on a living soul since we left the battle. Can't see any farms or houses downriver, can you? I think this must be ride-around country, like home." He frowned. "Haven't seen any livestock either, mind. So maybe nobody lives here at all. That'd be better for us, wouldn't it?"

Verjan looked away. "The further we go," he said, "the further we got to go back, once you've all seen sense. Look, even supposing we do make it to the sea, then what? Find a boat, he says. Dream on. And suppose we find a boat? We can't hire anyone to sail it; we've got nothing. Sure as hell we can't sail it ourselves. Down on the coast, anywhere there's likely to be boats, there's going to be a lot of people. We can't just go strolling about: we're the *enemy*."

"Doesn't follow." Trahidour joined them. "If we get some local clothes, cut our hair off, we're just half a dozen poor folks looking for work."

Verjan turned and poked Trahidour's forehead. "What about *that*? These people don't have the cuts. What're you going to do, wear a sack over your head?"

"No," Chanso said, "a hood. And we can pay for our passage, we got six good horses."

"Fine." Verjan was getting angry. "So we're going to walk all down through Blemya."

"No," Trahidour said calmly. "We're going to head for the marketplace, where there's always some of our people, and we're going to send home for them to come and get us. Or we borrow horses. If we get to Blemya, we'll be all right. I've been there; we can fit in easy, find work, we'll be safe there till we can get home. The main thing is to get the hell away from this war. I've had about as much of it as I want. Don't ever want to see those Teeth again."

"Exactly." Verjan got to his knees. "So we go back to Choris Anthropou, where they're on our side. Damn it, we've got pay owing to us there. We can hire a damn coach and four back home, forget about boats. But if you go with *him*, he'll get you killed. That I can promise you."

A shadow fell across Chanso's face; he looked round and saw Conselh standing behind him. "Him," he repeated. "And who might *he* be, Verjan?"

Verjan got up slowly. "You got lucky," he said. "There happened to be a gap and a river, and now they think you're a fucking prophet. Folha? Over here. I want three of those arrows."

Folha walked over. "What for?"

"I'm going back. This is stupid. I don't want to leave you boys with this crazy man, but I've had enough. So give me the arrows and I'll get going."

"Sorry," Conselh said. "We need them. Go if you must. You can take your horse, but that's it."

For a moment, Chanso thought Verjan was going to take a swing at Conselh; but instead he swung round and made a grab for the quiver at Folha's waist. Folha took a long step back; Verjan staggered and stooped. Then Conselh closed in behind him and punched him in the small of the back.

"Cut that out," snapped Clar, "you can hurt someone like that."

"So what," Conselh said. "He's my kid brother, I can treat him how I like." Verjan had dropped to his knees. Conselh came closer and kicked him in the face. "Should've done it days ago," he said, as Verjan rolled over on to his side and lay still. "I don't mind him bitching, I'm used to it, but I won't have him making trouble when we're in the shit like this." He took a long step back. "Don't think I didn't hear you last night," he said, "fixing to ride off and leave me. Well, you can if you want, though you won't last five miles. But he's through making trouble, and you're through listening to him. And that's straight from the shoulder."

Everyone was on his feet now, except Verjan. It was plain to Chanso that they were all afraid of him; probably all of them agreed with him, without Verjan wheedling in their ears, but Chanso wasn't sure that counted for very much any more. "Is he all right?" he thought, and heard himself say it aloud.

"Don't worry about him," Conselh said, "head thicker than a door. Here, you, get up." He kicked Verjan in the ribs, but he didn't move. "He'll be fine," Conselh said. "Come on, mount up. Plenty of light left."

They got on their horses. Verjan was still lying there, quite still. "You can't ride off and leave him," Folha said.

"Why not? He'll catch up, once he's done sulking."

They rode on and left him. Chanso risked a glance back over his shoulder, then saw Folha was riding next to him.

"You know," Folha said, "they reckon Senza and Forza Belot never got on. But they're sweethearts compared to Conselh and Verjan."

"I never had a brother," Chanso said.

"You're better off. Take those two. Been fighting all their lives. One says one thing, the other says the opposite." He shrugged. "I think this is as bad as it's ever got, but they've never been in so much trouble before. Just as well Verjan hadn't got his knife."

Chanso looked at him. "That bad?"

Folha nodded. "Conselh took it off him before we left," he said. "Don't suppose he'll get any sleep tonight. His own stupid fault, mind. Still, he was right about the gap."

"Do you think we should be heading south?"

"No," Folha replied, after a moment's hesitation. "I think we should've gone the other way first time Verjan suggested it. But we've come too far now to go back. And we've got nothing to carry water in, and we're lucky roast kite didn't give us all the draining shits."

From time to time, when he thought nobody was watching him, Chanso looked back over his shoulder. But there was no sign of a horseman hurrying to catch them up. Had Conselh actually killed him? Verjan hadn't been moving when they left him.

There were fish in the river. If you looked long enough you could see them, perfectly still with the current flowing all round them. Clar had heard somewhere that you could catch them with your bare hands if you were patient enough. It didn't take long to find out that he wasn't; but Folha managed to shoot one. The trick, he said, was to aim just behind the tail, to allow for the picture in your eye getting bent by the water. They cooked it over a dogwood spit and got half a mouthful each. It tasted of grit.

They slept in a dense clump of dogwood shoots, tall enough to hide the horses. Chanso woke up to find Folha sitting on a large stone on the bank, patiently stripping reeds with the head of an arrow. "I fancy these'll shoot," he explained. "Good enough for fish, anyhow."

Nine of the twelve reeds he'd prepared broke on the bow. He missed with two, and pinned a small brown fish to the riverbed with the third. "I reckon the dogwood sticks would do better," Trahidour said. "I heard that's what they use for arrows in these parts."

But Conselh wasn't prepared to spend a morning making arrows. "Maybe this evening," he said. "Right now, I want to get moving. We've still got a fair way to go."

Still no sign of Verjan. The others reckoned he must've taken his own advice and headed for Choris. "If he was following us he'd have caught up to us by now, the way we've been dawdling," Folha said.

"There'll be ducks in these reeds, bet you anything you like," Clar said, and Chanso was inclined to agree with him. "Conselh, what about it?"

"No nets," Conselh called back without turning round.

The reeds filled a slow bend of the river, which they were skirting, since Conselh reckoned the lower ground might be soft. "Don't need nets," Trahidour said. "Wind's downstream. If we light the reeds, they'll all get up in a covey, we can brown it with stones. Bound to hit something, and we only need three or four. What about it, Conselh? Folha?"

Folha thought for a moment. "Best place would be there," he said, pointing to a place where the river ran between a high bank and a clump of willows. "They'll have to bunch up going through there: it might work. And they're not our reeds and stones cost nothing. Why not?"

"Haven't you boys figured yet, this isn't a pleasure trip?" Conselh still hadn't turned round. "Further downstream there's a big wood, I saw it from that hill a way back. There'll be deer in that, probably tame as dogs. Folha can shoot one this evening, when it's getting dimpsy. If we fire those reeds, we're telling everyone in these parts who can see exactly where we are."

"You said the Ironshirts have given up by now," Clar pointed out. "Look, there's nobody here. You seen anyone? I haven't."

"All the more reason a cloud of smoke's going to draw attention," Conselh said calmly. "Forget it, Clar. You can go duck-hunting when we get home."

Trahidour turned to Chanso. "What do you think?"

Chanso hesitated before answering. "I think Folha's right, that high bank's a great place to stand. Do we have to fire the reeds? Two of us could drive them, and then there'd be no smoke."

Clar clapped his hands together. "I knew we brought him for a reason," he said. "The boy is smart. You any good with a stone?"

Chanso shook his head.

"Fine. You and me'll drive, the rest can throw. Conselh? What do you say?"

"Oh, for God's sake." Conselh stopped his horse. "Fine. But I'll drive. That reed bed's likely to be mighty soft, Clar, it'd gobble up a short-arse like you and we wouldn't know you'd gone."

Clar grinned, and Chanso guessed he preferred throwing stones to wading waist-deep in mud. For some reason. "You all right driving?" Conselh asked.

"Like I said, I'm a lousy thrower."

"Fine. And you're taller than these midgets." He held Chanso's horse as he dismounted. "Right, we'd better work a long way back, so as not to spook them. You three, get picking stones. And be ready. I don't want you standing round yapping when the birds are in the air."

Conselh led him a good half-mile; dead silence, since the wind was from them to the birds. On the way, they picked up a pair of hand-sized stones each, to bang together and make a racket when the time came. "You done this before?" Conselh whispered, as they approached the start of the reeds. Chanso nodded.

"Good boy," Conselh said. "Reckon it's shallow enough to wade here. You stay this side: come on when you hear me."

As Chanso stooped to take off his boots, Conselh disappeared into the reeds. Not long after, Chanso heard him hollering and clashing stones. He scrambled down into the water, and the mud gushed up round his ankles. He wasn't sure he liked that, so he waded across until he hit the riverbed itself. The water was up around his knees and the stones were treacherously smooth and slippery, but at least it was firm. He yelled – he'd dropped the stones wobbling through the mud – and took a long, tentative stride forward.

Clar had been right about the ducks. There were about three dozen, sitting in the middle of the river. He advanced on them but they didn't seem too bothered, so he carefully stooped and picked out a large stone, which he hurled into the middle of the group. That, apparently, was a different matter entirely. The ducks got up in an explosion of wings and spray; low and straight as an arrow downstream, right through the trap. As they flew between the high bank and the rocks they were barely a wingspan apart; and, sure enough, Chanso saw one fold in the air, then another two, then one more. He whooped with joy and splashed ahead, only to lose his footing and go down sideways. The water closed over his head, but he found his feet without too much trouble and stood up again, water streaming out of his hair and down his nose. Victory, he thought.

He trudged and splashed his way back to the bank, not fussed about slipping since he was drenched already. He wiped the mud off his legs the best he could with a handful of short reed, then crammed them back in his boots. Four birds he'd definitely seen go down, could well be others; judging by the way they'd flown, they were lazy and fat, good eating. He ran back to join the others, and saw four ducks spread out on the grass, and Folha gutting a fifth with the head of an arrow.

"Folha got three," Trahidour called out to him, "Clar and me got one each. Couldn't miss, hardly. Where's Conselh?"

Chanso looked back. "He went the other side of the river," he said. "Maybe he's gone on up a way."

Trahidour shrugged, broke a thorn off a bush and picked up a duck. Chanso sat down beside him and took out his pocket knife.

"Went in, I see," Folha said.

Chanso grinned. "Slipped on the stones."

"They can be the devil. Didn't know you got a knife."

"Forgot I had it."

"That'll come in handy," said Clar. "Not much you can do without a knife, and Conselh made us leave ours home."

Awkward silence; then Trahidour said, "Where's he got to, anyhow?"

Folha and Clar looked at each other. Then Folha put down his half-dressed duck. "Guess I'd better go look for him."

"I'll go," Chanso said. "I'm wet already."

He walked back along the edge of the reeds until he saw the trampled place where he'd come out. "Conselh?" he called out. Strange. He knew sound carried well here. He called again, then shed his boots and waded back into the mud, looking for the reeds Conselh had trampled on his way across.

The trail was easy to follow and he found him about twenty yards downstream, face down in the mud, the back of his head stove in. The hair was black with blood and mud; a bloody stone lay next to him. There were no footprints, so Verjan must have thrown it from the riverbank, probably hiding behind the clump of briars ten yards away. Good throw; amazing what you can do when you set your mind to it.

After a short discussion they agreed there was no point fishing him out; they had no tools to bury him with, and come the spate the river would wash up silt and do it for them. Nor was there anything to be gained chasing after Verjan. If he was a danger to them, he'd come to them and they'd deal with him; if not, let him go. "What he's done is punishment enough," Folha said, and there was no arguing with that.

"Beats me how he followed us and we didn't see him," Clar said, for the third time. "He must've been riding, couldn't keep pace with us on foot. I figure he must've gone out wide, over the skyline, then headed back in from time to time to see where we'd got to. Then, when he saw we'd stopped, he figured what we were about and saw his chance." He shivered; he'd been the one who suggested the duck hunt in the first place. And Conselh had taken his place in the driving squad, making himself exposed and vulnerable. "If he comes back, I'll see to him, you bet."

"He won't be back," Folha replied. "He had no quarrel with us. He'll be well on his way to Choris by now. Got to prove he was right, see."

They'd stopped for the night on the edge of the big wood Conselh had spotted earlier; they felt they had to, somehow, since he'd ordered it. Chanso had found a hand-sized piece of dry, sound beechwood; he sat by the fire whittling: something to give his attention to so he didn't have to look at their faces.

"He was my mother's brother's eldest son," Folha told him. "We're all cousins, one way or the other. Clar there's his nephew."

The shape of the wood told him it should be a bear; a big black bear, standing upright. "Two of my cousins were in our squadron," he said, "and four of my friends I grew up with. I don't suppose they made it. I hadn't thought about that, till now."

"You don't know," Trahidour said. "I don't suppose we were the only ones made it out; the Ironshirts can't have got them all. Maybe they'll be there waiting for you when you get home."

Chanso shook his head. "I'm all that's left," he said. "Which is stupid, because they were all better than me, smarter, all that. Makes you wonder—" Who decides these things, he didn't say, because whoever it is had a strange way of going about it. Unless He wanted the good ones, and left the rubbish behind. That he could understand.

"So," Clar said. "Do we keep on going?"

Folha threw a handful of sticks on the fire. "Or what? Don't see there's any choice. Stay here? No, we're going home. That's what he decided. And I figure they'll need us, if we can get there. It's going to be hard going back home, with so many of us—" He shook his head. "I know, you figure, when folks go off to the war, some of them won't be coming back. But all of us—"

"I reckon that's what happened here," Clar said quietly. "I

mean, it's not natural, how empty it all is. Someone ran sheep here not long ago, but I don't see anybody. I reckon they all went to the war, and nobody came back." He lifted his head. "Say, do you suppose, if it goes on much longer, there'll be anybody left at all?"

Folha sat up straight. "Means there'll be plenty of grazing and flocks for them that make it back," he said. "Sounds harsh, that's true, but let's face it, if we get back we won't be poor. Just means we'll have to work damn hard, that's all, just us to do everything." He yawned. "All the more reason for going on," he said. "Look at it this way, boys: we're a valuable commodity. So let's all take care and try not to do anything really stupid."

Chanso finished the carving the next evening, just as it got too dark to see. It wasn't bad. He threw it in the river; for Conselh, he thought.

In the morning, just after sunrise, Folha shot a deer. They dressed it out and slung it over the spare horse. "That'll keep us going for a bit and we won't have to keep stopping," Folha said.

"Do you think this river goes all the way to the sea?" Clar asked.

"That's what rivers do," Folha replied gravely. "At least, I'm hoping."

Trahidour shook his head. "I'm pretty sure the country changes," he said. "It's all farmland and fields nearer the coast. We saw it from the ship, remember."

"One tiny bit of it," Clar pointed out. "Could be it's like this all the way; we just don't know. Anyhow, I hope it stays like this, it's not so bad."

"Does anyone know what language they speak?" Chanso asked.

It was soon clear that nobody had thought about that. "It's a good point," Clar said. "I'm betting they talk Ironshirt. Anyway, it won't be anything we can understand. Going to make it hard for us to get a boat ride home."

"We'll make for a big city," Folha said: "some place they're used to strangers. My uncle used to go with the trade caravans; they were always doing deals with people they couldn't talk to. You wave your hands and make faces. Usually works, in the end."

"I knew a man who went to Blemya," Trahidour said. "Big cities, thousands of people crammed into tiny spaces lined with bricks. He said the smell took your head off." He looked at Chanso. "You ever been to a city?"

"Me? God, no. We're all grasslanders where I come from."

"Same here," Folha said. "Conselh was on about going to Blemya, when they had the trouble with the bad people: figured they'd be paying good wages. But all that fell through, of course. Probably just as well," he added. "Those Blemyans didn't have a clue about the bad people; it was only the Belots who could handle them."

Chanso asked, "Is it true the king of Blemya's a woman?"

"Queen," Folha said gravely. "Young girl your age, so they say."

"That's crazy."

"Never been there, so I wouldn't know. One thing I've learned on this trip, different people do things different ways, but the mistakes are always the same. I reckon a woman can make a fuck-up of ruling people just as well as a man can. Or a kid, come to that."

"They say," Clar said, "one of the emperors appointed his dog chief magistrate."

Folha nodded. "I had a dog like that once," he said.

They came to a cabin, so well hidden among the willow brakes that they didn't realise it was there until they passed it. The windows were shuttered and the door had been boarded up. "Maybe they left something inside," Trahidour said.

They agreed it was worth a look. They stove in the door with the biggest rock that Folha and Clar could lift out of the riverbed. Inside, they found four blankets, two changes of clothes for a man significantly taller than any of them, a shovel, a pick, a sledge-hammer, a knife, a side axe, a heavy-duty clay bottle (empty; faint lingering smell of beer) and a bucket of nails. Folha figured that the shed must've been there for men who worked on the river, maintaining the fords, that sort of thing. It hadn't been used for a long time. Come to that, they hadn't seen a ford yet.

"Never mind," Folha said. "We'll sling it all on the spare horse. Who knows what might come in handy? Here, Clar, you could stand on my shoulders and we could wear the coat."

"A blanket each," Trahidour said. "Now there's luxury."

That evening they saw two riders, a man and a woman. Not for long; the riders must have seen them, because they turned round and went back the way they had come, at speed. Chanso didn't like the look of that, but Folha said he wasn't worried. "Maybe she wasn't his wife," he said. "I'd clear out, if someone saw me. They were a long way off, they couldn't see who we were, so I don't suppose they were scouts for the Ironshirts. Could be they're just wary of strangers. In which case, they'll be as keen to stay clear of us as we are of them."

But he wouldn't let Clar light a fire, and Chanso noticed him sitting up late into the night, keeping watch, as Conselh had done. He had the bow and arrows with him, and the bow was strung.

Folha must have fallen asleep sometime between midnight and dawn, because they came with the first light of the rising sun, and nobody heard them until it was too late.

Chanso was jerked awake by a shout. He sat up, and a foot hit him in the face, accidentally or deliberately; there was a scuffle: three men were pulling a fourth to the ground, Chanso couldn't see who it was. Then he heard the solid, chunky noise of something hard hitting bone, and more shouting in a language he didn't understand. He jumped up, and something hit him in the small of the back; he spun round, and a man hit him on the forehead with a long stick. It wasn't hard enough to knock him down, but his ears rang and his vision blurred for a moment, and the pain made everything else irrelevant. Then the stick caught him under the ribs. He staggered backwards and sat down hard, unable to breathe. He realised he was waiting for the third blow, but it didn't come.

And they kept on shouting, whoever they were; angry, urgent, insistent; they were furious about something, but the words made no sense. A man came up to him, stopped a few inches from him; he was big, huge, with a broad, flat face and a black beard, and he was holding an axe in one hand and a knife in the other. He yelled; Chanso realised he was yelling at him, demanding the answer to a question, very angry because he wasn't getting an answer. "I don't understand," Chanso said, and that got him the poll of the axe on his collarbone. He screamed and the man kicked his head.

Two men were holding Folha's arms. The man who'd just kicked Chanso went over to Folha in two giant strides and put the blade of his knife under his chin. Then he looked round – at Chanso, and Clar and Trahidour, who were lying on the ground with men standing over them – and started shouting again; a question, definitely that, but still completely incomprehensible. He waited, then shouted it again, only louder. Trahidour said, "We can't understand you," in a faint, weak voice. Somebody kicked him. The man with the knife bellowed out his question a third time. Then he said three words, evenly spaced with gaps, like a man counting. Then he cut Folha's throat.

The men who'd been holding Folha came forward and pulled Clar to his feet. The shouting man rested the knife on his throat and asked the same meaningless question. Then the count – something, then Chanso thought the second syllable might have been *dui*, then the third word, and then he cut Clar's throat, too. Trahidour tried to jump up, he was yelling now; one of the men kicked him, probably missed, because the kick landed on the ball of his shoulder, and Trahidour ignored it; "We don't know your language, you stupid fucking—" A man behind him hit the back of his head with an axe handle and he dropped flat on his face. They hauled him up and put the knife to his throat. The man with the knife turned and looked straight at Chanso. This time he spoke rather than shouted, in the voice you use when your anger is beyond mere yelling. He repeated the question, slowly and clearly. He repeated it again. He began the count; *ang, dui*. "Please," Chanso shouted, "we can't understand." *Tin*, said the man with the beard, and killed Trahidour.

Up to that moment, Chanso had been frozen stiff. But when they tried to grab him, he sprang backwards, landed badly, picked himself up; he saw two men dart to either side, while two more came straight at him. He spun round and started to run; he managed four long strides, then something caught his ankle and he went down. The impact knocked him breathless; he kicked wildly to free his leg, connected with something, two, three times and then his foot was free. He scrambled up again and a man loomed in front of him. He jumped like a cat, grabbing for the man's throat with both hands; the man sidestepped. Chanso landed on his outstretched hands, pushed with his legs, ran himself upright. Five strides, and something impossibly hard and heavy slammed into the side of his head. He felt the ground hit his face. He tried to get up, but there was a weight on his back he couldn't shift, so heavy it was going to snap his spine. He twisted sideways, shifted the weight; a man fell across him, he scrabbled with both hands, found a face, ripped at it with his nails. The man shrank back, enough for him to slither free, dig his feet into the ground, get up again. Two hands clamped on his arm; he tugged, trying to dislodge the hands or rip his arm out of the socket. Someone had got his other arm; they were both pulling, stretching him. He kicked sideways, connected; the man on his left went down but didn't let go, pulled him down, too. He pushed with his legs and back against the ground, trying to free himself of his own arms, the way you try and burst through when you're all tangled up in briars. Someone trod on the inside of his left knee, folding his leg to the ground and put an elbow round his throat. He strained against it, pitting his windpipe against bone. He couldn't breathe at all. His strength drained out of him and he hung still.

He could see the man with the knife approaching. That brought his strength back, but he had nothing to push with or against. He knew the man with the knife would ask him the question, repeating it three times. Then he'd count, ang, dui, tin. And then he would slice his throat.

The man with the knife stopped, an arm's length away. He held out the knife until its point touched Chanso's eyebrow; he pressed, quite delicately but firmly, until blood dripped into Chanso's eye and closed it. Then he cut a line, along the eyebrow to the top of the nose, down the nose, through the lips, around the curve of the chin, stopping just short of the soft neck under the jaw. He asked the question, quite calmly, the first time.

"I can't understand you," Chanso said.

The elbow round his throat tightened, levering his head up, lifting his chin away from the point of the knife. Chanso looked into the eyes of the man with the knife; they were deep and brown. The man said something different; it would be something like, be reasonable, I don't want to have to do this. Chanso opened his mouth; it was full of blood, and he made a spluttering noise. The man asked the question the second time, and Chanso thought: it doesn't matter, it's time now, it's over and it won't hurt. He took a deep breath.

Someone shouted, a different voice, somewhere behind the man with the knife. Chanso couldn't understand it, but it made the man with the knife look round. He said something; he sounded angry, offended, how dare you interrupt me? The distant voice spoke again. The man with the knife shouted furiously, and turned back to Chanso. He started to repeat the question. Then Chanso heard a familiar whirring noise, and a thump, and saw an arrowhead appear between the knifeman's eyebrows.

For a moment, the man with the knife was quite still; then he fell forward. His head cracked down on to Chanso's forehead – he could feel his brain move inside his skull; then his arms were suddenly free. Unsupported, he fell, his face bumping hard on the back of the dead man's head. Another whirring noise, another, three more. Then dead silence; then the sound of approaching footsteps. And then a pleasant voice said, "Are you all right?"

Another voice said, "Sergeant, that's a bloody stupid question", and he heard boot leather creak as someone knelt down beside him. A hand gently raised his chin; a moment later, someone caught hold of his arms and raised him to his feet; like kind-hearted bystanders at an accident.

One eye was still full of blood and he couldn't open it. Through the other he saw two faces; one young, with red hair; the other older, with grey hair. The older man said, "What's your name?"

Chanso swallowed the blood in his mouth and said, "Chanso."

"The woodcarver?"

"I don't—" He had to stop and rest, and try again. "I don't understand."

"Are you Chantat mi Chanso, the woodcarver?"

"That's my name. I don't understand."

The older man turned his head and nodded. The younger man gave him something. He held it up so Chanso could see. It was the bear he'd whittled and thrown in the river.

"Did you do this?" the older man asked.

He was on the point of denying it; but he said, "Yes."

The older man grinned at him, then turned back and called out something in another language. The sound of it brought the fear rushing back. He was just about to move when the older man said, "It's all right, you're fine. You're safe. Nobody's going to hurt you. Let go of him," he added, and the hands let go. Chanso swayed for a moment, then found his feet. It was essential that he should stay upright, unhelped. He straightened his back.

"Boy, are we glad to see you," the older man said. "We've been chasing after you for days; we were sure we'd lost you. And talk about cutting it fine." He grinned. "You're in a bit of a mess," he said. "Let's sit you down and see what we can do."

They led him to the riverbank. The sun was up now, and he could see them: six men in plain grey coats, with quivers and longbows as tall as they were, such as the Ironshirt foot soldiers used. Four of them were incredibly tall, like giants. They sat him down on a tree trunk, and the red-headed giant knelt beside him and dabbed away the blood from his face with a tuft of wool dipped in water.

The older man sat next to him. "Look at me," he said. "How many fingers am I holding up?"

"Two."

"Splendid. Do you feel sick? Dizzy?"

"No."

The older man raised an eyebrow. "You must have a skull like a rock," he said. "Does it hurt when you breathe in?"

"No. A little."

"If you had broken ribs, you'd know about it. No, amazingly, I think you're basically in one piece. Obviously you're built to last, down south. Now then, my name's Myrtus, and this is Sergeant Teucer. If you don't mind, we'd like you to come with us."

From where he was sitting, Chanso could just see the feet of one of the dead men. "You can speak our language."

Myrtus nodded. "We're educated," he said. "Smart lads, all of us."

"Who were those men? Why did they—?"

Myrtus pursed his lips. "I don't honestly know," he said. "But the question they kept asking you was, what have you done with our sheep? So I guess they were shepherds, and they thought you were thieves." He frowned. "My fault," he said. "I lost your trail back by the reed beds, and I didn't pick it up again till it was almost dark. Like a fool I said, let's wait here and catch them up in the morning. Well," he added, "I wasn't to know, was I? Still, it's a mess, and I expect I'll get shouted at for it in due course. Wouldn't be the first time."

"Who are you?" Chanso asked.

"Ah." Myrtus seemed amused by the question. "That may take some explaining, unless your uncle happens to be a blacksmith. Well? Is he?"

"No. Both my uncles are shepherds."

"Ah, well. In that case, we're your guardian angels and the patron saints of woodcarvers. And I'm afraid you're coming with us, whether you like it or not." He paused, and said, "If I were you, I'd like it. You're in no fit state not to. Talk about your dramatic last-minute rescues," he added cheerfully. "You're lucky that Sergeant Teucer here's the best shot in the entire human race. Forty-five yards, and in rotten light, got him right plumb in the head. If it had been anyone else, you'd be dog food by now."

They buried all the bodies, side by side. They did a proper job. They didn't seem to be in any hurry.

"Basically, we're—" Myrtus paused and frowned. "All right," he said, "basically, we're *priests*." He spoke the word as though he was ashamed of it, he didn't mean it, there was something wrong with it. "We're priests," he repeated, "and we believe that exceptional people – exceptionally talented people, like you – are a gift from, um, God, and you should be looked after and kept safe and brought together to serve, well, God, by doing the things you do so well for, ah, in His service." He groaned slightly. "It's so much more complicated than that, but your language just doesn't have the words, I'm sorry, or if it does they didn't teach them on the course I went on. The point is, we're going to take you to a place where they'll explain all this properly and teach you some other stuff you need to know, and then we'd like it very much if you'd come and work for us building our temple. Which isn't a temple, needless to say, but I'm sure you get the idea."

"Excuse me," Chanso said. "You must've got it wrong. I'm not anybody."

Myrtus smiled at him. "I have to beg to differ on that one," he said. "Our people identified you back in your own country, from some carvings you'd done there, and then they found out you'd come over here for the war, so we went scurrying off to Rasch to look for you while the siege was on, but it was – well, difficult, let's say, and by the time we'd sorted out which unit you were with, you'd left there and were headed back this way. And of course we had no idea about the battle, that really threw us, so by the time we'd been through everything on the battlefield – didn't help that bloody Ocnisant got there before we did, so we had to buy about six hundred dead bodies off him, just to be sure none of them were you. Anyway, what with one thing and another, we've been chasing around like idiots trying to catch up with you, and it's more luck than judgement we found you at all, since you weren't with your unit. We just latched on to the few groups of your people that managed to get away from the battle. As luck would have it, I got sent to follow the group you turned out to be with. There's a dozen other parties like mine buzzing round the place after the other survivors; I imagine they'll have given it up as a bad job by now, or made contact and found out you're not there. Not that any of that matters a damn, because we found you and you're safe. Just as well you're on the tall side, for your lot. I'm guessing that's why the shepherds saved you till last, assumed you were the oldest, therefore the leader. Either that, or it was pure fluke. They're simple folk, the locals, and thick as bricks."

"You collect *people*?" Chanso said.

They were riding beside the river again, two ahead, two behind, and Chanso in the middle with Myrtus on one side of him and the tall sergeant on the other. "Put like that it does sound a bit dubious," Myrtus said, "but I guess it's true, yes, we do. The Eastern emperor collects silver, books, old coins, all sorts of junk, and the Lodge collects people. But we put them to work, doing good things. You ask the sergeant here, he'll tell you. We collected him, and he's never looked back. Isn't that right?"

The red-haired man smiled.

"We picked him up because he's an amazing shot," Myrtus went on. "And you're an amazing carver. Can I keep this, by the way?" He took the bear out of his pocket and put it straight back again; *no* clearly wouldn't be an acceptable answer. "Thanks. Probably be worth good money in a year or so. No, we hit on you because our – well, one of the top men in the Lodge is crazy about your no Vei primitive-naturalist figure carving, he wants it all over the beams in the Great Hall at Central. I gather we're on the track of a couple more like you, so with any luck you'll have people from home to talk to when you get there."

Chanso was quiet for a while. "You did all that," he said, "just to get someone to carve wood for you?"

Myrtus shrugged. "The Eastern emperor just turned down a chance to end the war to get a—" words Chanso didn't understand. "Pretty silver things," Myrtus glossed. "About yay big, smaller than the palm of your hand. And, actually, I can see his point. I think any of us in the Lodge would've done the same thing."

They were friendly and smiled a lot, and they'd bound up his ribs with bandages just in case, and they had the most amazing food. But Myrtus and Teucer rode just close enough to him that there was no chance of making a run for it, and there were the two horsemen behind, and the two in front. "We look after what we truly value," Myrtus explained gravely. "You don't mind, do you?"

He didn't answer that. Instead he asked, "Where are you taking me?"

Myrtus shook his head. "I could tell you, but it wouldn't mean a damn thing to you, I don't suppose. Let's just say far, far away and leave it at that. Somewhere you'll be well fed and you won't get beaten up any more. How does that sound?"

He paused for a moment before replying. "Fantastic," he said.

"It's perfectly simple," the sergeant told him. "All you need is this." He opened the flap of the right-side pannier and drew out a strange copper thing. It was circular and flat, the size of a big pancake or a small shield, and it had flanges all round, forming a raised rim, and a handle, and the inside was silvery with fresh tin. "This," the sergeant said proudly, "is a Western army regulation service-issue twelve-inch field duty frying pan. We buy them off Ocnisant, a hundred at a time." He let Chanso hold the handle, then took it back and packed it away. "You stick that over a fire, pour in just enough oil to cover the bottom, let it warm up. While it's doing that, you chop up four onions into tiny bits. Chuck 'em in the oil, add a few ground-up herbs, throw in your meat, a bit of cheese, a bit of flour, lentils, milk if you've got it, ditto vegetables, cut up really small, give it a stir from time to time and there you go. Dead simple, works with any damn thing." He frowned. "Except pork," he added.

"Pork."

"Yes. You know, pork? From pigs?"

"You eat pigs."

The sergeant grinned. "Sorry, forgot. The captain says it's because you're herdsmen, always on the move, and what you're not used to; you think it's nasty. Mind you, we're the same about spiders, and I've met people who say there's nothing better, fried in batter. Don't worry," he added quickly, "we've got quail, partridge, hare, basically anything that doesn't know to hide when it sees me coming. I shoot it, I cook it, that's what they keep me around for. Learned how to at Beal Defoir. That's where you'll be going. You'll like it there, I promise you."

"That's what they eat at – where you said?"

"No. Much, much better. There was a lad when I was there, sharp as a razor, every year he failed the tests on purpose just so he could stay and enjoy the food. Reckoned he'd hang around until he'd learned everything, and then they'd make him a professor and he'd never have to leave."

Chanso sat down on the grass. A few yards away, the troopers were watering the horses, while Myrtus scowled at a map. It didn't mean they were lost, the sergeant had explained, just that his eyesight wasn't what it was.

"Sergeant," he said. "Why did the shepherds kill my friends?"

The sergeant looked down at the grass. "We reckon they thought you were sheep thieves," he said. "That's bad, these days. The army foragers took most of the sheep. They can't spare any more."

Chanso nodded. He could understand that. "Ever since the battle," he said, "everyone gets killed and there's only me left. And all I can do is try not to think about it."

The sergeant smiled at him. "That's why you need to go to Beal Defoir," he said. "They'll explain it to you there, about the Lodge, and how it all makes sense. I lost my family, too, and all my friends. But once they explain it to you, you understand and it's fine. You don't believe me, of course you don't, but it's true. Suddenly everything falls into place, and you'll never be unhappy again."

They passed through a sequence of abandoned villages, one after another, on the edge of what had once been cultivated land. A road had recently been cut through head-high tangles of briars; Myrtus explained that the briar thrives on fertile ground, especially where it's been ploughed and manured for centuries. There were thorn thickets, the stems as thick as Chanso's wrist, where the bushes had self-seeded from hedges. Vast holly brakes crowded out what had once been coppiced woods, and where stands of mature timber had been felled, the ground was reed marsh, briar and scrub. Even the grass pastures were wet as sponges; ploughed land does that, apparently, when you stop ploughing it. Myrtus found it all fascinating – his family were landowners far away in the Mesoge, and improvement had been their hobby for generations. If he had the management of it, he declared, and about a hundred thousand prisoners of war, he'd have a crop off it in ten years, fifteen at the most. "But what they'll probably do is turn the whole lot over to sheep," he said sadly. "If my grandchildren ever come here, they'll find nothing but gorse and heather." Every half-mile or so they passed a charcoal pit, just starting to disappear under ivy and bindweed.

But the food just kept getting better and better, and his ribs stopped hurting, and the cuts on his face scabbed over nicely without infection. "You'll have a sweetheart of a scar," Myrtus told him cheerfully. "But I don't suppose that'll bother you."

Chanso considered explaining about the house marks on his forehead, but decided not to bother.

"My cousin," Myrtus went on, "he's had these terrible scars on his face ever since he was a kid. I can't say it's held him back particularly. He's a musician. Actually, he's more of a teacher, though he doesn't really do any teaching. It's complicated. The point is, a few red squiggles on your face needn't be the end of the world. And it's not like you're missing an ear or anything yucky like that."

Somehow, Chanso wasn't keen on dwelling on his future disfigurement. "How can someone be a teacher and not teach?" he asked.

Myrtus scratched his ear. "It's sort of the way we do things. If a man's a really good teacher, we stop him teaching and make him an organiser. Don't ask me to explain because you probably can't grasp the advanced concepts involved. Anyway, he still makes up music. I don't think he's supposed to, but he's so grand these days, nobody can stop him."

Beyond the spoiled farmland the country rose steeply. They rode across moors, and skyline-to-skyline expanses of ankle-high tree stumps, where a great pine forest had been cut down. Props, Myrtus explained; when you're laying siege to a city, you dig tunnels under the walls to undermine them, and you need wooden props to keep the tunnels from falling in. All this – he waved his arm vaguely at the unending row of stumps – went to underpin the siege works at (some place or other; Chanso didn't catch the name), about ten years ago; he couldn't remember now whether the city fell or not, but they moved a lot of earth and used up a lot of props. Fifty years of pine needles had so poisoned the ground that nothing would grow between the stumps except bracken and flags.

"Civilisation," Myrtus said, pointing. "See, over there, in the steep-sided valley between the two mountain ranges. That's Ioto. Nice place, if you don't mind breathing soot."

Once the heather gave way to grass, they started seeing sheep on the hillsides, and small herds of short, hairy ponies – bred for the mines, Myrtus said, these hills were practically solid iron, and Ioto was the iron-founders' town. And over there – he pointed to a range of hills scarred by deep brown gorges – that was where they dug coal to feed the foundries. Coal? Ah. It's a sort of black rock, and it burns like charcoal, only better. No, seriously.

When they were two days away from the city, Chanso asked about the stuff on the grass. It was like hoar frost, only black. Soot, Myrtus explained.

The sky behind the city was brown, and the sun was a red, sore gleam. Ten miles from the city gates, the drop-hammers had sounded like tinkling bells. Once inside the walls, the noise was a low ceiling inside your head that stopped you thinking beyond the simple and immediate. The buildings were black, the streets narrow and blocked with carts, whose wheels ran half-spoke deep in mud-bottomed ruts. There were high, arched wooden bridges over the main thoroughfares, because crossing at street level was impossible, and had been so for as long as anyone could remember.

It was strange to see people again; very strange indeed to see so many of them. Seventy thousand, Myrtus said; of course, the city had grown enormously during the war. All the country people for miles around had come in to town, to be safe and to find work. Even so, the foundries and the munitions factory were desperately short of workers; they had to pay ridiculously high wages, which was why everything in Ioto was five times the price you'd pay elsewhere. Ocnisant's third biggest competitor, the Ministers of Grace, were based here. Apart from them, and the general stores, commissaries and mercantiles, everyone worked for the war, making arrowheads. Just arrowheads, nothing else.

The Lodge had a house in Ioto, or, rather, a cellar: a huge cellar, like underground caverns. Two hundred feet down, it was quiet and cool and the air was relatively clean; water came from an underground cistern. It was clear, and more or less safe to drink if you boiled it first. Chanso was terrified; he felt like he was in a grave, and he couldn't understand why the roof didn't cave in, with the weight of all those buildings on top of it. They ate in a long, deserted hall with a stunningly carved and gilded roof, and slept in a little stone box, like the ones Chanso had seen in Blemya, for keeping ice through the summer.

"It's called tea," Myrtus said. "You make it by boiling leaves in water. Some people add honey and spices. It cuts the dust like nothing else, and you can drink it all day without falling over."

Turned out it didn't taste of anything, which was just fine. "Tell me about the Lodge," Chanso said.

Myrtus was quiet for a long time, until Chanso had decided he'd asked a rude question and was being ignored. Then Myrtus swallowed all his tea in one gulp and said, "The Lodge is—" And then he stopped.

"I'm sorry," Chanso said. "Is it something you're not supposed to tell me?"

"What? God, no. It's just so hard to explain." He looked round for a while, then raised his hand and waved it. The waving became a beckoning, and then he lowered it again. "I can't answer you," he said, "but this lady can." He called out in the horrible foreign language, and Chanso saw someone in a long grey gown coming towards them. "Siarma," he said. "Someone I want you to meet."

Siarma was female; about Chanso's mother's age, very tall and beautiful. She sat down next to Myrtus and lifted the cowl off her face. "Nice to see you, too, Captain. Who's this?"

Myrtus grinned. "He's probably got a catalogue number by now, but his name's Chanso, as you'll have gathered he's no Vei, and he'd like someone to explain to him about the Lodge. I thought, you'll do it so much better than me, and it'll give you a chance to polish up your irregular verbs."

She turned her head and smiled at Chanso. "It's always a pleasure to speak your language," she said, and unlike Chanso she had no trace of an accent. "I learned it for five years before I even met a no Vei, so you'll have to forgive me if I get things wrong."

"You're doing fine," Chanso said. "Really."

Myrtus laughed. "She's head of the faculty of southern languages," he said. "Means she knows more about it than you do."

"Ignore him," Siarma said. "One of my least promising students. What can I tell you about the Lodge?"

Chanso hesitated. Then he said, "Everything."

"Oh, that." She frowned. "Myrtus, be a darling and get us some more tea, this is ice-cold. And see if they've got any of those nice biscuits."

Myrtus grinned and went away. "You don't know anything at all?" she said.

"No."

"Very well." She laced her fingers together and rested them on the table. "In that case, let me tell you a story."

"Once upon a time," she said, "there was a blacksmith. He lived in a city, or a village, or a tent in the grass country, and people from miles around used to come to him for the tools and the other things they needed.

"Every day, just before daybreak, he would build a great fire, as hot as the sun. He crushed ore, mixed it with lime and charcoal and loaded it into a crucible; with the bellows he made the fire roar, until the iron sweated out of the rock and pooled in the pig slots he'd cut into the floor. Or he would take scrap from the scrap heap, heat it until it was soft, flatten it, draw it out, fold it and weld it and fold it again and again, then draw it down into bars over a swage block. When they were cool he put the pigs and bars up on a rack, ready to be made into whatever he needed to make.

"Many things were asked of him, from gates to spoons to needles, hooks to hinges to arrowheads. For each purpose he chose the most suitable material: plain iron for those things that neither bend nor flex, steel for those things that flex and carry an edge. He heated the material in the fire, worked it between hammer and anvil, stretched it, jumped it up, bent it, flattened it, twisted it and drew it out; he could make thick bars and thin plates, straight lines and every possible curve; he could make steel so hard it could cut steel, or sheet so thin you could crumple it in your hand. He could make springs that bent double on themselves and sprang back into shape. He could make wire that twisted and stayed twisted. Everything he made was different, but it all came from the same ore and passed between the same hammer and anvil; and everything he made was for a purpose, and everything, *everything* he made was good.

"The people would come and take away the things he made; and some of them were wise and used them well, and some of them were stupid, and used them badly. They broke them, bent them, twisted and distorted them; and then they would bring them back to the smith and say, this thing you made for me is no good, fix it or make me another.

"The smith would look at the work he had made and others had spoiled, and decide what was to be done. Because he loved the things he'd made, he would use all his skill and patience to straighten the bent and the twisted, to weld the broken, to braze and solder, to retemper the steel that had lost its memory. But sometimes the damage they had done was too great; so he put the thing he had made in the fire to soften it, until all its shape and memory were lost, and he hammered and folded and welded it back into bar stock, and began again, as if with fresh iron.

"Now, you must have seen some of the work that this smith made. You will have seen the sun and moon, which rise and set with such extraordinary precision, and the seasons that come round so reliably we can live by them, though we can't see the ratchets and the pawls. You will have seen the earth, which gives us bread and meat; you will have seen the body, which is the most perfect tool for all our needs, which responds to our quickest thought and our deepest memory. In everything that works and functions you've seen his hand; the mere fact that we can live, that we have a sun to warm us and food we can eat – if you want proof of this smith and his skill, look about you, look at everything useful and helpful and good, and ask yourself: Why does water refresh us and food nourish us? Why is there summer to grow the grain and winter to cool the earth? Why is there a sun to give us light and darkness to let us sleep? Or, if you prefer, who designed us so that we can live in the world, digesting bread and meat and water, being warmed by sunlight and cooled by shade, seeing in daylight and sleeping in the dark? You know there can only be one answer.

Because a great craftsman made all of these things, and everything he makes is good.

"And then reflect; he made me, and he made you. He made us for a purpose.

"Now the foolish people he makes things for sometimes forget or fail to understand what the purpose of his work might be. Because they're so foolish, sometimes they ask, why did he make the hurricane or the murderer or the disease? They fail to understand what they see when they look around them, at all the wonderful things he made, that serve their purpose, that work so well. They don't understand; if he made the sun, and the sun is good, and he made you and me – how can we be bad? They fail to understand that everything is good, applied to its proper purpose.

"And that," she said, "is the Lodge. In a nutshell." She poured herself a cup of the allegedly ice-cold tea, blew on it and sipped it. "Does that answer your question?"

"So you're priests," Chanso said. "Like he said."

"Priests." She looked offended. "Oh dear. No, we aren't priests, because we don't pray, and we don't have temples, and I'm not sure we have any gods, even. I think some of us believe in an old man in a leather apron. Some of us simply feel it's logical to assume that a world that functions must have a function. But priest is a bit of a rude word. You weren't to know that."

"But you believe—"

She shrugged. "So do you. You believe that if I drop a stone on your foot, it'll hurt. Well?"

"Well, yes. Obviously."

"I see. You believe in a machine – call it the world – which makes dropped things fall. Not just sometimes, not even most of the time, but always. You're halfway there, at the very least." She smiled. "I think where priests go wrong is asking people to believe in magic. Which is silly. They invent gods who can do stuff which is impossible; and when you stop and think about it, you *know* it can't be true. You can't split mountains down the middle with a frown, or fly without wings, or turn water into milk or wake the dead, and any system of values predicated on magic is obviously garbage. No, we believe in real stuff, like summer and sunrise and the germination of the seed, just as miraculous but we know it's real, because we can see it. We can see people who need to eat bread to live, and we know that if you put a wheat seed in the ground and come back later, you've got bread to eat. Coincidence? I really don't think so, do you?"

Chanso frowned. "But you said murderers and diseases—"

She nodded. "He made them, therefore they must be good, good for something. Yes, I believe that. It's the logical consequence of everything I see around me. All things have been made well, but some things are misused and some things are misunderstood, therefore some things are damaged and broken. And some things must be beaten and twisted if they are to be saved." She smiled. "I never said it was easy, or pleasant. I never said he's kind or loving or even fair. Actually, I don't see where blame and fault and good and evil come into it; it's just a case of foolish people using the wrong tool for the wrong job. And, of course, that's where the Lodge comes in."

He was about to ask, but decided to think about it for himself. "The right tool for the right job."

She was pleased with him. "Precisely," she said. "To take a very simple example: some fool took a woodcarver and tried to use him as a soldier. Easily put right; and that's what we've done. Usually it's not as simple or straightforward as that. Quite often we're dealing with fools who take craftsmen – Lodge people – and try and use them as targets or chopping blocks; or other fools who mistake people for chess pieces. And sometimes we find someone and even we can't figure out what the hell he's good for. Is he a hoe, a corkscrew or a doorstop? Is he a tool, an ornament or a weapon?" She frowned. "You'd be amazed how many people turn

out to be weapons. But as often as not, a weapon can only save a
life by taking one. I've had a good few students in my classes that
were almost too dangerous to handle, but they all turned out good
in the end, once we figured what they were for. There are no bad
things and no bad people. Just bad uses." She smiled again. "Are
we getting there?"

"I think so," Chanso said. "I'm not sure I agree, but—"

"You understand." She nodded. "That's the main thing.
Agreeing can wait. Sooner or later, nearly everyone accepts that
the sun is warm and water is wet. And once you've accepted that,
all the rest will inevitably follow. Meanwhile—" over her shoulder
he could see Myrtus coming back with a teapot and a plate "—I
suggest you enjoy the free food and the safety. They're both hard
to come by anywhere else."

Myrtus went to find out the news and came back looking thoughtful. Senza Belot, it was reliably confirmed, had survived the battle.
He'd stayed to the bitter end, then rushed off alone with five hundred lancers chasing him, but he'd made it to the border and was
now back in Choris, in prison, awaiting the emperor's justice.

Forza Belot was also confirmed alive. He had been ordered to
report to Iden Astea, to explain to his emperor why deliberately
losing seventy thousand men in one battle could possibly be
construed as a victory, or a good idea. He had not yet obeyed the
order, and his whereabouts were not known. Meanwhile, press
gangs were frantically recruiting all over the Western empire,
and no man over twelve or under seventy was safe; the emperor
was reported to be offering ridiculous money for mercenaries,
with the result that the few soldiers he still had were deserting
from the regular army and signing on with the free companies.
Rasch Cuiber, which had been well fed throughout the siege,
was now starving because all the farms for miles around were
deserted; instead of coming back when the Easterners left, the

country people were staying hidden in the wilderness, for fear of the recruiting sergeants. Attempts to send a relief caravan had foundered because there were no carts, no horses and no carters willing to risk impressment. The emperor was therefore seriously considering evacuating Rasch, sending its people to Iden and burning the city itself to the ground, to keep such a well-fortified stronghold from falling into enemy hands.

Ioto was forty-eight miles from the coast, sixty if you took the flat, straight road that skirted the mountains; sometimes it was quicker, sometimes not, depending on the state of the mountain passes. The iron wagons took the long road, and it was crowded with them – some days, they reckoned, you could walk to the sea across the beds and booms of carts, and get there quicker. There were six famous inns on the long road. "We'll go that way," Myrtus decided. "It's not like we're in a tearing hurry."

Much as he'd like to, Myrtus explained, he wasn't going to Beal Defoir. At the coast he'd hand Chanso over to another agent, get his next assignment and be off again, unless his luck was in and there were orders waiting for him to head for Division or Central. No, he had no idea who the agent would be— "though if you're really lucky, you might just get my wife. You'll like her, and she'll get you there quickly with the minimum of aggravation. Her name's Tenevris: tall, bony woman with bushy red hair. Light of my life. If you do see her, give her my love."

The Crown of Absolution was as full as Myrtus had ever seen it, mostly with carters; no hope of a bed for the night, or even a designated area of straw. And then Myrtus asked various questions about the innkeeper's uncle, and suddenly there was a room, in fact there were two, and dinner was on the house.

Chanso, who'd only slept under a roof twice before, lay awake most of the night staring out of the window, trying not to think what would happen if the rafters gave way. As is often the way, he fell asleep shortly before dawn and was hard to wake up.

"Breakfast," Sergeant Teucer bellowed in his ear. "Come on, while there's some left."

Chanso wasn't hungry; he'd done nothing but eat and sit on a horse for days, like a wise old man, and he was starting to suffer from stomach cramps and wind. But he'd taken a liking to tea, and there was plenty of that. "What are those men over there doing?" he asked.

Myrtus was eating bread and smoked sausage. "Where? Oh, them. They're playing cards." He did the little frown that meant he was about to explain. "It's just a way of gambling for money. You don't want to bother with any of that."

"A game?"

"Sure. A bit of fun, passes the time. Except, like I said, they think they'll get rich. Which they won't, believe me."

"The things in their hands," Chanso said. "We've got something like them at home."

Myrtus, his mouth full, stopped chewing. "You don't say."

"Yes. Only ours are thin sheets of brass, with the numbers and shapes stamped into them. We don't have any with pictures. They use them to read the future."

Myrtus and the sergeant looked at each other. "No pictures," the sergeant said.

"No, just shapes. Spears, wheels, that sort of thing. Like, if it's got five wheels stamped on it, it's the Five of Wheels. A prophet reads them for you when you're born, and when you get married, and if you're about to do something important and you want to know how it'll turn out. I don't think it works very well," Chanso added. "Mine when I was born said I'd be a great warrior leading a mighty army, and a wise and powerful priest, and one day I'd destroy a mighty empire. I think they just say what the parents want to hear, to be honest."

Myrtus was looking at him very strangely, but his voice sounded normal. "Actually," he said, "we do something a bit like that in the Lodge, though strictly speaking we're not supposed to. But everybody does it." He looked away and added, "I can do it for you, if you want."

"Do you believe in it, then?"

"No, not really," Myrtus said. "Except – well, we all secretly believe in fortune-telling, don't we? Deep down, I mean. Even though we know it's all garbage."

"I don't," Chanso said. Then he caught sight of Myrtus' face and added, "But go on, why not? It'll be interesting to see if you do it like back home."

They went outside and found an empty space in a semi-derelict trap-house. Myrtus and Sergeant Teucer sat on the floor, insisting that Chanso should have the upturned bucket. "It's important that the subject – that's you – is higher than the reader," Myrtus explained. "God knows why but there it is." He felt in his pocket and swore. "Left my cards in my saddlebag," he said. "Got yours, Sergeant?"

Sergeant Teucer nodded and took a thin wooden box from his sleeve. Someone had made it from offcuts of veneer, and when he opened it Chanso saw veneer rectangles with things drawn on them in ink. He spread them out in a fan and started sorting them, or deliberately mixing them up. Some of them were crudely drawn pictures, but the others were the familiar marks from back home: spears, cups, wheels, swords. Then he stacked them together neatly and handed them to Myrtus, who did exactly the same thing over again. Then he handed them to Chanso.

"Take six cards off the top," Myrtus said, "and lay them down on the floor, face upwards. Face means the picture."

Chanso did as he was told. "That's odd," he said.

Myrtus was watching him like a hunter watching a skittish deer. "What?"

"You remember I said they did this when I was born? Well,

there weren't any pictures then, of course. But these—" He pointed. "With just the markings. They're the same ones."

Myrtus looked as if he was about to be sick. "Is that right?" the sergeant said.

"Yes. Eight of Spears, Two of Wheels, Four of Cups, Nine of Spears. My mother told me, and my uncle. That's weird." The way the two of them were looking at him made him feel uncomfortable; he wished he hadn't agreed to it. "All right, then," he said. "What does it mean?"

Myrtus pulled himself together with an effort. "Well," he said. "It means you're going to go back to your own country one day, and you'll be rich and happy, and you'll have four wives and nine sons. Lucky you," he added.

"Really?"

Myrtus shrugged. He seemed better now. "That's what it says."

"*Four?*" Chanso scowled. "What happens to them? Do three of them die or something?"

"It could mean daughters," the sergeant said quickly. "Four daughters and nine sons. I thought you people had more than one wife."

"No."

"Then it's daughters," Myrtus said firmly. "There, isn't that nice?"

"How do you know it says that?"

"Divine insight," Myrtus said, sweeping up the cards and cramming them back in the box so hard he made a small split in the lid. "Actually, there's a handy crib you can buy for a stuiver, tells you what they all mean. Thank you, Sergeant. And for pity's sake buy yourself a decent pack, those are a disgrace." He stood up. He seemed to be fizzing with energy, though not particularly happy. "Time we made a move," he said, "before the road gets clogged up with bloody wagons."

*

For the rest of the journey, Myrtus and Teucer were rather more distant, if no less friendly. They answered questions pleasantly enough, but offered no unsolicited information, and most of the time the troop rode on in silence. Chanso was slightly surprised by this but he didn't really mind. It gave him time to think about what he'd already been told, and other things. The conclusion he reached was that he was in no danger while he was with these people, whereas his chances of getting home, alone, were more or less zero. He got the impression it would be different once he'd done what they wanted him to; once he'd been to the teaching place, and then the place where he had to carve roof timbers. After he'd done that, presumably, they'd have no further use for him and he could go; and nothing had been said about it, but he was fairly sure he'd get paid for his work, because that was how things were done in the empires, and these people seemed to be honourable and decent. The money he earned would get him home, quite possibly with something left over. Four wives and nine sons, or four daughters. He hoped it wouldn't be wives. How could anyone expect to find the girl of his dreams four times in a row? Better odds playing knucklebones.

He was terrified on the boat, just like the last time. How anybody could think it was a good idea to float across an infinity of restless water in a small wooden box defeated him entirely.

The courier they'd handed him over to was a large, cheerful grey-haired woman who laughed at all sorts of things, not all of them funny, and beat him four times at arm-wrestling. She spoke no Vei with a strong nasal accent and only ever used the present tense. He asked her if it was usual in the empire for women to work at jobs on their own, away from their homes and families. She laughed; no, it was highly unusual: only the Lodge allowed it, because the Great Smith made us all useful, even thieves and arsonists and lepers and women. And just as well, or when her husband died in the war she'd have been eating turnip tops and sleeping under bridges, and thank God they'd never had kids. All that was changing, though, because of the war, and so many men getting killed. Some places she'd been, she'd seen women ploughing, carting, mending roads, even a woman cooper, and another one apprenticed to a tinsmith. It was like the draught stock shortage, she said; if you couldn't get horses to pull your cart, then you used oxen, and very glad of them, even if they take three times as long and eat twice as much.

He beat her the fifth time, but he was sure she'd let him win.

A white island in a dark blue sea.

The dock was a single narrow wooden jetty, poking out into infinity. Ships didn't linger at Beal Defoir, and only came in close when the sea was calm. Every so often, she told him, there was a storm and the jetty just snapped off, leaving the island cut off until it could be rebuilt with lumber shipped from the mainland. No trees on Beal, scarcely anything grew there at all. The cliffs ran right around it, and the only way up was a single winding path from the one tiny beach. But you'll like it once you get there, she added.

No horses, either. Too steep to get them up there, nothing for them to eat if you could. She gave him a big smile and waved as he started to climb. It took him a very long time, and he had to stop halfway up.

Incredibly, they'd built a twenty-foot wall all around the top, all gleaming white stone. The path stopped at a gate, whitewashed. She'd told him to knock hard and be patient.

She'd also given him a piece of paper, folded as small as a dried fig and sealed. When eventually a porter in full Ironshirt armour opened the wicket, Chanso handed it over. The door shut in his face. Quite some time later, it opened again, and a short, slim young man with long hair in braids beckoned to him to follow.

"You're no Vei," Chanso said.

"That's right," the young man said. "That's why I'm here, to make you feel at home. By the way – and it doesn't matter a damn to me, but you ought to know for later – I'm actually quite grand and important, and if there's anyone else around you've got to call me sir or your grace. My name's Lonjamen, by the way. And you're Chanso?"

"That's right. Sir."

Lonjamen gave him a mock scowl. "I said when there's other people about. Come on, I'll show you what to do."

Chanso followed him through the doorway and saw a vast square courtyard, paved with white stone, surrounded on all sides by cloisters; their roofs were green copper, with tall chimneys. In the middle of the square was a statue, gold or gilded, forty feet high; a smith standing beside his anvil, raised hammer in one hand, tongs in the other, and from the anvil rose a fountain. "That's Old Wisdom," Lonjamen told him. "You wouldn't believe the trouble we have keeping that damn fountain going. There's cisterns deep down in the rock and pipes going right into the sea, and the only place you can see the wretched thing from is inside this quadrangle." He grinned. "We're a bit like that generally. But we're all right really."

Beyond the statue was a tall building with a burnished copper dome, and that, it turned out, was where they were going. "We'll get you signed in and spoken for, and then they'll find you a place to doss down and keep your stuff, and someone'll be along to fill you in on the routine and so on. Probably me, actually. All the other no Vei speakers are even grander than I am."

There were guards on the gleaming brass doors, twice as high as a man and embossed with the most amazingly lifelike figures Chanso had ever seen. The thought that he'd come here to learn carving horrified him, if they expected results like that. Beyond the doors was a square hall whose roof was the ceiling of the dome. If anything could possibly be higher than the sky, that was it. The floor was, of course, white stone, polished so it looked like it was running with water.

"Is this the headquarters?" Chanso asked. "Of the Lodge, I mean?"

"This place? God, no. Far too grand. The higher up the Lodge you go, the less you show off. This is just a school. We inherited it from the people who were before the empire. Bit of an embarrassment, really."

Lonjamen marched him up to a desk, over against a far wall. There he spoke to a clerk in the language Chanso couldn't understand. Then Lonjamen handed over the scrap of folded paper, and the clerk put it between the pages of a ledger, which he then closed.

"All done," Lonjamen said: "you're now official. Means they know you're here, and it's somebody's job to feed you. They may even wash your shirts if you're lucky. Come on, this way."

Chanso, Lonjamen and the clerk appeared to be the only living creatures in the whole vast hall. "Are there many people here?" he asked.

"About five thousand," Lonjamen replied, "on average. Now, mind you look about you and take note of where we go. This place is like an anthill."

They came to a stretch of wall with dozens of identical doors. Lonjamen opened one and stood back to let him through. Then they were in a corridor, white floor and ceiling, the wall covered with blinding gold mosaic. "First thing you'll need to do is learn to talk Imperial. Don't pull faces, it's easy. After that they'll put you through the basic catechism, so you'll understand what we're all about, and after that you'll be working on your special skill. Silverwork, isn't it?"

"Carving."

"Of course, woodcarving. You do realise, every last scrap of wood we use here has to come up that path on some poor bugger's shoulder. No pressure," he added pleasantly. "Marble we can just chip off the scenery, it's the only thing we're self-sufficient in. That and rainwater, if we're lucky."

Chanso thought for a moment. "Should I be learning stone-carving, then?"

"Of course not. Fat lot of use that'd be for decorating a wooden roof. No, the point is, while you're here, you're the centre of the universe: nothing's too much trouble. You want it, you ask for it, it comes on a boat and they carry it up the hill for you. Live crocodiles? Of course, sir, how many? Enjoy it while you can," he added. "Real life on the outside isn't like that." He grinned. "So they tell me, anyway."

It sounded like there ought to be a *but* coming; if so, Lonjamen didn't get round to it. They walked the length of the corridor, through a bronze gate (half the size of the front gate; still massive) and out into a narrow street. The shadows of the tall buildings on either side were so deep it could almost have been night, and the ground was paved with split flints. "Mind how you go," Lonjamen advised him over his shoulder. "Bloody slippery, have you over. You get used to it in time."

It was like walking down the bed of a river, and quite soon Chanso's ankles ached. The street wound round, a bend every few yards and identical unmarked doors everywhere he looked. It was inconceivable that anyone could ever find his way here or remember where he'd been or where he was supposed to go. Chanso tried counting his paces, but the awkwardness of walking made that pointless.

"Two meals a day," Lonjamen was saying – he'd gone on ahead. Chanso couldn't keep up with him without slipping and falling over, "and if you're peckish in between, go and be nice to the buttery: they're the ones with the real power around here. If they like you, this is paradise. If not, probably best to jump off the wall now and save yourself the agonies of frustration. This is your chapter house," he added, pushing open a door. "Number

One Six Three, in case you haven't been counting." He grinned. "Count everything, all the time. Becomes second nature after a while, like with musicians. Up the stairs to the top landing, seventh door on your right." He paused, then added, "I know what you're thinking. For weeks when I first got here, I thought I'd go out of my mind, being indoors, under roofs and ceilings. Don't worry, you'll adapt. This place grinds you down to begin with, but then you fit in and it's wonderful. See you later, probably."

Chanso had no idea how long it took him to learn Imperial. Afterwards he could remember days of unbelievable effort, when his mind was more utterly exhausted than his body had ever been in his life, followed by nights dreaming in a strange language, where he could make out one word in ten, then in four, then in three; and then there was the morning when he dragged himself up the eight flights of stairs to the rooftop where Domna Herec taught him, and she looked at him sourly and told him to go away.

He felt as though he'd been kicked in the face. "Why?" he asked. "What have I done?"

'Na Herec was eighty years old and the most terrifying human being he'd ever encountered. She must have been six feet tall when she was younger, and very beautiful. Now she had one appalling eye, sparse white hair scraped back into a bun and a tone of voice like fingernails digging into a burn. He'd spent every waking hour with her for as long as he could remember; ten days, possibly twelve.

"You've finished, that's what," she said. "Go away, I'm busy."

He felt terrible; all the effort she'd put in, all the patience she'd wasted on him, all the furious anger at his ineptitude she'd bottled up behind that one piercing eye, and finally she'd decided he was hopeless and she'd given up on him. "I'm sorry," he blurted out. "Please, can't we try again? I'll do better, I promise. I'll try really hard."

She gave him that look. "What language are we speaking?"

"Oh."

"Go away," she repeated, "and come back this time tomorrow; we'll be starting the next course. Try not to be late, if you can possibly manage it."

The next day she told him it was probably because he'd never learned to read. Illiterates (that was him) found it much easier to pick up new languages, because their minds and memories hadn't been spoiled: they still worked like a child's. And now, she went on, I'm going to teach you to read.

Reading was easy; it was like sheep tallies, except that each mark stood for a sound rather than a number or a place or ewe or ram. The hardest part was learning how to hold the stick. To start with, he gripped it so firmly it broke. Then he pressed down too hard, and went right through the half-inch of beeswax and split the wood. For a carver, she told him, he was incredibly cack-handed; is that how he handled his chisels and gouges?

What are chisels and gouges? he asked.

This, said Domna Seutz, is a chisel and this is a gouge. You can tell them apart because the chisel is flat and the gouge is half round. And what in God's name do you carve with where you come from if you don't know about chisels? What, *that*?

There were twenty-six chisels on Domna Seutz's rack, all different, and sixteen gouges. 'Na Seutz was younger than 'Na Herec, a short, solid woman with a man's hands and a humped back. Her eyes, she said, weren't what they were, so she had a round piece of glass, flattish, with thin edges and a thicker centre, mounted in a gold setting with wires sticking out of it. The wires fitted into carefully sewn sleeves in the linen band she wore round her forehead, and kept the glass a constant three-quarter inch from her right eye. When Chanso looked through it at his fingernail, it was nearly twice its normal size. No, he couldn't have one; these glasses had been made in Mezentia, a thousand years ago or something like that. There were only a few left, and nobody had been able to figure out how to make more of them. This one was Lodge property, on loan to her for the rest of her working life. Nobody knew what it was worth, but Emperor Glauca had one like it in his collection, and he'd traded the city of Scand Escatois to the Aelians to get it.

'Na Seutz wasn't nearly as fierce as 'Na Herec, but she was much harder to please. She didn't like the primitive style, she told him. What's that? It's what you do, she explained. She preferred Classical and Mannerist, though she didn't mind Formalism. The idea of art, she explained, is not to show things as they are, but as they could be. Only the Great Smith could make something perfect – everything he made was perfect – but surely it was the duty of his servants to come as close to perfection as they could. Therefore, let every man be handsome, every woman beautiful, every tree and flower grace-fully formed, every mountain symmetrical, every dog and squirrel as close to the ideal as possible. Portraits, in her opinion, were an abomination; a deliberate record of human inferiority and diver-gence from the ideal form. However, she recognised that Chanso had been sent to Beal to learn to be the best possible primitive-style carver he could become, so it wasn't her place to try and influence him in any way. But if he could possibly make his people's faces just a bit less ugly, she would take it as a personal favour.

Chanso reckoned she was probably mad. But she taught him a lot of very useful stuff about using the new, strange tools, and once he'd got used to them he found them quite helpful – if nothing else, they were quicker than gnawing away a flake at a time with a knife, and you could do straight lines and square edges, assuming you wanted to. And she could get an edge on a blade better than anyone he'd ever known, including his Uncle Vastida.

"You might want to take a look at this," she said, on the day he finished his first large piece for her. He was proud of it – a stag pulled down by dogs, with the huntsmen closing in; she said it was a bit too busy for her taste, but she was pleased that he'd finally grasped the concept of proportion, and the dogs' heads were the right size for their bodies.

He looked at the thing she'd put on the bench in front of him. "It's a book," she explained. "You read it."

"All of it?"

She looked at him. "Yes."

He picked the book up and opened it. "Both sides?"

"Give it here." She took it from him and turned the pages. "All of them," she said. "Both sides."

"My God."

He took the book back to his cell that evening, lit the lamp, put the book down on the floor and lay on his stomach, his head propped on his hands. Extraordinary thing; the black letters on the smooth, flat white page were so much easier to make out than the scratches in the beeswax – a clever bit of design, he had to admit – and after a while he found he didn't have to say the words aloud. They seemed to talk to him inside his head; they sounded rather like 'Na Herec, but without the seething impatience. He couldn't actually follow any of it – lots of names of people he hadn't heard of and words he didn't know; it was supposed to be about carving, but there was nothing about work-holding or following the grain, or how to get the last little flakes and fibres out of a corner – but that hardly seemed to matter. It was like a vision, or eavesdropping on angels. Sobering thought, that the people who lived in this unbelievable place read books all the time. He carried on until all the oil in his lamp was burned up; then he rolled on to his back (one thing he hadn't mastered yet was beds; there was nothing to stop him rolling off while he was asleep, and he had bruises he hoped he'd never have to explain) and dreamed of a great voice from heaven denouncing neo-formalism, while the sea rose up and lashed at the white encircling walls.

*

He was quite used to eating alone. The kitchens served two meals a day, but 'Na Herec and 'Na Seutz didn't approve of eating and wouldn't let him leave while there was still light in the sky just because of food. So when it was dark and they reluctantly let him go, he counted doors to the buttery and looked pathetic and sad until one of the bakers took pity on him. Pity usually took the form of that morning's bread (officially stale and only for pigswill; it was the most wonderfully soft bread he'd ever tasted) and whatever the bakers were having for dinner. They kept trying to get him to drink beer; he took it away in a brown jug and poured it down the drain outside his chapter house. Apart from the bakers and his teachers, he hadn't spoken to anyone since he arrived, but it didn't seem to bother him. The streets were usually deserted when he walked through them, and the people in the neighbouring rooms were all still asleep when he got up in the morning and out when he got back at night. He no longer winced when he heard Imperial spoken; he was beginning to think in it, and it was disconcerting sometimes when there was something he wanted to say and he realised there was no way of saying it. "Quite," 'Na Herec said, when he told her about the problem. "Imperial isn't a very good language. No Vei's much better for thinking big thoughts in, and Aelian is so much better for logical arguments. Imperial's good for laws and legal documents, and that's about all. But we're stuck with it, and there it is." She gave him that look. "I never could understand why a bunch of savages like your lot should have produced a language ideally suited for metaphysical debate, it seems such a waste."

Then 'Na Herec said she didn't want to see him again; he was fluent in Imperial, he could read adequately and his handwriting, though dreadful, was no worse than that of the Dean of Humanities. Instead, he was to report to Domna Lysao for his Ordinary Catechism—

"But I've done that," he said. "We did it together. You said I was—"

"Yes, and you are. But that's the Simple Catechism. Now you're going to do the Ordinary Catechism, which is different. Fairly different," she amended. "It covers the same basic core material, but this time you've got to show you understand it."

He looked at her. "Couldn't you—?"

Maybe just a tiny movement at the corner of her mouth, using the muscle other people used for smiling. "Yes, but I'm sick to death of the sight of you. Also, believe it or not, you're not the only student at Beal Defoir. I, however, am the only teacher who knows Erech Nichar. So Lysao gets you, and I wish her the very best of luck."

Two days before 'Na Lysao wanted to see him. An opportunity to lie in in the morning. But Lonjamen came and hammered on his door at the crack of dawn and dragged him down to breakfast.

"Are all the teachers here women?" he asked.

"What? No, of course not. About half and half, actually. You haven't got a problem with that, have you? They speak very highly of you."

That made no sense. "What, you mean 'Na Seutz and 'Na Herec? They both think I'm a disaster."

Lonjamen grinned. "Shows exceptional promise, unusual aptitude, rare to find such a combination of ability and diligence."

"'Na Seutz said that?"

"No," Lonjamen said. "She said you're naturally gifted but open-minded and eager to learn." He poured Chanso some tea. "Don't worry," he said. "I had 'Na Herec when I first got here. She made me feel like something you wipe off your shoe, but she taught me Imperial in no time flat. Marvellous woman. Her husband was sixth in line to the throne." He made that gesture with forefinger and throat. "That was fifty years ago. She's been here ever since."

"She *likes* me?"

Lonjamen laughed. "She's got a soft spot for all us no Vei," he said. "But what impresses her is talent. And if she's impressed, so am I. Try the pancakes, they're not bad."

A bit like saying the sea is perceptibly moist. "I thought she couldn't wait to see the back of me," he said with his mouth full.

"Well, there you go. Anyway, you get full marks and a gold star. Doesn't mean anything, but it's nice to know. You'll continue with 'Na Seutz, of course. Did she make you read Herennius on style and form?"

"Yes. I think so. I mean, I'm only about a quarter of the way through."

"It comes with practice," Lonjamen said. "Like everything. And 'Na Lysao for catechism." He paused, a scrap of pancake frozen in the air between mouth and plate. "You mustn't mind her," he said. "She's got a slightly unfortunate manner."

Chanso stared at him. "Like 'Na Herec?"

"Oh, Herec's a pussycat, everybody knows that. But Lysao can be—" He shrugged. "She's had a hard life. Make allowances."

The rule was that letters, notes, memoranda and the like should be written on wax tablets rather than paper or parchment, and everywhere you went there were bins and buckets to dump used tablets in; they were collected up at the end of the day, the wax was melted and refreshed, ready for reuse. On his way to his first lesson with 'Na Lysao, Chanso dutifully binned the tablet on which she'd written the time and the place, an action he regretted for the rest of his life.

The New Building (one of the oldest structures on Beal, needless to say) was part of the west wing of the main citadel. To get there, you had to thread your way through the narrowest streets on the island, steadily climbing until your heels were raw and your calves felt they were about to burst, until you came to a massive gateway flanked by two enormous stylised alabaster lions. Two armed guards were on duty at the gate; they smiled at Chanso as he passed, then carried on their conversation about the cock-fighting. From the gateway, a long stair rose up between tall buildings until he reached another gate, guarded by two more armed men. Behind them was a pair of doors, with six hinges on each side and four locks. Beyond the door was another stair, at the top of which stood two guards in gilded parade-ground armour. One of them asked his name, calling him "sir". He told them; they replied that he was expected, go on up. At the top of the stairs, outside a simple wooden door, an archer sat on the top step, bow drawn, arrow on the string; a no Vei. He stood up, smiling, and said something Chanso didn't understand. The archer repeated it, and Chanso realised he was speaking no Vei; "Are you here for the lesson?" Yes, he replied in Imperial, and gave his name. The archer nodded, rapped on the door and opened it for him.

She was standing by an open window, her back to him; all he saw was a slight, short woman with reddish-brown hair in a long braid. She turned and faced him.

She was neither beautiful nor pretty; a small, quite plain face and a thin body. She was probably ten years older than him. His mouth was suddenly dry and he'd forgotten his own name.

"Are you Chanso?" she said.

He nodded. She gave him a slight frown. "Sit down," she said.

Chanso looked round desperately for a chair, then realised his leg was touching one. He sat in it. She perched on a window seat, one foot resting on a pile of books, the other on the floor. "You're no Vei, aren't you?" she said. "One of Senza Belot's men."

He could never describe the way she said the name, though afterwards he did his best many times, when called on to do so. But as soon as she said it, he remembered where he'd heard her name before. It had been all over the camp. Lysao: the woman Senza Belot loved to the point of insanity, who'd left him.

She was waiting for an answer. He nodded.

"Were you in the battle?" she said. "Oh, for God's sake say something, instead of just waggling your head."

"Yes, my lady."

"Don't call me that. Did you see General Belot? Did you see him die?"

"No, my— No, I didn't."

She held him with her eyes for what felt like a very long time, then let him go. "I didn't say which General Belot," she said. "I meant the younger brother, Senza."

"No. I didn't see him, but that was three days earlier."

She picked up a book and opened it. "We're going to be doing the Ordinary Catechism. Have you read it?"

"No."

She frowned. "You can read."

"Yes."

"That's all right, then." She threw the book to him; he caught it, just about, before it hit his head. "Start at the beginning," she said. "If there's any words you don't understand, ask me."

He thought; well, that explains the guards, and why she's in the most inaccessible place on the island. Rumour had it that Senza had made a standing offer of a million gold angels to anyone who brought her to him. He opened the book, cleared his throat –

"You've got it upside down."

– turned it the right way up and started to read. "The Ordinary Catechism of the United Company of Smiths, in which—"

"You can skip all that. Start on page one. It's got the figure one at the bottom."

He found it. His hands were shaking so much he tore the paper slightly as he turned the leaves. Of course, she had to know about the bounty. How could you live with something like that hanging over you?

"I believe," he read, "that in the beginning was the fire. And—"

"Hold it there," she said. "Well, do you?"

"I'm sorry?"

"Do you believe?" She waited, then said, "Go on. It's a simple question."

"No," he said.

"Mphm." She looked up at the ceiling and for the first time he noticed that it was painted; a fresco of what he took to be the damned, in some version of an afterlife. They were being speared by dog-headed demons. Melodrama. "Let's see, now. The no Vei believe that the Skyfather created the earth out of the bones of the Primal Cow. Isn't that right?"

He hesitated, then said quickly, "That's what they taught us. But we—" He swallowed. "Most people think it's just a story. Only the old people believe in Skyfather any more."

She looked at him. "Skyfather, not *the* Skyfather. Thank you, I didn't know that. So you don't believe in anything."

He thought before he spoke. "I believe in what I can see and feel," he said.

She nodded, a very small movement. "You can see the sky."

"Yes."

"Isn't Skyfather just a way of talking about the sky, what we call personification? Like you might say, my boots are killing me. But your boots are dead, they can't *do* anything, they certainly can't exercise malice. I put it to you, you believe in the sky, therefore you believe in Skyfather."

"I don't believe he made the world out of a dead cow."

She laughed, and he'd never felt happier in his entire life. "Yes, well. Do you know what a metaphor is?"

'Na Herec had told him about all that. "Yes."

"Fine. Isn't Skyfather and the cow just a metaphor, for the wind and the rain grinding out the valleys and rounding off the tops of the hills?"

He thought about that, too. "No," he said.

She raised her eyebrows. "Most people say yes," she said. "But I'll accept your answer. You don't believe in the Great Smith."

"No."

"Me neither." She grinned slightly at his reaction. "What I mean is, I don't believe in Old Wisdom out there, with his hammer and apron. Have you noticed, by the way, that Old Wisdom has bare feet? And did you ever meet a smith who didn't wear the strongest, thickest boots he could get?" She took a bit of linen from her sleeve and touched her nose with it, then sniffed. "I'm like you: I believe in what I can see. What can you see?"

There was only one answer to that, but he didn't dare give it. "Um. Things around me. The sky, the ground, buildings—"

"Things around you," she said. "Haven't you done this bit already?"

He nodded. "The world works," he said. "It gives us everything we want, and it doesn't need to. I mean, the sun could be too cold to make the grass grow, but it isn't. That sort of thing."

She looked at him. "You're not convinced. Don't worry, you don't have to believe to pass this module, you just have to understand what the rest of us believe in."

"Do you?" he said, before he could stop himself.

"I'm not important," she said briskly. "Read on. You'd got as far as the fire."

Whether he'd learned anything he had no idea. He walked slowly down the endless stairs, hardly noticing the guards or the doors. Outside it was overcast and cold. He turned the wrong way out on to the street and quickly lost count of doorways. He couldn't remember if he had any other classes.

Senza Belot had put a value on her, for all the world to know: one million angels. In Aelia, where they bought and sold people like livestock, he'd heard that a good field hand was worth half an angel, while a pretty girl was sixty-five stuivers. Back home, if you killed a man in a fight, you paid compensation to his family – the starting point was thirty ewes and a ram, and the council met to hear evidence to raise or lower the tariff. Under Imperial law, Myrtus had told him, all people except the emperor were nominally of equal value, though needless to say their possessions weren't; and hadn't he said something about an emperor who was captured by the Scrael and ransomed for half a million?

What I couldn't do, he thought, with a million angels.

"I know what you're thinking."

Lonjamen's voice made him jump out of his skin. He hadn't seen him standing in the doorway. He was wearing a purple gown with gold braid on the sleeves.

"You've just met 'Na Lysao," Lonjamen said. "Yes?"

"Yes."

"All right. But just think of the difficulties. Getting up there would be easy; then you'd have to punch out the archer at the top of the stairs and take his bow, then shoot the guards on the way down while dragging a screaming woman. You could knock her out and carry her on your shoulder but then how are you going to draw your bow? All right, you could leave the bow and just take one arrow, use it as a very short spear; if you stayed up in the tower till it was dark, then knocked her out and carried her – suddenly taken ill, you'd tell the guards, and they'd believe you just long enough for you to stab them – then through the deserted streets to the main gate, which would be shut; just suppose you could kill the porter, it'd be down that horrible path in the dark with her on your shoulder, then find a boat – how do you sail a boat? I wouldn't have a clue, how about you? And it's days across open water to the mainland." He paused. "That's what you were thinking, isn't it?"

Chanso said nothing.

"Don't worry, we all do. Some of my colleagues sit up at night discussing the most ingenious plans in the Common Room; I have an idea or two of my own that might even work, but I'm never going to find out, because nobody would ever actually try. Would they?"

"No."

"Quite. Oh, and by the way, for every guard you saw, there's a dozen you didn't see, but they saw you all right, believe me. Five yards, you'd be a human hedgehog. You know who usually sits at the top of those stairs? Sergeant Teucer – you met him, didn't you? Finest shot in the known world. I taught him myself, as it happens. That's what I teach, archery." He smiled. "I know," he said. "She had that effect on me the first time. I guess the reason Senza offered a million for her is that a million's all he's got." He guided Chanso through a doorway into a small room crowded with tables and chairs. "I know you don't drink, but I think this is an exception." He nodded to a man standing in the corner, who went away. "Now, for five million, I'm not saying I wouldn't be tempted. For about two seconds."

Chanso sat down. Lonjamen sat opposite him and yawned. "It wasn't coincidence, was it?" Chanso said.

"No," Lonjamen replied. "Of course it wasn't. One of my duties is 'Na Lysao's personal security. I have this little talk with all her students." The man came out with a small clay bottle and two tiny cups. "What he saw in her," Lonjamen went on, "doesn't need to be explained. What she saw in him, however, I never will understand. Well, at first, of course, it was a purely commercial transaction. But when she left him the first time, she'd taken him for enough money to buy the Vesani Republic; and then she went back to him, which is the part I just can't see. I asked her," he added. "She told me to mind my own something or other business."

Chanso burst out laughing, and laughed until his ribs ached. Lonjamen poured him a cup of whatever it was and said, "Here, drink this." When the world stopped spinning, he actually felt much better.

"We're all in love with her, of course," Lonjamen went on, "all the men and half the women. Actually, make that two-thirds. You can see why we've got her teaching catechism. She sort of proves the point, doesn't she?"

Chanso had been thinking that himself; what can you see? And, having seen, do you believe in a power that makes all things perfect? A trick question, but valid even so. "Have I got to take catechism?" he asked. "Couldn't I do something else instead?"

Lonjamen beamed at him. "My advice is, wear a hat," he said. "Drink plenty of fluids. Here," he added, pouring. "It sort of grows on you. Like leprosy."

Chanso looked at the bowl, picked it up and swallowed the contents. Then he said, "Can I ask you a question?"

"Depends what it is?"

Amazing how quickly that stuff could wear off. "'Na Lysao," he said.

The corner of Lonjamen's mouth twitched. "What about her?"

"Does she want to be here?"

All traces of expression left Lonjamen's face. He put his bowl down on the table. "Of course she does. I'm sorry, but that's a stupid question. Why don't you ask her?"

"I'm sorry," Chanso said. "I just got the impression—"

He tailed off. Lonjamen waited, then said, "What impression?"

"Oh, I don't know. I'm sorry."

"It's the only place in the world where she's safe," Lonjamen said. He picked up the bottle and moved it out of Chanso's reach. "I think we'll put that down to Aelian peach brandy. Seriously, if you don't believe me, ask her yourself. She will undoubtedly answer you. You'll wish she hadn't, but she will."

"I said I'm sorry. Can we forget it now, please? I didn't mean to give offence."

"None taken." Still the completely blank face. "But several good people died getting her here, and the next tide could bring five warships loaded down with marines; we could put up a pretty good fight, but we really don't want to have to. 'Na Lysao's previous entanglements aren't really a suitable subject for speculation: please bear that in mind. All right?"

The next day he got a summons to the Principal's office.

"You have to understand," the Principal said, "Beal Defoir works because everybody who lives on the island would rather be here than anywhere else in the whole world. We expect our students to be broken-hearted when they leave and spend the rest of their lives wishing they could come back." He leaned back in his chair and steepled his fingers. "How about you?" he said. "Where would you rather be, right now?"

It was a remarkable chair. Its legs were four sword blades, deliberately bent, the curves all inwards, like two pairs of Cs back to back. They were constantly flexing as the Principal shifted his considerable weight. He was tall, fat, bald, with a close-cropped black beard and forearms like a bear's, which poked out from the wide, short sleeves of his academic gown. He was missing the index finger of his left hand.

"Nowhere," Chanso said. "I like it here. Very much."

"Oh, sure. But you'd rather be home, wouldn't you, among your own people. We can fix that for you. We can send you home tomorrow, if you like. No charge. Comfortable ride in a coach all the way."

"No," Chanso said, a little bit too loud. "Thank you," he added. "What you said, about nowhere else you'd rather be. That's me. Really."

And deep, brown eyes, like a cow's. "Is that right?" he said. "That's saying something, bearing in mind you didn't ask to come here. You could almost say we brought you here against your will."

"Captain Myrtus saved my life."

There was a sheaf of papers on the desk. Needless to say, from where Chanso was sitting they were upside down, but he'd spotted his name all over them. "You're not a believer, are you?"

"I don't know," Chanso said. "I don't not believe, if you see what I mean. And now I'm here, it's beginning to make a lot of sense."

The Principal picked up one of the papers. Chanso couldn't read a word of it, because it was in 'Na Herec's handwriting. "Apparently you're an exceptional student with occasional flashes of genuine insight." He put the paper down gently, as if afraid of waking it. "The old bat never said anything nice like that about me. And 'Na Seutz says you're diligent, hardworking, eager to learn and a pleasure to teach." He shuffled the papers into a neat stack. "I'll let you in on a secret. 'Na Seutz loathes teaching. She says the students are all lazy and they take the edge off all her tools. You've made two very good friends since you've been here."

There was a *but* coming. It filled the air, like imminent thunder.

"I've had a formal complaint," the Principal went on, "from Procurator Lonjamen. You have a right to see the charges against you." He handed Chanso a slim roll of parchment in a brass tube.

"I don't understand," Chanso said. "I was talking to him yesterday. There was – I said something, I didn't know it was wrong. I said I was sorry."

The Principal was waiting. Chanso looked at the tube. How were you supposed to get the paper out? He tried poking one end with his finger, but that just squashed it up and jammed it. He tried again from the other end, and managed to nudge out a quarter-inch, just enough to get a grip with his fingernails. Eventually the paper slid out; he spread it out on his knee. The writing was very small.

"Well?" the Principal said.

"I don't understand."

He'd said the wrong thing. "You're charged with gross misconduct and conduct unbecoming a craft apprentice," the Principal said, "in that you suggested to Procurator Lonjamen that he should join with you in a conspiracy to abduct Domna Lysao and deliver her to the agents of General Belot in return for a substantial bounty. Further or in the alternative, you declared that you are in love with Domna Lysao." He paused. "What don't you understand about that?"

"It's not true."

"Procurator Lonjamen says it is," the Principal replied. "He has no reason to lie. You, on the other hand—" He raised his hands. "Slandering a procurator isn't going to help matters," he said.

"I suppose not."

"You suppose right." The Principal was looking at him. "In your defence, Lonjamen says that at the time of the incident you had been drinking, and you aren't used to strong liquor. I think he's inviting you to say that it was the drink talking, and you didn't mean a word of it. Well?"

"It's true," Chanso said. "Lonjamen bought me a drink—"

"You bought him a drink."

"I'm sorry," Chanso said quietly. "I must not be remembering straight. We had a drink together, and we don't have anything like that at home, and I said a stupid thing. I'm very sorry. I wouldn't ever do anything to harm 'Na Lysao, or anything that might get me sent away from here. I love it here. I didn't mean anything by it."

The Principal carried on looking at him for a while, as though he was waiting for something. Then, quite abruptly, he clapped his hands together. "I thought that must be how it was," he said. "When you're young and stupid and a long way from home, you do the occasional stupid thing, especially when there's peach brandy involved. I'm not saying that makes it any better, but at least it's understandable. Perhaps you're thinking we're being a bit harsh on you, for a matter of a few badly chosen words. But I ask you to consider what it must be like for 'Na Lysao, with that terrible weight hanging over her head all the time. If I was in her position, I don't know how I'd cope with it. Think what it would be like: every time somebody looks at you, they're seeing a million angels. Think how she'd feel if she knew that a student she has high hopes of was saying that sort of thing about her, even in jest."

"She doesn't know?"

That had come out far too quickly. But the Principal smiled. "I saw no need to distress her with it," he said, "and you can see for yourself, if she knew it'd make it very awkward for you to carry on as her student."

"She has high hopes—"

"Based on one lesson, yes."

"I can carry on going to her for catechism?"

The Principal frowned. "Well, that depends, doesn't it? These are serious charges. If you deny any part of them, there would have to be a hearing. If you admit them in full, I have the discretion to let them lie on the file – not dismissed, you understand, and not forgotten about, but not proceeded with, so long as nothing of the sort ever happens again. It's not the way we usually do things. But since you've had such excellent reports from two highly respected members of Faculty—" The Principal frowned and lowered his voice. "More to the point," he went on, "I have to tell you, Procurator Lonjamen spoke up very strongly on your behalf. He told me, he knows exactly what it's like for a young no Vei coming here for the first time: it's overwhelming, so totally different from anything you've ever experienced before. First you think you're less than nothing, an ant or a beetle; then, once it sinks in that you've been accepted, you go right to the other extreme, you think the place belongs to you and you're the equal of the gods and can do no wrong. In fact, Lonjamen's sticking his neck out for you, and you'd do well to remember that." He frowned some more, then said, "I'm prepared to let you stay here, on probation. From now on, you'll be the perfect student. You will not take one step out of line. If I ever hear your name again, it'll be because you've won a prize. And you won't just be very, very careful about what you say, you'll be very careful indeed about what you *think*; because there are a lot of extremely clever people here on this island, and from now on they'll be watching you. Do you understand?"

"Yes," Chanso said. "And I really am sorry."

"Good," the Principal said. "So I should think. You're a lucky man; you've got three very good friends on Beal Defoir. Do try not to let them down again."

Five days later she told him, "That's fine. You're all done."

"Excuse me?" he asked.

"The course is finished. You passed. Congratulations." She had her back to him; she was looking out of the window. For the last three days she'd had it shuttered, and they'd had their lesson by lamplight, even though it was mid-morning. "You can go."

It hadn't occurred to him that this might happen. There was still so much he didn't understand. All they'd done was read through the text, with a few rather strange discussions. "I don't – I mean, it doesn't feel like I've finished."

"You have, believe me. Well done, you're a smart boy. Usually this course takes fourteen days; you've done it in six. You're getting five stars and a commendation. What more could you want?"

He walked down the stairs in a daze. He'd passed, apparently; five stars and a commendation: the Principal would be pleased, and probably Lonjamen as well. And he'd never see her again.

"Human figures?" 'Na Seutz looked at him. "Why would you want to try that?"

Now that he wasn't doing catechism, he had double lessons with 'Na Seutz. She was very pleased with him. Most of the time, he was hardly aware of what he was doing. "I thought I'd like to try," he said.

"I thought representations of the human form were taboo in your culture."

He shrugged. "I'm not no Vei any more. Not really."

"Wash your mouth out with ashes and lye," she said sternly. "That's a terrible thing to say. Take me, for instance. I'm Euxentine. That's who I am, and I'm proud of it. The Lodge isn't a country. You are who you are."

He wasn't interested in the subject. "I just thought I'd like to try people," he said. "There's a long and noble tradition of human sculpture: look at Diagoras; look at the Sensualists. And I'm sick to death of carving squirrels."

Instead of answering, she reached up into the rack of fine timber that hung from the roof and took down a three-inch-square section, two feet long. "Sycamore," she said. "A bit pale for skin tones, but it's got that faint iridescence."

To see her, all he needed to do was close his eyes. He worked with the knife only, because it was slower. He made her stand at a window, half turned away. While he was doing the elbow, the knife slipped and cut his hand to the bone. Blood splashed on the wood; he wiped it off straight away, but of course there was a stain, on her shoulder and cheek.

"You're not usually that careless," she said, grabbing his hand and binding it with a bandage of fine muslin. She looked at his work; he thought, she doesn't approve. "I wouldn't do any more to that, if I were you," she said. "It's perfect. Anything else would spoil it."

He knew she was right, but it hurt worse than the cut. "Will that stain bleach out?"

"Not unless you want to raise the grain," she said. "And don't try sanding it, either; it's too deep. Just leave it. Actually, it looks sort of meant." She picked it up and moved it on to the windowsill. "Are you going to give it to her?"

"What?"

"To 'Na Lysao. She doesn't usually accept presents, but—" She turned it slightly, to adjust the play of light and shade. "She's only human."

"No," Chanso said. Then, without knowing why, he said, "You have it."

She stared at him. Then, "Yes, please," she said quickly.

'Na Seutz had four more blanks from the same tree. Three of them he made into near replicas of the first one, slightly adjusting the angle of her head, nothing else. For the fourth one, he made her sit, just like the first time he'd seen her. His hand was taking a long time to heal, there had been a slight infection, and he kept using the wound to press down on the back of the knife.

"You know," 'Na Seutz said gently, "that's the most amazing work I think I've ever seen. But maybe you should try doing something else next."

He looked at her. "Squirrels."

"You wouldn't go hungry. People will always want squirrels."

Just for her, he added a squirrel, sitting beside 'Na Lysao on the window seat. "Actually, it looks more like a friendly rat," she said. "But I like it, it's good." She peered at it, then added, "You know, in five hundred years' time people are going to be puzzled as hell about why you put in a rat."

"Symbolism," Chanso said.

"Ah."

He was dreaming about horses. His father had sent him to find the old white mare, but he couldn't find her. He rode for hours, covering extraordinary distances, but she was nowhere to be seen. He called her name, over and over again.

Something nudged him and he woke up. A man he knew vaguely by sight was standing over him. In his right hand was a drawn sword.

"It's all right," the man said. "Well, no, it's not. You need to get up, now."

He knew the man, but he couldn't remember where from. There

was light in the room, coming from the corridor outside: bright torches, or a lantern. "What's wrong?"

"The city's under attack," the man said. "Come on, get up. Report to the sergeant at the head of this staircase."

The man left him. He lay for a moment, then swung his legs out of bed, pulled on a shirt, stuffed his feet into his boots and staggered out into the corridor. A man pushed past him; in armour, holding a sheaf of spears tied up like a faggot of firewood with green twine. Chanso followed him. He could hear shouting – orders, not panic. Under attack? Made no sense.

On the landing he saw most of the occupants of the neighbouring rooms, men he'd seen now and again but never spoken to. They were in shirts or coats, and they looked bewildered and terrified. Two men in armour were handing out weapons.

"You," one of them said. "You're no Vei. You get a bow."

"I'm a terrible shot."

A bow and a quiver forced their way into his hands. "Bullshit. Archers to the front wall, fifth level. That's you," the man clarified. "*Move!*"

He had no idea how to get to the front wall, fifth level. But out in the quadrangle he saw a squad of archers, half a dozen or so, jogging grimly across the grass. He ran and caught up with them. He heard a horrible thumping noise that made the ground shake.

He grabbed the arm of one of the archers. "What's happening?"

"We're being attacked."

"Who by?"

The archer just looked blank. They started running up a long staircase, two steps at a time. Chanso kept up for as long as he could, but then they pulled ahead. He followed, gasping for breath.

At the top of the stairs he saw Lonjamen, talking to a man in armour. By the time he reached him, they'd finished their conversation and Lonjamen was walking away. Chanso called out his name.

Lonjamen glanced at him. "Get with the other archers," he said.

"What's going on? Who's attacking us?"

"I don't know, do I?" Lonjamen walked away, then turned. "Down the corridor, third left, brings you out on to the north gallery. Keep going till you see a staircase going up. Three flights, you'll be there. Good luck," he added, and disappeared through a doorway.

Another thump; the floor shook. Chanso slipped, fell on his left knee, jumped up again. Hell of a time for an earthquake. He did as Lonjamen had told him and came out into the night air. He was on a sort of huge balcony with a high stone wall in front of him. It was almost as bright as daylight, but the wrong colour.

"Get down," someone shouted at him. That made no sense. Then a heavy hand landed on his shoulder and a foot rammed the inside of his knee, forcing him into a crouch. "Shrapnel," a voice bellowed in his ear. "Bloody great chunks of flying rock. They'll take your head off."

"What's going on?" he asked.

A hand clamped to the back of his neck guided him tight up against the rampart. "Artillery," the voice said. "They got two barges anchored out there mounted with siege engines, mangonels probably. They splashed a couple of bulbs of Vesani fire against the walls, just so they could see to aim, and now they're trying to shoot out the gate."

Chanso turned his head and saw a helmet, Ironshirt type, with cheek-guards that almost met at the front. "Who are they?"

"Search me," said the helmet. "My guess is, somebody who wants a million angels. What else've we got worth taking?"

Something whistled through the air, a swishing sound, like a broom sweeping. Then a thump that made Chanso's ears ring, and the stonework under him trembled again. Then there was a lot of shouting. The helmet swore and stood up. A voice close by called out, "Archers front and centre!"

A hand grabbed Chanso's shirt. "That's us," the voice said. "Well, come on."

He stood up and followed the armoured man, who was running along the parapet. A line of archers were standing up out of the shadows. Chanso looked out over the parapet and saw the sea, gleaming with yellow. At least five black shapes broke up the pattern of the waves. Directly below where he was standing was the causeway that carried the path up to the main gate. The gate itself was gone, just a ragged hole in the stonework, ugly as smashed teeth. The walls looked like they were dripping with liquid fire.

Someone shoved him and told him to move, then pushed past him. He stayed where he was. Up the causeway, maybe two hundred yards away, something weird and shapeless was crawling up the causeway. He stared at it, then realised it was a long, dense column of men, with shields locked together in front and at the sides, marching in perfect step. He could hear a voice calling out, *ang, dui* – the same words the shepherd had used; of course, the Imperial for *one, two*.

"On my mark," someone yelled, about twenty yards away to his left. "Nock arrows."

Chanso remembered he was holding a bow. He considered it quickly. It wasn't anything like he was used to; it was long, taller than he was, and straight, made of one piece of wood. Primitive. He fumbled an arrow out of the quiver he'd been given. It was heavy, as thick as his little finger, and far too long for him. He clipped it on to the string. Presumably he was supposed to shoot at the men on the causeway, as soon as they came in range. It struck him as a bizarre thing to do. Even with the bright light of the burning stuff on the walls, it was far too dark for any sort of accurate aiming. He'd always been taught, don't shoot till you can see the whites of their eyes. And who were they, anyway?

"Draw," yelled the voice, so he drew. The bow was heavy, but instead of stacking, it drew evenly until his thumbnail brushed the corner of his mouth; at which point, the voice yelled, "Loose!" He hadn't been told what to aim at, so he held somewhere vague over the heads of the men on the causeway, and let the string pull through his fingers. He watched the arrow climb, ebb and drop; it clattered against the stonework, which told him he was six feet low.

"Nock," the voice commanded; by the time it said, "Draw", the line of shields was much closer, he could make out their burnished steel rims. He drew, holding a man's height above the line of advancing helmets. On "Loose", he let go, and watched his arrow into a shield. It stuck without penetrating, and the man carrying it kept on walking. No cast to these stupid bows. Now if he'd had his bow— He remembered that he no longer owned one: no bow; he didn't own anything any more. Instead, he belonged, to this strange island. He nocked before the order was called, looking for something sensible to shoot at; caught sight of a bare head, seventy yards away among the helmets. The voice told him to draw; he kept his eye fixed on the bare head, drew, lifting the arrowhead high; intuition whispered to him that a little bit of left wouldn't hurt. Loose, howled the voice, and his arrow soared, swooped, clattered off the point of a helmet a foot or so from the bare head, flicked up like a spark from a wet fire and flashed away out of sight. Close, but no bloody good at all.

His next four shots went high; then the voice was yelling something different: *down, down, off the wall*. Men were running past him; he didn't dare move for fear of being knocked off his feet. When a gap appeared, he darted into it and followed the man in front of him. No point asking where they were going, clearly nobody knew; something must be happening, whether it was good or bad was anybody's guess. As he ran, it occurred to him that he'd just tried to kill somebody, and felt relieved that he'd failed.

He was clattering down a spiral staircase, petrified of losing his footing, didn't dare slow down for fear of the man right behind him. Then a long sprint down a corridor, then more stairs, then a scrum, with the man behind him shoving him against the back of the man in front; he clung to the bow and managed to keep it from being wrenched out of his hand, but he lost his grip on the quiver and felt it being pulled from his fingers. A bow but no arrows. Then he stumbled out into fresh air. He turned to look for the quiver, but the men behind him wouldn't let him stop. The voice was calling, "Line out"; he didn't know what that meant, but the men in front of him and behind him did. He found himself standing in a line across one of the quadrangles – he didn't know which one – facing a gateway about forty yards away. The gate was closed. He turned to the man on his left, about six feet away. "Arrows," he called out. "I haven't got any." The man didn't seem to hear.

One of those terrible thumps, not quite so loud, and the ground didn't move; the sound bounced, like a beat on a drum. The voice yelled, "Nock"; he mimed nocking an arrow. Another thump, but different. It had a tearing undertone, the crackle of splintering wood, and Chanso realised it was the gate in front of him. He was suddenly terrified; on the other side of the gate was a monster so strong it could smash cross-plied oak. An urge to run swept over him, too strong to resist; he wanted to glance behind him, for somewhere to run to, but he didn't dare take his eyes off the gate. A third thump; the voice yelled, "Draw!" but nobody moved; the gate had flown open and was hanging like broken wings. "Loose," yelled the voice, but Chanso was backing away; he could see it coming through the smashed gate, the horrible thing with shields for scales. He dropped the bow and ran, dimly aware that he wasn't alone.

He was running at a wall, and he had no idea if there were doors in it, or where they led to, or how far behind him the monster was, whether it was gaining on him. Then his foot caught in something; he pitched forward, landed painfully on his knees and elbows; as he scrambled to get up, something landed hard in the small of his back and flew over his head, a swirling black shape like an enormous crow that turned into a man running, not looking back. He was winded, couldn't breathe. The ground he lay on was shaking. He forced himself to his feet, only to be knocked spinning by a hard, flat blow; then he was on his back, and a forest of boots was all around his head. He felt one land on his knee, another in his solar plexus; one pressed down on the side of his head but slipped off; he felt his scalp tear under the hobnails. He balled his hands into fists; the boots had swept over him and passed on. He heard shouting, and breaking wood.

He heard a voice, which he knew was the Great Smith, whispering: stay perfectly still; don't move. It was a clear voice, calm, very soft but he could hear it perfectly over all the noise. He did as he was told, awaiting further instructions.

He waited a long time, and no more instructions came. The other noises were further away now. He opened his eyes and saw the faint red of sunrise. He breathed in and out a few times; it hurt, but not badly. He rolled on to his side and held still while he counted: *ang, dui, tin*. Then, taking his time, he got to his feet and looked around.

The quadrangle was deserted, apart from a handful of body shapes on the ground, which didn't concern him. No sign of the monster, or the other archers. Behind him, much fainter, he could hear the roars and crunches of the monster; he guessed it had found its way through the solid wall and was busy elsewhere. He took a step, but his left knee yelled pain at him. Screw you, he told it, and limped the shortest way across the quadrangle until he came to a wall. Close by was a door, slightly ajar, with yellow light leaking out round it. He grabbed the handle, hung from it while he manufactured some strength, dragged the door open and fell through it, into an empty room; a scholar's room, with books and papers and a big, fat, wonderful chair. He closed the door, hobbled over to the chair and sat in it.

The light came from a lamp on a table. He considered it. Would light attract the monster? He gave it some thought and decided no, probably not. He looked down at his knee, which was a red, sticky mess, and his hands, which were in pretty fair shape. That's me done for today, he told himself. That's more than enough for one day.

He couldn't possibly have fallen asleep, not in the middle of a battle; but he opened his eyes suddenly, just as the door began to open. It swung wide towards him; and there in the doorway was the monster.

It had chosen to take the form of a gigantic steel man; an Imperial, a Blueskin – Chanso had heard of them but never seen one – unhelmeted, with a spreading mane of black hair pouring down over his shoulders like floodwater; in his hand was a sword, and the scales of his armour sparkled golden in the glow of the lamp. Chanso froze, just in case the monster might possibly overlook him if he kept perfectly still. But the monster's black eyes were on him, gazing at him, and he spoke—

The Angel, Reversed

Major Genseric opened the door and looked inside, but it was only someone's study. There was a boy, sitting behind a desk, probably a student or a servant. Not a threat. He looked petrified, and faintly comic.

"Where's the library?" Genseric asked.

The boy stared at him; scared, half-witted, maybe both. "The library," Genseric repeated slowly. "Big room full of books. Well?"

The boy struggled for a moment, then said, "Sorry, don't know."

Didn't know or wasn't telling; actually, *didn't know* was entirely possible, given the look on his face. Not just gormless; rather, a bottomless pit into which gorm falls and is utterly consumed. "Oh, for God's sake," Genseric snapped, and slammed the door.

There were three more doors in that section of wall. One opened on a steep staircase and the other two were locked, and there simply wasn't *time*— Come on, Genseric told himself, the most famous library in the known world, it's got to be somewhere. Damn this place to hell. Why couldn't someone have dug up a floorplan? Why couldn't there be any *signs*?

He was standing in the middle of the quadrangle feeling help-less and annoyed when Captain Sirubat turned up. "We've found it," he called out.

"Hoo-bloody-ray," said Genseric. "Where? No, don't point. Tell me, in words."

"Through that door there," said the captain, "up two flights, turn left down a corridor, third door on your right, brings you to some more stairs—"

Genseric held up his hand. "Anyway," he said, "you found it. Right, now we can get on. Where's the head man?"

"In the gatehouse," the captain said. Pause. "Through that arch there, left, you can't miss it."

The head man, Genseric reminded himself, was the Principal; not just the chief administrator of what was probably – grey area – a sovereign nation, but also a considerable scholar and the greatest living authority on metallurgy. He took several deep breaths to calm himself down, sheathed his sword and went in.

The gatehouse must've taken a direct hit from the mangonel, because half of it wasn't there any more. Most of the roof was on the floor, and the furniture was smashed under fallen rubble. The man he'd come to see was sitting on the only survivor, a small gate-leg table. He was dirty and covered in dust, but apparently otherwise unharmed. He looked stunned, as if he was trying to figure out if all this was real or just an elaborate practical joke.

"Principal Ertan," Genseric said. The wretched man looked up at him. "I'm Major Genseric. Your people are in my way."

The Principal opened his mouth but said nothing.

"You've got a hundred students crowded up the staircase to my lady's chamber," Genseric said. "Human shield, presumably. I really don't want to hurt them if I can help it."

No answer. Why do we have to do this? Genseric thought. It's so pointless, and these people aren't the enemy. They're just— He sighed. "So here's the threat," he said. "Clear them out of there, or my men will burn down your library."

For a moment, Genseric thought the Principal was going to choke to death. He wanted to help, but he wasn't sure he knew what to do. But then the Principal said, "You can't."

"Yes, I can. They tell me there's a quarter of a million books in there. I never realised there were that many in the whole world." He paused, then said, "Up to you. Let us take what we came for and we'll be on our way, no more fuss, nobody gets hurt, no more damage."

He counted to five under his breath. The Principal hadn't moved.

"We've done our best," he said. "We haven't shot a single arrow, and as far as I know, none of your people have been killed. You've been doing your damnedest to hurt us, but that's all right. I understand. But you've lost, there's nothing more you can do, so please be sensible and help me to keep the damage to a minimum."

He waited. Maybe the poor fool had lost the use of his tongue. It took some people that way, he'd read somewhere. "Oh, come on," he said. "Say something."

"No," the Principal said.

"What? For crying out loud, man, you're talking about several hundred lives. I'm a soldier, not a butcher. Do you understand what I'm saying? First I'll set fire to the library. Then I'll send my men in to clear the staircase. It'll be the greatest crime against humanity in all of history, and all because you're so damn stubborn. Don't you get it? It's over. You can't stop me. What you can do is help me prevent a fucking disaster. Well?"

He realised he'd been shouting, which he hadn't wanted to do. But the fool was just sitting there, understanding and not giving in. Ridiculous. Unbelievable. And then a thought occurred to him, and he thought, Of course, brilliant.

He turned to the captain, who was right behind him. "Did we get any of this man's personal staff?"

"Two, sir. Chief secretary and deputy principal."

"They'll do." The Principal's eyes were wide with horror. "Oh, pull yourself together, I'm not going to hurt them," Genseric snapped. "Right, fetch them in here, quick as you like."

Curious specimens: one was a youngish no Vei, the other a middle-aged woman. The no Vei was missing his right thumb; Genseric was pleased to see his people had bandaged it neatly, properly. The woman had blood on her dress, but seemed unhurt. "Names," he snapped.

The woman gave him a murderous scowl. "I'm Lonjamen," the no Vei said quickly. "This is Emphianassa."

"Fine," Genseric said. "Now listen to me. I've just told your chief here that if he doesn't get his human shield off the stairs to the top tower, I'm going to burn the library."

The woman yelled something at him that he decided he hadn't quite heard. "And then," he went on, "I'll have no choice but to clear that stair, any way I can. Your chief's just told me, go ahead. Is that what you want? You two. Don't look at him, I'm talking to you."

The woman had gone white as linen. The no Vei was staring at him as though at an approaching tidal wave. "No," he said. "I take it there's an alternative."

"Of course there is," Genseric said. "Seems to me, if your boss here were to see sense, he'd send one of you two to give the order. Well? Yes or no."

The woman was in tears. "Yes," said the no Vei. "That'd be me."

"Fine. So it's not him I need to convince that I'm serious, it's you. Look at me," he said, taking a step closer. "Are you convinced?"

The no Vei nodded quickly. "If I do it, will you let the students on the stairs go?"

"I promise," Genseric said. "Soon as we've got what we want, we'll be off and out of your hair before you can say snap. Or the streets can run with blood. You decide. I really don't care any more. I've had about as much of you people as I can take."

The Principal jumped up and started yelling; Genseric knocked him to the floor with the back of his hand, skinned his knuckles on the fool's bony jaw. Trouble with me, he thought: I don't know my own strength. "Ignore him, he doesn't matter. It's all up to you. I'm going to count to five."

"All right," the no Vei said, before he could start. The Principal, on his hands and knees, was mumbling through a mouthful of blood and loose teeth. The woman looked like she was about to start screaming. Civilians, Genseric thought. No more idea than my mother's cat.

All but a dozen of the students obeyed the order to evacuate the staircase; the remainder weren't hard to remove, with a little help from both ends of a spear or two. It was as the last of them were being bundled away that Genseric remembered a story his uncle had told him. He swore loudly, looked round for someone to give orders to, found nobody, broke into a run. This horrible place, all doors and corridors.

More by luck than judgement he came out in the main quadrangle, where he'd posted two troopers and a sergeant. He was too blown from running to explain, so he grabbed the sergeant by the wrist and towed him like a barge, with the two troopers trotting behind like carriage dogs.

In the ruins of the gateway he stopped, looked down the causeway, then up and down the rampart. Nothing. "There's got to be another way on and off this horrible rock," he said. "Sergeant?"

He knew the man: smart, reliable. "Only the one place you can put in a boat, sir."

"Fine. So there must be another way down to the beach." He screwed his eyes shut, trying to think. "There isn't, is there?"

"Wouldn't have thought so, sir."

"My Uncle Aimeric," Genseric said, "had the best collection of early Republican silver in the East. So what he did was, he built this vast, impregnable strongroom, bolts and bars and two-inch-thick doors. And he kept the actual stuff in a couple of apple barrels in the hay barn. She's not in that damned tower, Sergeant. They'll have her stowed in some broom cupboard somewhere, and a quick and easy way off the rock in case of trouble. Which means a sally-port and a watergate tucked away round the side somewhere, and hope they can keep us busy long enough for her to get clean away." He took a deep breath. He was, he realised, utterly exhausted. "Get down to the ship," he said, "tell the captain. They're looking for something small and fast, on the shortest course to the mainland." His mind had gone blank. "Which would be Blemya, God help us, and once she's there we can't do a damn thing. It's probably too late by now, but it's got to be worth a try."

It was the sloop from the main troop carrier that captured the prize, at the very last moment, with the golden blaze from the Blemyan lighthouse roof already in sight. The scholars' pinnace was fast but the sloop was faster; they managed to grapple at extreme range and winch in close enough to board. There was an ugly little fight – four scholars dead, two marines – but the young lieutenant commanding the sloop found the girl hiding behind some barrels and dragged her out by the hair, whereupon the scholars gave up and were quiet. They scuttled the pinnace to save time, and picked up a fresh breeze back to Beal Defoir.

Genseric had spent the time waiting for news of the interception exploring the tunnels that led down through the rock to the hidden landing bay, the whereabouts of which he'd extracted from the Principal with eloquent words and the toe of his boot. It was a remarkable piece of engineering; there was a winch-operated lift running up and down a sheer-sided brick-lined shaft (so even if an attacker knew about the watergate, he couldn't get in to the fortress that way); you could get from the winch-head in the basement of the chapel to the watergate in just under ten minutes, and the whole thing was hydraulically powered by submerged waterwheels; just pull on a lever to engage the gear train and away you went.

"We ought to clear this lot out and take this place for ourselves, sir," Captain Orderic said. "It's the most amazing fortified position; you could hold it indefinitely with a hundred men."

Genseric smiled. "They had a hundred. Hundred and twenty, in fact."

"I was meaning soldiers," the captain said. "And you'd need a drawbridge on that causeway, and artillery. But it's perfect. And just sitting here doing nothing."

Genseric considered explaining, but he didn't have the energy. "Write a report," he said, "I'll see it's passed on." To join all the other reports, he didn't add. He'd read them all before embarking on this horrible job. But none of them had mentioned a secret watergate. He felt rather pleased about that.

All in all, it had gone off well. The scholars and marines on the boat had been the only lives lost; thirty-odd scholars had been injured, and twelve marines, but nothing too dreadful. The gatehouse was a complete write-off and there were a few smashed-up doors and broken windows. For his report, Genseric put the value of the damage at five thousand angels: on the generous side. The Principal had been stunned to hear that he'd be getting compensation. "Who from?" he'd asked, and Genseric had smiled and told him he wasn't at liberty to say.

He was marginally less pleased when the captain of the main transport told him where they'd put the girl: in Genseric's cabin, because it was the only enclosed space big enough and comfortable enough for honoured guest quarters that could be guarded to the required level of security. Genseric, the captain suggested, might like to bunk in the mess hall, or share with one of his officers. "Couldn't you put her in the cargo hold?" Genseric said; but, no, there were rats, and women don't like rats, everyone knows that. So he had them rig him up a tent on the aft deck, and prayed it didn't rain.

He wasn't looking forward to what came next, but it had to be done.

She was sitting on what had been his bunk, reading the copy of Eleutherius that he'd neglected to take with him, and which he knew he'd never get back. She looked up at him and scowled.

"Where's Senza?" she said. "When can I see him?"

"Sorry." Genseric braced himself. "Wrong brother."

She went completely still.

"It was your blasted Lodge that gave us the idea," he explained. "Get hold of something they want, something they'll give anything for. In their case, some religious artefact for that nutcase Glauca. Then General Belot – sorry, our General Belot, Forza – got to thinking. And of course, we knew exactly where to find you."

She looked straight at him. He felt cold all over.

"The Lodge will crucify you," she said. "You do know that, don't you?"

The same thought had crossed his mind; but it was much harder to dismiss it when she said it. "I obey orders," he said.

"That won't save you."

"No, I don't suppose it will."

She was quiet for a long time. Then she said, "Where are you taking me?"

"Sorry, I can't tell you."

"Do you know?"

He shook his head. "That's why I can't tell you. I hope it's not far. I'm sleeping in a tent on the deck."

Maybe he'd got used to girls laughing at his jokes. Not this one. Not that he'd expect her to. And it's probably not a good idea to try and raise a laugh from the Angel of Death. "Well," she said. "Don't let me keep you."

He turned away. She called him back. "You'd have done it, wouldn't you?"

"Excuse me?"

"Killed all those people. Just to get to me."

He turned back. "Dear God, no. And I wouldn't have burned their precious library, either. No, if I hadn't managed to bully that clerk, I'd probably have tried smoking them out – bit of a fire, open all the doors, throw on plenty of wet blankets. That place was a chimney. But I didn't want to, in case the fire got out of hand and I burned down half the school." He risked a smile. "Don't flatter yourself," he said. "I don't do massacres for anyone. Or human sacrifices."

"I expect you had orders."

Just a guess? Probably. But she said it like she knew. "Of course," he replied. "And I carried them out, and nobody got hurt." He paused. Worth a try. "Disappointed?"

She gave him a look that convinced him it hadn't been worth a try after all. "I hope the Lodge spares you," she said. "I want Senza to deal with you."

He winced slightly. Not given to idle threats, by the sound of it. "I take what comes," he said. "It's my job."

"Senza's got a bath," she said. "He fills it with milk and honey. Anybody he doesn't like goes in the bath, all tied up tight, and he leaves them in the sun for a day or so. The honey and the sour milk attract flies, and the flies lay eggs. He'll see to it you get food and water, whether you like it or not." She gave him a smile. "In the end, they strip you to the bone. The Lodge would just stab you in your sleep. Where's the play value in that?"

It took him a lot of effort to keep his voice steady. "I can see why he likes you," he said. "If you need anything, just shout."

Two days of beautiful refreshing boredom, blue sky and calm sea. Then she sent for him.

"I'm sick to death of being cooped up in this kennel," she said. "I want to go up on deck."

"Your wish is my command," he said politely. "I'll ask the captain if it's convenient."

"I want to go up on deck *now*."

"Of course." He closed the door on her, then went and sat in the sun for a couple of hours, eating grapes and watching the flying fish. Then he went back down and fetched her.

"You got that from my copy of Eleutherius," he said. "About the bath full of honey. I knew it sounded familiar."

"I imagine that's where Senza got the idea," she replied. "He's a great reader." She pushed past him and came out into the light. "Been thinking about it, have you? What it'll be like?"

He took a couple of long strides to overtake her. Everyone on deck had stopped what they were doing. "Senza Belot doesn't go in for macabre forms of torture," he said. "He's bound by the Joint Protocols of Conduct, same as everybody else. Glauca would have his head on a pike if he caught him doing something like that."

"You believe that? How sweet."

He let the crew stare. Either she'd enjoy it, which might sweeten her temper, or it'd embarrass her, which might take the edge off her self-confidence. He guided her well away from the rail; it was a calm day, but he was a weak swimmer.

"A million angels, Major Genseric," she said. "That's a lot of money."

"Indeed it is," he said. "To put it in context, though, my great-grandfather once bet a hundred thousand on which of two snails would be first to reach the top of a wall. His son, my great-uncle, spent a quarter of a million on a palace for his wife, but she didn't like the view, so he had the tops of the mountains cut off. My Uncle Theuderic—"

"Your father was indicted for high treason and all his property was confiscated," she said. He shivered. How could she possibly—?

"True," he conceded. "But my Aunt Segimer owns three valleys and a city; she's unmarried and ninety-one. Besides, I've got my army pay. And if you insult me again, I'll smack your head till it rings."

She gave him a startled look. "I didn't mean to insult you."

"That's why I didn't hit you." He lifted his eyes just a little, over her head, to look at Captain Orderic, who was hovering just behind her, to her left. He took the hint and moved a little closer to the rail. "Now some of the officers and men on this ship aren't quite so fortunate as me, financially speaking. I'll ask you not to unsettle them by putting silly ideas in their heads." He paused for a moment, then went on: "I get the impression you don't like getting hit. Normally I wouldn't dream of it, but according to you I'm a dead man already, so why the hell not?" He gave her his prettiest smile. "If Forza asks about the bruises, I'll tell him you walked into a door. All my men will back me up. Do you understand?"

She looked at him as though she'd recognised someone she used to know. "Perfectly."

"Splendid. Would you like some tea?"

"No, thank you. I'd like to go back to my cabin now."

When he closed the door on her, he began to shake. That bothered him.

"Pure poison," Captain Orderic said. "We ought to throw her over the side."

"What, and kill all those fish?" Genseric poured himself a

drink: a much smaller one than he'd have liked. "For the avoidance of doubt," he said, "if anyone lays a finger on that woman, I'll hang him. Pass it on, would you?"

Orderic grinned. "Except you?"

"Including me. I've never hit a woman and I don't intend to start now. Unacceptable behaviour." He sipped, and pulled a face. Should've looted the cellars of Beal Defoir while he had the chance. "No, I got the impression she knows all about being knocked around. Only weak spot I've detected so far. Therefore, I make empty threats."

"I'd sort of gathered that's why she left Senza," Orderic said.

"Oh, you hear all sorts of stories." Actually, the stuff grew on you, once you'd weathered the initial shock. "But I don't think so. I think if he had, that'd have been it, finished. And she went back to him the first time, remember."

Orderic shrugged. "I wish I knew where we were going," he said. "To be honest with you, I'm not great on boats."

"Landlubber," Genseric said equably. "Nor me. My father had a ship when I was a kid; we used to all pile on board and go off visiting. Those aren't happy memories."

He'd offered the opening, and Orderic accepted it. "What she said, about your father. Is it true?"

"I assumed you knew. Yes. And, yes, he was guilty. That is, he was an idealist: he wanted the empires reunited. And he was stupid enough to think it could be done by men of goodwill discussing things in a reasonable manner." He finished his drink. "I've got his skull somewhere," he said. "A sergeant of mine stole it off the spikes above the arch at Cripplegate, thought I might like it. Hell of a nice thing to do, don't you think?"

"Who was that? Old Eusto?"

Genseric shook his head, "No, it was a chap called Sirupat, before your time. We lost him at Antecyra Fords, poor devil." He looked at the bottle. It was beautiful, but he was strong. "Aelian," he went on: "they make the best sergeants, in my experience. Bear that in mind when you have a command of your own."

Orderic nodded briskly. "About her Ladyship."

"Oh, God, her."

"I was thinking," Orderic said. "There wouldn't be anything, well, sharp in that cabin, would there?"

Genseric looked at him. "Yes, there is," he said. "There's my nail scissors, for a start, and we've been letting her have glass and pottery cups and plates. Just as well one of us has got a brain."

Orderic grinned. "I'll see to it."

"No need to be tactful. Let's see," he went on, "someone on this ship's bound to have lifted some of that fancy silver tableware back on the island. She can have that instead. And have them cut her food up small, so she doesn't need a knife."

"When we were up on deck," Orderic said, "I could tell she was thinking about it. What does she imagine Forza's going to do to her, for God's sake?"

Genseric frowned. "My guess is, it's more a case of what he might use her *for*. As in, he can't trade her for anything if she's dead." He thought about that for a moment, then added, "Not that I think she's in any hurry to do herself in, not if she can see her way round it. But let's keep our eye on the mark, shall we, just in case?"

She sent for him.

He took a bottle of wine, a plate of honeycakes and two volumes of Idealist poetry with the Beal Defoir crest embossed on the tubes, which he'd confiscated from a lance corporal of marines. "No thank you," she said. "I don't read pornography."

"It's thousand-year-old pornography," he said, "which means it's literature, so it's all right. Suit yourself," he added, putting the tubes back in his sleeve. "Can't offer you anything else, I'm afraid."

"Those belong to the Lodge."

"I know, that's why I confiscated them. They'll be sent back in due course." He smiled. "Though what all those scholars want with classic Euxentine erotica, I can't begin to imagine."

"It's literature," she said.

"Of course." He offered her the honeycakes. She shook her head. "You wanted to see me."

"Yes." She indicated the chair with a slight movement of her head. He sat down. "About your father."

"Mphm. Could this possibly wait? I'm rather busy."

"I knew him."

Genseric's heart sank. "Oh, yes?"

"Professionally." She smiled viciously at him. "I thought you might like to know that."

"I don't think I believe you," he said. "He's been dead ten years."

"Oh, I started young. Very young. That's how he liked them." She paused, taking stock of the damage she'd done. "If you still don't believe me, I can tell you things about him."

"No," Genseric said. "Please don't."

"Why not? I'd have thought you'd have been interested. I'll bet I could tell you about a whole side of his personality you never knew anything about. See this?" She rolled up her sleeve. Just below the wrist was a white, shiny scar. "Would you like to hear how I got it?"

"Not really, no."

"Oh, go on. Pour me a drink and we can swap stories about the old devil. When I heard what had happened to him I went about smiling for a week. How's your mother, by the way? I could tell you a thing or two about her, as well. Very broad-minded woman. Very."

"She's dead."

"You're just saying that to cheer me up."

Genseric leaned back in his chair and stretched his hands

wide on his knees. "What is all this?" he said. "Are you trying to provoke me?"

She shook her head. "Though you did say, if I insulted you—"

"You're insulting my parents, not me."

"Can the truth be an insult?"

"Worst sort, I've always thought. Anyway, I didn't mean what I said."

"Didn't you now."

"Empty threats," Genseric said. "It's what I'm best at. So, why are you doing this?"

She shrugged. "Maybe I enjoy hurting people. Habit I picked up from someone I used to know when I was young. Thirteen, actually."

"I don't think so," Genseric said. "I think it's just long-range bombardment, to soften me up. It's the sort of thing Senza would do." He smiled. "They warned me you were a handful."

"But you like a girl with spirit."

"No, not really."

"You don't like girls."

"I don't like you," Genseric said mildly. "But you're not typical, so that's all right." He stood up. "I don't believe a word of what you said about my father," he said. "I think you'd heard of him, and therefore me, because it was a big story at the time and you've got a very good memory. I think you threatened me with details of moles and birthmarks because you knew I'd shy away." He paused for a couple of heartbeats, then went on, "I think you were trying to get me to hit you, because you've figured out how disgusted I'd be with myself afterwards; and that might just be an opening, a bit of guilt you could work on. Or I don't know, maybe you really are just sharpening your claws on the furniture. I wouldn't blame you if you were: it passes the time and makes you feel you're doing something. But you're going to Forza and that's that. Sorry."

She looked at him again. "Do you know what he'll do to me?"

"Not a clue."

"He'll send me back to Senza. Oh, he'll want the East in exchange, but that's beside the point. Senza will give it to him, and Forza will send me back."

Genseric frowned. He'd promised himself he wouldn't get involved, but it was very hard to resist. "Which is what you want."

"Are you mad? Why do you think I've spent the last three years trying to get away from him?"

"What do you know," Genseric asked, "about shipping lanes?"

Orderic gave him a blank stare. "You should ask the captain about that."

"I'm asking you."

"Nothing," Orderic replied.

Genseric rested his folded arms on the rail. "Nor me," he said. "I know that even though it's a very big sea, ships tend to go along these invisible roads, and it's something to do with prevailing winds and stuff like that. I'm assuming that explains *them*."

He dipped his head slightly towards the stern. Orderic, who knew him well, didn't look round, just moved his eyes and then moved them back. "Four sails."

"Is it four now? I only counted three."

"My eyesight's better than yours."

"Maybe." Genseric yawned. "I'm assuming," he said, "that they're four ordinary, harmless merchant ships following a shipping lane which happens to be the one we're using. That's a perfectly logical explanation, isn't it?"

"Yes."

"And we've got, what, sixty-five marines on board, and this is a pretty fast ship, apparently. It's not like we've got anything to worry about."

Orderic massaged his forehead with his fingertips. "No luck finding out where we're going, I suppose."

"No, but I haven't tried violence yet."

They both turned slowly, so that they were facing the ship's launch. "Apparently," Orderic said, "the correct name for it's a catboat."

"Is that right?"

"Because it's got just the one mast, right at the back. Sorry, astern. Why that makes it a catboat I don't know, but it does."

"How many will it carry?"

"Depends on who you ask," Orderic replied. "The consensus would seem to be, somewhere between six and ten."

"I don't see how we could manage with less than seven," Genseric said, after a pause for thought. "You, me, her. Someone to steer the boat, someone to do whatever it is you do with the sails. And two marines, to keep the sailors in order. Seven. Plus food and water for at least six days."

"Ten," Orderic said. "I have this recurring nightmare where I'm in a small boat in the middle of the sea, and there's no food or water. Let's be on the safe side."

"We must be nearly there by now, surely," Genseric said angrily. "We've been on this horrible ship for days, and we haven't had storms or anything to blow us off course. And for all I know, they're sending out escorts to bring us in safe."

"You'd have thought so."

Genseric straightened up. "I think I'll go and make some empty threats," he said. "You find out which sailors we should take, and choose two marines."

"And supplies for ten days?"

"Six," Genseric said. "Save weight; go faster. We're not sailing round the world, for crying out loud."

The captain had his orders. He was answerable to his superiors, according to the chain of command, in which Genseric didn't feature. Genseric and his damned marines were simply passengers, nothing more. The orders explicitly stated that their destination was not to be divulged to any unauthorised person. Genseric was not authorised. Therefore—

"These orders," Genseric smiled. "In writing, presumably."

"Of course."

He nodded over the captain's head. "Sergeant, search the captain's cabin. Bring me any paper with writing on it."

He couldn't do that, it was outrageous. It was mutiny. Genseric had no authority—

"No," Genseric said. "But I have got sixty-five obedient marines."

"All right." The captain got up and walked to the rail. "I'll tell you. But—"

Something in his voice. Not just fury and outraged sensibilities. Fear? "No, don't bother," Genseric said, resting his hand on the captain's shoulder just firmly enough to push him back into his seat. "Sergeant, carry on."

The search was commendably quick and thorough. It produced the captain's document case, containing his charts and recent correspondence, including the written orders. Genseric read them with interest, while two marines held the captain's arms.

"Full cooperation with the officer commanding," he read out: "keep him fully informed at all times." He lowered the paper. "Not what you said. Nothing about not telling us where we're going; in fact quite the opposite." He put the orders back in the document case and took out one of the charts. "Of course, I can't read these things," he said. "But I imagine someone on this boat can, beside yourself. I'll bet you anything you like, wherever the hell we are, it's not the shortest route from Beal Defoir to Callinica Bay. Also," he went on, as the captain turned his head to avoid looking at him, "I think this thing can go much, much faster, and that makes me wonder why it isn't. You wouldn't be dawdling so someone can catch us up, would you?"

The captain didn't say anything. Genseric held out his hand; the sergeant who'd done the search handed him a small rosewood box. "One last thing," Genseric said. "Are these yours?"

No reply. Genseric opened the box and looked at the pack of cards; beautiful work, scrimshaw on thinly sawn whalebone. "Card-playing and other forms of gambling are strictly forbidden on board all navy ships," he said. "Play a lot, do you?"

The captain gave him a look of genuine terror. "It's just a pack of cards," he said.

"Of course it is," Genseric said. He extended his hand over the side and dropped the box into the sea. "Careless of me," he said. "Now I haven't got any evidence against you." He leaned forward, bringing his mouth close to the captain's ear; at the same time, he caught hold of the captain's thumb and levered it back until he felt significant resistance. "Don't feel bad about it," he said quietly; "you did your best. Now, unless you want to go and fetch your cards, how soon before those Lodge ships catch us up?"

For a moment he thought the captain wouldn't speak. Then: "Tomorrow, first light."

"That's fine," Genseric said. "Now, what I want you to do is increase speed; not too much, just enough to make it so they don't catch up till, let's say, a couple of hours after noon tomorrow. I'm sure you can manage that, and if you can't, Sergeant Laxa here will cut your head off. All right?"

The ship's first officer could read a chart just fine. He told them they were two days from Zatacan, on the Blemyan coast. He plotted them a course for the nearest Western port: three days with a good wind, five if they were unlucky. He was pleased and terrified to find that he was now in effective command, and promised to do exactly as he'd been told. He personally vouched for the loyalty of his helmsman, who could read a chart and lay in a course as well as anyone in the fleet.

"You'll have a job, though," he said. "The catboat's fast, but so are those sloops following us. You sure you don't want to stay and see if we can't make a fight of it?"

Genseric pulled a sad face. "Personally, I think we could," he said. "I don't think Lodge people can fight worth a damn, from what I saw back at Beal. But I can't risk it. We'll do it my way."

The catboat had to be hauled up on to its derricks and lowered into the sea, with its crew on board. It swung wildly on the way down, nearly spilling Orderic into the sea; he grabbed for the side and got the helmsman instead, and they collapsed in a heap in the bottom of the boat. Fortunately it was too dark to see the look on her face.

Needless to say, they couldn't risk a lamp or a lantern. The sky was overcast; good from the point of view of getting away without the sloops seeing them, disastrous for navigation. The helmsman had brought a small piece of stone, mounted on a small piece of wood, and a shallow bowl; fill the bowl with water and float the wood in it, and the stone, being magic, would always point north. When Orderic had been told that that was how they'd be finding their way, in the dark, in the infinite sea, he'd had a panic attack and Genseric had seriously considered leaving him behind.

"Of course," the helmsman had said, "if it's a dark night I won't be able to see the lodestone. But that's all right. Come first light, if we're astray, we just change course."

The catboat had a tiny canvas cabin, big enough for two people to sit side by side if they didn't mind touching knees. Genseric decided he minded, so he assigned Orderic the first shift of guard duty.

All night and most of the first day she sulked and didn't say a word. Genseric took that as a good sign.

The helmsman was a short, spare man, about fifty, with a big nose and long black hair in a single braid. He gave the impression that he was having the time of his life. His first command, he explained. Genseric gave him an uneasy grin and congratulated him. He learned a lot about him during the course of the first day; how his family had been fishermen for generations, but his eldest brother had got the boat when the old man died and he didn't fancy shipping on a merchantman, so he joined the navy, just in time for the Battle of Tragous, which had been a shambles and no mistake, but he'd been lucky: he'd been with the squadron that showed up late and missed out, basically they'd turned up, seen what was happening and got out quick, and after that he'd been on troop transports for six years, and now he was helmsman on the *Achiyawa*, which was a good ship, don't get him wrong, but a man wasn't going to get anywhere, if the major saw what he meant, and besides, this war, everywhere you looked there was some bugger making a fortune out of it, every fool with a boat bigger than a walnut shell, it broke a man's heart to see all those opportunities slipping by, and knowing that any moment the *Achiyawa* could be ordered into battle, and no disrespect, but the command in this war, not fit to run a ferry across a small river. No, if he had his chance, he knew what he'd do.

Genseric waited for a natural break, then said, "Tell you what. If you can get this thing landed anywhere in the Western empire, you can keep it. Yours, free and clear, and an honourable discharge from the Service to go with it. How would that suit you?"

"Can you do that?"

"If I can get that bloody woman safely delivered to Forza Belot, I can do anything I like."

The helmsman grinned. "Shouldn't be a problem," he said.

She was seasick. It was the first sign of humanity she'd shown. At first, Genseric suspected she was faking it; but nobody could vomit that hard at will, he was sure of it, and the shade of green her face had turned was entirely authentic, in his not inconsiderable experience. Orderic and one of the marines were similarly afflicted, but for once Genseric wasn't bothered at all. He sat in the prow most of the time, watching the horizon for any trifling irregularity that could mean land. There was no sign of the sloops, or any other ships at all.

The first bit of Western territory they would reach, the helmsman informed him, was an island, Pandet or some such name; it was four miles out from the mainland, and there ought to be a squadron of ships there, unless they were on patrol. In any event there would be a dockyard and a garrison, and sloops and cutters to carry Genseric and his party to Atrabeau. He sounded so confident that Genseric's heart sank, but the helmsman promised him faithfully that Atrabeau was massively defended and no real use to anybody, and the Easterners hadn't been near it since the war started; it was only twelve miles from the Blemyan frontier, so it'd be incredibly tactless for the East to attack it, not if they wanted to be friends with Blemya. This time tomorrow, he said, if this wind keeps up. We're practically there.

Those familiar with the stretch of coast between Atrabeau and Zatacan know just how quickly the Creed squalls can get up, and how ferocious they can be. Opinions differ as to the origin of the name. Some hold that it derives from the length of the average storm – just long enough to recite the Confession, the Five Pillars and the Exeat – while others maintain that reciting the offices is a sure way to still the winds and subdue the waters, which is why a storm lasts as long as it does.

Genseric, huddled in the bottom of the catboat, could hear someone screaming scripture into the wind. Coming from a family with a long and proud tradition of unbelief, he didn't know the words and couldn't join in, but he paraphrased as best he could: *Lord, whoever you are, please make it stop.* That, apparently, wasn't good enough. An empty water barrel fell on his back, and he stopped, in case his imperfect prayers were annoying the Divine.

"Where is this?" Orderic asked.

It was a stupid question, not deserving a reply. The beach the storm had pitched them up on was broad, flat and featureless; the sand was white, there were no rocks, precious little driftwood or seaweed. In the distance, Genseric could just make out the dark green of a pine forest.

The helmsman was gazing at his bribe, the foundation of his future prosperity, which was now just so much firewood. They'd hit something on the way in which had torn the bottom out of her, and she'd shed strakes all the way up the beach. The mast was somewhere in the deep water, a long way away. A few bits and pieces were bobbing up and down thirty yards or so out, but the captain showed no inclination to go and fetch them.

"I didn't see any island," Orderic was saying. "Or is this the island? It's too big, isn't it? I thought you said there was a town."

Genseric didn't think it was the island. He hadn't really been keeping track of their progress during the storm, but it had been horribly fast, at least until they lost the mast, and, as for direction, he didn't have a clue. But wherever they were, he was quite sure it wasn't where they were meant to be. One of his many regrets was that his armour was at the bottom of the sea. He'd taken it off in case he had to do any swimming, and it had gone the way of the rest of their cargo when the catboat was holed. Orderic still had his sword, but that was their entire defensive capability.

He got up and trudged across the soft sand to where she was sitting, with her back to the keel, staring at her bare feet as though she'd never seen them before. Her hair was a sodden rope and her arms were covered in sand. "I don't suppose you know—"

"No."

He sat down beside her. "Well," he said, "I suppose we ought to make a move. It won't be that long before it gets dark."

"I haven't got any shoes."

"That's unfortunate. But we can't stay here forever. We've got to find out where we are."

She wasn't looking at him. Neither was anyone else; they were all giving their entire attention to something on the landward side of the wreck. He saw it quickly enough: a dozen or so horsemen, hurrying towards them. Ah, well, he thought.

It wasn't long before he could tell they were soldiers, twelve lancers and an officer in a red cloak with a fur collar. He stood up and went to meet them.

The officer was light-skinned but the features of his face were pure Imperial; a young man, maybe twenty-four or five, in gilded parade armour, with an ivory scabbard for his sword. "Who the hell are you?" he said.

"We were shipwrecked," Genseric said.

"I didn't ask how you got here."

"My name's Genseric."

He was annoying the young officer. "East or West?"

Something in the way he said it, a hint of distaste for both alternatives. "Excuse me," Genseric said, "but is this Blemya?"

"East or West?"

"West," Genseric said. "We were heading for Atrabeau, and there was this sudden storm which came out of nowhere. We don't want to be any trouble to anyone, so if you could just—"

"Sergeant," the officer said. At once, the troopers fanned out, forming a half-circle. Their lance points were universally level with Genseric's head, a really quite impressive display of drill. One of them slid out of his saddle, planted his lance firmly in the sand, advanced on Genseric and pulled his hands behind his back. "Tell your men to put down their weapons."

"We haven't got any," Genseric said; then he remembered

Orderic's sword. "We're on a diplomatic mission," he said, but nobody seemed interested.

The officer had ridden past him, and was looking at Lysao. "Who's that?" he said.

"We're on a diplomatic mission," Genseric repeated, "escorting a representative of a—"

"This man is armed," the officer snapped. The half-circle shifted and reformed around the ship, as Orderic raised both his hands in the air. "If you're diplomats, where's your credentials?"

"We lost them in the shipwreck," Genseric said, "along with everything else, but I can assure you, we're properly accredited—"

"He's lying."

She hadn't shouted, but she didn't need to. There was a nasty moment of silence, and then she went on, "I'm a citizen of Beal Defoir, an independent state recognised by the Blemyan crown. Several days ago these men attacked my home and abducted me by force. I demand that you arrest them."

Genseric recognised the glazed look that froze on the young officer's face. He'd worn it himself, in his time, when some routine job had suddenly sprouted horns and wings and metamorphosed into something horribly difficult. Under other circumstances he'd have sympathised. "Don't listen to her," he said, trying to sound scornfully confident. "The fact is, she's a convicted criminal. Extraditing her was our mission. She'll say any damn thing just to keep from being taken to Atrabeau."

The officer looked at him, then back at Lysao. There was a wretched weariness in his face that would have melted a heart of stone. "Has anyone got any papers or means of identification?" he said. No answer. "Fine," he sighed. "Corporal, go back and get seven horses, no, forget that, bring a cart. The rest of you, I want this wreck searched. Anything you find, bring it to me." He slid off his horse and tethered it to the keel, then wiped sweat out of his eyes with the back of his hand. "Sergeant, gather this lot up and keep them together, I don't want any of them going anywhere."

Genseric watched the corporal gallop away. One less, he thought; that's probably as good as it's likely to get. She had a particularly insufferable smirk on her face. He glanced at Orderic, who was looking straight at him, waiting; he didn't dare nod, but he flicked his eyes quickly at the officer, then at the sergeant, then looked away. He let his left hand hang by his side, closed his fist, lifted first the thumb, then the index finger, middle finger, ring finger, little finger; and then he threw himself at the officer and dragged him to the ground.

The cloak helped; Genseric was able to drag it over the officer's head with his left, which meant he could draw that handsome ivory-hilted sword with his right and use it to stab its owner just above the thigh, where there's a gap between the bottom row of plates of the regulation cuirass and the top of the cuisse. He put an extra bit of strength behind it, just to relieve his feelings, until he felt the blade grate on bone; then he jumped up, letting the impetus drag the sword out of the wound, and looked round to see if Orderic had read his signals. Apparently yes: the sergeant was staggering backwards, as Orderic lunged forward to stab one of the troopers, who'd been a bit slow figuring out what was happening. Then another trooper monopolised his attention for a moment or so; a tricky customer who feinted a skull-splitting chop to bring his guard up, then started to shift into a groin-level stab; Genseric read him right, pivoted on his back foot and cut down on his outstretched arm, catching him just above the wrist. He was overdoing it – the hand came off and went flying, and Genseric stumbled forward, briefly losing his balance. That could have been disastrous if there'd been anyone behind him, and it was pure luck that there wasn't. But he recovered well and was nicely poised on the balls of his feet when a trooper lunged at him with a lance. He shifted left, caught the lance just below the head with his left hand, reeled the trooper in like a fish and cut his throat with a little backhand flick. As the trooper went down, he saw the helmsman topple over backwards; he reversed the dead soldier's lance and threw it at the man who'd killed the helmsman, missed but drew him forward into a simple feint-high-cut-low. As he killed him, he thought he saw a shadow cross the dying man's face; without looking, he pulled out the sword, reversed it and stabbed blindly behind him, registered an impact against something too hard to pierce; turned as tightly as he could and brought his sword up just in time to block a half-hearted cut; angled his blade so the cut would slide off and converted the block into a downward thrust that slithered off the scales of the cuirass down into an improvidently advanced knee. The pain and shock of that bought him enough time for a step back and a rather belated assessment of the situation, which he concluded with a rising cut under the chin – again, overdoing it, he cut right through to the poor devil's teeth. Another step back and count the men standing – three. Orderic, one marine and the other sailor. Victory, apparently. He caught his breath and forced his mind clear, so difficult to do after a scrimmage. He was covered in blood, but he was pretty sure none of it was his, so that was all right.

An awful thought struck him and he looked round; but she was still there, frozen stiff, a look of pure horror on her face. "Get her," he snapped, and Orderic snapped out of whatever dream he'd been in, bounded across and grabbed her by the wrist; she screamed, and Orderic bellowed, "Quiet!", and she stopped. Genseric stooped over the fallen marine; all over with him, poor sod, his head was split open down to his eyebrows. The helmsman he knew about. "You," he called to the marine, "get those horses."

"Major." Orderic pointed with his sword at the dead bodies. Yes, but there wasn't time: the corporal would be back with his cart – the corporal, who'd heard everything, names, the request for asylum; damn. His idea had been to leave the mess and let the sea clean it up; by the time the bodies were found, they'd be over the border. He'd forgotten about the corporal. But an extra enemy might well have turned the fight against them, he'd done well to shorten the odds; it's never perfect, and you have to do the best you can. He shook his head. "Get her on a horse," he said. "Better tie her to the girth or something, I can't be bothered with any more fuss."

Fortuitously there was some rope, just about enough, one end of a broken line tied to a cleat hook on the side of the catboat. He guessed she was still in shock; it occurred to him for the first time that maybe she'd never seen anything like this before – if so, a slice of luck, she'd be numb with it and no bother to anyone. Now then, which way? Happily, even he knew the answer to that one. The sea is north, therefore left is west, just follow the coast to the border. As he hauled himself into the dead officer's saddle his mind was buzzing with mental arithmetic; let x be the time it takes for the cart to get here, plus another x for it to go back, a third x for the soldiers to arrive—

Orderic handed him the reins of her horse. He didn't look round. This was going to be hard enough as it was.

Maybe an hour later. The sun was going down. Orderic said, "We could lay up for the night in that stand of trees over there."

Genseric shook his head. "Let's keep going," he said. "It can't be much further, surely."

"I don't like riding at night without a lantern," Orderic said. "And the horses need a rest: they're dead beat."

Genseric wasn't listening. He was looking straight ahead, unable to be sure what he'd just seen in the failing light. "It can't be," he said. "How could they have got ahead of us?"

Fanning out from the wood were at least fifty horsemen, possibly more; small men on light, slim horses; not something you want to see in Blemya. He heard Orderic sigh and say, "Well, that's that, then."

"It's a shame," Genseric said. "We must be nearly there."

"You did your best," Orderic said.

Yes, but that wasn't the point. Maybe if this had happened before they'd killed the patrol; no, still not the point. Failure; it was all that mattered. He could hear his father saying, "The best man always wins". With a sigh, he drew his sword and dropped in on the ground; then he unwrapped the reins of her horse from his wrist and dropped them, too. "I hate losing," he said.

"I'd sort of gathered."

"None of the evil crap you do matters if you win." He turned round in his saddle and looked at her. "Horse-archers," he said. "We don't mess with them. You're free to go."

She looked at him, then nudged her horse forward. "Don't do that," he said, "it'll step in its reins and get tangled. Here." He swung out of the saddle – God, but his legs were stiff – picked up the reins and handed them to her. "You might put in a good word for us," he said. "We tried to be nice. Really."

She looked down at him, and the question that had been at the back of his mind all quietly answered itself. Worth every stuiver, he thought. "I will," she said.

He told the whole story, complete and accurate, to the Blemyan officer at the fort. When he'd finished, the officer called for the guards and had him marched off to the cells.

He didn't think much of them. They were wood, not stone; a glorified shed, with a tiled roof and just one bolt on the door. But he was worn out, and he hadn't slept properly since before the raid. I'll escape later, he promised himself, and went to sleep.

When they woke him up, it was screaming bright sunlight outside; he was politely escorted into the drill yard, where he saw Orderic sitting on a mounting block, polishing his boots.

"I get the impression they don't know what to do with us," Orderic said cheerfully. "Are we murderers, prisoners of war or very badly behaved diplomats? By the way, I don't know about where they put you, but mine was so flimsy I wouldn't keep a goat in it. And the stables are over there." He indicated the direction with the slightest of nods. "I'll give it a go if you want."

Genseric shook his head. "Have you seen her Ladyship?"

"No. Better quarters than ours, I'd imagine. Is it true Beal Defoir counts as an independent sovereign state?"

"No idea. And I don't suppose they know, either."

"We could try and snatch her," Orderic said, with a marked lack of enthusiasm. "I mean, there's two of us and only a hundred or so of them."

"They don't pay me enough," Genseric said firmly. "I suggest we stay quiet and try not to annoy them any more. The way things are going, we could probably do worse than sit out the rest of the war in a nice sunny place like this."

Orderic beamed at him. "Restful," he said. "I think I'd like that. I wonder if the food's any good."

Three days of peace and rest under a blue sky; and, yes, the food was perfectly acceptable –

("What the hell is this supposed to be?" Orderic demanded. "It looks like maggots. I'm not eating this."

"Your loss," said the guard. "It's yummy. Also, it's all there is. We call it *rice*."

"What is it, some kind of edible larvae?"

"It's basically grass seeds. I'll have it if you don't want it.") – once you got used to it, and the guards lent them a chess set and some bowling balls – no, sorry, no cards, strictly forbidden to military personnel. And when they found out that Genseric played the rebec and Orderic knew the flute, they lent them instruments and made up a quintet. Their repertoire was limited (Scantia, Procopius, Ermanaric; do you know any Oida? Yes, but nobody's perfect) but they were competent and enthusiastic musicians, and it had been a long time since Genseric had heard anything decent. "The truth is," Captain Dapha, the guard commander, told him, confirming his suspicions, "we aren't really sure what you are. So we're treating you as honoured guests who aren't allowed to leave. I hope that's all right."

A sharp poke in the ribs. Genseric opened his eyes, but it was too dark to see.

"On your feet."

"Dapha?" Genseric scrubbed his eyes with his knuckles. "What's the matter?"

"On your feet," Dapha repeated. "You're moving out."

"All right, just give me a moment."

A hand closed in his hair and pulled up. He rose, protesting, and something hard hit him in the pit of the stomach. Through the partition, he heard Orderic shout something and then abruptly fall silent. Ah, he thought. Clarification of status has been received.

He was being towed by his hair. "Can I put my boots on?" he asked, and took the impact of a spear butt against his ear as meaning no, he couldn't. Well; he couldn't blame them. Nobody wants to get into trouble.

Outside in the yard, by torchlight, he saw a coach. It wasn't an elegant thing; it was built of inch planks, like floorboards, and there were no windows. Nothing to sit down on, either. Once he and Orderic were inside, the door slammed and he counted three bolts. He realised he hadn't had an opportunity to ask about his men – the marine and the sailor – but consoled himself with the thought that he wouldn't have been given an answer.

"What d'you reckon?" Orderic said. "Sit up against the wall, or flat on the floor?"

It was so dark he couldn't tell which side of him Orderic was on. "Don't suppose it'll matter much."

He heard someone shouting something: couldn't make out the words. "Do you think this is it?" Orderic asked. "You know."

"Oh, be quiet," he said.

When at last the door opened, the light burned his eyes and he cringed away from it; and he heard a voice saying, "Dear God, look at the state of you." The voice's tone was not sympathetic.

He was hauled out by a man in uniform into a wide paved yard surrounded on all four sides by tall, impressive buildings. He was too weak to stand up, but they didn't hit him. Someone said, "They can't go in looking like that. Get them cleaned up and find them something to wear."

Nothing about food or drink, which was a pity, but Genseric was largely past caring. The coach had stopped at least a dozen times, but only for the time it takes to change horses. The rest of the time it had kept up a horrible bruising pace, no suspension on badly rutted roads. He felt like he'd been in a fight for days on end, and never landed a single punch. They had to carry Orderic out, like a sack of logs.

He was helped rather than dragged across the yard, through an arch into a stable yard. There they sat them both down on a mounting block, peeled off their clothes and washed them down with brooms, brushes, curry-combs and cold water from a bucket until their skins were raw but perfectly clean. Long woollen gowns were then dragged down over their heads, and wooden-soled sandals strapped to their feet. A seven-foot sergeant in award armour stood over Genseric with a comb in his hand and looked at his loosened, tangled hair, shook his head and tossed the comb into the bucket, along with the contaminated brushes. "They'll do," said a young man in a shiny gold breastplate. "Come on, move. You know what she's like if she's kept waiting."

Genseric started to get up, but his knees failed; they caught him before he pitched on to his face and put him back on the mounting block. "You'll just have to chair them," the golden boy said. "At least as far as the portico."

Four men crowded round Genseric with spears. For a moment, all he could think of was Orderic's question – do you think this is it? – but apparently not; one spear was for him to sit on, one went under the joints of his knees; the other two ran lengthways, to support his arms. It was actually quite comfortable, even at the jogtrot.

Out into the yard again – that horrible coach had gone, thank God; death rather than another ride in that thing – and up the steps of the biggest, tallest building, through two impossibly tall bronze gates embossed with stylised fighting eagles, across a marble-floored hall to another set of bronze doors; then they were lowered until their feet touched the ground, the spears were slid out from under them and they were lifted upright and left to fend for themselves. Someone whispered in Genseric's ear, "If you fall over, I'll kill you." He made an effort and put one foot in front of another. It was hard, like walking with numb feet, just before the pins and needles set in – but he reckoned it was worth the effort. The vast doors opened and a hand in the small of his back propelled him forward, into what appeared to be the House of God.

It was slightly smaller than the great hall of the Imperial palace at Rasch, and the roof wasn't quite as high as the Golden Mountain temple; nevertheless, Genseric realised at once just how country cousin and provincial those two places were: sad imitations of the real thing, in which he now stood. The floor was porphyry, polished to a watery gloss. The walls and ceiling blazed with gold mosaic, scenes that cried out and demanded to be gazed at, studied in detail and adored. Two rows of fluted, gilded columns strode down the hall, where stood a raised dais of white marble, supporting a throne tall and wide enough for the King and Queen of Heaven to sit comfortably side by side. As he tottered towards it, there was some bizarre optical illusion that made it look as though it was rising up into the air – and then he realised it was no illusion: that monstrous, unbelievable weight really was slowly lifting upwards, floating with no apparent support. There were people in the hall, row upon row of them, like worshippers in Temple; they weren't looking at him, only at the slowly rising throne. When he was fifty yards away from it, he thought he could just make out a tiny human figure, probably a child, perched on the cloth-of-gold-drape bench seat. At twenty yards, a hand on his shoulder stopped him and pushed him gently to his knees. It never occurred to him not to kneel; he'd been waiting for an opportunity.

Then he saw something else. On the marble dais, next to where the throne must have rested before it began to float, was a single straight-backed wooden chair. In it sat Lysao, in a snow-white gown, and she was looking straight at him. Oh, he thought. But never mind. No doubt at some point they'd kill him, probably in a very unpleasant way, but that scarcely seemed to matter. They could only damage his body, and already he felt that he had passed beyond all that, that he was no longer flesh but spirit. If they killed his flesh and his spirit could stay here, that wouldn't be so bad. In fact—

"That's her up there," he heard Orderic whispering next to him. "Must be."

He had to think for a moment, and then he remembered. They were in Blemya; and the one thing everybody knew about Blemya was that it was ruled by a woman; by a little girl. He looked up, but all he could see was a suit of extraordinary clothes – a long purple gown, glittering with gold thread and seedpearls like a dragon's underbelly; a shining gold sash, coiled round the folds of the gown like a python; a monstrous crown like a weathervane, three times the size of a human head. The fact that the clothes sat upright instead of crumpling in a heap suggested there must be someone inside there, but he or she was completely invisible.

Genseric realised someone was speaking; had been, for some time. He caught his own name, but the echo caught everything else and made it a reverberating jumble, one voice bickering with a thousand copies of itself. He tore his eyes away from the throne and located a bald man in a gown rather like the one he was wearing, standing a few yards away, talking up to the bundle of clothes. For a moment, he wondered what was going on, and then it dawned on him. The bald man was the prosecutor.

Under other circumstances, it would've struck him as unfair that he couldn't understand what was being said against him. But the reasoning behind it came in a flash of intuition. The acoustics of this place were pitched so that the occupant of the throne, so high up and far away, could hear every word; nobody else mattered. Almost certainly, whoever it was up there knew all the facts already, could read minds and hearts, could count all the grains of sand on the seashore and all the stars in the sky. There were certain formalities, but that was all they were. Judgement, when it came, would be undeniable and perfect. Arguing the toss would be unthinkable; obscene.

Then he caught Lysao's eye again, and shivered.

The prosecutor had finished and backed away, out of sight among the congregation. For one horrible moment, Genseric wondered if he was supposed to say something. But he was spared that. Lysao stood up, made a perfunctory nod at the base of the throne, and began speaking. Again, he couldn't make out any of it, but he fancied he could guess what the gist of it was. The echo swirled her voice, mixed it up with itself, bounced it off the walls and ceiling like a ball. There was no beauty in it now: it was harsh, shrill, querulous. He guessed she couldn't hear herself, because otherwise she'd stop, appalled. He felt ashamed of himself for ever having been born.

At last she finished whatever it was she'd been saying; she did the offensive nod once again, sat down and looked bored. There was a moment of silence which went on and became awkward. Then she spoke to him.

He heard his name, clear as flute music, so close he started to look round to see who was right beside him. He heard it again and realised where it was coming from. He looked up at the distant figure. "Your Majesty," he said.

"Do you wish to say anything?"

His words were still swooping and filling the air around him; he'd heard them only as a sort of confused howling. He shook his head, realised she probably couldn't see him. "No, your Majesty," he said, and winced at the horrible noise. Everyone was looking up at the throne, waiting. He wished the moment could last for ever.

"The appellant Lysao," said the heavenly voice, "claims to be a citizen of Beal Defoir, which I am informed is recognised by this house as a sovereign nation. She further claims that she was abducted against her will by soldiers of the Western emperor, led by Major Genseric, who is before us. The Domestic of the Bedchamber claims that Major Genseric has told the representatives of this house that the appellant is a fugitive from justice in the West, and that he was executing a lawful warrant. Major Genseric has declined to speak in his own suit."

A brief silence. There were no echoes to die away.

"This house recollects," the voice went on, "that no treaty of extradition exists or has ever existed between Blemya and either empire. Therefore this house cannot hear any request for extradition, and indeed, none has been formally made."

Genseric felt delighted and confused. He'd been sure he was the one on trial, for killing the soldiers. Or hadn't they got that far yet?

"The appellant claims," said the voice, "that as a priestess she is entitled to sanctuary as against Major Genseric. However, she has neglected to furnish any proof that the West seeks to extradite her in connection with any alleged offence related to the office of priest, and therefore her claim in this regard must be refused."

Another pause. Orderic was tugging at his sleeve. He ignored him.

"The Domestic claims that Major Genseric and his companions killed twelve soldiers of the coast patrol in an attempt to resist arrest. However, the Domestic has not furnished sufficient corroborative evidence for this claim to enable this house to hear the matter, and that claim is also dismissed."

Genseric felt his jaw drop open. He let it hang. He had no strength left.

"This house confesses to a certain difficulty in deciding what should become of the parties in this case. The appellant is not obliged to go with Major Genseric, nor has she any standing to stay in Blemya. There seems to be no obligation on this house to incur the trouble and expense of conveying her home to Beal Defoir. The appellant further claims that her life would be in danger were she to be conveyed by land to the frontiers of either the Western or Eastern empires, but offers no proof of this claim other than hearsay. This house finds that it is under no obligation to the appellant, other than the simple and basic duty of hospitality. This house has always held that duty in the highest possible regard, and therefore resolves that the appellant be allowed to stay in Blemya, as the guest of this house, until suitable arrangements can be made for her return to Beal Defoir. As for Major Genseric and his three companions, they are to be escorted with all due expedition to the Western frontier and allowed to depart in peace."

"We're going to be in so much trouble," Orderic muttered. "They aren't going to like this one little bit."

"Be quiet," Genseric said absently. His mind was still just full enough of the visions he'd seen to be peacefully numb, but every word Orderic spoke made it harder to keep it that way. He glanced up at the sun and figured it must be mid-afternoon. They'd reach the border by nightfall, they'd assured him, guaranteed. This time they were on a magnificently kept road in a well-sprung chaise bearing the livery of the royal messengers. He kept expecting to wake up and find himself in the other coach; except that in the other coach sleep had been impossible.

"All we've achieved," Orderic said, "was to take her out of somewhere where she was vulnerable and put her in what's probably the safest place on earth right now. Oh, and along the way we violated Blemyan territory and killed a dozen of their soldiers. Is Forza going to be pleased with us? I think not."

"I thought I told you to be quiet," Genseric said, yawning. "That's an order."

"I don't think you'll be in a position to give orders much longer," Orderic replied sadly. "Me neither. I don't know which'd be worse, strung up or broken back to the ranks and sent to the front. Why the hell didn't you say something while you had the chance? You could tell she was bending over backwards to find a reason for helping us. Last thing she wants is to piss off both the Belot brothers simultaneously, but thanks to you—"

"If you don't shut your face," Genseric said, "I'll shut it for you. Got that?"

There now; he'd shocked and offended his friend. He leaned back in his seat and admired the sky. "Back there," he said. "I think I may have had a spiritual experience."

"Bullshit," Orderic said crisply. "It was just acoustics and hydraulics. I don't even think that was the real queen."

"It was her," Genseric said. "Don't you ever read the monthly reports? There's been all sorts going on in Blemya. She's back in control."

Orderic stared at him. "You might have told me."

"I assumed—" He shrugged. "Makes no odds," he said. "But

that . . . place we were in; that was the Great Hall, the real thing. When the old guard was still in control, she wasn't allowed to use it, she had to make do with the New Hall. It's a close replica, but it doesn't have that amazing acoustic effect. When they built the New Hall they tried to copy it exactly, but they got it very slightly wrong, so it doesn't work there. Sorry, I thought you knew."

Orderic scowled at him, then shrugged. "Well, anyway," he said, "at least you admit it's all cleverness and trickery and not the Voice of God. You went all to pieces in there. Admit it."

"Freely," Genseric said. "I looked up, and I saw judgement looking down at me. I was quite prepared to go to the gallows, accepting the fairness of its decision. But I was accorded grace, and here I still am."

"For now, anyway," Orderic said. "When we get back—"

Genseric sat up. "When we get back," he said, "we're going to be asked a lot of very detailed questions about everything we saw in the palace. It ought to save our necks; might even do us some good, if we're lucky. You don't get it, do you? By sheer dumb luck, we're the first Westerners with official standing to have seen the new regime in Blemya. I don't care how mad Forza is at us, we did good." He closed his eyes for a moment. "That's why I regard it as a spiritual experience," he said. "Soon as I heard that garbled echo, I knew; Great Hall, that's a statement if ever there was one. She's in charge and she wants everybody to know it; and that's why she let us go, because she wants a rapprochement with the West, or at least, she wants us to think she does." He yawned again. "Put it another way," he said. "From the depths of failure, grace caught us and drew us up into the light. Instead of outcasts, we'll be heroes. Lucky old us."

The interrogation and debriefing lasted four days; approximately three hours for every minute they'd spent in the Great Hall. Every detail, from the brightness of the candles to the colour of the acolytes' chasubles; in a society so completely marinaded in ritual as Blemya, the slightest thing could be enormously significant – indeed, subtle details were more likely to carry true significance than overt statements. Genseric was quite right; the return of the Queen of Blemya to the Great Hall completely eclipsed the failure of their mission – which, having failed, was not to be talked about and probably had never happened; the attack on Beal Defoir was almost certainly pirates dressed up as Imperial forces, wearing armour and uniforms bought from Ocnisant. As for Forza, nobody seemed to know where he was or what he was doing; he was busy with some new idea and couldn't be bothered with the fallout from the old one.

While Genseric was in the South Wing, he did pick up one interesting piece of news. Domna Lysao wasn't in Blemya any more. She'd left the sanctuary of the royal palace, taking with her a horse and a number of small, valuable items (retrospective gifts, according to unofficial Blemyan sources) and vanished into the night; a corresponding time later, a woman on a horse of the same colour and stature as the one missing from the royal stables had crossed the frontier, narrowly evading the border guards—

"But that's crazy," Orderic protested, when Genseric told him. "We went to all that trouble, nearly got ourselves disgraced and killed, and then the bloody woman trots off into the West of her own free will. It's enough to make you give up soldiering and join a monastery."

"I said she'd crossed the frontier," Genseric said gently, "I didn't say which one. She crossed into the East."

Four weeks later, Genseric was back on the front line. A large contingent of Eastern cavalry had broken through in the north, and General Dipaza had asked for him by name.

It was a long, gruelling march, in the rain and bitter cold, and when they got there the Easterners had retired into the foothills of the mountains, where only an idiot would follow them. They'd left behind them the usual trail of burned and deserted villages; that was all they'd achieved, so technically their withdrawal constituted a victory. Nevertheless, some form of token reprisal was called for. Dipaza couldn't be bothered to go himself, so Genseric had the honour of leading one infantry battalion and two squadrons of Cassite lancers across the border, with instructions to burn a minimum of two hundred farmsteads and appropriate at least a thousand head of cattle. There would be no resistance, and the operation shouldn't take longer than three weeks. He could kill civilians if he wanted to, but it wasn't essential. He could use his own judgement on that.

The Cassites felt the cold. It was hard, even for an Imperial like Genseric, to see how that was possible. Cassite lancers wear scale armour from head to toe; under the armour they have padded jacks and breeches an inch thick, and regulations permit the wearing of surcoats, cloaks and scarves, as well as the traditional Cassite arming cap, a full pound weight of wool quilted into a tulip shape, with earflaps and neck guard, worn under the massive full-face helmet. Cassites were prized by both sides because they alone could survive in all that impossible gear (which made them pretty well invulnerable) without dying of heat exhaustion; attempts to equip non-Cassite units with the same kit had always ended in disaster or mutiny. And, anywhere north of the Lakes, they felt the cold dreadfully and whined about it incessantly, and you had to be nice to them or they'd desert to the enemy without a moment's hesitation. Not that they were unreliable or treacherous; far from it. You couldn't persuade a Cassite to change sides by bribing him, or holding his children hostage. But if his fingers went numb and his teeth started to chatter – essentially, at any temperature below the melting point of copper – either you gave him firewood and extra blankets or you lost him forever. Simple as that.

Genseric had served with Cassites before, so he knew what was needed. He filled four carts with enough blankets to bow the axles, assigned two companies of infantry to wood-foraging duties and commandeered a large consignment of rolls of felt, fortuitously held in bonded store at Prahend awaiting shipment downriver to the hatmakers of Rasch. The felt made all the difference. The Cassites cut it into strips and jammed it between their armour and their clothing, and cautiously predicted that they might not freeze to death after all.

For all that, the Sausagemen proved to be highly effective at trashing farmsteads. Orderic reckoned it was simply a matter of motivation; burning thatch offered warmth. Genseric felt there was probably rather more to it than that, but he wasn't inclined to think about it too deeply. The mission was going well but he wasn't enjoying it.

"We're on target for houses," Orderic reported, as the sparks rose, "but we're a bit behind on the livestock. A lot behind, in fact. You'd think they'd go together, farms and farm animals, but apparently not."

There spoke the city boy, who didn't realise that houses can be rebuilt in a few months, but flocks and herds take years. They hadn't seen a living soul for days, which confirmed it; the locals had driven off their livestock to somewhere remote and well hidden, trusting to snowfall to cover the tracks. Caves, possibly, if there were any in the foothills of the mountains; if not, there would be sheltered combes, steep-sided river valleys, maybe even large patches of clear-fell in the pine forest where sheep at least could graze long enough for the monsters to go away. Finding them, of course, would be next to impossible without ridiculous luck or local knowledge. In fact, the only way Genseric could see of losing a significant number of his men was launching off into the wild looking for such places. Burned houses would have to do. Stealing cattle was specialised work, and for some reason it hadn't featured in his otherwise faultless education.

Luck, however, seemed determined to be on his side, whether he wanted it or not. Two stray sheep, big stocky animals with heavy, briar-clogged fleeces, crossed their path, stared at them and bolted back up the hillside. Genseric roared at the men closest to him to follow; they jumped down from their horses and scrambled dangerously up the snow-covered shale, while Orderic halted the line. The scouts were a long time returning; when they did, they reported fresh tracks in the snow on the other side of the ridge. Genseric sent them back again, with instructions to follow the tracks as far as they could. When they got back, just after sunset, they said the trail led to a steep gorge, dropping away sharply to a folded-over combe with a stream at the bottom. They hadn't gone too far, because they could hear more sheep, a lot of them, but they could see glimpses of green between the rocks, suggesting the combe was sheltered and warm.

"And, you can bet your life, closed off at both ends," Orderic said cheerfully, while the Cassites were dismounting. Horses couldn't go where they were going. "Secure the ends and nothing can get out."

"Except sheep," Genseric replied. "Sheep can get out of anything, trust me. My father used to say that's why sheep are so evil. It's no good sending them to Hell; they only get out again." He lifted his helmet, considered the weight and all the uphill that lay ahead and decided not to bother; the mail coif would do instead, and he could take it off and sling it through his belt. "Ah well," he said. "The exercise will do us good."

By the time they reached the top of the ridge overlooking the southern entrance to the combe, even the Cassites were warm, though naturally they didn't admit it. The climb had taken them from sunrise to mid-morning, and Genseric was glad of the excuse of getting his forces in position. He sat down on the ground with his back to a thorn tree and caught his breath. He'd allowed the Cassites plenty of time to get round the side of the steep to cover the north entrance of the combe; he was staying on the south side, with half the infantry; the rest were down below, looking after the horses. That gave him a total of three hundred and fifty men; against what? Three dozen shepherds? Even so, he told himself, do it properly. The very worst words a commander can ever utter are *I never thought of that.*

He therefore gave the Cassites an extra five general confessions to get into place, then lifted his arm and waved Orderic and the first two companies of infantry into motion. They scrambled down the slope, and as soon as they'd reached the bottom, he followed with the third company.

The combe was a beautiful place; green in winter, with thorn and wild plum trees lining a straight, fast-running stream. The whole of one bank was carpeted with sheep; a thousand, easily. As he'd anticipated, the sides were too steep for a man to climb without ropes and hooks; even the sheep had to turn back halfway, as their hooves lost grip on the thin, easily uprooted heather and moss. He'd overestimated the enemy numbers by a factor of three. There were a dozen shepherds, mostly boys, two old men and an even older woman. They stood up and stayed perfectly still, which suggested they knew the rules only too well.

"Now what?" Orderic said, wiping his forehead. "Sorry, but my mother didn't raise me to be a shepherd. You know all about this stuff, don't you?"

Genseric frowned. "In theory," he said. "My father owned twenty thousand sheep, among other livestock. But we left the more technical side of it to the professionals. Sergeant," he called out. "Any farm boys in your platoon? I need this lot rounded up and driven back the way we just came."

The infantry, Genseric quickly discovered, were men of many skills and talents – fishermen, quarrymen, brickmakers, sawmill hands, dockers, porters, roadmenders, even a few refugees from proper trades such as weavers, coopers, tanners, wheelwrights, chandlers, foundrymen, stonemasons, cartwrights, fullers and one bankrupt coppersmith. No shepherds. The Cassites, of course, knew livestock better than anyone – they lived by driving their vast flocks across dune and desert – but, they objected, they'd been hired as soldiers, not stockmen; besides, any fool knows you round up stock on horseback, not on foot. And you have dogs. Without dogs–– They shrugged regretfully and sat down on the grass, shivering.

"It's ridiculous," Genseric said angrily, "they shouldn't be in the army, they're tradesmen, they should be in a factory somewhere, making munitions. The regulations specifically say––"

"Major."

Orderic was pointing at something. He followed the line of his outstretched arm, and on the skyline he saw a man, several men, a row of them, evenly spaced like fence posts. They were archers. He swung round; they were lined out on the other side of the combe, too. That's it, then, he thought.

"They've blocked both ends," Orderic said. His voice was low and remarkably steady, in the circumstances. "I thought––"

"Shut up," Genseric snapped. "Let me think."

"What about? They've got us. We're dead."

They weren't the only ones to have noticed. Captains and sergeants were yelling orders, ranks were forming, the men were kneeling, lifting their shields. Pointless. They couldn't climb the sides, and a dozen men could hold either end of the combe against a thousand. He started counting the archers, but gave up when he reached treble figures.

"There's always the reserve," Orderic said. "We've still got the men we left with the horses."

"Want to bet?" He looked round one more time. Whoever had set the trap and lined out the archers clearly knew what he was doing, there was no point even trying to fight. But they weren't shooting; not yet. "I think we'd better surrender," he said quietly. "Stand the men down. I'll go and see if I can find someone to talk to."

They found him; two of them, a slight, grey-haired man and a red-headed giant. There was some way down through the rocks that they knew, though there was nothing to see; they appeared suddenly, walking across the grass, unarmed and looking as though they'd come to buy the sheep. He walked over towards them, with Orderic just behind him; ten yards away, the older man gestured for them to stop. "Just you, Major," he called out. "Not the captain."

Genseric hesitated. He wasn't wearing any badge of rank, and neither was Orderic. "Better do what they want," he said. "Wait here."

He followed them up the slope and talked to them for a while. Then he came down again. Orderic was waiting exactly where he'd left him. He took a moment to catch his breath, then said, "It's all right."

"Major?"

"They're letting you go. Tell the men to pile up their weapons and dump their armour, helmets, too. When they've done that, you can lead them out on the north side, where we came in. I'm afraid the rest of the battalion wasn't so lucky: they tried to put up a fight. Oh, and they're keeping the horses, so you're going to have to walk. But apart from that, you should be fine."

Orderic had noticed the pronouns. "You're not coming with us."

"You've got to deliver a message to regional command. Basically, it's this. There's now a third party in this war. They aren't bothered if East and West stick to killing each other, but if we carry on burning out farms and forcibly enlisting the country people, we shouldn't expect them to be so kind-hearted in future. Apparently they did the same thing to an Eastern division last week, away up in the Rhus country; the Easterners chose to make a fight of it, and they won't be going home. They appreciate that it'll take quite a few demonstrations of this sort before anyone takes them seriously, but they've got to start somewhere. Just deliver the message," Genseric added. "That's all they want from you. All right?"

"Who are they?"

Genseric looked at him for a moment. "I get the impression this deal is conditional on me not answering that question," he said. "I think I know, but I'm only guessing."

"You're not coming."

"No." Genseric looked away. "No, I've got to go with them, and I can't tell you why. It's all right," he added quickly. "I've known all along, ever since Beal Defoir, that someone was going to get stuck with the tab eventually. It's like she said, it was just a matter of time. But that's none of your business. Get on and do what they want, before they change their minds."

Orderic started to say something, but he turned his back on him and walked away, up the slope.

The Cherry Tree

They'd been issued with a jar of honey. "I think you're supposed to wrap it in cheesecloth first," Teucer said, but Myrtus didn't think so. "Just stick it in," he said, "bung the lid on and melt some beeswax round it. I really don't want to look at it any more than I can help."

It was a tight fit. Whoever issued the jar had probably been thinking of a smaller man. The ears wedged against the rim, and Teucer had to use considerable force to get it inside; honey welled up all round it and slopped out on to his hands. Even then, the hair wouldn't go in at all. "Cut it off, then," Myrtus ordered.

"You sure that's all right?"

"It'll have to be, won't it?" Myrtus drew his knife and sawed through the thick braids; finally, the lid fitted, just about. "I'll hold it shut," Myrtus said. "Get the beeswax."

Teucer came back with a block of wax and a small copper pan. He heated the pan over the fire till the wax went clear; it smelt of honey, a scent Myrtus was rapidly growing sick of. He held the jar up and turned it slowly while Teucer poured. The result was a mess, but airtight.

"What do you suppose they want it for?" Teucer asked.

Myrtus shivered a little. "Proof, mostly. And they'll stick it up on a spike on a gate somewhere. Ironic," he added. "The poor devil's father ended up the same way. Runs in families, evidently."

Teucer was frowning. "Well, he asked for it, didn't he?"

"He was a brave soldier," Myrtus said, "who died to save his men." He put the jar down, then wiped his hands vigorously on the grass. "That's the thing," he said. "Your soldierly virtues, like courage and self-sacrifice. It's bloody disconcerting when you see the enemy has them, too. Life would be much easier if they were all treacherous cowards, but they aren't. You're right, though," he added. "He had it coming."

"Happiest days of my life, Beal Defoir." Teucer picked up the jar and loaded it carefully into a strong hessian sack. "What about the body?" he asked.

"Leave it. Must be a few crows around here somewhere."

Myrtus picked up the axe and took it down to the stream; he washed it off, then pulled a clump of reeds and scrubbed his hands until they hurt. He'd got honey on his sleeves, too, but he didn't have a spare shirt; the corpse had one, but it was sodden with blood. There wasn't much to choose between them, but on balance he preferred the honey. I get all the rotten jobs, he told himself, and rinsed his hands one more time in the cold, swift water.

"Scouts are back," Teucer reported on his return. "They say the column's reached the road and they're making good time."

Myrtus nodded his approval. "I don't think we'll have any trouble from them," he said, "I think he had them pretty well trained. But you'd better have the scouts keep an eye on them till we're safely back in the mountains." He looked up and indicated the pile of weapons and armour with a slight tilt of his head. "What do you reckon we should do with that lot?" he said.

Teucer thought about it. "Worth money," he said.

"Yes, but it's a hell of a lot of junk to cart up all those hills. The hell with it, we'll leave it. The locals can sell it to Ocnisant, if they can be bothered." He looked round, and was satisfied. "In which case," he said, "I think we're about done here. All turned out fairly well, if you ask me."

Teucer took the axe from him and slung it on the packhorse, with the rest of the tools. "I'm glad we didn't have to fight," he said.

Myrtus grinned. "Balls," he said, "you were itching to show off, I could tell. You like to impress your students."

"On targets, yes," Teucer said. "It still doesn't feel right, shooting at people." He gathered the reins of the packhorse. "The first thing they tell you back home, when you pick up a bow, don't point it at anyone. It goes against the grain. I keep expecting someone to smack me round the face and tell me not to be so bloody stupid."

Myrtus laughed. "That's war for you," he said. "All the things that used to be forbidden are suddenly compulsory, but it's all right because the government says so. No, I agree with you, it's a very strange way to behave, when you stop and think about it."

Halfway through the morning after next, Teucer asked, "Who runs the Lodge?"

Myrtus gave him a sideways look. "Well," he said, "there's the Council of Privileges, who do the day-to-day administration, and they answer to the commissioners. Why?"

"I know that," Teucer said. "But who chooses them? Someone must, but nobody seems to know who."

"The commissioners choose the council."

"All right. How about the commissioners?"

"That I don't know," Myrtus said. "Nor do I want to. Logic dictates that there must be someone higher up than the commissioners, but logic isn't everything. I don't know. Maybe the Great

Smith comes to them in visions. Why? Thinking of running for office?"

Teucer laughed. "Sergeant's plenty good enough for me," he said. "How about you? What's the next step up from major?"

"There isn't one," Myrtus replied. "From major you get shoved back into the civilian grades, and I don't fancy that at all. They make you a field agent and you can get sent anywhere and told to do anything. One week you could be ambassador to the Jazygite Alliance; next week they could send you to be the cook in a tea house, with all the Lodge business for half a province to do in your spare time. We dread promotion. It's why the Lodge works."

"There must be someone right at the top, though," Teucer said. "Must be. Like the emperors, or kings, or high priests. You need someone like that. Like a body needs a brain."

"You seem to manage just fine without."

The question stayed in Myrtus' mind, and he thought about it on the long ride back to Central, and again when he presented himself for debriefing, until he happened to look through the window and something altogether more compelling drove it out—

"That's new," he said.

"Yes." She pursed her lips. "You don't like it."

He poured them both some tea. "It's not a question of liking it," he said, unable to tear his eyes away. "It's a perfectly nice tree, what's not to like? It's just a bit—"

"Inappropriate? Blasphemous? An abomination?"

"Obvious." He sipped the tea, acknowledging the grace notes of pepper and jasmine. "A cherry tree, for crying out loud, in the middle of the main square. I mean, why not a thirty-foot black obelisk with *The End Is Nigh* picked out in gold lettering?"

"Cost too much, for one thing. You have no idea how far over budget we are. Anyway, it's there, most people seem to like it, and if it gets chopped down in the middle of the night I'll know who to suspect. How was lovely pastoral Rhus?"

"That wasn't me," he said. "I went the other way, remember?"

"So you did," she corrected. "Well? How did you get on?"

So he told her about it, in proper military terminology, interceptions and ravelins and extractions. She didn't seem to be listening. She was gazing out of the window, in the direction of that horrible tree. He skipped the last trivial incidents of their journey home, and waited till she remembered he was there.

"So," she said. "Do you think it's going to work?"

"That's not for me to—"

"An opinion, Major." She smiled at him. "Go on. What do you think?"

He frowned. "I'm not sure," he replied. "I think, as soon as news gets back to Rasch and Choris, all hell's going to break loose."

"We've been through all that. They can't spare the men."

"How many men does it take?" He shrugged. "Let's think about it. I ambushed a battalion and two squadrons of Cassites. Suppose they send two battalions to teach those villages a lesson. With local knowledge and help from the villagers, I could probably – I say probably – see them off with five hundred archers. That's two-thirds of our military capability here at Central. Of course, they don't know that; they think this is an uprising by the villagers themselves, and by now they really don't know how many people are left up here; almost certainly they think there's more than there really are. Even so, what happens after that? Do you really think they're going to go meekly away and write off the north as a dead loss?"

"You've seen the casualty reports from the Belot brothers' latest reunion. They'll have no choice. They haven't got the manpower."

"So you say." He picked up his teacup, then put it down again. "Just for once," he said, "level with me. I know there's another agenda behind this. I'd really like it if you'd tell me what it is."

He was sure she'd deny it, or refuse. Instead, she shrugged her wonderful slim shoulders. "Not an agenda, as such. More the hope of useful consequences."

"Ah."

She paused, then went on. "We anticipate that there will be reprisals," she said, "and we won't be able to protect all the villages, though we'll do everything we can. The people won't just sit still and let themselves get burned out and their flocks stolen. They'll clear out."

"Like they're doing now. And their homes are trashed, and their crops are ruined—"

She shrugged. "They'll clear out," she said, "and we'll be there to tell them, come north. Come over the mountains and the moors, they won't follow you there. Come and live with us. We've got plenty of land, we'll tell them, and we'll protect you."

Myrtus opened his mouth, paused, thought for a moment. "We're going to recruit an army from these people."

"More than that." He couldn't miss the new tone in her voice. "Not just an army, a country. A new nation. That's what Central's all about. What we've built here isn't just a new headquarters for the Lodge, we don't need one, we've managed splendidly without one for a thousand years. No, what we're building is the capital city of a new nation. First all the empty land in the Rhus country, then gradually we work our way south, taking over all the land they've emptied with their ridiculous war, resettling all the refugees hiding in swamps and mountains; it's the obvious solution, don't you see? We're never going to reunite the old empire, it's too divided and too damaged for that. The only chance is to start all over again – get rid of the empires and the emperors, take charge ourselves; give the power to the only people on earth who can be trusted with it: us. Think about it. We've got all the best people, from artisans to administrators to soldiers. We've got all the knowledge, we've been thinking about exactly these problems for centuries. We can start with a clean slate. That's the amazing thing, which has never happened before, ever. We don't have to keep on making the same old mistakes. We can start from a point where there's nothing settled, nothing established; no vested interests, no power blocs, nobody to interfere with doing it *right*, for a change. What's the biggest slogan in the Lodge? Revaluation of all values. He made everything, and therefore everything is good. It's our time, Myrtus. This war is our chance. We've kept it going so long that both sides are completely worn out and the world is sick of them. Now—"

He stared at her. "*We've* kept it going?"

"Oh, don't be naïve. Of course. Every step of the way. We've kept the balance; no side ever has the advantage. That's why, when we thought Forza was dead, we had a dozen different plans in hand for killing Senza. That's what we needed Lysao for. And that's why you and your boy Teucer have been training all those archers. Look; we've got a capital city, we've got an army, we've got a government, the best possible government in the world. All we need now is a nation. Naturally, it's going to take time—"

She stopped and looked at him; imploringly, almost. He took a moment to calm himself down.

"You shouldn't have told me all that," he said.

"Why not? One of our most pressing needs right now is a really good general. Why do you think you're here? The commission has asked me—"

"Dear God." He jumped up. "That's just not funny. I couldn't—"

"You'll do as you're told." Then she grinned. "Like we all do. That's the point, isn't it? We all do this out of love; that's why we stand a chance when nobody else in history ever stood any chance at all."

"For pity's sake," he said. "Are you seriously ordering me to go out and conquer the world?"

She was silent for a moment. Then she smiled and said, "Yes."

He saw her again the next day. He asked her, "What if we lose?"

She smiled. "We can't."

"Don't you believe it," he said angrily. "One defeat, that's all it'd take. If we were to lose a hundred men, even—"

"It's all right," she said. "We're not going to."

He wasn't about to make the same mistake twice. "What else haven't you told me?"

She sat down on the porch. In front of them was the cherry tree. A gardener was raking mulch round its base. "We can't lose," she said. "Friends in high places."

"For God's sake don't be so damned mysterious. What friends?"

"It's easy to beat an enemy who doesn't want to win," she said.

She'd given him one more day to make up his mind. He went to look for Teucer.

He found him in a hayloft above a semi-derelict barn, out on the very edge of town. He was sitting in the loft door, his legs hanging out over the drop.

"I keep forgetting," he said. "You were born here."

"Not here." Teucer pointed. "Over there, just behind that hill. I went out there six months ago; there's nothing left now. They pulled it down and took the stones, for the Temple." He shrugged. "I don't mind. I guess they're my stones now. They're welcome to them."

Myrtus sat beside him and looked out. From where they were, he could see over the new town and the wall. Beyond there was just moorland, and on the skyline the low hill that masked Teucer's home.

"That's where our butts used to be," Teucer said. "That's where I shot my first possible. It's a thing in archery," he said, "it's when—"

Myrtus smiled. "I know," he said. "You told me, and it's in your file."

"I've lost count of how many possibles I've done since then," Teucer said. "You know what? I met someone the other day, and he told me, officially, I'm the best archer in the world. Officially."

"Yes," Myrtus said.

"How can they possibly know that?"

"They know everything."

Teucer pulled a face. "It's bullshit," he said. "There's got to be loads of archers better than me."

"Actually," Myrtus said gently, "no, there aren't. The Lodge identified you – actually, I identified you, when you were sixteen. I saw your name in a bunch of reports from field agents, read what they'd written about you; based on my knowledge and experience in such matters, I figured that you were shaping up to be the very best. So, when you were nineteen, I had you rounded up and taken to Beal. After that, I assigned you to field duty to sharpen your skills in the real world, and then I took you on for my own command." He paused to pick a wisp of straw out of his hair. "Remember Lonjamen, at Beal? He used to be the best, until you came along. One of these days I'd love to see you two shoot a match. Anyhow, he agrees with me. That's why he got taken off the line and put into Beal, to teach you. He'll be coming up here quite soon. He's looking forward to seeing you again."

Teucer looked stunned. "Really? Professor Lonjamen? He thinks—" Teucer shook his head. "Oh, I don't know," he said. "Did you really – I mean, was it really you who chose me? I thought you were just a—" He stopped short. "Sorry," he said.

"That's perfectly all right. That's the Lodge for you. All of us get all the rotten jobs, all of the time. Doesn't matter how grand you are. Generally speaking, the grander, the rottener." He looked down at his hands. "They want me to be a commissioner," he said.

Teucer's eyes went wide. "That's amazing," he said. "I bet you're pleased."

"You haven't listened to a word I've said," Myrtus snapped. "In the Lodge, the last thing you want is promotion." He breathed out slowly, letting the anger dissipate. "There's a vacancy," he said. "Someone's got to fill it. Someone I know and trust and thought of as a dear friend told them—" He shrugged. "My wife, as a matter of fact. Dear God, if you'd ever met some of the other commissioners—" He drew his knees up under his chin. "The point is," he went on, "I'm entitled to a personal assistant. If I choose someone, they don't have any say in the matter, they're assigned to me and that's that. So I thought I'd ask you first."

"Me?"

"What did I ever do to you, you mean?"

Teucer shook his head. "What I mean is, you sure you want me and not someone else?"

Myrtus laughed. "I need someone I can rely on," he said. He turned his head away. "Yesterday, I'd have said there were two of you. Now it's just you. If I were you, I'd refuse. If you do, chances are that sooner or later you'll be sent to Beal to take over Lonjamen's job. You liked Beal, or so you keep telling me. If you go with me, I don't suppose that'll happen. Not for a long time, anyway."

"I wouldn't want that job," Teucer said. "Not being a professor. I wouldn't know what to say."

"Think about it," Myrtus said; it came out like thunder, a command from God. "At least think about it." He turned his head back again. "You know that question you asked me. About who runs the Lodge."

"You said—"

"It started me thinking," Myrtus said. "So I asked someone who ought to know."

"What did he say?"

"She. She said she doesn't know. I believe her. And if anybody should know, it's her."

"Well," Teucer said. "Thanks for trying."

He still had three hours of his day of indecision left; but he went to see her anyway.

He found her in one of the small tower rooms in the cartulary, which someone had told him she'd appropriated for her own use. He could believe it; the walls were covered in icons and there were books all over the floor. She was reading at a desk by the window, and didn't look up when he came in. But she said his name. "Come over here," she said. "You want to see this."

"I wanted to ask you—"

"Later." She beckoned him, her eyes still on the roll of parchment. "I don't know if you've made your mind up yet, but just you take a look at this. I think it's the clincher."

He came closer. "What is it?"

She looked up, handed him the roll. "It's a copy of Emperor Glauca's will," she said. "You really don't need to know how we got it, but, believe me, it's the goods."

He gazed at her. "Friends in high places?"

"Oh, yes. The people crossed out in red are dead, incidentally. Oh, and the reason we wanted to see it was, we had a chat with Glauca's doctor. He figures the old fool is good for another eight years."

He read it.

A traditionalist to the core, Glauca had left the Eastern empire to his closest living relative, his nephew, the Western emperor, his deadly enemy; in eight years, give or take six months or so, the two empires would be reunited, regardless of what happened in the war. There was a brief note of explanation: the war was necessary and Glauca regarded it as his solemn duty, because he was the lawful ruler of the whole empire and his nephew was a traitor and a usurper. He therefore intended to take back what was rightfully his, regardless of the cost. However, the fact remained that his nephew was his rightful heir, and so long as either of them lived, no one else would ever sit on the Eagle Throne. He also pointed out that Blemya was a province of the empire, currently in revolt; should he die before reconquering it, he laid the sacred charge on his successor.

In the event that his nephew predeceased him, the throne would pass to the next closest relative. The candidates were listed, in order of priority of entitlement; the first sixteen names had been crossed out in red. The seventeenth—

Myrtus let go of the paper; it rolled itself back into a scroll. "No," he said. "That's unthinkable."

"Agreed."

He scowled at her. "Oh, come on," he said. "By your reasoning, he's the perfect choice."

She shook her head slowly and solemnly. "Absolutely not," she said. "You can't have been listening. The empire's got to go, remember? We need to start from scratch, a blank page. No, I agree with you entirely, it'd be a disaster. The worst possible outcome."

He took a deep breath. "All right," he said. "I think I—"

"Wait," she said, "there's more. Little bit of news just in. Three days ago, someone broke into Glauca's tower in Choris, with a knife. Came this close to killing him, only a servant managed to stop him. The man who does his toenails, would you believe. And—" she went on, before he could speak, "on the same day, at almost exactly the same time, in the royal apartments at Iden Astea—"

"Dear God."

She shook her head. "Also unsuccessful," she said, "though they managed to stick one in him; nasty flesh wound but he'll live." She took the scroll away from him and locked it in a small boxwood chest. "You realise what this means."

"You don't think *he*—?"

"Oh, no." She sounded quite definite. "He wouldn't know what was in Glauca's will. But someone does." She poured cherry brandy into a small horn cup and handed it to him. He loved her for that. "Well? Made your mind up?"

He swallowed the brandy and looked at her. "Do you seriously believe I'd last one minute against either of the Belot boys? With eight hundred men?"

She sighed. "I *told* you. Won't happen. It's not that sort of war."

"In that case." He paused. There was no turning back, but he wanted the moment before the world changed forever to last just a little longer. "Yes," he said. "I'll conquer the universe for you, if that's what you want."

"Thank you," she said, and kissed him on the cheek.

extras

about the author

K. J. Parker is the pseudonym of Tom Holt, a full-time writer living in the south-west of England. When not writing, Holt is a barely competent stockman, carpenter and metalworker, a two-left-footed fencer, an accomplished textile worker and a crack shot. He is married to a professional cake decorator and has one daughter.

Find out more about K. J. Parker and other Orbit authors by registering for the free newsletter at www.orbitbooks.net.

if you enjoyed

THE TWO OF SWORDS:
VOLUME 2

look out for

THE TWO OF SWORDS:
VOLUME 3

also by

K. J. Parker

To Saevus Andrapodiza, all human life had value. This revelation came to him in a moment of transcendent clarity as he looked out from the summit of Mount Doson over the fertile arable plains of Cors Shenei in central Permia. Every man, woman and child, regardless of age, ability, nationality, religion, sexual orientation or social class was valuable and must be treated as such. His task, he realised, was finding someone to buy them all.

As a native of East Permia, he was free from the restrictive laws of the two empires, where slavery had been illegal for a hundred and fifty years, ever since excessive reliance on servile labour had threatened to wipe out the yeoman class, from whom the Imperial army was almost exclusively drawn. In Permia, with the lowest level of population per square mile in the inhabited world, there were no such considerations. When Saevus embarked on his mission, the price of a field hand in Permia was nine oxen, thirty ewes or forty pigs, making good help unaffordable to the hard-working farmers who were the backbone of the nation. He set out to change all that.

He considered the proposition from the supply end. Because Permia had been at peace with its neighbours for generations, the supply mostly came from breeders, who naturally had to recoup the costs of fifteen years of careful nurture, together with the ongoing expense of the brood stock. But there were wars practically everywhere else; stockades crammed with surrendered prisoners, the women and children of captured cities slaughtered simply because they weren't worth anything to anybody. Prices at the pithead, so to speak, were ridiculously cheap; the real expense lay in transporting the goods to Permia, across some of the worst roads in the world.

Perhaps Saevus' greatest gift was his vision, his ability to see clearly, his sense of perspective. Before he entered the business, slave caravans limped through the high mountain passes between Rhus and Permia in gaggles of ten or twenty, moving at the pace of the slowest lame man or sickly child; and why? Because the traders were small operators, undercapitalised, inefficient. Saevus had a ship built, at that time the biggest merchant vessel ever constructed. With a full load of seven hundred, it could cover the distance between Aelia Major and Permia in ten days, as opposed to the six weeks needed by an overland caravan to cover the same distance. The cost of the ship was staggering, but, from the moment its keel bit the surf, Saevus was saving money. Marching rations of a pound and a half of barley bread per day for six weeks amounted to sixty-one pounds of bread, at a cost of an angel sixteen. Shipboard rations, a generous pound per day for ten days – ten pounds, nineteen stuivers, a saving of eighty-five per cent. Furthermore, the mortality rate overland was between forty and sixty per cent, so half the outlay was liable to be wasted, expensive bones bleaching by the roadside, dead loss. Aboard Saevus' ship, the death rate was a trivial fifteen per cent.

War is always with us; even so, it wasn't long before Saevus Andrapodiza had dried up the pool of young, able-bodied men available for purchase, or at least generated a demand that far outstripped supply. By keeping his prices to the end user as low as he possibly could, he'd stimulated the Permian economy, doubling grain yields in under a decade, with the result that more and more

Permians were able to afford a slave, or two, or five. Land which since time immemorial had been dismissed as useless was now coming under the plough, as thousands of reasonably priced hands swung picks and mattocks, shifting millions of tons of stones and hacking out terraces on windswept hillsides. More and better farms called for more and better tools, which someone had to make, from materials that someone had to fell or mine; and more money in circulation meant more people could afford the better things in life, and the craftsmen who supplied them couldn't cope without help. Permia was crying out for manpower, but all the wars in the world couldn't keep pace. For a while, Saevus looked set to be the victim of his own success.

It's a true measure of the man that he made this setback into an opportunity. Obviously, perfect physical specimens were the ideal; but life, he argued, isn't like that. Take any small family-run farm or workshop; look at who actually does the work. It's not just the man and his grown-up son. Everyone is involved – women, children, the old folks, the feeble, the sick. Saevus often talked about a farm he'd visited as a boy, where the farmer's aunt, seventy years old and missing an arm, still made a precious contribution keeping an eye on the sheep, collecting the eggs, leading the plough-horses, sorting through the store apples. Everyone is valuable – not necessarily of equal value, it goes without saying, but that's just a matter of appropriate pricing, and there were smallholders and small-scale artisans who'd be glad of any help they could get, assuming the price was one they could afford to pay. What was more, these hitherto neglected categories of livestock came with hidden benefits. Children grew into adults. Old men had skills and valuable experience. Many women had significant recreational as well as practical value. A one-legged crone might look like she's not worth her feed, but she's bound, over the course of a long life, to have learned how to do something useful, and you don't need two legs to card wool or ret flax or plait straw or sort and bag up nails, all the tedious, repetitive, time-devouring little jobs that somehow have to get done if the householder's hard work in the field or at the workbench is to be turned into money.

Saevus built a fleet of new ships, each one capable of transporting twelve hundred head, with a ninety per cent survival rate. The unit cost of getting a potential worker from battlefield or burned-out city to Permia fell by a breathtaking thirty-seven per cent. As his overheads fell, so did his prices. Now, practically everybody could afford to own a functional, useful human being.

Sadly, Saevus didn't live to see the outbreak of the East–West war, but his son Saevus II, universally known as Saevolus, was ideally placed to take full advantage when the Eastern emperor Glauca repealed the anti-slavery laws throughout his dominions, shortly followed by his nephew in the West. And only just in time. War losses and economic devastation had led to attrition of manpower on such a scale that it was virtually impossible to make up the losses of the endless sequence of major battles, or keep anything like a serious army in the field. Slave labour, however, would enable the empires to take thousands of men from the plough and the forge, freeing up whole regiments for service, while ensuring uninterrupted supply of equipment and materiel for the war effort from slave-staffed State arsenals.

The simple inscription on the base of Saevus' statue reads: *He saw the worth of every man. We shall not look upon his like again.*

When Procopius (the great composer) was fourteen years old his uncle sent him to the Imperial Academy of Music at Tet Escra to study harmonic theory under the celebrated Jifrez. Aware that the journey would involve crossing the notorious Four Fingers Pass, Procopius' uncle provided him with an escort of six men-at-arms, two archers, a personal attendant and a cook; he also sent with them the full cost of his nephew's tuition and maintenance: five thousand angels in gold. A cautious man, he had made proper enquiries about the eight soldiers, and the servant had been with the family for many years. The cook was a last-minute addition to the party. He seemed like a respectable man, and he came recommended by a noble family in the south.

The party crossed the Four Fingers without incident and began the long climb down Castle Street to the river valley. On the fourth day, just before sunrise, Procopius woke up to find the cook standing over him with a filleting knife in his hand.

"What's the matter?" he asked. The cook bent down and stabbed at him with the knife.

It was probably his phobia about blades that saved him. He rolled sideways as the blow fell, so that the knife struck him on the shoulder rather than in the hollow between the collarbones, as the cook had intended. The cook yelled at him and tried to stamp on his face; he caught his attacker's foot with both hands and twisted it, toppling him; then he jumped up and ran, passing the dead bodies of the soldiers and his servant, all with their throats cut. The cook threw the knife at him, but it hit him handle first, between the shoulders. He kept running, until he was sure the cook had given up chasing him.

Although he'd escaped the immediate danger, his situation was about as bad as it could be. The cut in his shoulder was bleeding freely. He was still five days from the nearest known settlement, with nothing except his shirt. His feet were bare. The surrounding countryside was shale rock, with a few clumps of gorse. He had no idea if there were any streams running down off the mountain; he couldn't see any, and was reluctant to leave the road to go exploring. It was a reasonably safe assumption that the cook would be following the road – where else would he go? – and he would be on horseback, most likely armed with a selection of the dead soldiers' weapons. Procopius had never fought anyone in his life. He seriously considered staying where he was and waiting for the cook to find him and kill him; he was going to die anyway, and a knife would be quicker and easier than hunger, exposure or gangrene.

It was only the thought that, if he let himself be killed, the cook would prevail and thereby in some vague sense prove himself the better man; the sheer unfairness of it that convinced him to keep going and do his best to survive.

Fortuitously, the road at this point was steep and made up of loose, dry stones; a horseman would have little advantage over a man on foot. He kept up the best pace he could manage, stopping only to listen for the sound of his pursuer, until nightfall. Then he left the road and hid as best he could in the gorse, waiting for sunrise. He was so tired he fell asleep for a few hours, but was wide awake long before the sun rose.

As soon as it was light enough to see by, he carefully made his way back uphill, parallel to the road, about fifty yards off on the eastern side, until he reached the place where the cook had camped for the night. He covered his advance by using the cook's horse as cover. He took an arrow from the quiver hanging from the saddle, crept in slowly and quietly and stabbed the cook through the ear without waking him.

He made an effort to cover the body with stones but soon gave up; the clouds were gathering, and he understood the merit of getting as far along the road as he could before the rain started to fall. As well as the money, the cook had brought two full waterskins and a sack of food, mostly cheese, dried sausage and apples; also two blankets and an oilskin cape. There were also various weapons, but Procopius left them behind, as he had no idea how to use them. He took a small knife and the cook's boots, which were much too big for him.

The next two days were fairly straightforward, although he led the horse rather than rode it, even though his feet were horribly sore. On the third day, however, he came to the place where the Blacklode crosses the road. Heavy rain on the Four Fingers had swollen the normally shallow river into a flood. Procopius had no experience with such matters, but he recognised at once that he had no hope of crossing the river in that state. With no map, he had no way of knowing if there were any alternative fords or crossings. He'd been careful with the food, but at best he had just enough for another four days. He couldn't get his head far enough round to see properly, but he had an idea that the wound in his shoulder had gone bad; it was warm and tender to the touch and hurt more now than it had earlier, and he felt weak and decidedly feverish. He decided that honour had been satisfied by his defeat of the cook, and there was nothing inherently shameful in this situation about death by exposure. He sat down beside the river, cleared his mind and fell asleep.

He woke up to find a man leaning over him, in more or less the same attitude as the cook. This time, though, he didn't instinctively flinch, mostly because he was too weak and sick to move. He noticed that the stranger wasn't holding a knife.

"You all right?" the stranger said.

"No."

The stranger frowned. "How'd you get yourself all cut up like that?"

Procopius took a deep breath and explained, as lucidly as he could; he'd been sent on a journey with a large sum of money, one of the servants had tried to kill him for the money but he'd managed to get away, and now here he was, lost and alone and very sick. The stranger nodded, to show he'd understood.

"Will you help me?" Procopius asked. "Please?"

The man smiled. "Wish I could," he said. "But don't worry, it'll be all right. What happened to your face? It's a real mess."

Procopius explained that, when he was eighteen months old, his father had murdered his mother and then tried to kill him too. "Is that right?" the stranger said. "You've had a pretty rough old time, one way and another. Still, it'll all come right in the end. Believe it or not, you'll look back on all this someday and understand it was all for the best."

"Look," Procopius said, "please, can you help me? At least give me a leg up so I can get on the horse. I haven't got the strength."

The stranger smiled. "In that case, that horse isn't much use to you, is it? So, really, I might as well have it, save me footslogging it all the way to the nearest town to fetch help. I hate walking. I get blisters."

"You can't have it."

"Sorry." The stranger's smile grew wider, if anything. "You can't use it, and you can't stop me taking it, so tough. Tell you what I'll do. I'll buy it off you."

"I don't want to sell it. I need it."

"No you don't," the stranger said gently. "But I'm going to give you a good price for it. I'm no thief."

He gathered the reins, put his foot in the stirrup and hoisted himself into the saddle. All the provisions and the other stuff were in the saddlebags. "It'll be all right," he said, "I promise you. You're going to be fine, just you wait and see."

Procopius watched him until he was out of sight; a long time, because, from where he was, he could see the road for ten miles, so at least an hour, during which time the horse and rider gradually grew smaller and further away before dwindling down into a dot, and then nothing. During that long time, he resolved not to die, because he needed to follow the thief, catch up with him and deal with him the way he'd dealt with the cook, for roughly the same reason. But this time it looked as though that wasn't going to be possible. He was getting weaker, it was harder and harder to stay awake; when he wasn't burning hot he was freezing cold, and, really, what was the point? His weakness had proved him to be inferior. If he didn't deserve to live, he didn't deserve to live. Simple as that.

He woke up lying in the bed of a cart. The driver and his wife were taking a load of cheese to market; you poor thing, they said, whatever happened to you? And they were very kind and looked after him, they took him to the inn at Loscobiel and stayed with him until he was better, and then took him on to Tet Escra, where he was able to get a letter of credit from his uncle's bank that made good his losses and enabled him to give the cheesemonger and his wife a proper reward, appropriate to his dignity and station in life, so that was all right.

On his first day at the Academy, he presented the Principal with a manuscript: a flute sonata in three movements. He didn't mention the background to the piece, how the shape of it had come to him as he lay among the rocks hoping to die, after the thief stole his horse, because that wasn't relevant, and he didn't suppose the Principal would be interested. The Principal put the manuscript on his desk and said he'd be sure to look at it some time, when he had a moment.

Two days later, he was sent for.

"Did you write this?" the Principal asked him. He looked fierce, almost angry.

"Yes," Procopius said.

"Think carefully, and I'll ask you again. Did you write this?"

"Yes."

"All on your own?"

Procopius suppressed a smile. Very much all on his own. "Yes. Sir," he added, remembering his manners. Then he couldn't resist asking, "Did you like it?"

The Principal didn't answer that. Instead, he gave a ferocious lecture on the evils of plagiarism. It had been known, he said, for students from wealthy families to hire penniless young composers to write works which the students then passed off as their own; behaviour the Principal confessed he couldn't begin to understand, because surely anybody who did such a thing would be eaten away with shame, and what possible pleasure could anyone get from being praised and rewarded for something he hadn't done? In such cases, the penalty was instant expulsion from the Academy. He wanted Procopius to understand that; and now he'd ask the question a third time, and if the answer was yes, there'd be no penalty, not this time. Did you write this piece of music?

"Yes," Procopius said. "Sir. I mean, like you said, why would I want to pretend if I hadn't? I've come here to learn, not to show off."

"I see," the Principal said. "In which case, that'll be all. You can go."

The Principal never liked him after that, because he'd made a serious accusation against him and it turned out to be wrong. But all the teachers loved him and said he was the most remarkable talent they'd ever come across, and it was a privilege to be part of the making of someone who would undoubtedly turn out to be the finest musician of his generation. Procopius wasn't sure about all that. The teachers had shown him all sorts of clever ways to turn the shapes in his mind into music; he'd been shocked and appalled by his own ignorance and the fact that he hadn't been able to figure out such things for himself but had had to be shown. That felt like cheating, though apparently it was quite legitimate. For the rest of it, the shapes just came to him, without any real work or effort on his part, certainly no skill or engagement with excellence. He was given them, unearned, just as he'd always been given everything, his whole life, undeserved, simply because he was the son and sole heir of a rich man who died relatively young, and the nephew of a rich, doting uncle.

So, for a while, he made sense of it the best he could. He thought about the man who'd taken his horse. You'll be all right, the man had said, just you wait and see. And he'd said he wasn't a thief, and he'd pay a good price for the horse; and that was when young Procopius began to see the shapes, and calling that a coincidence was stretching belief much further than it could possibly go. He could make no sense of it, of course – because what would a god or similar supernatural agency want with a horse, or feel the need to pay for a perfectly unremarkable thirty-thaler gelding with such a precious and valuable commodity? – but the fact that he couldn't make sense of it certainly didn't mean that it didn't make sense, only that he wasn't smart enough to figure it out. Later, he realised that he'd simply exchanged one insoluble problem for another, with a garnish of the supernatural to excuse him from having to analyse it rationally, and simply accepted; he was one of those people from whom things are taken and to whom things are given, not necessarily proportionately; a conduit for the remarkable and the excessive, himself unremarkable and lacking in any real substance, either for good or evil.